读真题
记单词

大学英语四级词汇

(2009.12-2005.6)

李立新 主　编

傅芳欣 吴嘉平 王彦琳　副主编

710分

- 收词齐全　历年真题词汇一网打尽
- 注释精准　词条重点突出循环记忆
- 全面扩充　同义反义同根全面囊括
- 精准译文　巩固记忆写译双重提高

CET-4

中国出版集团
中国对外翻译出版公司

图书在版编目（ＣＩＰ）数据

读真题记单词大学英语四级词汇／李立新主编. 一北京：
中国对外翻译出版公司，2010.1
ISBN 978-7-5001-2388-0

I. 读… II. 李… III. 英语－词汇－高等学校－水平考
试－自学参考资料 IV. H313

中国版本图书馆CIP数据核字（2010）第015524号

出版发行／中国对外翻译出版公司
地 址／北京市西城区车公庄大街甲4号物华大厦六层
电 话／（010）68338545 68353673 68359101
邮 编／100044
传 真／（010）68357870
电子邮箱／book@ctpc.com.cn
网 址／http://www.ctpc.com.cn

策划编辑／吴良柱 顾 强
责任编辑／韦 薇 张 星

印 刷／北京富泰印刷有限责任公司
经 销／新华书店

规 格／787×1092 毫米 1/16
印 张／16.5
字 数／330 千字
版 次／2010 年 1 月第 1 版
印 次／2010 年 1 月第 1 次

ISBN 978-7-5001-2388-0 定价：25.00 元

前 言

突破四级并不难，关键要过词汇关。众所周知，熟练掌握大纲要求的词汇是顺利通过四级考试的基石，所以选择一本最有效的词汇参考书至关重要。对于备考四级的同学来说，大纲和真题是最权威的复习资料。真题除了用来熟悉出题思路，提高解题技巧之外，还是记单词的经典蓝本，因为真题几乎涵盖了大纲词汇，而且体现了高频词汇，所以在真题中记单词使得备考更有针对性。此外，把单词放在真题语境中，记单词就会更高效。因此读真题记单词无疑是一种非常有效的方法。

本书具备以下特色：

一、涵盖历年真题词汇，注释精准重点突出

本书收录了 2005 — 2009 年的大学英语四级考试真题。所有词条的选择和注释都既严格按照大纲的要求，又考虑到考生的需求。所注词条包括真题中所有疑难词汇和词组，以及读写常用搭配，而且重点高频单词、词组在不同的篇章重复出现，便于读者巩固记忆。

本书的注释不求全面，但求精准、重点突出。每个单词和词组的第一个义项都是在对应的真题语境中的意义，随后是常用义项。考生掌握后就能轻松应对四级考试中的熟词生义、一词多义现象。

二、全面扩充核心词汇，囊括同义反义同根词组

笔者根据大纲的要求，考虑到实战需要，根据各类词汇的不同特点，对核心词汇进行了全面扩充，附有常用的同义词、反义词、同根词及词组，方便考生通过联想扩大词汇量。

三、在语境中记单词，从容应对新四级

虽然新四级不再有词汇题，但词汇测试渗透到了每个题型中，而且大纲要求更加注重在语篇中综合运用词汇的能力，这从 2006 年新四级真题的选词填空、完型填空以及翻译题中可见一斑。在真题语境中记住的单词和词组才可以灵活运用，才可以在考试中以不变应万变。

愿此书伴您走向成功！

编 者
2010 年 1 月

目 录

Is there enough oil **beneath** the Arctic National Wildlife *Refuge* (保护区) (ANWR) to help **secure** America's energy future ? President Bush certainly thinks so. He has argued that tapping ANWR's oil would help ease California's **electricity crisis** and provide a major **boost** to the country's energy independence. But no one knows **for sure** how much **crude** oil lies buried beneath the frozen earth with the last government survey, **conducted** in 1998, projecting **output** anywhere from 3 billion to 16 billion **barrels**.

The oil industry goes with the high end of the range, which could equal as much as 10% of U.S. **consumption** for as long as six years. By **pumping** more than 1 million barrels a day from the **reserve** for the next two three decades, lobbyists claim, the nation could **cut back on** imports **equivalent** to all shipments to the U.S. from Saudi Arabia. Sounds good. An oil **boom** would also mean a multibillion-dollar *windfall* (意外之财) in tax **revenues**, *royalties* (开采权使用费) and **leasing fees** for Alaska and the Federal Government. Best of all, **advocates** of **drilling** say, damage to the environment would be **insignificant**. "We've never had a document case of oil rig **chasing** deer out onto the pack ice." says Alaska State Representative Scott Ogan.

Not so far, say environmentalists. Sticking to the low end of government **estimates**, the National Resources Defense Council says there may be no more than 3.2 billion barrels of economically **recoverable** oil in the coastal plain of ANWR, a drop in the bucket that would do **virtually** nothing to ease America's energy problems. And consumers would wait up to a decade to gain any benefits, because drilling could begin only after much bargaining over leases, environmental permits and **regulatory** review. As for ANWR's impact on the California power crisis, environmentalists **point out** that oil is **responsible** for only 1% of the Golden State's electricity output—and just 3% of the nation's.

文章词汇注释

▶▶ **beneath** [bɪ'ni:θ]

[释义] *prep.* ①在…下方 ②在底下 ③在…的掩盖下

[同义] under, below, underneath

[反义] above

▶▶ **secure** [sɪ'kjuə]

[释义] *v.* ①使安全，保护 ②保证获得 *a.* ①安全的 ②安心的 ③有把握的

[同义] guarantee, make safe

[同根] security [sɪ'kjuərɪtɪ] *n.* ①安全 ②保护物 ③保证 ④确信，把握

[词组] be secure of 对…有把握，确信
feel secure about/as to 对…（觉得）放心
secure (sth.) against/from 使（某物）免遭

▶▶ **electricity crisis** 电力危机

▶▶ **boost** [bu:st]

[释义] *n.* ①推动（力）②提高 *v.* ①举，推 ②推动，提高 ③增加

[同义] enhancement

▶▶ **for sure** 确切地，毫无疑问，肯定地

▶▶ **crude** [kru:d]

[释义] *a.* ①天然的 ②简单的 ③粗鲁的 ④未加修饰的 *n.* 原油，石油

[同义] natural, primitive, raw

[反义] refined

[同根] crudity ['kru:dɪtɪ] *n.* ①粗糙，粗野 ②粗鲁的行为

▶▶ **conduct** [kən'dʌkt; -dəkt]

[释义] *v.* ①做，进行，管理 ②为人，表现 ③给…做向导 ④指挥 ['kɒndʌkt; 'kɑ:n-] *n.* ①实施（方式），经营（方式）②行为，品行 ③指导，领导

[同义] do, perform, manage, behave

[同根] conduction [kən'dʌkʃn] *n.* ①传导，传导性 ②输送，输导
conductor [kən'dʌktə] *n.* ①指导者 ②售票员 ③指挥家 ④导体
conductive [kən'dʌktɪv] *a.* 传导的，传导性的，有传导力的

▶▶ **output** ['autput]

[释义] *n.* ①产量 ②产出，生产 ③（工、农业等的）产品，（文艺方面的）作品

▶▶ **barrel** ['bærəl]

[释义] *n.* ①桶，一桶之量 ②圆筒 ③许多，大量 *v.* 把…装桶

▶▶ **consumption** [kən'sʌmpʃən]

[释义] *n.* ①消费量，消耗量 ②消耗，消费，浪费

[反义] conservation

[同根] consume[kən'sju:m] *v.* ①消耗，耗尽 ②吃完，喝光 ③毁灭 ④挥霍
consumer [kən'sju:mə] *n.* ①消费者，用户 ②消耗者，毁灭者

▶▶ **pump** [pʌmp]

[释义] *v.* ①（用泵）抽（水），抽吸 ②灌输，注入 *n.* 泵，抽水机

[词组] pump out 抽空

▶▶ **reserve** [rɪ'zɜ:v]

[释义] *n.* ①（常作 ~ s）（矿）藏量，储量 ②贮备金，储藏量 *v.* ①保留 ②预订 ③把…专门留给 *a.* ①保留的 ②留出的 ③后备的，预备的

[同义] store

[同根] reservation [,rezə'veɪʃən] *n.* 保留，（旅馆房间等）预定，预约
reserved [rɪ'zɜ:vd] *a.* ①留作专用的，储备的 ②预订的，预约的 ③有所保留的 ④拘谨的

[词组] keep in reserve 留作预备
with reserve 有保留地
without reserve 无保留地，无条件地

▶▶ cut back on ①减少，削减，缩减 ②倒叙

▶▶ equivalent [ɪ'kwɪvələnt]
[释义] a. ①相等的，相同的 ②同等重要的 n. 等价物
[同义] equal, similar
[同根] equivalence [ɪ'kwɪvələns] n. 相等，等价，等效，（词语的）等义
[词组] be equivalent to ①相等于…，等（同）于 ②与…等效

▶▶ boom [bu:m]
[释义] n. ①迅速发展，繁荣 ②隆隆声 v. ①繁荣 ②发出隆隆声 a. 繁荣的
[同义] prosperity, flourish
[同根] booming ['bu:mɪŋ] a. ①趋于繁荣的，迅速发展的 ②隆隆作响的

▶▶ revenue ['revɪnju:]
[释义] n. ①（国家的）岁入，税收 ②尤指（大宗的）收入，（从地产、投资等所得的）收益
[同义] income
[词组] revenue tax（旨在筹措财政收入的）岁入税

▶▶ lease [li:s]
[释义] v. 出租（土地等），租得，租有（土地等）

▶▶ fee [fi:]
[释义] n. ①费（如手续费，会费等），服务费，酬金 ②赏金，小费
[同义] charge
[词组] hold in fee 占有，拥有

▶▶ advocate ['ædvəkeɪt]
[释义] n. ①拥护者，提倡者 ②辩护者，律师 v. ①拥护，主张
[同义] supporter, promoter, backer
[反义] opponent

[同根] advocacy ['ædvəkəsɪ] n. ①拥护，提倡 ②辩护，辩护术
advocator ['ædvəkeɪtə] n. ①拥护者，提倡者 ②辩护者

▶▶ drilling ['drɪlɪŋ]
[释义] n. ①钻孔，钻井 ②操练，演习 a. ①钻孔的 ②辛辣的，尖刻的
[同根] drill [drɪl] v. ①在…上打眼（或钻孔）②训练，演练 ③通过练习传授 n. ①钻头，钻机 ②训练，演练

▶▶ insignificant [ˌɪnsɪg'nɪfɪkənt]
[释义] a. ①可忽略的，微小的 ②不重要的，无意义的
[同义] unimportant, trivial
[反义] significant
[同根] insignificance [ˌɪnsɪg'nɪfɪkəns] n. ①微小 ②不重要，无意义

▶▶ chase [tʃeɪs]
[释义] v. ①驱逐，赶出 ②追赶，追捕，追寻 ③追求，向…献殷勤 n. ①追赶，追捕 ②追寻，追求 ③被追猎的动物
[同义] drive out, pursue, run after, hunt
[词组] chase up ①追上 ②为某一目的而寻找

▶▶ estimate ['estɪmeɪt]
[释义] n. ①估计，估计量 ②看法，判断 v. ①估计，估价 ②评价，判断
[同根] overestimate [ˌəuvə'estɪmeɪt] v. 过高估计，评价过高
underestimate [ˌʌndər'estɪmeɪt] v. 低估，看轻
[词组] by estimate 据估计
make an estimate of 给…作一估计，评价

▶▶ recoverable [rɪ'kʌvərəbl]
[释义] a. ①可重获的 ②可恢复的，能复原的 ③能追回的，（债务等）能收回的
[同根] recover [rɪ'kʌvə] v. ①追回，收复 ②挽回，补偿 ③恢复（健康等）

recovery [rɪ'kʌvərɪ] n. ①追回，收复
②恢复，复苏 ③康复，痊愈

▶▶ **virtually** ['vɜ:tʃʊəlɪ]

[释义] ad. 实际上，事实上，差不多

[同义] in fact, almost, nearly

[同根] virtual ['vɜ:tjuːəl;-tʃʊəl]
a. ①实际上的，事实上的 ② [计] 虚拟的

▶▶ **regulatory** ['regjʊlətərɪ]

[释义] a. ①管理的，控制的 ②调整的，调节的 ③受控制的

[同根] regulate ['regjʊleɪt] v. ①管理，控制 ②调整，调节 ③使规则化 ④调

整，校准

regulation [regjʊ'leɪʃən] n. ①规则，条例 ②管理 ③校准，调整

▶▶ **point out** 指出

▶▶ **responsible** [rɪ'spɒnsəbl]

[释义] a. ①承担责任的，应负责任的 ②有责任能力的

[反义] irresponsible

[同根] responsibility [rɪˌspɒnsə'bɪlɪtɪ] n. ①责任，职责 ②责任感，责任心

[词组] be responsible for 是造成…的原因，为…负责

选项词汇注释

▶▶ **exhaust** [ɪg'zɔːst]

[释义] v. ①用尽，耗尽 ②使精疲力竭 ③把…的内容抽空，排完 n. ①（废气等的）排出，放出 ②排气装置 ③（排出的）废气，废液

[同义] use up, wear out

[反义] supply, refresh, renew

[同根] exhausted [ɪg'zɔːstɪd] a. ①用完的，枯竭的 ②极其疲惫的，精疲力竭的

exhausting [ɪg'zɔːstɪŋ] a. 使之用完的，使人精疲力竭的

[词组] be exhausted by/with 因…而疲劳

▶▶ **yield** [jiːld]

[释义] n. ①收益 ②产量 v. ①出产，生产 ②产生（效果等）③使屈服，使投降 ④让出，放弃

[同根] yielding ['jiːldɪŋ] a. ①出产的 ②易弯曲的 ③柔顺的，屈从的

[词组] yield to 屈服于，让步于

▶▶ **reliance** [rɪ'laɪəns]

[释义] n. ①依靠，依赖 ②信任，信心 ③受信赖的人（或物）

[同义] dependence

[同根] rely [rɪ'laɪ] v. ①依靠，仰仗 ②信赖，相信，指望

reliable [rɪ'laɪəbl] a. 可靠的，可信赖的

reliant [rɪ'laɪənt] a. ①信赖的，依靠的 ②有信心的，自力更生的

[词组] place reliance on/upon 信任

▶▶ **drain** [dreɪn]

[释义] v. ①（使）逐渐消耗 ②排干积水 n. ①消耗，耗尽 ②排水沟

[同义] exhaust

[同根] drainage ['dreɪnɪdʒ] n. ①排水，排泄 ②排泄物 ③排泄设备

[词组] drain away 使排出，流出
drain of 使逐渐消耗

▶▶ **commercial** [kə'mɜːʃəl]

[释义] a. ①商业的 ②商品的 ③商业广告性的 n. （广播、电视等的）商业广告

[同义] business-related

[同根] commerce ['kɒmɜːs] n. ① 商业，贸易 ②社交，（意见等的）交流

▶▶▶ **exploitation** [ˌeksplɔɪ'teɪʃən]

[释义] n. ①（资源等的）开发，利用 ②剥削，榨取

[同义] development, utilization, use

[同根] exploit [ɪk'splɔɪt] v. ① 开 发，开采 ②利用 ③剥削

exploitative [ɪk'splɔɪtətɪv] a. ①开发的，开采的 ②剥削的，榨取的

▶▶▶ **optimistic** [ˌɒptɪ'mɪstɪk]

[释义] a. 乐观的，乐观主义的

[同义] hopeful, cheerful

[反义] pessimistic

[同根] optimism ['ɒptɪmɪzəm] n. ①乐观 ②乐观主义

optimist ['ɒptɪmɪst] n. 乐观主义者

▶▶▶ **get under way** 开始进行

"Tear 'em **apart**!" "**Kill** the fool!" "**Murder** the *referee*（裁判）!"

These are common **remarks** one may hear at various sporting events. At the time they are made, they may seem **innocent** enough. But let's not kid ourselves. They have been known to influence behavior in such a way as to lead to real **bloodshed**. **Volumes** have been written about the way words affect us. It has been shown that words having certain *connotations*（含义） may cause us to **react** in ways quite foreign to what we **consider** to be our usual **humanistic** behavior. I see the term "**opponent**" as one of those words. Perhaps the time has come to **delete** it from sports terms.

The dictionary meaning of the term "opponent" is "adversary", "enemy", "one who opposes your interests." Thus, when a player meets an opponent, he or she may tend to treat that opponent as an enemy. At such times, winning may **dominate** one's **intellect**, and every action, no matter how **gross**, may be considered **justifiable**. I recall an incident in a handball game when a referee refused a player's request for a **time out** for a glove change because he did not consider them wet enough. The player **proceeded** to rub his gloves across his wet T-shirt and then **exclaimed**, "Are they wet enough now?"

In the heat of battle, players have been observed to throw themselves across the court without considering the **consequences** that such a move might have on anyone in their way. I have also **witnessed** a player reacting to his opponent's international and **illegal** blocking by **deliberately** hitting him with the ball as hard as he could during the course of play. Off the court, they are good friends. Does that **make any sense**? It certainly gives proof of a court attitude which **departs from** normal behavior.

Therefore, I believe it is time we *elevated* (提升) the game to the level where it belongs thereby setting an example to the rest of the sporting world. **Replacing** the term "opponent" **with** "associate" could be an **ideal** way to start.

The dictionary meaning of the term "associate" is "colleague", "friend", "**companion.**" Reflect a moment! You may soon see and possibly feel the difference in your reaction to the term "associate" rather than "opponent."

文章词汇注释

▶▶ **tear apart** ①把…批评得体无完肤 ②彻底搜查（某处）

▶▶ **murder** [ˈmɜ:də]
[释义] v. ①谋杀，残杀，屠杀 ②扼杀（真理、艺术等）n. ①谋杀，谋杀罪，②〈口〉（对语言等的）破坏，糟蹋
[同义] kill, slaughter, massacre
[同根] murderer [ˈmɜ:dərə] n. 杀人犯，凶手

▶▶ **remark** [rɪˈma:k]
[释义] n. ①言辞，言语，评论 ②注意，觉察 v. ①说，评论 ②注意，觉察
[同义] comment, statement
[同根] remarkable [rɪˈma:kəbl] a. ①不平常的，非凡的 ②显著的，值得注意的 n. 引人注目的事，知名人物
[词组] make/pass a remark on 就…发表意见，对…品头论足
remark on/upon 谈论，议论，评论

▶▶ **event** [ɪˈvent]
[释义] n. ①比赛项目 ②（常用复数）时事，时局 ③事件，事变
[词组] at all events 无论怎样
in any event 无论如何
in the event of 万一，如果…发生
in no event 决不能

▶▶ **innocent** [ˈɪnəsənt]
[释义] a. ①无害的 ②无罪的，清白的 ③单纯的，坦率的 ④幼稚的，无知的，头脑简单的 n. ①无罪的人 ②天真无邪的人（尤指孩子）③头脑简单的人，无知的人
[同义] guiltless
[反义] guilty
[词根] innocence [ˈɪnəsns] n. ①无罪，清白 ②率直，天真无邪 ③无知，头脑简单

▶▶ **bloodshed** [ˈblʌdʃed]
[释义] n. ①杀戮 ②流血

▶▶ **volume** [ˈvɒlju:m; (US)-jəm]
[释义] n. ①书卷，卷 ②体积，容量 ③份量，额 ④音量
[词组] speak volumes (for sth.) 有力地说明，充分证明

▶▶ **react** [rɪˈækt]
[释义] v. ①做出反应 ②影响，起作用 ③反抗，反对
[同义] respond
[同根] reaction [ri:ˈækʃən] n. ①反应 ②看法，态度 ③反动，对抗

▶▶ **consider** [kənˈsɪdə]
[释义] v. ①认为，把…看作 ②考虑，细想 ③体贴，照顾
[同义] think, believe
[同根] consideration [kənsɪdəˈreɪʃən] n. ①考虑 ②需要考虑的事项 ③体

贴，关心

considering [kən'sɪdərɪŋ] *prep.* 考虑到，就…来说

considerable [kən'sɪdərəbl] *a.* ①相当大（或多）的 ②重大的，重要的，著名的

considerate [kən'sɪdərɪt] *a.* ①关切的，体贴的，体谅的 ②考虑周到的

▶▶▶ **humanistic** [ˌhjuːmə'nɪstɪk]

[释义] *a.* 人道主义的，人文主义（者）的，人文学科的

[同根] human ['hjuːmən] *n.* 人，人类 *a.* ①人的，人类的 ②有人性的，通人情的

humanity [hjuː'mænɪtɪ] *n.* ①人道，仁慈，博爱 ②人类 ③人性

humanism ['hjuːmənɪzəm] *n.* 人道主义，博爱精神

▶▶▶ **opponent** [ə'pəʊnənt]

[释义] *n.* 对手，反对者 *a.* ①对立的，敌对的 ②对面的

[同义] rival, challenger

[同根] oppose [ə'pəʊz] *v.* ①反对，抵抗 ②阻挡，妨碍 ③使相对，使对抗

opposite ['ɒpəzɪt] *a.* ①对面的 ②截然相反的 ③反对的，对立的

opposition [ɒpə'zɪʃən] *n.* ①反对，敌对 ②反对党 ③对面的位置

▶▶▶ **delete** [dɪ'liːt]

[释义] *v.* ①删除，划掉 ②消除，擦去

[同义] cross out, erase

[同根] deletion [dɪ'liːʃən] *n.* ①删除 ②删除部分

▶▶▶ **dominate** ['dɒmɪneɪt]

[释义] *v.* ①支配，控制 ②俯瞰，俯视 ③在…中占首要位置

[同义] control, rule

[同根] dominant ['dɒmɪnənt] *a.* ①占优势的，统治的 ②（在数量、分布等方面）占首位的，主要的 *n.* 占优势者

dominance ['dɒmɪnəns] *n.* 优势，统治或支配的地位，最高权力

domination [dɒmɪ'neɪʃən] *n.* 支配，统治，控制

▶▶▶ **intellect** ['ɪntɪlekt]

[释义] *n.* ①理智，智力 ②理解力，领悟力 ③才智非凡的人，[总称] 知识界

[同义] mind

[同根] intelligence [ɪn'telɪdʒəns] *n.* ①智力，才智 ②情报

intellectual [ˌɪntɪ'lektʃuəl] *n.* 知识分子 *a.* ①知识的，智力的，理智的 ②用脑力的，需智力的 ③智力发达的，理解力强的

▶▶▶ **gross** [grəʊs]

[释义] *a.* ①恶劣的，严重的 ②粗俗的，下流的 ③总的，毛的 *n.* ①总量，总额 ②多数，大多数 *v.* 赚的总收入或毛利

▶▶▶ **justifiable** ['dʒʌstɪfaɪəbl]

[释义] *a.* 无可非议的，正当的

[同义] justified, reasonable, correct, right, proper

[反义] unreasonable

[同根] justify ['dʒʌstɪfaɪ] *v.* ①证明…正当，为…辩护 ②证明…无罪 ③证明…合法

justification [ˌdʒʌstɪfɪ'keɪʃn] *n.* ①认为有理，认为正当 ②正当的理由，借口

▶▶▶ **time out** ① [体]（球类等比赛进行中的）暂停 ②（工作等活动中的）暂停时间，休息时间

▶▶▶ **proceed** [prə'siːd]

[释义] *v.* ①继续进行，进而做 ②进行，开展 ③行进，前进

[同根] process ['prəʊses] *n.* ①过程，变化过程 ②步骤，加工方法 ③（时

间等）进行，进展 v. ①对…进行加工 ②使接受处理（或检查，审议）
procedure [prə'si:dʒə] n. ①程序，步骤 ②常规，传统做法 ③ [计] 过程
procession [prə'seʃən;prəu-] n. ①行列，队伍 ②连续，一（长）排 ③列队行进

▶▶ **exclaim** [ɪk'skleɪm]
[释义] v. ① (表示抗议等) 大声叫嚷 ② (由于痛苦等) 呼喊，惊叫
[同义] cry, shout
[反义] whisper
[同根] exclamation [,ekskle'meɪʃən] n. ①喊叫，惊叫 ②感叹词

▶▶ **consequence** ['kɒnsɪkwəns; (US) 'kɒnsɪkwens]
[释义] n. ①结果，后果 ②重要性，价值
[同义] result, effect
[词根] consequent ['kɒnsɪkwənt] a. ①作为结果（或后果）的 ②合乎逻辑的，合理的 n. 结果，随后的事（或事件）
consequently ['kɒnsɪkwəntlɪ] ad. 因此，所以
[词组] as a consequence 因而，结果
in consequence 因此，结果
of no consequence 不重要的，无足轻重的
without negative consequence 没有副作用

▶▶ **witness** ['wɪtnɪs]
[释义] v. ①目击，注意到 ②为…作证，证明 ③作…的证人 n. ①见证人 ②证据，证词 ③可作证据的人（或物）
[词组] bear witness 作证，证明，表明
in witness of 作为…的证明，为…作证

▶▶ **illegal** [ɪ'li:gəl]

[释义] a. 违反规则的，不合法的，非法的
[同义] unlawful
[反义] legal

▶▶ **deliberately** [dɪ'lɪbərətlɪ]
[释义] ad. ①故意地，蓄意地 ②慎重地，审慎地 ③从容地
[同义] on purpose, purposely, with intent, by design
[同根] deliberate [dɪ'lɪbəreɪt] v. ①仔细考虑 ②商议 [dɪ'lɪbərət] a. ①慎重的 ②蓄意的 ③从容的
deliberation [dɪ,lɪbə'reɪʃən] n. ①细想，研究 ②审议，商议 ③审慎，从容
deliberative [dɪ'lɪbəreɪtɪv] a. ①审议的，有审议权的 ②考虑过的，慎重的

▶▶ **make any sense** 有意义，有道理，讲得通
▶▶ **depart from** ①违反，背离 ②离开，从…出发
▶▶ **replace...with...** 用…替代…

▶▶ **ideal** [aɪ'dɪəl]
[释义] a. ①理想的，完美的，典型的 ②空想的，想象中的 n. ①理想 ②完美，典型 ③努力目标，最终目的 ④设想，想象中的事物
[同义] unrealistic, romantic
[反义] realistic
[同根] idealism [aɪ'dɪəlɪzm] n. ①唯心主义，唯心论，观念论，理念论 ②理想主义
idealist [aɪ'dɪəlɪst] n. 理想主义者，空想家
idealistic [aɪ,dɪə'lɪstɪk] a. ①理想主义（者）的，空想（家）的 ②唯心主义（者）的

▶▶ **companion** [kəm'pænjən]
[释义] n. ①同伴,伴侣 ②成对（副、双）

的东西之一 v. ①陪伴，与…为伴 ②结伴，交往

[同义] friend

[同根] company ['kʌmpənɪ] n. ① 公司，商号 ②陪伴，交往 ③一群人 ④同伴（们），朋友（们）a. ①待客

的 ②公司的

companionable [kəm'pænjənəbl] a. 友善的，好交际的

companionship [kəm'pænjənʃɪp] n. ①伴侣关系 ②交际，交往

选项词汇注释

▶▶ **athlete** ['æθliːt]

[释义] n. ①运动员，选手 ②身强力壮的人

[同义] sportsperson

▶▶ **harsh** [hɑːʃ]

[释义] a. ①苛刻的，严厉的 ②毛糙的 ③刺目的 ④崎岖不平的

[同根] harshly ['hɑːʃlɪ] ad. 严厉地，苛刻地

▶▶ **short-tempered** [ʃɔːt'tempəd]

[释义] a. 脾气暴躁的，易发怒的

[同义] quick-tempered, irritable, impatient

[反义] patient

▶▶ **offend** [ə'fend]

[释义] v. ①使生气，冒犯，得罪 ②违犯，违反

[同根] offence [ə'fens] n. ①冒犯，得罪 ②犯法（行为），过错 ③引起反感的事物 ④进攻

offensive [ə'fensɪv] a. ①得罪人的，无礼的 ②攻击的，进攻性的

▶▶ **rival** ['raɪvəl]

[释义] n. ①竞争对手，敌手 ②可与之匹敌的人（或物）a. 竞争的，对立的 v. ①与…竞争 ②努力赶上（他人的事业等）③与…匹敌，比得上

[同义] competitor, opponent

▶▶ **illegally** [ɪ'liːgəlɪ]

[释义] ad. 违反规则地，违法地

[同义] unlawfully

[同根] legal ['liːgəl] a. ①法律（上）的 ②合法的 ③法定的

legalize ['liːgəlaɪz] v. 使合法化，使得到法律认可

▶▶ **keep on** 继续，保持

▶▶ **scream** [skriːm]

[释义] v. ①（因恐惧等而）尖声叫喊 ②（机器等）发出尖锐刺耳的声音 ③纵声大笑 ④强烈要求 n. ①尖叫声，惊叫声 ②尖锐刺耳的声音

[反义] whisper

[同根] screaming ['skriːmɪŋ] a. ①发出尖叫的 ②引人注目的 ③引人捧腹大笑的

[词组] scream for 强烈要求

scream out 大叫

▶▶ **protest** ['prəʊtest]

[释义] n. ①抗议 ②申明 v. ①申明 ②抗议 a. 抗议性的，表示抗议的

[同义] objection

[词组] under protest 被迫地，持异议地，不情愿地

without protest 心甘情愿地，无异议地

▶▶ **call on** ①呼吁，要求 ②访问，拜访，探望 ③邀请

▶▶ **sense of responsibility** 责任感

Passage ③

Consumers are being confused and **misled** by the *hodge-podge*（大杂烩）of environmental claims made by household products, according to a "green labeling" study published by Consumers International Friday.

Among the report's more *outrageous*（令人无法容忍的）findings—a German **fertilizer** described itself as "earthworm friendly", a brand of **flour** said it was "**non-polluting**" and a British **toilet paper** claimed to be "environmentally friendlier."

The study was written and researched by Britain's National Consumer Council (NCC) for lobby group Consumer International. It was **funded** by the German and Dutch governments and the European Commission.

"While many good and useful claims are being made, it is clear there is **a long way to go** in ensuring shoppers who are adequately **informed** about the environmental impact of products they buy," said Consumers International director Anna Fielder.

The 10-country study surveyed product **packaging** in Britain, Western Europe, Scandinavia and the United States. It found that products sold in Germany and the United Kingdom made the most environmental claims on average.

The report focused on claims made by **specific** products , such as *detergent*（洗涤剂）and **insect sprays**, and by some garden products. It did not test the claims, but **compared** them **to** labeling guidelines set by the International Standards Organization (ISO) in September, 1999.

Researchers **documented** claims of environmental friendliness made by about 2, 000 products and found many too **vague** or too misleading to meet ISO standards. "Many products had specially-designed labels to make them seem environmentally friendly, but in fact many of these symbols mean nothing," said report researcher Philip Page.

"**Laundry** detergents made the most number of claims with 158. Household cleaners were second with 145 separate claims. While paints were third on our list with 73 .The high numbers show how very confusing it must be for consumers to **sort** the true **from** the misleading." he said.

The ISO labeling standards ban vague or misleading claims on product packaging, because terms such as "environmentally friendly" and "non-polluting" cannot be **verified**. "What we are now pushing for is to have **multinational corporations** meet the standards set by the ISO." said Page.

文章词汇注释

▶▶▶ **mislead** [mɪsˈliːd]

[释义] v. ①把…引错方向，把…引入歧途，误导 ②使产生错误想法

[同义] misdirect

[同根] misleading [mɪsˈliːdɪŋ] a. ①迷惑人的，使人产生误解的 ②引入歧途的

▶▶▶ **fertilizer** [ˈfɜːtɪlaɪzə]

[释义] n. ①肥料（特指化肥）②使丰富者，促进发展者

[同根] fertilize [ˈfɜːtɪlaɪz] v. ①施肥于，使肥沃 ②使丰富，促进…的发展
fertile [ˈfɜːtaɪl; ˈfɜːtl] a. ①肥沃的，多产的 ②可繁殖的 ③想象力丰富的，富于创造的

▶▶▶ **flour** [ˈflaʊə]

[释义] n. ①面粉，（谷物等磨成的）粉 ②粉状物质

▶▶▶ **non-polluting** [ˈnɒnpəˌluːtɪŋ]

[释义] a. 不污染的，污染极小的

▶▶▶ **toilet paper** 卫生纸，手纸

▶▶▶ **fund** [fʌnd]

[释义] v. 为…提供资金 n. ①资金，基金，专款 ②储备，蕴藏 ③ [pl.]（银行）存款，现款 ④特别基金管理机构

[同义] finance, sponsor

▶▶▶ **a long way to go** 有很长的一段路要走

▶▶▶ **informed** [ɪnˈfɔːmd]

[释义] a. ①了解情况的，见多识广的 ②有教养的，开明的

[同义] learned

[同根] inform [ɪnˈfɔːm] v. ①通知，告诉，报告 ②告发，检举
information [ˌɪnfəˈmeɪʃən] n. ①通知，报告 ②消息，资料 ③知识

▶▶▶ **packaging** [ˈpækɪdʒɪŋ]

[释义] n. ①包装，打包 ②包装物，包装术，包装业

[同根] pack [pæk] n. 包裹，背包 v. 包装，捆扎，塞满，压紧
package [ˈpækɪdʒ] n. ①包裹，小盒 ②包装袋 ③一揽子交易（或计划等）v. ①包裹，把…打包 ②包装（商品）③把…组合成一体

▶▶▶ **specific** [spɪˈsɪfɪk]

[释义] a. ①明确的，具体的 ②特有的，独特的

[同根] specify [ˈspesɪfaɪ] v. 具体指定，详细说明
specification [ˌspesɪfɪˈkeɪʃən] n. ①具体指定，详细说明 ② [常作~s] 规格，工程设计（书），详细计划（书），说明书

▶▶▶ **insect spray** 杀虫剂

▶▶▶ **compare...to...** ①把…和…比较 ②把…比作…

▶▶▶ **document** [ˈdɒkjumənt]

[释义] v. ①用文件等证明，为…提供文件 ②为（书等）引证 ③用记实材料作成（影片等）n. ①文献，公文

②证件，单据

[同根] documental [ˌdɒkjuˈmentəl] *a.* ①文件的，公文的 ②记录的，记实的

▶▶ **vague** [veɪɡ]

[释义] *a.* ①模糊的，含糊的 ②没有表情的，茫然的

[反义] clear

[同根] vagueness [ˈveɪɡnɪs] *n.* ①含糊，模糊 ②不明确的事，模糊的东西

▶▶ **laundry** [ˈlɔːndri]

[释义] *n.* ①〈口〉所（送）洗的衣物 ②洗衣房，洗衣店

▶▶ **sort...from...** 把…从…挑出来，区分，区别

▶▶ **verify** [ˈverɪfaɪ]

[释义] *v.* ①证明，证实 ②核实，查对，查清

[同义] confirm, prove

[反义] disprove

[同根] verification [ˌverɪfɪˈkeɪʃən] *n.* ①证明，证实 ②核实，查对，查清

verifiable [ˈverɪfaɪəbl] *a.* 可证实的，可核实的

▶▶ **multinational corporation** 跨国公司

选项词汇注释

▶▶ **outrageous** [aʊtˈreɪdʒəs]

[释义] *a.* ①令人不能容忍的 ②凶暴的 ③肆无忌惮的 ④极棒的

[同根] outrage [ˈaʊtreɪdʒ] *n.* ①肆无忌惮的恶行，不法行为 ②侮辱，冒犯 *v.* ①激怒 ②伤害（感情等）③对…施暴行

▶▶ **become aware of** 发觉，注意到

▶▶ **inform...of...** 通知…，告诉…

▶▶ **revise** [rɪˈvaɪz]

[释义] *v.* ①修改，改正 ②修订，校订

[同义] modify, adjust

[同根] revision [rɪˈvɪʒn] *n.* ①修订，修改 ②校订本，订正版

▶▶ **arouse** [əˈraʊz]

[释义] *v.* ①引起，激起 ②使…奋发，使…行动起来 ③唤起，唤醒

[同义] stimulate, stir

▶▶ **widespread** [ˈwaɪdspred; -ˈspred]

[释义] *a.* ①普遍的，广泛的 ②充分伸展的 ③分布广的

[同义] extensive, general

[反义] limited

▶▶ **tempt** [tempt]

[释义] *v.* ①诱惑，引诱 ②吸引，引起…的兴趣 ③冒…的风险

[同义] appeal, attract

[同根] temptation [tempˈteɪʃən] *n.* ①诱惑，引诱 ②诱惑物

tempting [ˈtemptɪŋ] *a.* 诱人的，吸引人的

▶▶ **satisfy** [ˈsætɪsfaɪ]

[释义] *v.* ①符合，达到（要求等），满足（需要等）②使满意

[同根] satisfaction [ˌsætɪsˈfækʃən] *n.* ①满意，满足 ②使人满意的原因，乐事

satisfied [ˈsætɪsfaɪd] *a.* 感到满意的，满足的

satisfactory [ˌsætɪsˈfæktəri] *a.* 令人满意的

Passage ④

Two hours from the tall buildings of Manhattan and Philadelphia live some of the world's largest black bears. They are in northern Pennsylvania's Pocono Mountains, a home they share with an **abundance** of other wildlife.

The streams, lakes, *meadows*（草地）, mountain **ridges** and forests that make the Poconos an ideal place for black bears have also attracted more people to the region. Open spaces are threatened by plans for housing **estates** and important *habitats*（栖息地）are **endangered** by highway **construction**. To protect the Poconos' natural beauty from **irresponsible** development, the *Nature Conservancy*（大自然保护协会）named the area one of America's "Last Great Places".

Operating out of a century-old schoolhouse in the village of Long Pond, Pennsylvania, the **conservancy**'s bud Cook is working with local people and business leaders to **balance** economic growth **with** environmental protection. By **forging partnerships** with people like Francis Altemose, the Conservancy has been able to protect more than 14, 000 **acres** of environmentally important land in the area.

Altemose's family has farmed in the Pocono area for generations. Two years ago Francis worked with the Conservancy to include his farm in a county farmland protection program. **As a result**, his family's land can be protected from development and the Altemoses will be better able to provide a secure financial future for their 7-year-old grandson.

Cook **attributes** the Conservancy's success in the Poconos **to** having a local **presence** and a **commitment** to working with local **residents**. "The key to protecting these **remarkable** lands is **connecting with** the local community, " Cook said. "The people who live there respect the land. They value quite forests, clear streams and abundant wildlife. They are eager to help with conservation effort".

For more information on how you can help The Nature Conservancy protect the Poconos and the world's other "Last Great Places, " please call 1-888-564 6864 or visit us on the World Wide Web at www.tnc.org.

文章词汇注释

▶▶ **abundance** [ə'bʌndəns]

[释义] n. ①大量，丰富 ②富有，富裕

[同义] large quantity, plenty

[反义] scarcity

[同根] abundant [ə'bʌndənt] a. ①大量的，充足的 ②丰富的，富裕的

▶▶ **ridge** [rɪdʒ]

[释义] n. ①山脊，分水岭 ②（人、动物的）脊梁 ③田埂，犁垄 ④屋脊

▶▶ **estate** [ɪ'steɪt]

[释义] n. ①地产，房产 ②遗产 ③（在乡村的）大片私有土地，种植园

▶▶ **endanger** [ɪn'deɪndʒə]

[释义] v. 危及，使遭危险，危害

[同根] endangered [ɪn'deɪndʒəd] a. ①（生命等）有危险的 ②有灭绝危险的

▶▶ **construction** [kən'strʌkʃən]

[释义] n. ①建造，建设 ②建筑物，结构 ③建造术

[同义] building

[反义] destruction, ruination

[同根] construct [kən'strʌkt] v. ①建造，构成 ②对…进行构想 ③（人为地）制造，编造
constructive [kən'strʌktɪv] a. ①建设性的 ②结构（上）的

▶▶ **irresponsible** [ˌɪrɪ'spɒnsəbl]

[释义] a. ①不负责任的，无责任感的 ②无责任能力的

[同根] irresponsibility [ˌɪrɪpɒnsə'bɪləti] n. ①不承担责任 ②不承担责任的行为（或人）③（尤指智力，或财力上）无责任能力
irresponsive [ˌɪrɪ'spɒnsɪv] a. ①无反应的，无答复的 ②不承担责任的

▶▶ **operate** ['ɒpəreɪt]

[释义] v. ①运作，运转 ②活动，行事 ③动手术 ④经营，管理

[同义] carry on, conduct, manage, handle

[同根] operating ['ɒpəreɪtɪŋ] a. ①操作的，运转的 ②经营的，营业的
operation [ˌɒpə'reɪʃən] n. ①运转，操作 ②经营 ③手术 ④作用，效力
operational [ˌɒpə'reɪʃənl] a. 操作的，运作的

[词组] operate on/upon sb. 给某人动手术

▶▶ **conservancy** [kən'sɜːvənsɪ]

[释义] n. ①（自然资源）保护机构（或区）②（对自然资源的）管理，保护

[同根] conserve [kən'sɜːv] v. ①保护 ②使（能量等）守恒
conservation [ˌkɒnsɜː'veɪʃən] n. ①保存,（对自然资源的）保护 ②森林（或其他自然资源）保护区
conservative [kən'sɜːvətɪv] a. ①保守的，传统的 ②稳当的，保险的 ③稳健派的 n. ①保守者，小心谨慎者 ②稳健派人 ③防腐剂

▶▶ **balance...with...** 平衡…与…，权衡…与…，斟酌…与…

▶▶ **forge** [fɔːdʒ]

[释义] v. ①锻造，使形成，制作 ②把…锤炼成 ③伪造（货币等）④编造（故事等）

▶▶ **partnership** ['pɑːtnəʃɪp]

[释义] n. ①合作关系，伙伴关系 ②合伙企业，全体合伙人

[同根] partner ['pɑːtnə] n. ①伙伴，同伙 ②合伙人，股东 ③搭档，同伴 ④配偶 v. ①使结伙 ②成为…的伙伴，作…的搭档

▶▶▶ **acre** ['eɪkə]

[释义] n. 英亩

▶▶▶ **as a result** 结果

▶▶▶ **attribute...to...** 把…归因于…

▶▶▶ **presence** ['prezns]

[释义] n. ①存在 ②出席，在场人物 ③（某人的）所在地方，面前

[同义] existence, being, appearance, attendance

[反义] absence

[同根] present [prɪ'zent] v. ①呈现，出示，提出 ②引见 ③给，赠送 ④上演 ['prezənt] n. 礼物，现在 a. 现在的，出席的
presentation [ˌprezen'teɪʃən] n. 介绍，陈述，赠送，表演

[词组] in the presence of sb. 在…面前，在（某人）眼前

▶▶▶ **commitment** [kə'mɪtmənt]

[释义] n. ①许诺，承诺 ②交押，收监 ③托付，交托

[同义] promise

[同根] commit [kə'mɪt] v. ①犯（罪），做（错事等）②把…交托给 ③使做

出保证
committee [kə'mɪtɪ] n. 委员会

▶▶▶ **resident** ['rezɪdənt]

[释义] n. ①居民，住户 ②（旅馆等的）住客，寄宿者 a. ①定居的，常住的 ②住校的，住院的 ③（鸟类等）无迁徙习性的

[同义] dweller, occupant, inhabitant

[同根] residence ['rezɪdəns] n. ①住宅，住处 ②居住，定居
residency ['rezɪdənsɪ] n. ①住宅，住处 ②居住，定居 ③住院医生实习期
residential [ˌrezɪ'denʃl] a. ①居住的，住所的 ②学生寄宿的

[词组] be resident at/in 住在…

▶▶▶ **remarkable** [rɪ'mɑ:kəbl]

[释义] a. ①非凡的，奇异的 ②值得注意的 n. 引人注目的事件，知名人物

[同根] remark [rɪ'mɑ:k] v. ①说，评论 ②注意，觉察 n. ①言辞，评论 ②注意，察觉

▶▶▶ **connecting with** ①和…联合，和…结合 ②由…联想到…

选项词汇注释

▶▶▶ **population** [ˌpɒpjʊ'leɪʃən]

[释义] n. ①人口 ②（具有共同特点的）一类人 ③（某地或某类）物品的总数 ④ [生] 居群，种群

[同义] inhabitants, residents, populace

[同根] populate ['pɒpjʊleɪt] v. ①（大批地）居住于 ②构成…的人口（或动植物的总数）③（事物等）在…中占有位置，占据
populace ['pɒpjʊləs] n. 平民，百姓

▶▶▶ **wildlife** ['waɪldlaɪf]

[释义] n. 野生生物

▶▶▶ **die out** 灭绝，逐渐消失

▶▶▶ **cooperation** [kəʊˌɒpə'reɪʃən]

[释义] n. ①合作，配合 ② [经] 合作，合作性团体

[同根] cooperate [kəʊ'ɒpəreɪt] v. 合作，进行经济合作

▶▶▶ **inclusion** [ɪn'klu:ʒən]

[释义] n. ①包含，含括 ②内含物

[同义] enclosure

[反义] exclusion

[同根] include [ɪn'klu:d] v. ①包括，包

含 ②列为…的一部分 ③包住，关住
inclusive [ɪnˈkluːsɪv] a. 包括的，包含的
including [ɪnˈkluːdɪŋ] prep. 包括

▶▶ **region** [ˈriːdʒən]
[释义] n. ①地区，区域 ②行政区 ③领域，界 ④范围，幅度
[同根] regional [ˈriːdʒənl] a. ① 地区的，地域性的 ②局部的 n. 地区分支机构
[词组] in the region of 在…附近，在…左右（指数字）

▶▶ **consideration** [kənsɪdəˈreɪʃn]
[释义] n. ①考虑 ②体贴，关心
[同义] thought, deliberation, reflection
[同根] consider [kənˈsɪdə] v. ① 考虑 ②认为，把…看作 ③体贴，顾及

considerable [kənˈsɪdərəbl] a. ①值得考虑的 ②相当大（或多）的
considerate [kənˈsɪdərɪt] a. ①关切的，体谅的 ②考虑周到的，周密的
considering [kənˈsɪdərɪŋ] prep. 考虑到，就…来说
[词组] take into consideration 考虑到，顾及
in consideration of 考虑到，由于
be under consideration 在考虑中，在研究中

▶▶ **establishment** [ɪˈstæblɪʃmənt]
[释义] n. ①建立，确定 ②法典，法规
[同义] founding, formation, creation
[同根] establish [ɪˈstæblɪʃ] v. ①建立，创立 ②安置，安顿 ③确立 ④证实，表明

Just five one-hundredths of an inch thick, light golden in color and with a perfect "saddle curl", the Lay's potato chip seems an unlikely weapon for global domination. But its maker, Frito-Lay, thinks otherwise. "Potato chips are a snack food for the world," said Salman Amin, the company's head of global marketing. Amin believes there is no corner of the world that can resist the charms of a Frito-Lay potato chip.

Frito-Lay is the biggest snack maker in America owned by PepsiCo and accounts for over half of the parent company's $3 billion annual profits. But the U.S. snack food market is largely saturated, and to grow. The company has to look overseas. Its strategy rests on two beliefs: first a global product offers economies of scale with which local brands cannot compete. And second, consumers in the 21st century are drawn to "global" as a concept. "Global" does not mean products that are consciously identified as American, but ones that consumes—especially young people—see as part of a modem, innovative (创新的) world in which people are linked across cultures by shared beliefs and tastes. Potato chips are an American invention, but most Chinese, for instance, do not know that Frito-Lay is an American company. Instead, Riskey, the company's research and development head, would hope they associate the brand with the new world of global communications and business.

With brand perception a crucial factor, Riskey ordered a redesign of the Frito-Lay logo (标识). The logo, along with the company's long-held marketing image of the "irresistibility" of its chips, would help facilitate the company's global expansion.

The executives acknowledge that they try to swing national eating habits to a food created in America, but they deny that amounts to economic imperialism. Rater, they see Frito-Lay as spreading the benefits of free enterprise across the world. "We're making products in those countries, we're adapting them to the tastes of those countries, building businesses and employing people and changing lives, " said Steve Reinemund, PepsiCo's chief executive.

文章词汇注释

▶▶ **saddle** ['sædl]

[释义] n. ①鞍状物 ②鞍，鞍具 ③脊，后背部 v. ①给马等装鞍，上鞍 ②使负重担，使承担责任 ③强加

[词组] get into the saddle ①上马 ②就职
in the saddle ①骑着马 ②在位，掌权
put the saddle on the right (wrong) 责备理应（不该）受到责备的人

▶▶ **domination** [dɒmɪ'neɪʃən]

[释义] n. ①支配，控制 ②在…中占首要地位

[同根] dominative [dɒmɪ'neɪtɪv] a. ①支配的，决定性的 ②有支配欲的 dominant ['dɒmɪnənt] a. ①占优势的 ②居高临下的 ③占首位的 n. 占优势者

▶▶ **potato chip** 炸土豆片

▶▶ **snack food** 快餐食品

▶▶ **account for** ①（数量等）占 ②解释，说明

▶▶ **annual** ['ænjuəl]

[释义] a. ①年度的，每年的 ②一年一次的 n. ①年报，年鉴 ②一年一度的事件

[同根] annually ['ænjuəlɪ] ad. 一年一次地，年度地

▶▶ **saturate** ['sætʃəreɪt]

[释义] v. ①使（市场）饱和 ②使充满 ③使饱享 ④浸透，使湿透

[同根] saturation [ˌsætʃə'reɪʃən] n. ①饱和（状态）②饱享 ③浸透
saturated ['sætʃəreɪtɪd] a. ①饱和的 ②充满的 ③浸透的，湿透的

▶▶ **strategy** ['strætɪdʒɪ]

[释义] n. ①战略，策略，计谋 ②战略学 ③战略部署

[同根] strategic [strə'tiːdʒɪk] a. ①根据战略的，战略上的 ②关键性的，对全局有重大意义的

▶▶ **scale** [skeɪl]

[释义] n. ①规模，范围 ②刻度，标度 ③衡量标准，尺度 ④等级，级别

[词组] in scale 成比例，相称
out of scale 不成比例，不相称
scale up 按比例增加
scale down 按比例减少

▶▶ **economy of scale** 规模经济

▶▶ **compete** [kəm'piːt]

[释义] v. ①竞争，对抗 ②比赛 ③（事物）媲美，比得上

[同根] competition [kɒmpɪ'tɪʃən] n. ①竞争 ②比赛，竞赛，赛会
competitive [kəm'petɪtɪv] a. ①竞争（或比赛）的 ②好竞争的 ③有竞争力的
competent ['kɒmpɪtənt] a. ①有能力的，能胜任的 ②合格的，合适的
competence ['kɒmpətəns] n. 能力，称职，胜任

▶▶ **consciously** ['kɒnʃəslɪ]

[释义] ad. 自觉地，有意识地

[同义] intentionally, knowingly, on purpose

[反义] unintentionally

[同根] conscious ['kɒnʃəs] a. ①意识到的，感到的 ②神志清醒的 ③有意的，存心的
consciousness ['kɒnʃəsnɪs] n. ①感觉，知觉，自觉 ②意识，观念
unconscious [ʌn'kɒnʃəs] a. 失去知觉的，无意识的
subconscious [sʌb'kɒnʃəs] a. 下意识的

▶▶ **crucial** [ˈkruːʃəl]

[释义] *a.* ①决定性的，至关重要的 ②严酷的，极为困难的

[同义] vital, critical, important

▶▶ **irresistibility** [ˌɪrɪˈzɪstəblɪtɪ]

[释义] *n.* 不能抵抗，不能抗拒

[同根] irresistible [ˌɪrɪˈzɪstəbl] *a.* ①不可抗拒的 ②不能反驳的 ③极为诱惑人的

▶▶ **facilitate** [fəˈsɪlɪteɪt]

[释义] *v.* ①使容易，使便利 ②促进，推动 ③帮助，援助

[同根] facility [fəˈsɪlɪtɪ] *n.* ①容易，便利 ②熟练，灵巧 ③设备，工具 facilitation [fəˌsɪlɪˈteɪʃn] *n.* ①简便化 ②使人方便的东西，辅助物

▶▶ **expansion** [ɪkˈspænʃn]

[释义] *n.* ①扩大，扩张 ②张开，展开 ③膨胀 ④扩大物，扩展部分

[反义] shrinkage, contraction

[同根] expand [ɪkˈspænd] *v.* ①发展，扩展，扩充 ②张开，展开

expansive [ɪkˈspænsɪv] *a.* ①扩张的，膨胀的 ②广阔的，全面的

expansively [ɪkˈspænsɪvlɪ] *ad.* 扩张地，全面地

▶▶ **acknowledge** [əkˈnɒlɪdʒ]

[释义] *v.* ①承认，确认 ②对…打招呼 ③对表示谢意

[同义] admit

[反义] deny

[同根] acknowledgement [əkˈnɒlɪdʒmənt] *n.* ①承认，确认 ②致谢

▶▶ **swing to** 使（态度或习惯）改变，转变

▶▶ **deny** [dɪˈnaɪ]

[释义] *v.* ①否认 ②拒绝相信 ③拒绝给予，拒绝某人的要求

[词组] deny oneself 节制，戒绝 deny oneself to 不会见，谢绝

▶▶ **adapt...to** 使…适应于…

选项词汇注释

▶▶ **suit one's need** 适应…的需要

▶▶ **promising** [ˈprɒmɪsɪŋ]

[释义] *a.* 有希望的，有前途的，有出息的

▶▶ **in the interest of** 为了（或符合）…

的利益，有助于

▶▶ **spoil** [spɔɪl]

[释义] *v.* ①破坏，损害 ②毁掉 ③宠坏，溺爱 ④（食物）变坏，变质

Passage ②

    In communities north of Denver, residents are **pitching in** to help teachers and **administrators** as the Vrain school **District** tries to solve a $13.8 million budget shortage **blamed** on **mismanagement**. "We're worried about our teachers and principals, and we really don't want to lose them because of this," one parent said. "If we can help ease their financial burden, we will."

Teachers are **grateful**, but know it may be years before the district is *solvent*（有综合能力的）. They feel really good about the parent support, but they realize it's impossible for them to solve this problem.

The 22,000-student district discovered the shortage last month. "It's extraordinary. Nobody would have imagined something happening like this at this level," said State Treasurer Mike Coffman. Coffman and district officials last week agreed on a state emergency plan freeing a $9.8 million loan that enabled the *payroll*（工资单）to be met for 2, 700 teachers and staff in time for the holidays.

District officials also took $1.7 million from student-activity **accounts** of its 38 schools. **At** Coffman's **request**, the District Attorney has begun investigating the district's finances. Coffman says he wants to know whether district officials hid the budget shortage until after the November election, when voters approved a $212 million **bond** issue for schools.

In Frederick, students' parents are buying classroom supplies and offering to pay for **groceries** and **utilities** to keep first-year teachers and principals in their jobs.

Some $36, 000 has been raised in **donations** from Safeway. A Chevrolet dealership donated $10, 000 and **forgave** the district's $10, 750 bill for **renting** the driver educating cars. IBM **contributed** 4, 500 packs of paper.

"We employ thousands of people in this community," said Mitch Carson, a hospital chief executive, who helped **raise funds**. "We have children in the school, and we see how they could be affected."

At Creek High School, three students started a website that **displays** newspaper articles, district information and an email *forum*（论坛）. "**Rumors** about what's happening to the district are moving at **lightning** speed," said a student. "We wanted to know the truth, and spread that around instead."

文章词汇注释

▶▶▶ pitch in ①齐心协力，作出贡献 ②…投入，把…扔入 ③动手干，使劲干

▶▶▶ administrator [əd'mɪnɪstreɪtə]
[释义] n. ①管理人员，行政人员 ②行政官员
[同义] manager, supervisor

20

[同根] administer [əd'mɪnɪstə] v. ①掌管，管理 ②执行，处理
administrate [əd'mɪnɪstreɪt] v. ①掌管，管理 ②执行，处理
administration [ədmɪnɪs'treɪʃən] n. ①管理，行政 ②管理部门 ③官员任期
administrative [əd'mɪnɪstrətɪv] a. 行政的，管理的，政府的

▶▶ **district** ['dɪstrɪkt]
[释义] n. ①区，行政区 ②地区，区域 ③选区 v. 把…划分成区
[同义] region, area

▶▶ **blame** [bleɪm]
[释义] v. ①归咎于 ②责备，责怪
n. ① （过错、失败等的）责任 ②责备
[同义] attribute to, hold responsible
[词组] blame on/onto 把…归咎于…

▶▶ **mismanagement** [ˌmɪs'mænɪdʒmənt]
[释义] n. 管理不善，处理不当
[同根] manage ['mænɪdʒ] v. ①处理，管理，经营 ②完成，设法办到
mismanage [ˌmɪs'mænɪdʒ] v. 对…管理不善，对…处理不当

▶▶ **grateful** ['greɪtful]
[释义] a. ①感激的 ②令人快意的，令人舒适的，使人感激的
[同义] thankful, appreciative
[反义] ungrateful
[词组] be grateful to sb. for sth. 为某事而感谢某人

▶▶ **account** [ə'kaunt]
[释义] n. ①户头，账户 ②解释 ③记述，报导，报告 ④理由，根据 v. ①解释，说明 ②报账 ③（指数量等）占 ④认为，把…归结于
[同根] accounting [ə'kauntɪŋ] n. ①会计，会计学 ②帐，记帐，清算帐目
accountant [ə'kauntənt] n. 会计（员），会计师
accountancy [ə'kauntənsɪ] n. 会计师之职，会计学
[词组] balance accounts with sb. 与某人结清账目

▶▶ **at sb.'s request** 应某人要求

▶▶ **bond** [bɔnd]
[释义] n. ①公债，债券 ②联结，联系 ③联结物，绳索 ④契约 v. 粘合
[同义] share, stock, tie, link, connection

▶▶ **grocery** ['grəusərɪ]
[释义] n. ①食品杂货 ②（美）食品杂货店，食品杂货业
[同根] grocer ['grəusə] n. 食品杂货商

▶▶ **utility** [ju:'tɪlɪtɪ]
[释义] n. ①器械，设施 ②公用事业 ③功用，效用
[同根] utilize ['ju:tɪlaɪz] v. 利用
utilization [ˌju:tɪlaɪ'zeɪʃən] n. 利用

▶▶ **donation** [dəu'neɪʃən]
[释义] n. ①（给慈善机关等的）捐赠物，捐款 ②捐赠，赠送
[同义] contribution
[同根] donate [dəu'neɪt] v. 捐赠，赠予

▶▶ **forgive** [fə'gɪv]
[释义] v. ①豁免，免除 ②原谅，宽恕 ③容许（失误等）

▶▶ **rent** [rent]
[释义] v. ①租借，租用 ②出租，出借
n. ①地租 ②租金 ③出租的房屋（或土地）
[同根] rental ['rentl] n. ①租费，租金收入 ②租赁 ③出租的财产 a. 供出租的

▶▶ **contribute** [kən'trɪbju:t]
[释义] v. ①捐献，捐助 ②投（稿）③贡献，提供
[同义] donate

四级词汇

[同根] contribution [ˌkɒntrɪˈbjuːʃən] n. ①贡献 ②（投给报刊等的）稿件
contributor [kənˈtrɪbjuːtə] n. ①捐助者，捐款人 ②贡献者 ③投稿者
[词组] contribute to 捐献，贡献给，有助于

▶▶ **raise funds** 筹集资金

▶▶ **display** [dɪˈspleɪ]
[释义] v. ①展示，显示 ②陈列，展览

③炫耀，夸示 n. ①陈列，展览 ②展示，显示 ③展览品
[同义] show
[词组] on display 正在展览中

▶▶ **rumor** [ˈruːmə]
[释义] n. 谣言，传闻 v. 谣传，传闻
[同义] gossip

▶▶ **lightning** [ˈlaɪtnɪŋ]
[释义] a. 闪电般的，极快的 n. 闪电

选项词汇注释

▶▶ **arise** [əˈraɪz]
[释义] v. ①产生，出现 ②上升，升起 ③（由…）引起，产生

▶▶ **quit** [kwɪt]
[释义] v. ①离开，辞职 ②停止，放弃 ③使摆脱，使免除 n.（美口）离开，辞职
[同义] resign, leave, abandon
[词组] be quit of 摆脱，脱离，免除

▶▶ **personnel** [ˌpɜːsəˈnel]
[释义] n. ①全体人员，员工 ②人事（部门）a. ①员工的 ②有关人事的
[同义] staff

▶▶ **accuse** [əˈkjuːz]
[释义] v. ①控告，指责 ②归咎于
[同义] blame, charge
[同根] accused [əˈkjuːzd] a. 被控告的 n. 被告
accusation [ækjuːˈzeɪʃn] n. ①控告，指控，指责 ②罪状，罪名
[词组] accuse sb. of… 指控某人…

▶▶ **pool** [puːl]
[释义] v. ①集中（钱、力量等）②共同承担 ③（使）形成池塘 n. ①池塘，

游泳池 ②水洼，小水坑

▶▶ **demand** [dɪˈmɑːnd]
[释义] v. ①要求，请求 ②需要 ③查问，询问 ④强要，强令 n. ①要求 ②要求物 ③需要，需求
[同义] ask, call for, require
[同根] demanding [dɪˈmɑːndɪŋ] a. 要求高的，需要技能的，苛求的
[词组] have many demands upon/on one's time 时间不够支配
in (great) demand ①需要量很大 ②许多人都需要
make demands of/on 对…提出要求，有求于
meet the demand 满足需要，符合要求

▶▶ **in the view of** 按照…的观点（或看法、见解）

▶▶ **insolvable** [ɪnˈsɒlvəbl]
[释义] a. 不能解决的，不能解答的
[同根] solve [sɒlv] v. ①解决，解答 ②阐明，解释 ③清偿，解除 ④溶解
solution [səˈluːʃən] n. ①解，解法 ②解决，解决办法 ③溶液，溶剂
solvable [ˈsɒlvəbl] a. 可解释的，可

解决的

▶▶ **irreversible** [ˌɪrɪˈvɜːsəbl; -sɪb-]

[释义] a. ①不可挽回的，不可改变的 ②不能倒转的，不能撤回的

[同根] reverse [rɪˈvɜːs] n. ①相反情况，对立面 ②反面，背面 v. ①（使）反向 ②彻底改变，撤销 ③调换 a. ①相反的 ②背面的，反面的

reversal [rɪˈvɜːsəl] n. ①反转，颠倒 ②撤销，废弃 ③翻转 ④逆转，恶化

reversible [rɪˈvɜːsəbl] a. ①可反向的，可翻转的 ②可逆转的，可废弃的

▶▶ **cover-up** n. ①掩盖，掩饰手段 ②罩衫，罩袍 a. 掩盖的，掩饰的

▶▶ **extent** [ɪkˈstent]

[释义] n. ①范围，程度 ②广度，长度，大小

[同义] degree

[词组] to a certian extent 在一定程度上，有几分，部分地

to some extent 某种程度上，（多少）有一点

to the extent of 到…的程度

▶▶ **attention** [əˈtenʃən]

[释义] n. ①注意，留心 ②注意力 ③关心，照料

[同义] care, concern

[同根] attentive [əˈtentɪv] a. ①注意的，留心的，关心的 ②殷勤的，有礼貌的

[词组] call/draw/invite/direct sb.'s attention to sth. 促使某人注意某事

catch/arrest sb.'s attention 引起某人的注意

devote/focus/give one's attention on 把注意力集中在…

with attention 留心地，注意地

▶▶ **appeal to** ①呼吁，恳求 ②诉诸，求助 ③上诉 ④对…有吸引力，投合…的心意

▶▶ **expose** [ɪkˈspəuz]

[释义] v. ①揭露，揭发 ②使处于…作用之下 ③陈列，展出 ④暴露

[同义] uncover, display

[反义] hide, cover, conceal

[同根] exposition [ˌekspəˈzɪʃən] n. ①说明，阐述，评注 ②博览会，展览会

exposure [ɪkˈspəuʒə] n. ①暴露，显露 ②揭露，揭穿 ③陈列 ④曝光

expositive [ɪkˈspɒzɪtɪv] a. 说明的，解释的，评注的

expository [ɪkˈspɒzɪˌtəri] a. 说明的，解释的，评注的

[词组] expose their plot 揭穿了他们的阴谋

▶▶ **properly** [ˈprɒpəlɪ]

[释义] ad. ①正确地，准确地 ②适宜地 ③有礼貌地，体面地

[同义] correctly, appropriately

[同根] proper [ˈprɒpə] a. ①适宜的 ②合乎体统的 ③正确的，准确的

▶▶ **crisis** [ˈkraɪsɪs]

[释义] n. ①危机，危急关头 ②转折点，关键时刻

[同义] disaster, emergency

[同根] critical [ˈkrɪtɪkl] a. ①批评的，评论的 ②爱挑剔的 ③危急的

[词组] at a crisis 在紧急关头

face a crisis 面临危局

pass a crisis 度过危机，脱离危险期

Passage ③

"Humans should not try to avoid stress any more than they would shun food, love or exercise." Said Dr. Hans Selye, the first physician to document the effects of stress on the body. While here's on question that contin-uous stress is harmful, several studies suggest that challenging situations in which you're able to **rise to the occasion** can be good for you.

In a 2001 study of 158 hospital nurses, those who faced **considerable** work demands but **coped with** the challenge were more likely to say they were in good health than those who felt they stress that you can manage also boost *immune*（免疫的）function. In a study at the Academic Center for Dentistry in Amsterdam, researchers **put** volunteers **through** two stressful experiences. In the first, a **timed** task that required memorizing a list followed by a short test, subjects through a *gory*（血淋淋的）video on **surgical procedures**. Those who did well on the memory test had an increase in levels of immunoglobulin A, an **antibody** that's the body's first line of **defense** against **germs**. The video-watchers experienced a **downturn** in the antibody.

Stress **prompts** the body to produce certain **stress hormones**. In short **bursts** these hormones have a positive effect, including improved memory function. "They can help **nerve cells** handle information and put it into storage," says Dr. Bruce McEwen of Rockefeller University in New York. But in the long run these hormones can **have a harmful effect on** the body and brain.

"**Sustained** stress is not good for you," says Richard Morimoto, a researcher at Northwestern University in Illinois studying the effects of stress on **longevity**, "It's the occasional burst of stress or brief exposure to stress that could be protective."

文章词汇注释

▶▶ **rise to the occasion** 起而应变，得体地应付突如其来的情况

▶▶ **considerable** [kən'sɪdərəbl]
[释义] *a.* ①相当大的，很多的 ②重大

的，值得考虑的
[同义] great
[同根] consider [kən'sɪdə] *v.* ①考虑，细想 ②认为，断定 ③体贴，考虑到

consideration [kənsɪdə'reɪʃən]
n. ①考虑 ②要考虑的事，动机 ③体贴
considerably [kən'sɪdərəbəlɪ] *ad.* 相
当大地，在很大程度上

▶▶ **cope with** ①应付，对付 ②同…
竞争

▶▶ **put through** ①通过…检查、检验
②做成，完成 ③办理…的手续 ④接
通（电话）

▶▶ **timed** [taɪmd]
[释义] *a.* ①定时的 ②在特定时刻发生
（或完成）的

▶▶ **surgical** ['sɜːdʒɪkəl]
[释义] *a.* 外科的，外科手术的
[同根] surgery ['sɜːdʒərɪ] *n.* ①外科，
手术 ②手术室 ③（英）诊所
surgeon ['sɜːdʒn] *n.* 外科医生

▶▶ **procedure** [prə'siːdʒə]
[释义] *n.* ①步骤，过程 ②常规，传统
做法 ③[计] 过程
[同根] proceed [prə'siːd] *v.* ①（尤指
停顿或打断后）继续进行 ②进行，
开展 ③进而做，开始做 ④行进，
前进
process ['prəʊses] *n.* ①过程 ②步
骤，方法 ③（时间等）进行，进展
v. ①对…进行加工
procession [prə'seʃən; prəʊ-] *n.* ①（人，
车等的）行列，队伍，列队行进
②连续，一（长）列

▶▶ **antibody** ['æntɪˌbɒdɪ]
[释义] *n.* [生] 抗体

▶▶ **defense** [dɪ'fens]
[释义] *n.* ①防御，守卫 ②防御物，防
御能力 ③辩护，答辩 ④被告方
[反义] offence, attack
[同根] defend [dɪ'fend] *v.* ①保卫，防

御 ②为…辩护
defensive [dɪ'fensɪv] *a.* 防御性的，
防卫的
[词组] in defense of ①保卫，捍卫
②为…辩护

▶▶ **germ** [dʒɜːm]
[释义] *n.* 微生物，细菌

▶▶ **downturn** ['daʊntɜːn]
[释义] *n.* ①衰退，下降趋势 ②下翻，
下转

▶▶ **prompt** [prɒmpt]
[释义] *v.* ①刺激，引起，激起 ②促使，
怂恿 ③提示，提词 *a.* 敏捷的，及
时的
[同义] stimulate, encourage
[同根] promptive ['prɒmptɪv] *a.* 敦促
的，激励的

▶▶ **stress hormone** 应激激素

▶▶ **burst** [bɜːst]
[释义] *n.* ①突发，一阵迸发 ②突然破
裂,爆炸 *v.* ①（使）爆炸,胀裂 ②冲,
突然显现 ③爆发，突然发作
[词组] at a burst 一阵，一口气，一举，
一下

▶▶ **nerve cell** 神经细胞
▶▶ **have a harmful effect on** 对…有害，
对…有不良影响

▶▶ **sustain** [sə'steɪn]
[释义] *v.* ①保持，使持续 ②赡养，供
养 ③支撑，承担 ④忍受，经受住
[同根] sustainable [sə'steɪnəbl] *a.* ①可
持续性的 ②能承受的

▶▶ **longevity** [lɒn'dʒevɪtɪ]
[释义] *n.* ①长寿，长命 ②寿命 ③长期
供职，资历

选项词汇注释

▶▶ **manageable** ['mænɪdʒəbl]
[释义] a. ①可控制的 ②可管理的 ③可设法做到的
[同根] manage ['mænɪdʒ] v. ①处理，经营 ②控制，驾驭 ③使用，操纵 ④设法做到
management ['mænɪdʒmənt] n. ①管理，经营 ②管理部门，资方

▶▶ **stay away from** 离开，远离，不出席

▶▶ **run out of** 用完

▶▶ **cut down on** 削减，减少

▶▶ **experience** [ɪk'spɪərɪəns]
[释义] v. 经历，体验 n. ①经历，阅历 ②经验，感受

[同根] **experienced** [ɪk'spɪərɪənst]
a. 有经验的，老练的，有见识的
experienceless [ɪk'spɪərɪənslɪs]
a. 无经验的，缺乏经验的，不老练的
experiential [ɪk,spɪərɪ'enʃəl] a. 经验的，来自经验的

▶▶ **determine** [dɪ'tɜːmɪn]
[释义] v. ①确定，决定 ②下决心，决意 ③测定，查明
[同义] decide
[同根] **determined** [dɪ'tɜːmɪnd] a. ①已下决心的，决意的 ②坚决的，坚定的
determination [dɪ,tɜːmɪ'neɪʃən]
n. ①决心，坚定 ②决定，决断

Passage 4

If you want to teach your children how to say sorry, you must be good at saying it yourself, especially to your own children. But how you say it can be quite **tricky**.

If you say to your children "I'm sorry I got angry with you, but..." what follows that "but" can render the apology **ineffective**: " I had a bad day" or "your noise was giving me a headache " leaves the person who has been injured feeling that he should be apologizing for his bad behavior in expecting an apology.

Another method by which people appear to apologize without actually doing so is to say "I'm sorry you're **upset**" , this **suggests** that you are somehow **at fault** for allowing yourself to get upset by what the other person has done.

Then there is the general, all covering apology, which avoids the necessity of identifying a specific act that was particularly hurtful or **insulting**, and which the person who is apologizing should promise never to do again. Saying "I'm useless as a parent" does not **commit** a person to any specific improvement.

These **pseudo**-apologies are used by people who believe saying sorry shows weakness, Parents who wish to teach their children to apologize should see it as a sign of **strength**, and therefore not **resort to** these pseudo-apologies.

But even when **presented** with examples of genuine contrition, children still need help to become aware of the **complexities** of saying sorry. A three-year-old might need help in understanding that other children feel pain just as he does, and that hitting a playmate over the head with a heavy toy requires an apology. A six-year-old might need **reminding** that spoiling other children's expectations can require an apology. A 12-year-old might need to be shown that raiding the biscuit tin without asking **permission** is **acceptable**, but that borrowing a parent's clothes without permission is not.

文章词汇注释

▶▶ **tricky** [ˈtrɪkɪ]

[释义] a. ①微妙的 ②难处理的，棘手的 ③足智多谋的 ④诡计多端的

[同义] delicate

[同根] trick [trɪk] v. ① 欺骗，愚弄 ②变戏法 ③开玩笑，戏弄 n. ①戏法，把戏 ②技巧，窍门 ③诡计，花招 ④恶作剧 a. ①变戏法用的 ②欺诈的 ③有诀窍的
trickily [ˈtrɪkɪlɪ] ad. 用欺骗手法

▶▶ **ineffective** [ˌɪnɪˈfektɪv]

[释义] a. ①无效的，用处很小的 ②无能力的，不能干的

[同义] useless, futile

[反义] effective

▶▶ **upset** [ʌpˈset]

[释义] a. ①心烦意乱的 ②不适的，不舒服的 v. ①弄翻，打翻 ②搅乱，打乱 ③使心烦意乱，使不适

[同义] unhappy, annoyed, irritated

[反义] pleased, happy

▶▶ **suggest** [səˈdʒest]

[释义] v. ①使人想到，使人联想到 ②建议，提议 ③暗示，启发

[同根] suggestion [səˈdʒestʃən] n. ①建议，意见 ②暗示，启发
suggestive [səˈdʒestɪv] a. 提示的，暗示的，引起联想的

▶▶ **at fault** ①有过错，有责任 ②感到困惑，不知所措 ③出毛病，有故障

▶▶ **insulting** [ɪnˈsʌltɪŋ]

[释义] a. ①侮辱的，污蔑的，无礼的 ②损害人体的

[同义] offensive, abusive, rude

[反义] polite

[同根] insult [ˈɪnsʌlt] n. ①侮辱 ②损伤 v. ①侮辱，辱骂 ②损害，危害 ③攻击，袭击

▶▶ **commit** [kəˈmɪt]

[释义] v. ①使做出保证，使承担义务 ②把…交托给 ③犯(罪)，做(错事等)

[同根] commitment [kə'mɪtmənt] n. ①托付，委托 ②许诺，保证
committee [kə'mɪtɪ] n. 委员会

[词组] commit oneself on 对…表态
commit oneself to ①委身于 ②专心致志于

▶▶ pseudo ['sju:dəʊ]

[释义] a. 假的,冒充的 n.〈口〉假冒者，伪君子

▶▶ strength [streŋθ]

[释义] n. ①优点，长处 ②强度，牢度 ③力量，力气，实力

[同义] power, force, might, vigour

[反义] weakness

[同根] strengthen ['streŋθən] v. ① 加强，巩固，使坚强 ②增加…的艺术效果

▶▶ resort to ①采用，使用（手段）②诉诸（法律）③常去

▶▶ present [prɪ'zent]

[释义] v. ①提供，赠送 ②表示，致以（问候等）③提出，递交 ④显示，呈现 ['prezənt] n. ①礼物，赠品 ②目前，现在 a. ①出席的，到场的 ②现在的，目前的

[同根] presentation [,prezen'teɪʃən] n. ①介绍 ②陈述 ③赠送 ④表演

▶▶ complexity [kəm'pleksɪtɪ]

[释义] n. ①复杂（性），错综（性）②错综复杂的事物

[同义] complication

[反义] simplicity

[同根] complex ['kɒmpleks] a. ①由部件组成的，组合的 ②复杂的，难懂的 n. ①综合体，集合体 ② [心] 情结

▶▶ remind [rɪ'maɪnd]

[释义] v. ①提醒，使想起 ②使发生联想

[同根] remindful [rɪ'maɪndful] a. ①起提醒作用的，提示的 ②牢记的，留意的

[词组] remind sb.of… 使某人想起…

▶▶ permission [pə'mɪʃn]

[释义] n. 允许，准许，许可

[同义] agreement

[反义] prohibition

[同根] permit [pɜ:'mɪt] n. 许可证，执照 v. ①允许，许可 ②使成为可能
permissive [pɜ:'mɪsɪv] a. ①给予许可的，准许的 ②宽容的，放任的

▶▶ acceptable [ək'septəbl]

[释义] a. ①可以接受的，可忍受的 ②合意的，受欢迎的

[同根] accept [ək'sept] v. ①接受，收受 ②答应，承认 ③认可，允许 ④赞同，赞成
acceptance [ək'septəns] n. ①接受，接纳 ②赞同，赞成 ③承认，认可

选项词汇注释

▶▶ owe [əʊ] v. ①欠 ② 应给予，应该（或有必要）做 ③应把…归功于 ④应感激

[反义] repay

[同根] owing ['əʊɪŋ] a. 该付的，未付的

[词组] owe it to oneself 认为自己有责任
owe sth. to 把…归功于，为…而应

感谢

▶▶ take...into account 考虑…，斟酌…

▶▶ set a good example 树立一个好榜样

▶▶ patient ['peɪʃnt]

[释义] a. 忍耐的，有忍耐力的，有耐心的 n. ①病人 ②（美容院等的）顾客

[反义] impatient

[同根] patience ['peɪʃəns] n. ①忍耐，容忍 ②耐心，耐性，坚韧

▶▶ tolerant ['tɒlərənt]

[释义] a. ①忍受的，容忍的 ②能耐…的 ③有免疫耐受性的

[同义] patient

[反义] intolerant

[同根] tolerate ['tɒləreɪt] v. ①忍受，宽恕 ②容许，不干预 ③对…有耐力

tolerance ['tɒlərəns] n. ①宽容，容忍 ②忍耐力 ③［医］耐受性，耐药量

toleration [tɒlə'reɪʃən] n. ①宽容，忍受，容忍 ②容许，默认 ③耐受性

[词组] be tolerant of (toward) 对…人能容忍（或宽容）

▶▶ call for 需要，要求

▶▶ progress ['prəʊgres; (US)'prɑ:gres]

[释义] n. ①进步，前进 ②行进 v. ①前进，进步，发展 ②行进，进行

[同义] advancement, improvement

[反义] retreat

[同根] progressive [prə'gresɪv] a. ①进步的，先进的，革新的 ②前进中的，发展中的 ③渐次的，循序渐进的

Interest in pursuing international careers has soared in recent years, enhanced by *chronic* (长久的) personnel shortages that are causing companies to search beyond their home borders for talent.

Professionals seek career experience outside of their home countries for a variety of reasons. They may feel the need to recharge their batteries with a new challenge. They may want a position with more responsibility that encourages creativity and initiative. Or they may wish to expose their children to another culture, and the opportunity to learn a second language.

When applying for a job, one usually has to submit a resume or curriculum vitae (CV). The two terms generally mean the same thing: a one—or two—page document describing one's educational qualifications and professional experience. However, guidelines for preparing a resume are constantly changing. The best advice is to find out what is appropriate regarding the *corporate* (公司) culture, the country culture, and the culture of the person making the hiring decision. The challenge will be to embrace two or more cultures in one document. The following list is a good place to start.

● Educational requirements differ from country to country. In almost every case of "cross-border" job hunting, just stating the title of your degree will not be an adequate description. Provide the reader with details about your studies and any related experience.

● Pay attention to the resume format you use—chronological or reverse-chronological order. Chronological order means listing your 'oldest' work experience first. Reverse-chronological order means listing your current or most recent experience first. Most countries have preferences about which format is most acceptable. If you find no specific guidelines, the general preference is for the reverse-chronological format.

● If you are submitting your resume in English, find out if the *recipient* (收件人) uses British English or American English because there are variations between the two **versions**. For example, university education is often referred to as "**tertiary** education" in the United Kingdom, but this term is almost never used in the United States. A reader who is **unfamiliar** with these variations may assume that your resume contains errors.

文章词汇注释

▶▶ **soar** [sɔː;sɒr]

[释义] v. ①猛增，剧增，高涨 ②高飞，升腾

[同义] ascend, leap, skyrocket

[同根] soaring ['sɔːrɪŋ] a. ①剧增的，高涨的 ②高飞的，翱翔的

▶▶ **shortage** ['ʃɔːtɪdʒ]

[释义] n. ①不足，缺乏 ②缺乏的量

[同义] scarcity, lack

[反义] excess

▶▶ **border** ['bɔːdə]

[释义] n. ①边界 ②边缘，界线 v. ①邻接，毗连 ②形成…边界 ③（常与 on, upon 连用）近似，接近 a. 边界的，形成边界的

[同义] boundary

[同根] borderland ['bɔːdələnd] n. 边疆，边境，边沿地区
borderline ['bɔːdəlaɪn] n. 边界线，界限 a. 边界线上的，边界附近的

[词组] on the border of ①在…的边界上 ②将要，濒临于

▶▶ **talent** ['tælənt]

[释义] n. ①有才能的人 ②天资，天才，才干

[同义] genius

[同根] talentless ['tæləntlɪs] a. 没有天赋的，无才能的
talented ['tæləntɪd] a. 天才的，有才干的

▶▶ **recharge** [ˌriːˈtʃɑːdʒ]

[释义] v. ①再充电 ②再猛攻，反击 ③再控告，再指控

▶▶ **battery** ['bætərɪ]

[释义] n. ①电池（组）②一套，一批，一系列

▶▶ **responsibility** [rɪˌspɒnsəˈbɪlɪtɪ]

[释义] n. ①责任，职责 ②责任感，责任心

[同义] duty

[反义] irresponsibility

[同根] responsible [rɪˈspɒnsəbl] a. ①认真负责的 ②承担责任的，有责任能力的 ③责任重大的

[词组] take the responsibility for 对…负有责任

▶▶ **initiative** [ɪˈnɪʃətɪv]

[释义] n. ①首创精神 ②主动的行动 ③（前面与 the 连用）主动权 a. 开始的，创始的

[同义] inventiveness

[同根] initiate [ɪˈnɪʃɪeɪt] v. ①开始，发起 ②把（基础知识）传授给（某人）③让…加入 ④倡议，提出（措施等）
initial [ɪˈnɪʃəl] a. 开始的，最初的 n. 首字母
initiation [ɪˌnɪʃɪˈeɪʃən] n. ①开始，创始 ②入会，加入组织 ③指引，传授

[词组] have the initiative 掌握主动权
on (one's) own initiative 主动地
take the initiave 采取主动，首先采取

行动

▶▶ **apply for** 申请，请求

▶▶ **submit** [səb'mɪt]

[释义] v. ①提交，呈递 ②（使）服从，（使）屈服 ③听从，忍受

[同义] present

[反义] withdraw

[同根] submission [səb'mɪʃən] n. 屈服，降服，服从

[词组] submit to ①提交给… ②服从于，屈从于

submit oneself to 甘受，服从

▶▶ **resume** ['rezju:meɪ]

[释义] n. ①（求职者的）履历，简历 ②摘要，概略

[rɪ'zju:m] v. ①（中断后）再继续，重新开始 ②恢复，重新得到 ③接着说

▶▶ **curriculum vitae** [kə'rɪkjuləm'vi:taɪ]

[释义] n. （求职者的）履历，简历

▶▶ **generally** ['dʒenərəlɪ]

[释义] ad. ①一般地，大体 ②普遍地，广泛地 ③笼统地，概括地

[同义] in general, by and large, normally

[同根] general ['dʒenərəl] a. ①总的，普遍的 ②一般的，通常的 ③笼统的，大体的 n. 将军，军事家，战略家
generalize ['dʒenərəlaɪz] v. ①对…进行概括 ②使一般化
generalization [,dʒenərəlaɪ'zeɪʃən] n. 概括，普遍化

▶▶ **describe** [dɪ'skraɪb]

[释义] v. ①描写，叙述 ②画出（图形），描绘

[同义] depict

[词组] describe sb. as 把某人说成是（称作）

▶▶ **constantly** ['kɒnstəntlɪ]

[释义] ad. ①不断地 ②坚持不懈地

[同义] always, often

[同根] constant ['kɒnstənt] a. ①不变的，固定的 ②时常发生的，连续不断的 ③忠实的，忠心的 n. ①不变的事物 ②常数，衡量
constancy ['kɒnstənsɪ] n. ①持久不变 ②忠实 ③永久性的事务

▶▶ **embrace** [ɪm'breɪs]

[释义] v. ①包括 ②（欣然）接受 ③包围，环绕 ④拥抱 n. 拥抱，包围

[同义] hold, include

▶▶ **cross-border** a. 跨国界的

▶▶ **job hunting** 求职

▶▶ **state** [steɪt]

[释义] v. ①陈述，声明 ②规定 n. ①状况 ②心情，心态 ③国家，领土 ④州，邦

[同根] statement ['steɪtmənt] n. ①（正式的，或肯定的）说法 ②（正式的）声明 ③陈述

▶▶ **degree** [dɪ'gri:]

[释义] n. ①学位 ②程度 ③（等级中的）级 ④度，度数

[词组] to a degree ①（英口）非常，极其 ②稍微，有点
to the last degree 极度地

▶▶ **adequate** ['ædɪkwɪt]

[释义] a. ①充分的，足够的 ②适当的，胜任的

[同义] ample, sufficient, enough, satisfactory

[词组] be adequate for 足够…，适合…

▶▶ **detail** ['di:teɪl;dɪ'teɪl]

[释义] n. ①细节，详情 ②详述 ③详图 v. ①详述 ②列举

[同根] detailed ['di:teɪld] a. ①详细的，细致的，精细的 ②复杂的

[词组] go into details 详细叙述，逐一说明
in detail 详细地

▶▶▶ **related** [rɪ'leɪtɪd]

[释义] *a.* ①有关的，相关的 ②有亲戚（或亲缘）关系的 ③叙述的，讲述的

[同义] connected, linked, associated

[反义] unconnected

[同根] relate [rɪ'leɪt] *v.* ①讲述，叙述 ②（使）互相关联，证明…之间的必然联系

relation [rɪ'leɪʃən] *n.* ①关系，联系 ②叙述，故事 ③亲戚关系，亲戚

relationship [rɪ'leɪʃənʃɪp] *n.* ①关系，关联 ②亲属关系

relative ['relətɪv] *a.* ①有关系的 ②相对（性）的，比较的 *n.* 亲戚

▶▶▶ **format** ['fɔ:mæt]

[释义] *n.* ①格式，形式 ②（出版物的）开本，版式 *v.* 安排…的格局（或规格），[计] 格式化（磁盘）

▶▶▶ **chronological** [ˌkrɒnə'lɒdʒɪkəl]

[释义] *a.* 按年代顺序排列的

▶▶▶ **variation** [ˌveərɪ'eɪʃən]

[释义] *n.* ①变化，变更 ②变异，变种

[同义] change, alternation

[同根] vary ['veərɪ] *v.* 改变，变化

variety [və'raɪətɪ] *n.* ①变化，多样性 ②种种 ③种类

various ['veərɪəs] *a.* ①各种各样的 ②许多的 ③多方面的，具有多种特征的

▶▶▶ **version** ['vɜ:ʃən]

[释义] *n.* ①（一事物的）变化形式，变体 ②版本 ③译本，译文

▶▶▶ **tertiary** ['tɜ:ʃərɪ]

[释义] *a.* 第三位的，第三级的，第三的

▶▶▶ **unfamiliar** [ˌʌnfə'mɪlɪə]

[释义] *n.* ①不熟知的，不通晓的 ②不熟悉的，陌生的

[同义] new, novel

[同根] familiar [fə'mɪlɪə] *a.* ①熟悉的，通晓的 ②常见的，普通的

familiarity [fəˌmɪlɪ'ærɪtɪ] *n.* ①熟悉，通晓 ②亲近，亲昵 ③随便，放肆

选项词汇注释

▶▶▶ **original** [ə'rɪdʒənəl]

[释义] *a.* ①独创的，新颖的 ②最初的，原来的 ③原版的 *n.* 原物，原作

[同义] innovative, inventive, creative

[同根] origin ['ɒrɪdʒɪn] *n.* ①起源，来源，起因 ②出身，血统

originate [ə'rɪdʒɪneɪt] *v.* ①发源，产生 ②发明，创作 ③创始，开创

▶▶▶ **expand** [ɪk'spænd]

[释义] *v.* ①扩展，扩大，扩充 ②张开，展开

[同义] enlarge

[反义] shrink, contract

[同根] expansion [ɪk'spænʃən] *n.* ①扩大，扩张 ②张开，展开 ③膨胀 ④扩展部分

expansive [ɪk'spænsɪv] *a.* ①扩张的，膨胀的 ②广阔的，全面的

▶▶▶ **skill** [skɪl]

[释义] *n.* ①能力，熟练性 ②（专门）技术，技艺

[同义] proficiency, technique, craft

[同根] skilled [skɪld] *a.* ①熟练的，有技能的 ②需要（专门）技术的，需

要熟练能力的的

▶▶▶ **take into consideration** 顾及，考虑到

▶▶▶ **impress** [ɪm'pres]

[释义] v. ①使留下深刻印象，使铭记 ②印，盖（印、邮戳等）于

[同义] make an impression on, make an impact on

[同根] impression [ɪm'preʃən] n. ①印象 ②压印，印痕 ③影响，效果

impressive [ɪm'presɪv] a. ①给人深刻印象的，感人的 ②威严的，使人敬畏的

▶▶▶ **highlight** ['haɪlaɪt]

[释义] v. ①强调，使显著 ②（绘画或摄影中）用强光突出 ③以强光照射，照亮 ④为…中最突出的事物 n. ①强光（效果），最亮部分 ②最突出的部分

▶▶▶ **keen** [kiːn]

[释义] a. ①强烈的，深切的 ②热衷的，渴望的 ③锐利的，锋利的 ④敏锐的

[同义] intense, eager, enthusiastic

[词组] be keen on 热衷于，对…着迷

▶▶▶ **be aware of** 知道，意识到

▶▶▶ **recipient** [rɪ'sɪpɪənt]

[释义] n. ①接受者 ②容器 a. 容纳的，愿意接受的

[同根] recipience [rɪ'sɪpɪəns] n. ①接受，容纳 ②感受

recipe ['resɪpɪ] n. 食谱，烹饪法

receipt [rɪ'siːt] n. 收条，收据

▶▶▶ **with regard to** 关于

▶▶▶ **distinctive** [dɪs'tɪŋktɪv]

[释义] a. 独特的，与众不同的

[同义] unique, characteristic

[反义] common

[同根] distinct [dɪs'tɪŋkt] a. ① 独特的，截然不同的 ②清楚的，明白的 ③清晰的，明显的

distinction [dɪs'tɪŋkʃən] n. ①区分，分清 ②差别 ③特点，特性 ④显赫，声望

distinguish [dɪs'tɪŋgwɪʃ] v. ①区分，分清 ②辨别出，看清 ③使杰出，使著名

Passage ②

Educating girls quite possibly yields a higher rate of return than any other **investment** available in the developing world. Women's education may be unusual **territory** for economists, but enhancing women's contribution to development is actually as much an economic as a **social issue**. And economics, with its emphasis on *incentives*（激励）, provides **guideposts** that **point to** an **explanation** for why so many girls **are deprived of** an education.

Parents in **low-income** countries fail to invest in their daughters because they do not expect them to make an economic contribution to the family: girls grow up only to marry into somebody else's family and bear children. Girls are thus seen as less valuable than boys and are kept at home to do housework while their brothers are sent to school—the *prophecy*（预言）

becomes **self-fulfilling**, **trapping** women **in** *a vicious circle* (恶性循环) of neglect.

An educated mother, on the other hand, has greater **earning** abilities outside the home and faces an entirely different set of choices. She is likely to have fewer but healthier children and can **insist on** the development of all her children, ensuring that her daughters are given a **fair** chance. The education of her daughters then makes it much more likely that the next generation of girls, **as well as** of boys, will be educated and healthy. The vicious circle is thus **transformed into** a **virtuous circle**.

Few will dispute that educating women has great social benefits. But it has **enormous** economic advantages as well. Most obviously, there is the direct effect of education on the wages of **female workers**. Wages rise by 10 to 20 per cent for each additional year of schooling. Such big returns are **impressive** by the standard of other available investments, but they are just the beginning. Educating women also has a significant impact on health practices, including family planning.

文章词汇注释

▶▶▶ **investment** [ɪn'vestmənt]
[释义] *n.* ①投资 ②（时间等的）投入
[同根] invest [ɪn'vest] *v.* ①投（资）
　②耗费，投入（时间等）
　investable [ɪn'vestəbl] *a.* 可供投资的，可用于投资的
[词组] make an investment in 投资于…

▶▶▶ **territory** ['terɪtərɪ]
[释义] *n.* ①（活动、知识等的）领域，领土 ②地区，地方
[同义] area, field

▶▶▶ **social issue** 社会问题

▶▶▶ **guidepost** ['gaɪdpəust]
[释义] *n.* ①路标，指向牌 ②指导方针，指导原则 ③准则

▶▶▶ **point to** ①指明，指出 ②指向，朝向 ③显示，证明

▶▶▶ **explanation** [,eksplə'neɪʃən]
[释义] *n.* ①解释，说明 ②辩解，辨明
[同根] explain [ɪk'spleɪn] *v.* ①解释，说明…的含义 ②辩解，辩护
　explanatory [ɪk'splænətərɪ] *a.* 解释的，说明的
[词组] in explanation of 解释

▶▶▶ **be deprived of** 被夺去了…的，被剥夺了…的

▶▶▶ **low-income** *a.* 低收入的

▶▶▶ **self-fulfilling** [selfful'fɪlɪŋ]
[释义] *a.* ①（预言等）本身自然会实现的 ②自我实现的，实现自己抱负的

▶▶ trap...in 使…陷入圈套，使…受限制

▶▶ earn [ɜ:n]
[释义] v. ①赚得，挣得 ②赢得，获得，使得到 ③招致，惹起
[同义] make money
[反义] consume, spend
[同根] earnings ['ɜ:nɪŋz] n. ①工资，收入 ②（由投资等）赚得的钱，收益，利润

▶▶ insist on ①坚持，强调 ②坚决主张，坚决要求

▶▶ fair [feə]
[释义] a. ①公平的，公道的 ②合理的，正当的 ③还可以的，尚可的 ④天气晴朗的 n. ①美好的事物，美人 ②集市
[同义] just, reasonable
[同根] fairly ['feəlɪ] ad. ①公平地，公正地 ②相当地，尚可地 ③完全，简直

▶▶ as well as 和，除…之外（也）

▶▶ be transformed into 被转变为…

▶▶ virtuous circle 良性循环

▶▶ enormous [ɪ'nɔ:məs]
[释义] a. ①巨大的，庞大的 ②穷凶极恶的，横暴的
[同义] giant, great, huge, large, vast
[反义] little, small, tiny
[同根] enormously [ɪ'nɔ:məslɪ] ad. 非常地，巨大地

▶▶ female worker 女工

▶▶ impressive [ɪm'presɪv]
[释义] a. 给人深刻印象的，显著的，感人的
[同义] remarkable, notable, striking

选项词汇注释

▶▶ argue ['ɑ:gju:]
[释义] v. ①主张，认为 ②争论，争执 ③说服，劝说
[同义] think, believe, consider, dispute
[同根] argument ['ɑ:gjumənt] n. ①争论，争辩，争执 ②说理，论证 ③理由，论据，论点
[词组] argue about 辩论（或争论）某事

▶▶ developing country 发展中国家

▶▶ labor-saving [ˌleɪbə'seɪvɪŋ]
[释义] a. 节约人工的，省力的

▶▶ prophecy ['prɒfɪsɪ]
[释义] n. ①预言 ②预言能力 ③预示，先兆

▶▶ be discontented with 对…不满，对…不满意

▶▶ turn out to be 原来是，结果是，最后证明是

▶▶ turn into （使）变成，（使）成为

▶▶ beyond reach 够不着，拿不到，影响不到，无法理解

▶▶ gain [geɪn]
[释义] v. ①获得，博得，赢得 ②增加 ③（经过努力）到达 n. ①获得，取得 ②增加，增添 ③获得的东西，取得的进展
[同义] acquire, earn, get, win
[反义] lose
[同根] gainable ['geɪnəbl] a. 可得到的，可赢得的

▶▶ arouse the interest of 引起…的兴趣

▶▶ well-educated a. 受过良好教育的

Passage 3

Speeding off in a stolen car, the thief thinks he has got a great catch. But he is in for an unwelcome surprise. The car is fitted with a remote *immobiliser* (锁止器), and a radio signal from a control centre miles away will ensure that once the thief switches the engine off, he will not be able to start it again.

The idea goes like this. A control box fitted to the car contains a mini-cellphone, a micro-processor and memory, and a *GPS*（全球定位系统）satellite positioning receiver. If the car is stolen, a coded cellphone signal will tell the control centre to block the vehicle's engine management system and prevent the engine being restarted.

In the UK, a set of technical fixes is already making life harder for car thieves. "The pattern of vehicle crime has changed," says Martyn Randall, a security expert. He says it would only take him a few minutes to teach a person how to steal a car, using a bare minimum of tools. But only if the car is more than 10 years old.

Modern cars are far tougher to steal, as their engine management computer won't allow them to start unless they receive a unique ID code beamed out by the *ignition*（点火）key. In the UK, technologies like this have helped achieve a 31% drop in vehicle-related crime since 1997.

But determined criminals are still managing to find other ways to steal cars, often by getting hold of the owner's keys. And key theft is responsible for 40% of the thefts of vehicles fitted with a tracking system.

If the car travels 100 metres without the driver confirming their ID, the system will send a signal to an operations centre that it has been stolen. The hundred metres minimum avoids false alarms due to inaccuracies in the GPS signal.

Staff at the centre will then contact the owner to confirm that the car really is missing, and keep police informed of the vehicle's movements via the car's GPS unit.

文章词汇注释

▶▶ **catch** [kætʃ]
[释义] *n.* 值得获得的物或人

▶▶ **be in for** ①肯定会经历，注定要遭受 ②参加（竞赛等）

▶▶ **unwelcome** [ʌn'welkəm]
[释义] *a.* 讨厌的，不受欢迎的
[同义] unwanted, uninvited
[同根] welcome ['welkəm] *a.* ①受欢迎的 ②被允许的，不受限制的 *v.* ①欢迎，迎接 ②款待，接待 *n.* ①欢迎，接受 ②欢迎词

▶▶ **fitted with...** 安装有…配件/设备

▶▶ **remote** [rɪ'məut]
[释义] *a.* ①遥控的，远程的 ②远的 ③边远的，偏僻的 ④关系疏远的
[同根] remotion [rɪ'məuʃən] *n.* 远离，遥远

▶▶ **signal** ['sɪgnl]
[释义] *n.* 信号 *a.* 信号的 *v.* 发信号，用信号通知
[同义] indication
[同根] sign [saɪn] *n.* ①符号，记号 ②征兆，预兆 ③手势，示意动作 ④招牌，指示牌 *v.* ①签（名）②以手势表示，示意 ③签署（信、文件等）④预示，表示

▶▶ **switch...off**（用开关）关掉，（用开关）切断（电流）

▶▶ **mini-cellphone** *n.* 微型手机，袖珍型手机

▶▶ **micro-processor** *n.* 微处理器

▶▶ **memory** ['memərɪ]
[释义] *n.* ①[计] 存储（器）②记忆，记忆力 ③回忆 ④纪念
[同根] memorize ['meməraɪz] *v.* 记住，熟记
memorial [mɪ'mɔːrɪəl] *a.* ①记忆的 ②纪念的 *n.* ①纪念物 ②纪念仪式 ③纪念碑，纪念馆
[词组] bear/have/keep in memory 记 在心里，没有忘记

▶▶ **satellite positioning receiver** 卫星定位接收器

▶▶ **vehicle** ['viːɪkl]
[释义] *n.* ①车辆，交通工具，机动车，运载器 ②传播媒介，手段

▶▶ **engine management system** 发动机操纵系统

▶▶ **a set of** 一组，一套

▶▶ **fix** [fɪks]
[释义] *n.* 应急措施，补救办法

▶▶ **security expert** 安全专家

▶▶ **bare minimum** 最小量，最小限度，最低限度

▶▶ **ID code** 身份编码

▶▶ **beam out** 定向发射，发出（信号等）

▶▶ **achieve** [ə'tʃiːv]
[释义] *v.* ①（经努力）达到，得到 ②完成，实现
[同义] attain, accomplish, complete, finish, fulfill
[反义] fail, abandon, give up
[同根] achievement [ə'tʃiːvmənt] *n.* ①达到，实现 ②成就，成绩

▶▶ **determined** [dɪ'tɜːmɪnd]
[释义] *a.* 下定决心的，坚定的
[同义] resolute
[同根] determine [dɪ'tɜːmɪn] *v.* ①下决心 ②决定 ③是…的决定因素
determination [dɪ,tɜːmɪ'neɪʃən]

n. ①坚定，决断力 ②决心，决定

▶▶ **manage to** 设法做到

▶▶ **get hold of** 得到，获得，找到

▶▶ **tracking system** 跟踪系统

▶▶ **send a signal** 发送信号

▶▶ **operation centre** 操作中心

▶▶ **false alarm** 虚假警报

▶▶ **due to** ① 由于，因为 ②应归于，应归咎于

▶▶ **inaccuracy** [ɪnˈækjʊrəsɪ]

[释义] *n.* 差错,不精确(性),不准确(性)

[反义] accuracy

[同根] inaccurate [ɪnˈækjʊrɪt] *a.* ①不准确的，不精确的 ②错误的，不真实的

▶▶ **keep...informed of...** 使…跟踪了解 /调查…

▶▶ **via** [ˈvaɪə, ˈviːə]

[释义] *prep.* ①通过，凭借 ②经过，经由

选项词汇注释

▶▶ **automatically** [ɔːtəˈmætɪklɪ]

[释义] *ad.* ①自动地，自动化（操作、作用）地 ②机械地，无意识地

[反义] manually

[同根] automate [ˈɔːtəmeɪt] *v.* ①使自动化 ②用自动化技术操作
automatic [ɔːtəˈmætɪk] *a.* ①自动的 ②必然的，自然的 ③自发的
automation [ɔːtəˈmeɪʃən] *n.* ①自动化（技术）②自动操作

▶▶ **make an attack on** 对…进行攻击，抨击

▶▶ **make use of** 利用，运用

▶▶ **technology** [tekˈnɒlədʒɪ]

[释义] *n.* ①技术（学），工业技术 ②术语 ③技术应用 ④应用科学

[同根] technique [tekˈniːk] *n.* ①技术，工艺 ②技能，技巧 ③手段，方法
technical [ˈteknɪkəl] *a.* 技术的，技能的，工艺的
technician [tekˈnɪʃən] *n.* 技术员，技师

▶▶ **lose interest in** 失去…兴趣

▶▶ **ignition** [ɪgˈnɪʃ ən]

[释义] *n.* ① [机] 点火，点火装置 ②燃烧，着火

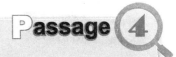

Passage **4**

Psychiatrists (精神病专家) who work with older parents say that **maturity** can be an asset in **child rearing**—older parents are more **thoughtful**, use less physical **discipline** and spend more time with their children. But raising kids takes money and energy. Many older parents find themselves **balancing** their limited **financial resources**, **declining** energy and failing health **against** the growing demands of an active child. Dying and leaving young children is probably the older parents' biggest, and often unspoken, fear. Having late-life children, says an economics professor often **means** parents, particularly fathers, "**end up retiring** much later." For many, retirement becomes an **unobtainable** dream.

Henry Metcalf. a 54-year-old **journalist**, knows it takes money to raise kids. But he's also worried that his energy will **give out** first. Sure, he can still ride bikes with his **athletic** fifth grader, but he's learned that young **at heart** doesn't mean young. Lately he's been taking *afternoon naps*（午睡）to **keep up** his energy. "My body is aging," says Metcalf, "You can't **get away from** that."

Often, older parents hear the ticking of another kind of biological clock. **Therapists** who work with middle-aged and older parents say fears about aging are nothing to laugh at. "They worry they'll **be mistaken for** grandparents, or that they'll need help getting up out of those little chairs in **nursery school**," says Joann Galst, a New York psychologist. But **at the core of** those little fears there is often a much bigger one: "that they won't be alive long enough to support and protect their child," she says.

Many late-life parents, **though**, say their children came at just the right time. After marrying late and **undergoing** years of *fertilily*（受孕）treatment, Marilyn Nolen and her husband, Randy, had twins. "We both wanted children," says Marilyn, who was 55 when she **gave birth**. The twins have given the couple what they desired for years, "a sense of family". Kids of older dads are often smarter, happier and more **sociable** because their fathers are more involved in their lives. "The dads **are** older, more mature," says Dr. Silber, "and more **ready** to focus on **parenting**."

文章词汇注释

▶▶ **maturity** [mə'tjʊərɪtɪ]

[释义] *n.* ①成熟，准备就绪 ②成熟（期），壮年（期）

[反义] immaturity

[同根] mature [mə'tjʊə] *a.* ①熟的，成熟的 ②成年人的，壮年的 *v.* ①（使）成熟 ②（票据、保险单等）到期

▶▶ **child rearing** 抚养孩子，养育孩子

▶▶ **thoughtful** ['θɔːtfʊl]

[释义] *a.* ①考虑周到的，体贴人的 ②沉思的，思索的

[同根] thoughtfully ['θɔːtfʊlɪ] *ad.* 考虑周到地，思虑地，沉思地
thoughtless ['θɔːtlɪs] *a.* 欠考虑的

▶▶▶ **discipline** [ˈdɪsɪplɪn]
[释义] n.①处罚②纪律，行为准则③（智力、道德的）训练 v.①训练，训导②控制③处罚，惩罚

▶▶▶ **balance...against...** 在…与…间进行权衡，比较，斟酌
▶▶▶ **financial resources** 财政或财力资源

▶▶▶ **declining** [dɪˈklaɪnɪŋ]
[释义] a.①衰退中的，下降的②倾斜的
[反义] growing
[同根] decline [dɪˈklaɪn] v.①下降，减少②衰退，衰落③婉辞，谢绝④使倾斜，使低垂 n.①下降，减少，落下②衰退，衰落③倾斜，斜坡
declination [ˌdeklɪˈneɪʃən] n.①下倾，倾斜②拒绝，婉言谢绝③衰退，衰落
[词组] on the decline 走下坡路，在衰退中
the decline of life 晚年，暮年

▶▶▶ **mean** [miːn,mɪn]
[释义] v.①意味着②意指，意谓③表示…意思 a.①吝啬的，刻薄的②卑鄙的③平庸的，低劣的
[同义] indicate
[同根] meaning [ˈmiːnɪŋ] n.①意义②重要性
meaningful [ˈmiːnɪŋful] a. 意味深长的，有意义的

▶▶▶ **end up doing** 以…结束/告终

▶▶▶ **retire** [rɪˈtaɪə]
[释义] v.①退休，退役②退出，退隐③后退 n.①退隐②退隐处
[同根] retired [rɪˈtaɪəd] a.①退休的，歇业的②离群索居的③引退的
retirement [rɪˈtaɪəmənt] n.①休退，退役②引退，退隐③退却，撤回
[词组] retire into oneself 不与人交往，

默不作声

▶▶▶ **unobtainable** [ˌʌnəbˈteɪnəbl]
[释义] a. 得不到的，无法得到的
[同义] unavailable, unattainable
[同根] obtain [əbˈteɪn] v.①得到，获得②通用，流行，存在
obtainable [əbˈteɪnəbəl] a. 能获得的，能得到的

▶▶▶ **journalist** [ˈdʒɜːnəlɪst]
[释义] n. 新闻记者，从事新闻杂志业的人
[同义] reporter
[同根] journal [ˈdʒɜːnl] n.①杂志，刊物，日报②航海日志，日记，日志

▶▶▶ **give out** ①用尽，精疲力竭②分发（试卷、金钱等）③发表，宣布④发出（光、信号等）

▶▶▶ **athletic** [æθˈletɪk]
[释义] a.①活跃的，强健的②运动的，运动员的③（体型）健壮的
[同根] athlete [ˈæθliːt] n.①运动员，体育家②身强力壮的人

▶▶▶ **at heart** ①内心里②本质上，实际上
▶▶▶ **keep up** ①保持，维持②（使）继续下去③（使）保持良好状态④不落后，并驾齐驱
▶▶▶ **get away from** ①逃脱，逃避②走开，离开

▶▶▶ **therapist** [ˈθerəpɪst]
[释义] n. 临床医学家，治疗专家

▶▶▶ **be mistaken for** 被误认为
▶▶▶ **nursery school** 幼儿园
▶▶▶ **at the core of** 在…的核心，在…的中心

▶▶▶ **though** [ðəʊ]
[释义] ad. 可是，然而，不过 conj.①虽然，尽管②即使③可是，然而，不过
[同义] however，nevertheless，

notwithstanding

[词组] as though 恰如，好象
even though 即使，纵然

▶▶ undergo [ˌʌndəˈɡəu]
[释义] v. 经历，经受，遭受
[同义] experience, endure

▶▶ give birth 生孩子，产崽

▶▶ sociable [ˈsəuʃəbl]
[释义] a. ①好交际的，合群的 ②社交的，交际的 ③群居的

[同根] social [ˈsəuʃəl] a. ①社会的 ②社交的，交际的 ③合群的
society [səˈsaɪətɪ] n. ①社会 ②（社会）阶层 ③社交界
socialize [ˈsəuʃəlaɪz] v. ①参加社交，交往 ②使社会化，使合群

▶▶ be ready to do ①乐意做，甘愿做 ②快要…的，就要…的，动辄…的

▶▶ parenting [ˈpeərəntɪŋ]
[释义] n. （父母对子女的）养育

选项词汇注释

▶▶ be experienced in 在…方面有经验
▶▶ bring up ①养育，教育 ②提出 ③（军队等）调上来 ④呕吐

▶▶ pension [ˈpenʃən]
[释义] n. ①养老金，抚恤金 ②津贴，补助金 v. 发给…养老金（抚恤金等）
[词组] pension off ①发给…养老金，使退役，使退休 ②因陈旧（或损坏）而不再使用

▶▶ dream of ①向往，渴望 ②梦想，幻想，想象 ③做梦，梦见
▶▶ be reluctant to 不愿意的，勉强的

▶▶ advanced [ədˈvɑːnst]
[释义] a. ①年迈的，上年纪的 ②超前的，先进的 ③高级的
[同根] advance [ədˈvɑːns] v. ①使向前移动 ②促进 ③提议，建议 ④提升
advancement [ədˈvɑːnsmənt] n. ①前进，促进 ②提升，晋升 ③提高，增加

▶▶ keep up with ①跟上（人、潮流、形式等）②保持联系
▶▶ pace of life 生活节奏
▶▶ be mistaken for 被误认为

Skimming and Scanning
Highways

Early in the 20th century, most of the streets and roads in the U.S. were made of **dirt**, brick, and **cedar** wood blocks. Built for horse, **carriage**, and foot **traffic**, they were usually poorly cared for and too narrow to *accommodate*（容纳）**automobiles**.

With the increase in **auto** production, private *turnpike*（收费公路）companies **under local authorities** began to **spring up**, and by 1921 there were 387,000 miles of **paved** roads. Many were built using **specifications** of 19th century Scottish engineers Thomas Telford and John Mac Adam (for whom the **macadam surface** is named), whose specifications stressed the importance of **adequate drainage**. Beyond that, there were no national standards for size, weight restrictions, or commercial signs. During World War I, roads throughout the country were nearly destroyed by the **weight** of trucks. When **General** Eisenhower returned from Germany in 1919, after serving in the U.S. Army's first **transcontinental** motor *convoy*（车队）, he **noted**: "The old convoy had started me thinking about good, **two-lane** highways, but Germany's Autobahn or **motorway** had made me see the wisdom of broader ribbons across the land."

It would take another war before the **federal government** would act on a national highway system. During World War II, a tremendous increase in trucks and new roads were required. The war demonstrated how critical highways were to the defense effort. Thirteen percent of defense plants received all their **supplies** by truck, and almost all other plants shipped more than half of their products by **vehicle**. The war also revealed that local control of highways had led to a confusing variety of design standards. Even federal and state highways did not follow basic standards. Some states allowed trucks up to 36,000 pounds, while others restricted anything over 7,000 pounds. A government study recommended a national highway system of 33,920 miles, and Congress passed the Federal-Aid Highway Act of 1944, which called for strict, centrally controlled design criteria.

The interstate highway system was finally launched in 1956 and has been hailed as one of the greatest public works projects of the century. To build its 44,000 mile web of highways, bridges, and tunnels, hundreds of unique engineering designs and solutions had to be worked out. Consider the many geographic features of the country: mountains, steep grades, wetlands, rivers, deserts, and plans. Variables included the slope of the land, the ability of the pavement to support the load, the intensity of road use, and the nature of the underlying soil. Urban areas were another problem. Innovative designs of roadways, tunnels, bridges, overpasses, and interchanges that could run through or bypass urban areas soon began to weave their way across the country, forever altering the face of America.

Long-span, segmented-concrete, cable-stayed bridges such as Hale Boggs in Louisiana and the Sunshine Skyway in Florida, and remarkable tunnels like Fort McHenry in Maryland and Mt. Baker in Washington, met many of the nation's physical challenges. Traffic control systems and methods of construction developed under the interstate program soon influenced highway construction around the world, and were invaluable in improving the condition of urban streets and traffic patterns.

Today the interstate system links every major city in the U.S., and the U.S. with Canada and Mexico. Built with safety in mind, the highways have wide lanes and shoulders, dividing medians or barriers, long entry and exit lanes, curves engineered for safe turns, and limited access. The death rate on highways is half that of all other U.S. roads (0.86) deaths per 100 million passenger miles compared to 1.99 deaths per 100 million on all other roads.

By opening the North American continent, highways have enabled consumer goods and services to reach people in remote and rural areas of the country, spurred the growth of suburbs, and provided people with greater options in terms of jobs, access to cultural programs, health care, and other benefits. Above all, the interstate system provides individuals with what they cherish most personal freedom of mobility.

The interstate system has been an essential element of the nation's economic growth in terms of shipping and job creation: more than 75 percent of the nation's **freight deliveries** arrive by truck; and most products that arrive by rail or air use interstates for the last **leg** of the journey by vehicle. Not only has the highway system affected the American economy by providing shipping routes, it has led to the growth of **spin-off industries** like service stations, **motels**, restaurants, and shopping centers. It has allowed the **relocation** of manufacturing plants and other industries from urban areas to rural.

By the end of the century there was an immense **network** of paved roads, **residential** streets, **expressways**, and **freeways** built to support millions of vehicles. The highway system was officially renamed for Eisenhower to **honor** his vision and leadership. The year construction began he said: "Together, the **united** forces of our **communication and transportation systems** are **dynamic** elements in the very name we bear—United States. Without them, we would be a mere **alliance** of many separate parts."

文章词汇注释

▶▶ **dirt** [dɜːt]
[释义] n. ①泥土，泥地 ②污物 ③肮脏（状态）

▶▶ **cedar** ['siːdə]
[释义] n. 雪松，西洋杉，香柏

▶▶ **carriage** ['kærɪdʒ]
[释义] n. （载客的）马车，运输工具

▶▶ **traffic** ['træfɪk]
[释义] n. ①交通，往来 ②流动的车辆及行人

▶▶ **automobile** ['ɔːtəməubiːl]
[释义] n. （主美）汽车

▶▶ **auto** ['ɔːtəu]
[释义] n. （美口）汽车

▶▶ **under local authorities** 在地方当局管理下，在地方当局控制下

▶▶ **spring up** ①涌现 ②（植物等）迅速生长，（友谊等）产生

▶▶ **pave** [peɪv]
[释义] v. ①铺（路），铺筑 ②为…作准备
[同根] pavement ['peɪvmənt] n. ①路面 ②（主英）人行道

▶▶ **specification** [ˌspesɪfɪˈkeɪʃən]
[释义] n. ①规格，标准 ②说明书，详述
[同根] specific [spɪˈsɪfɪk] a. ①明确的，具体的 ②特有的，独特的
specificity [ˌspesɪˈfɪsɪtɪ] n. 特性，特征，特殊性

▶▶ **macadam surface** 碎石路面

▶▶ **adequate** ['ædɪkwɪt]
[释义] a. ①适当的，充分的 ②足够的
[同义] proper, sufficient, enough
[同根] adequacy ['ædɪkwəsɪ] n. ①适当，恰当 ②足够

▶▶ **drainage** ['dreɪnɪdʒ]
[释义] n. ①排水系统，水道 ②排水

③排出的水 ④逐步流出，外流

[同根] drain [dreɪn] v. ①慢慢排出，放出 ②排去…的水 ③消耗 ④使精疲力竭 n. ①排水沟，阴沟 ②排水 ③（逐渐的）外流，耗竭

▶▶ **weight** [weɪt]

[释义] n. ①重压，压力 ②重量 ③重要（性），价值 ④势力，影响

[同根] weighty ['weɪtɪ] a. ① 重 的，笨重的 ②重大的，有影响的，权威性的

[词组] carry weight 有重要性，有影响，有分量，有价值

give weight to 重视…

lose weight 体重减轻，变瘦

put on weight 体重增加，发胖

throw one's weight about/around ①滥用权势，仗势欺人 ②耀武扬威

▶▶ **general** ['dʒenərəl]

[释义] n. 将军 a. ①一般的，普遍的 ②大致的，大体的，笼统的 ③（用于官职）总…，…长

[同根] generalize ['dʒenərəlaɪz] v. ①对…进行概括 ②概括出，推断出 ③推广，普及

generalization [ˌdʒenərəlaɪ'zeɪʃən] n. ①概括，归纳 ②推论，普遍原理（或原则）

[词组] in general 一般（或总的）说来，大体上

▶▶ **transcontinental** [ˌtrænzkɒntɪ'nentəl]

[释义] a. ①横贯大陆的 ②在大陆那一边的

▶▶ **note** [nəʊt]

[释义] v. ①说起，谈到，特别提到 ②注意，留意 ③着重，强调 ④记录，记下 n. ①记录，随笔 ②按语，注解 ③短笺，便条，④票据，钞票

[同义] say, remark, speak

[同根] noted ['nəʊtɪd] a. 著名的，知名的

[词组] change one's note 改变调子，改变态度

make a note of 记下，写下

of note ①显要的，有名望的 ②值得注意的，应重视的

take note 注意，留意

▶▶ **two-lane** a. 双车道的

▶▶ **motorway** ['məʊtəweɪ]

[释义] n. (英) 高速公路

▶▶ **federal government** 联邦政府

▶▶ **supply** [sə'plaɪ]

[释义] n. ①（军队等的）补给品，必需品 ②供应，供应的东西 v. ①供给，提供 ②弥补（缺陷等）③满足（需要等）

[同根] supplier [sə'plaɪə] n. ①供应者 ②原料（或商品）供应国（或地区）

[词组] in short supply 供应不足

▶▶ **vehicle** ['viːɪkl]

[释义] n. 车辆，交通工具，运载器

▶▶ **recommend** [rekə'mend]

[释义] v. ①推荐，建议 ②劝告，忠告

[同义] suggest, advise, propose

[反义] oppose

[同根] recommendation [ˌrekəmen'deɪʃən] n. ①推荐 ②推荐信 ③劝告

recommendable [ˌrekə'mendəbl] a. ①可推荐的，值得推荐的 ②可取的

▶▶ **interstate** ['ɪntəˌsteɪt]

[释义] a. 州与州之间的，州际的 n. 州际公路

▶▶ **launch** [lɔːntʃ, lɑːntʃ]

[释义] v. ①使投入，使运行 ②发射，投射 ③发动(运动等),发起 n. ①(船的)下水 ②发射 ③发行，投放市场

▶▶ **hail** [heɪl]

[释义] v. ①热情赞扬，欢迎，喝彩 ②招呼，高呼 n. ①欢呼 ②招呼

[词组] drink hail 干杯

▶▶ **solution** [sə'luːʃ(ə)n]

[释义] n. ①解决办法 ②解答，解法 ③溶液，溶剂

[同根] solve ['sɒlv] v. ① 解决 ②解释，解答 ③清偿，解除 ④溶解

▶▶ **work out** ①想出，设计出 ②理解，知道 ③使筋疲力尽，耗尽 ④计算出

▶▶ **geographic feature** 地理特征，地貌特征

▶▶ **variable** ['veərɪəbl]

[释义] n. 可变因素，可变物，变数，变量 a. 可变的，不定的，易变的

[同根] vary ['veərɪ] v. 改变，变化
varied ['veərɪd] a. 各式各样的，有变化的
various ['veərɪəs] a. 不同的，各种各样的
variety [vəˈraɪətɪ] n. ①变化，多样性 ②品种，种类
variation [ˌveərɪˈeɪʃ(ə)n] n. 变更，变化，变异，变种

▶▶ **slope** [sləup]

[释义] n. ①倾斜，坡度 ②斜面，斜线 ③斜坡 a. 倾斜的 v. (使) 倾斜

[同根] sloping ['sləupɪŋ] a. 倾斜的，有坡度的

▶▶ **intensity** [ɪn'tensɪtɪ]

[释义] n. ①强度，烈度 ②强烈，剧烈，紧张

[同根] intense [ɪn'tens] a. ① (指性质) 强烈的,剧烈的,激烈的 ② (指感情) 热烈的，热情的
intensify [ɪn'tensɪfaɪ] v. 加强，增强，(使) 变尖锐
intension [ɪn'tenʃən] n. ①增强，加剧 ②强度，烈度 ③紧张 ④专心致志

▶▶ **intensive** [ɪn'tensɪv] a. ① 加强的，集中的 ②集约 (经营) 的

▶▶ **underlying** [ˌʌndə'laɪɪŋ]

[释义] a. ①在下面的 ②基本的，根本的 ③潜在的

▶▶ **urban area** 城市地区

▶▶ **innovative** ['ɪnəveɪtɪv]

[释义] a. 创新的，革新的，新颖的

[同义] pioneering, inventive, original

[同根] innovate ['ɪnəveɪt] v. ① 革新，改革，创新 ②创立，创始
innovation [ˌɪnə'veɪʃ(ə)n] n. ①革新，改革，创新 ②新方法，新制度，新奇事物
innovator ['ɪnəveɪtə] n. 创新者，革新者

▶▶ **overpass** ['əuvəˌpɑːs]

[释义] n. (主美) 天桥 v. ①穿过 ②超越，超过，胜过

▶▶ **interchange** [ˌɪntə'tʃeɪndʒ]

[释义] n. ①道路立体枢纽交换道 ②交换，交替 v. ①交换，互换 ② (使) 交替发生，轮流进行

[同根] interchangeable [ˌɪntə'tʃeɪndʒəbəl] a. 可交换的，可交替的

▶▶ **run through** ①贯穿，穿过 ②匆匆处理，匆匆做

▶▶ **bypass** ['baɪpɑːs; (US)'baɪpæs]

[释义] v. ①绕过，避开 ②为…加设旁道 n. 旁道，旁路

▶▶ **weave one's way across** 迂回行进地穿过

▶▶ **long-span** a. 跨度的，跨度大的

▶▶ **segmented-concrete cable-stayed bridge** 混凝土斜拉桥

▶▶ **method** ['meθəd]

[释义] n. 方法，办法

[同义] approach, means

[同根] methodology [meθə'dɒlədʒɪ]
n. ①（学科的）一套方法 ②方法论

▶▶ construction [kən'strʌkʃən]
[释义] n. ①建造，建筑 ②建造术，建造式样 ③建造物
[反义] destruction, ruination
[同根] construct [kən'strʌkt] v. ① 建造，构筑 ②构想，设想
constructive [kən'strʌktɪv] a. ① 建设性的 ②结构的，构造的

▶▶ invaluable [ɪn'væljuəbl]
[释义] a. 非常宝贵的，无价的，无法估价的
[反义] valueless
[同根] value ['væljuː; -ju] n. ①价值 ②估价，评价 v. ①估价，评价 ②重视
valuable ['væljuəbl] a. 贵重的，珍贵的，有价值的
valueless ['væljuːlɪs] a. 没有价值的，毫无用处的

▶▶ condition [kən'dɪʃən]
[释义] n. ①状况，状态 ②健康状况 ③条件，前题
[同义] state, situation
[同根] conditional [kən'dɪʃnəl] a. 有条件的，视…而定的
conditioned [kən'dɪʃənd] a. ①受条件限制的，制约的 ②(to) 适应…的，习惯于…的
conditioner [kən'dɪʃənə] n. ①调节器，调节者 ②空气调节器，空调设备
[词组] make it a condition that... 以…为条件
on condition（that）... 如果，在…条件下
on no condition 决不
on this（that）condition 在这种（那种）情况下

▶▶ median ['miːdɪən]
[释义] n. 中线，中间分隔（分车）带

▶▶ barrier ['bærɪə]
[释义] n. ①栅栏，障碍物 ②关卡，屏障 ③障碍 ④界线 v. 以屏障隔开（隔绝）

▶▶ entry ['entrɪ]
[释义] n. ①入口，通道 ②进入，入场 ③门口，路口，河口
[同义] entrance, passage

▶▶ exit ['eksɪt; 'egzɪt]
[释义] n. ①出口 ②出去，退场 v. ①出去，退出 ②去世，死亡
[反义] entrance
[词组] make one's exit ①退出，离去 ②去世，死亡

▶▶ curve [kɜːv]
[释义] n. ①弯道，（道路的）弯曲处 ②曲线，弧线 ③[统] 曲线图表 v.（使）弯曲,（使）成曲线 a. 弯曲的，曲线状的

▶▶ limited ['lɪmɪtɪd]
[释义] a. ①有限制的，限制的 ② [商] 有限责任的
[反义] unlimited, limitless
[同根] limit ['lɪmɪt] n. ①限度，限制 ②范围，界限 ③限额 v. 限制，限定
limitation [,lɪmɪ'teɪʃən] n. ①限制 ②局限，缺陷 ③限度，限额

▶▶ compared to... 和…比较

▶▶ consumer goods [pl.] 生活资料，消费品

▶▶ rural area 农村地区

▶▶ spur [spɜː]
[释义] v. ①刺激，促进 ②急速前行，策马飞奔 n. 刺激，鼓励
[同义] stimulate, promote, encourage
[词组] on the spur of the moment 一时冲动之下，未经仔细考虑地，当即，当场

▶▶ **option** ['ɒpʃən]

[释义] *n.* ①选择，选择权 ②（供）选择的事物（或人）

[同义] alternative, choice

[同根] optional ['ɒpʃənəl] *a.* 随意的，任选的，非强制性的

▶▶ **in terms of** ①在…方面，从…方面来说 ②根据，按照

▶▶ **health care** 医疗保健

▶▶ **above all** 首先，尤其是

▶▶ **cherish** ['tʃerɪʃ]

[释义] *v.* ①珍爱，珍视 ②抱有，怀有

[同义] treasure, value

▶▶ **mobility** [məʊ'bɪlɪtɪ]

[释义] *n.* ①流动 ②流动性 ③机动性

[同根] mobile ['məʊbaɪl] *a.* 可移动的，易变的，机动的

mobilize ['məʊbɪlaɪz] *v.* ①动员②调动 ③使流通

mobilization [ˌməʊbɪlaɪ'zeɪʃən] *n.* ①动员 ②调动

▶▶ **creation** [kriː'eɪʃən]

[释义] *n.* ①创造 ②创作 ③创建

[同义] originality, inventiveness

[同根] create [krɪ'eɪt] *v.* ①创造，创作②创建，创设 ③引起，产生

creative [kriː'eɪtɪv] *a.* 有创造力的，独创性的

creativity [ˌkriːeɪ'tɪvətɪ] *n.* 创造力，创造性

▶▶ **freight** [freɪt]

[释义] *n.* ①货物 ②货运 ③货车，货轮

▶▶ **delivery** [dɪ'lɪvərɪ]

[释义] *n.* ①运载，运送 ②（邮件的）投递 ③讲话，表演 ④释放

[同根] deliver [dɪ'lɪvə] *v.* ①投递，运载 ②发表 ③释放，解救

[词组] take delivery of 收（货），提取（货物）

▶▶ **leg** [leg]

[释义] *n.* 旅程的一段

▶▶ **spin-off industry** 附带产业

▶▶ **motel** [məʊ'tel]

[释义] *n.* 汽车旅馆

▶▶ **relocation** [ˌriːləʊ'keɪʃən]

[释义] *n.* 重新定位，重新安置

[同根] relocate [ˌriːləʊ'keɪt] *v.* 重新定位，重新安置

▶▶ **network** ['netwɜːk]

[释义] *n.* ①网状系统，交通网 ②关系网 ③广播（电视）网 ④［计］网络

▶▶ **residential** [ˌrezɪ'denʃəl]

[释义] *a.* ①居住的，住所的 ②学生寄宿的

[同义] inhabited

[反义] migratory

[同根] reside [rɪ'zaɪd] *v.* 居住

residence ['rezɪdəns] *n.* ①居住，定居 ②住宅，住处 ③学生宿舍

resident ['rezɪdənt] *n.* ①居民，住户②（旅馆等的）住客，寄宿者 *a.* ①居住的，常住的 ②住校的，住院的

residency ['rezɪdənsɪ] *n.* ①居住，定居 ②住宅，住处

▶▶ **expressway** [ɪk'spresweɪ]

[释义] *n.* 高速公路，快速干道

[同义] superhighway

▶▶ **freeway** ['friːweɪ]

[释义] *n.* ① 高速公路 ②〈美〉免费高速公路，免费高速干道

[同义] expressway

▶▶ **honor** ['ɒnə]

[释义] *v.* ①向…表示敬意 ②给…以荣誉 ③尊敬，尊重 *n.* ①荣誉，光荣②名誉，信用 ③崇敬，敬意 ④礼仪，礼节

[同义] respect

[反义] dishonor

[同根] honorable ['ɒnərəbl] a. ①荣誉的，光荣的 ②可尊敬的 ③名誉好的，体面的

[词组] do honor to ①向…表示敬意，尊敬地对待 ②使增光，给…带来荣誉

in honor of 为了向…表示敬意，为庆祝，为纪念

on/upon one's honor 以名誉担保

▶▶ united [juˈnaɪtɪd]

[释义] a. ①联合的，共同的 ②团结的，一致的 ③联盟的

[同义] combined

[同根] unite [jʊ(:)ˈnaɪt] v. ①使联合，使混合 ②使团结，使统一

▶▶ communication and transportation system 交通运输系统

▶▶ dynamic [daɪˈnæmɪk]

[释义] a. ①有活力的，强有力的 ②力的，力学的 ③动力的，动态的

n. ①动力，动力学 ②活力，[喻] 动力

[同根] dynamics [daɪˈnæmɪks] n. ①力学，动力学 ②动力 ③动态

▶▶ alliance [əˈlaɪəns]

[释义] n. ①联盟，同盟，联姻 ②盟约

[同义] coalition, association, union

[同根] ally [əˈlaɪ; ˈælaɪ] v. ① (使) 联盟，结盟，联合 ②联姻 n. 同盟国

选项词汇注释

▶▶ make sense 有意义，有道理

▶▶ take action ①采取行动 ②提出诉讼 ③开始起作用

▶▶ in spite of 不顾，尽管，任凭

▶▶ highway system 公路系统

▶▶ military installation 军事设施

▶▶ in recognition of 公认，赏识，表彰

Reading in Depth
Section A

El Nino is the name given to the **mysterious** and often **unpredictable** change in the climate of the world. This strange phenomenon happens every five to eight years. It starts in the Pacific Ocean and is thought to be caused by a failure in the trade *winds*（信风）, which affects the ocean currents driven by these winds. As the trade winds **lessen** in strength, the ocean **temperatures** rise, causing the Peru current flowing in from the east to **warm up** by as much as 5℃.

The warming of the ocean has **far-reaching** effects. The hot, *humid*（潮湿的）air over the ocean causes severe **tropical thunderstorms**. The rainfall is increased across South America, bringing floods to Peru. In the West Pacific, there are **droughts** affecting Australia and Indonesia. So while some parts of the world prepare for heavy rains and floods, other parts face drought, poor crops and **starvation**.

El Nino usually lasts for about 18 months. The 1982-83 El Nino brought the most destructive weather in modern history. Its effect was worldwide and it left more than 2,000 people dead and caused over eight billion pounds **worth** of damage. The 1990 El Nino lasted until June 1995. Scientists estimate this to be the longest El Nino for 2,000 years.

Nowadays, weather experts are able to **forecast** when an El Nino will strike, but they are still not completely sure what leads to it or what affects, how strong it will be.

文章词汇注释

▶▶ **mysterious** [mɪˈstɪərɪəs]

[释义] a. ①神秘的，难以理解的 ②卖弄玄虚的，诡秘的

[同根] mystery [ˈmɪstərɪ] n. ①神秘（性）②神秘的事物，不可思议的事物，谜

▶▶ **unpredictable** [ˌʌnprɪˈdɪktəbl]

[释义] a. 不可预测的 n. 不可预测的事物

[反义] predictable

[同根] predict [prɪˈdɪkt] v. 预言，预料，预报

prediction [prɪˈdɪkʃən] n. ①预言，预料 ②预言的事物，预报的事物

predictive [prɪˈdɪktɪv] a. 预言性的，有预报价值的

▶▶ **lessen** [ˈlesn]

[释义] v. ①（使）变小，（使）减轻 ②贬低，降低

[同义] reduce, diminish

[反义] strengthen

▶▶ **temperature** [ˈtemprɪtʃə(r)]

[释义] n. ①温度 ②体温 ③热度

▶▶ **warm up** ①（使）暖起来 ②（使）热心起来 ③热身，（使）做（赛前）准备活动，（演奏或演唱前）（使）做准备练习

▶▶ **far-reaching** a. 深远的，广泛的

[同义] extensive, broad

▶▶ **tropical** [ˈtrɒpɪkl]

[释义] a. ①热带的，有热带特征的 ②炎热的，酷热的 ③热烈的，热情的

[同根] tropic [ˈtrɒpɪk] n. ①回归线 ②热带，热带地区 a. 热带的，热带地区的

▶▶ **thunderstorm** [ˈθʌndəstɔːm]

[释义] n. 雷暴，雷暴雨

▶▶ **drought** [draʊt]

[释义] n. ①干旱，旱灾 ②长期缺乏，严重不足

[同根] droughty [ˈdraʊtɪ] a. 干旱的，干燥的

▶▶ **starvation** [stɑːˈveɪʃən]

[释义] n. ①饥饿，饿死 ②（生活必须品的）匮乏

[同根] starve [stɑːv] v. ①饥饿，挨饿 ②（使）饿死 ③渴望，迫切需要
starveling [ˈstɑːvlɪŋ] a. 挨饿的 n. 挨饿者，缺乏营养的动物（或植物）

▶▶ **worth** [wɜːθ]

[释义] n. ①价值 ②作用 prep. 值…钱，相等于…价值 a. 值钱的，可贵的

[同根] worthy [ˈwɜːðɪ] a. ①有价值的，值得重视的 ②值得的，应得的
worthful [ˈwɜːθful] a. 有价值的，宝贵的，可贵的

worthless [ˈwɜːθlɪs] a. 无价值的，不值钱的，没用处的
worthwhile [ˈwɜːθˌwaɪl] a. ①值得的，值得做的 ②有真实价值的

▶▶ **nowadays** [ˈnauədeɪz]

[释义] ad. 现今，现在

▶▶ **forecast** [ˈfɔːkɑːst]

[释义] v. ①预测，预报 ②预示 ③预见到 n. ①天气预报，预测 ②预示

[同义] predict

[同根] forecaster [ˈfɔːkɑːstə] n. ①天气预报者，气象预报员 ②（经济形势等的）预测者，推测者

Section B
Passage One

Communications technologies are **far from** equal when it comes to conveying the truth. The first study to **compare** honesty across **a range of** communications **media** has found that people are twice as likely to tell lies in phone conversations as they are in emails. The fact that emails are automatically recorded—and can come back to *haunt* (困扰) you—appears to be the key to the finding.

Jeff Hancock of Cornell University in Ithaca, New York, asked 30 students to keep a communications diary for a week. In it they **noted** the number of conversations or email exchanges they had lasting more than 10 minutes, and **confessed** to how many lies they told. Hancock then worked out the number of lies per conversation for each medium. He found that lies **made up** 14 per cent of emails, 21 per cent of **instant** messages, 27 per cent of face-to-face interactions and an **astonishing** 37 per cent of phone calls.

His results, to be presented at the conference on human-computer interaction in Vienna, Austria, in April, have surprised psychologists. Some expected emailers to be the biggest liars, **reasoning** that because **deception** makes people uncomfortable, the *detachment* (非直接接触) of emailing would make it easier to lie. Others expected people to lie more in face-to-face exchanges because we are most **practiced** at that form of communication.

But Hancock says it is also crucial whether a conversation is being recorded and could be reread, and whether it occurs in real time. People appear to be afraid to lie when they know the communication could later be used to **hold** them **to account**, he says. This is why fewer lies appear in email than on the phone.

People are also more likely to lie in real time—in an instant message or phone call, say—than if they have time to think of a response, says Hancock. He found many lies are *spontaneous* (脱口而出的) responses to an **unexpected** demand, such as: "Do you like my dress?"

Hancock hopes his research will help companies work out the best ways for their employees to communicate. For instance, the phone might be the best medium for sales where employees are encouraged to **stretch** the truth. But **given** his results, work **assessment**, where honesty is a **priority**, might be best done using email.

文章词汇注释

▶▶▶ **far from** ①远非，完全不 ②远离

▶▶▶ **compare** [kəm'peə]
[释义] v. ①比较，对照 ②把…比作
[同义] contrast
[同根] comparison [kəm'pærɪsn]
　　n. ①比较，对照 ②相似，类似 ③比拟，比喻
　　comparative [kəm'pærətɪv] a. 比较的，比较研究的
[词组] bear/stand comparison with 不亚于，比得上
　　beyond comparison 天壤之别，不可相比
　　by comparison 比较起来，用比较方法
　　in comparison with 和…比较起来

▶▶▶ **a range of** 一系列，一排

▶▶▶ **media** ['miːdɪə]
[释义] (medium 的复数形式) n. 媒体

▶▶▶ **note** [nəut]
[释义] v. ①记录，记下 ②注意，留意 ③着重，强调 n. ①记录，随笔 ②按语，注解 ③短笺，便条 ④票据，纸币
[同义] write down, record
[同根] noted ['nəutɪd] a. 著名的，知名的
[词组] change one's note 改变调子，改变态度
　　make a note of 记下，写下
　　of note ①显要的，有名望的 ②值得注意的，应重视的
　　take note 注意，留意

▶▶▶ **confess** [kən'fes]
[释义] v. ① (to) 坦白，承认，供认 ②忏悔
[同根] confession [kən'feʃən] n. ①坦白，承认，供认 ②忏悔

▶▶▶ **made up** ①构成，组成 ②补充，弥补，补偿 ③捏造，虚构 ④化妆

▶▶▶ **instant** ['ɪnstənt]

[释义] *a.* ①事先未准备（或考虑）的，即兴的，即时的 ②立即的，马上的 ③（食品）速溶的，方便的 *n.* ①瞬息 ②（某一）时刻 ③速溶饮料

[同根] instantly ['ɪnstəntlɪ] *ad.* 立即，马上 *conj.* 一…（就）

[词组] on the instant 立即，马上
the instant(that) 一…（就）

▶▶▶ **astonishing** [əs'tɒnɪʃɪŋ]

[释义] *a.* 惊人的，令人惊讶的

[同根] astonish [əs'tɒnɪʃ] *v.* 使惊讶
astonishment [əs'tɒnɪʃmənt] *n.* ①惊讶，惊愕 ②令人惊讶的事物

▶▶▶ **reason** ['riːzn]

[释义] *v.* ①分析，推理 ②辩论，讨论 ③劝喻，说服 *n.* ①理由，原由 ②理智，判断力

[同根] reasoning ['riːzənɪŋ] *n.* ①推理，推论 ②论据，理由 ③评理，讲理 *a.* ①（有）理性的 ②推理的，推论的
reasonable ['riːznəbl] *a.* ①合理的，正当的 ②公平的，公道的 ③有理智的，明智的 ④通情达理的，讲道理的

[词组] beyond/out of/past all reason 毫无道理，全然无理
in（all）reason 合情合理，正当的

▶▶▶ **deception** [dɪ'sepʃən]

[释义] *n.* ①欺骗，蒙蔽 ②诡计，骗术 ③受骗

[同根] deceive [dɪ'siːv] *v.* 欺骗，诓骗，蒙蔽
deceit [dɪ'siːt] *n.* ①欺骗，欺诈 ②欺骗行为，欺诈手段，骗术

▶▶▶ **practiced** ['præktɪst]

[释义] *a.* ①熟练的，老练的 ②习得的，练成的

[同义] experienced

▶▶▶ **hold...to account** 使…承担责任

▶▶▶ **unexpected** [ˌʌnɪk'spektɪd]

[释义] *a.* 没有料到的，意外的，突如其来的

[同义] unanticipated, sudden

[同根] expect [ɪk'spekt] *v.* ①期待，盼望 ②预料，预期
expectation [ˌekspek'teɪʃən] *n.* ①期待，预期 ②希望，前景，前程

▶▶▶ **stretch** [stretʃ]

[释义] *v.* ①夸大，夸张 ②（使）延伸，（使）延续 ③舒展，伸长

[词组] at a stretch 不停地，连续地，一口气地
at full stretch ①尽量伸出手臂 ②极其紧张地，全力以赴地
beyond the stretch of 超出…范围以外

▶▶▶ **given** ['gɪvn]

[释义] *prep.* 考虑到

▶▶▶ **assessment** [ə'sesmənt]

[释义] *n.* ①评价，估计 ②被估定的金额

[同根] assess [ə'ses] *v.* ①估定（财产、价值）②确定（税款、罚款、赔款等）的数额 ③征收（税款、会费等）④评估（人物、工作等）

▶▶▶ **priority** [praɪ'ɒrɪtɪ]

[释义] *n.* ①优先考虑的事，优先配给 ②优先，优先权 ③（时间等方面的）在先，居前

[同根] prior ['praɪə] *a.* ①在先的，在前的，居先的 ②优先的，更重要的

选项词汇注释

▶▶▶ **trace** [treɪs]

[释义] n. ①痕迹，踪迹 ②（美）小路，小径 v. ①追踪，跟踪 ②追溯，追究，探索 ③查出，看出，找到

▶▶▶ **policy** ['pɒlɪsɪ]

[释义] n. ①策略，计谋，手段 ②方针，政策

▶▶▶ **relaxed** [rɪ'lækst]

[释义] a. ①放松的，轻松自在的 ②松弛的，宽松的 ③随和的

[同根] relax [rɪ'læks] v. ①（使）松懈，放宽 ②缓和,减轻 ③（使）轻松,(使)休息

relaxation [,ri:læk'seɪʃən] n. ①松弛，放宽 ②缓和，减轻 ③娱乐，消遣

▶▶▶ **restrained** [rɪ'streɪnd]

[释义] a. ①受限制的，受约束的，拘谨的 ②克制的，忍耐的

[同根] restrain [rɪ'streɪn] v. ① 抑制，遏制 ②控制，限制

restraint [rɪ'streɪnt] n. ①抑制，克制 ②控制，约束

▶▶▶ **impress** [ɪm'pres]

[释义] v. ①给…留下深刻印象，使铭记 ②印，盖（印）于

[同义] make an impression on, make an impact on

[同根] impression [ɪm'preʃən] n. ① 印象，感想 ②压印，印痕 ③影响，效果

impressive [ɪm'presɪv] a. ①给人深刻印象的 ②威严的

▶▶▶ **trustworthy** ['trʌst,wɜːðɪ]

[释义] a. 可信赖的，可靠的

Passage Two

In a country that **defines** itself by ideals, not by **shared blood**, who should be allowed to come, work and live here? **In the wake of** the Sept. 11 attacks these questions have never seemed more **pressing**.

On Dec. 11, 2001, as part of the effort to increase homeland **security**, federal and local authorities in 14 states **staged** "Operation Safe Travel"— **raids** on airports to arrest employees with false *identification*（身份证明）. In Salt Lake City there were 69 arrests. But those **captured** were anything but **terrorists**, most of them illegal immigrants from Central or South America. Authorities said the **undocumented** workers' illegal status made them **open to** *blackmail*（讹诈）by terrorists.

Many immigrants in Salt Lake City were angered by the arrests and said they felt as if they were being treated like **disposable** goods.

Mayor Anderson said those feelings were justified **to a certain extent**.

"We're saying we want you to work in these places, we're going to look the other way **in terms of** what our laws are, and then when it's **convenient** for us, or when we can try to **make a point** in terms of national security, especially after Sept. 11, then you're disposable. There are whole families being **uprooted** for all of the wrong reasons." Anderson said.

If Sept. 11 had never happened, the airport workers would not have been arrested and could have gone on quietly living in America, probably **indefinitely**. Aria Castro, a manager at a Ben & Jerry's ice cream shop at the airport, had been working 10 years with the same false Social Security card when she was arrested in the December airport raid. Now she and her family are living **under the threat of** *deportation* （驱逐出境）. Castro's case is **currently** waiting to be settled. While she awaits the outcome, the government has granted her permission to work here and she has returned to her job at Ben & Jerry's.

文章词汇注释

▶▶▶ **define** [dɪˈfaɪn]

[释义] v. ①规定，限定…的界线 ②解释，给…下定义

[同根] definition [ˌdefɪˈnɪʃ ən] n. ①定义 ②解释，下定义

definite [ˈdefɪnɪt] a. ①明确的，确切的 ②一定的，肯定的 ③限定的

▶▶▶ **shared blood** 共同的血统

▶▶▶ **in the wake of** ①在…之后，紧紧跟随…的 ②随着…而来，作为…的结果 ③仿效

▶▶▶ **pressing** [ˈpresɪŋ]

[释义] a. ①迫切的，急迫的 ②热切的，恳切的

[同义] urgent

[同根] press [pres] v. ①按，推 ②挤，榨取 ③催促，敦促 n. ①报刊，新闻界 ②印刷，印刷术 ③紧迫，匆忙

pressure [ˈpreʃ ə] n. ①压力 ②压迫感

▶▶▶ **security** [sɪˈkjuərɪtɪ]

[释义] n. ①安全，安全感 ②防御物，保护物 ③保证，担保

[同义] safety

[同根] secure [sɪˈkjuə] a. ①安全的，无危险的 ②安心的，无忧虑的 ③有把握的，确定无疑的 v. ①使安全，保卫 ②保证，担保

▶▶▶ **stage** [steɪdʒ]

[释义] v. ①筹划，发动 ②演出，上演 ③展现，呈现 ④分阶段实现，逐步进行 n. ①舞台 ②戏剧，戏剧艺术 ③阶段，步骤

[词组] on stage 在舞台上，当众

stage by stage 逐步地，循序渐进地

▶▶▶ **raid** [reɪd]

[释义] n. ①查抄，搜捕 ②袭击，侵袭 ③劫掠，掠夺 v. ①袭击 ②劫掠，劫夺

▶▶ **capture** ['kæptʃə]

[释义] v. 俘获，捕获，夺取 n. 捕获，战利品

▶▶ **terrorist** ['terərɪst]

[释义] n. ①恐怖（主义）分子 ②恐吓者，威胁者 a. 恐怖主义的

[同根] terror ['terə] n. ①恐怖 ②令人恐怖的人 ③恐怖时期 ④恐怖行动
terrorism ['terərɪzəm] n. ①恐怖主义 ②恐怖行动 ③恐怖统治

▶▶ **undocumented** [ˌʌn'dɒkjumentɪd]

[释义] a. ①未注册的，无正式文件的 ②无事实证明的

[同根] document ['dɒkjumənt] n. ①文献，公文 ②证件，单据 v. ①用文件等证明，为…提供文件 ②为（书等）引证 ③用记实材料作成（影片，小说等）
documental [ˌdɒkju'mentəl] a. ①文件的，公文的 ②记录的，记实的

▶▶ **open to** ①容易受到… ②对…开放 ③是…的自由 ④乐意接受，愿意考虑

▶▶ **disposable** [dɪ'spəuzəbl]

[释义] a. ①可（任意）处置的，可自由支配的 ②用后即丢弃的，不回收的 n. 一次性物品，不回收的物品

[同根] dispose [dɪ'spəuz] v. ①处理，处置 ②布置，安排
disposal [dɪ'spəuzəl] n. ①处理，处置 ②布置，安排 ③除掉，丢掉

▶▶ **mayor** [meə]

[释义] n. 市长

▶▶ **mayoress** ['meərɪs] n. ①女市长 ②女市长助理 ③市第一夫人

▶▶ **to a certain extent** 在一定程度上

▶▶ **in terms of** 根据，按照，在…方面

▶▶ **convenient** [kən'viːnɪənt]

[释义] a. ①方便的，便利的 ②近便的，附近的

[同根] convenience [kən'viːnɪəns] n. ①方便 ②便利设施

▶▶ **make a point** 表明一种看法，证明一种观点

▶▶ **uproot** [ʌp'ruːt]

[释义] v. ①连根拔起，[喻] 根除，灭绝 ②使离开家园

▶▶ **indefinitely** [ɪn'defɪnɪtlɪ]

[释义] ad. ①无限期地 ②不确定地

[同根] indefinite [ɪn'defɪnɪt] a. ①不确定的 ②无限期的 ③模糊的，含糊的
indefinitive [ˌɪndɪ'fɪnɪtɪv] a. ①不明确的 ②非决定性的

▶▶ **under the threat of** 受到…的威胁，在…的威胁之下

▶▶ **currently** ['kʌrəntlɪ]

[释义] ad. ①现在，当前 ②普遍地，通常地

[同义] at present, presently

[同根] current ['kʌrənt] a. ①现在的 ②通用的，流通的 n. ①潮流 ②水流，气流，电流 ③趋势，倾向
currency ['kʌrənsɪ] n. ①通货，货币 ②（货币的）流通，通行 ③流通时期

选项词汇注释

▶▶ **be composed of** 由…组成

▶▶ **offended** [ə'fendɪd]

[释义] a. 生气的
[同义] annoyed, angry

[同根] offend [əˈfend] v. ①冒犯,得罪,使生气 ②违犯,违反 ③使厌恶
offence [əˈfens] n. ①冒犯,得罪 ②犯法行为,罪行,过错 ③讨厌的东西 ④进攻,攻击
offensive [əˈfensɪv] a. ①冒犯的,无礼的 ②使人不快的,讨厌的 ③进攻的

▶▶▶ discouraged [dɪsˈkʌrɪdʒd]
[释义] a. 气馁的,灰心丧气的
[同义] depressed, disheartened, dispirited
[同根] discourage [dɪsˈkʌrɪdʒ] v. ①使泄气,使灰心 ②阻止,阻挡,劝阻
discouragement [dɪsˈkʌrɪdʒmənt] n. ①灰心,丧气 ②挫折,使人丧气的事情
discouraging [dɪsˈkʌrɪdʒɪŋ] a. ①令人丧气的,使人灰心的 ②阻止的

▶▶▶ target [ˈtɑːɡɪt]
[释义] n. ①对象,目标 ②靶子,标的 ③(想达到的)目标,指标 v. ①瞄准,对准,把⋯作为目标 ②为⋯定指标
[词组] off target 不对头的,不准确的
on target 击中要害的,准确的
hit a target ①射中靶子 ②达到定额,达到指标

▶▶▶ attack [əˈtæk]

[释义] v. ①(用武力)进攻,攻击 ②(用语言)攻击,抨击 ③(疾病等)侵袭,侵害 ④着手,投入,从事 n. ①攻击,抨击 ②(疾病)突然发作
[同义] aggression, strike, hit
[反义] defense

▶▶▶ take advantage of ①利用(时机,他人的无知,弱点等)②占⋯的便宜,欺骗

▶▶▶ turn a blind eye to 对⋯熟视无睹

▶▶▶ deport [dɪˈpɔːt]
[释义] v. ①把(外国人)驱逐出境 ②流放,放逐
[同根] deportation [ˌdiːpɔːˈteɪʃən] n. 驱逐出境,流放,放逐

▶▶▶ permanently [ˈpɜːmənəntlɪ]
[释义] ad. 永远地,永恒地,长期不变地
[同义] eternally, perpetually, enduringly, lastingly
[反义] temporarily
[同根] permanent [ˈpɜːmənənt] a. ①永久(性)的 ②长期不变的 ③耐久的
permanence [ˈpɜːmənəns] n. ①永久性,永恒 ②长期不变 ③耐久性

Skimming and Scanning
Six Secrets of High-Energy People

There's an energy crisis in America, and it has nothing to do with fossil fuels. Millions of us get up each morning already weary over what the day holds. "I just can't get started," people say. But it's not physical energy that most of us lack. Sure, we could all use extra sleep and a better diet. But in truth, people are healthier today than at any time in history. I can almost guarantee that if you long for more energy, the problem is not with your body.

What you're seeking is not physical energy. It's emotional energy. Yet, sad to say, life sometimes seems designed to exhaust our supply. We work too hard. We have family obligations. We encounter emergencies and personal crises. No wonder so many of us suffer from emotional fatigue, a kind of utter exhaustion of the spirit.

And yet we all know people who are filled with joy, despite the unpleasant circumstances of their lives. Even as a child, I observed people who were poor, or disabled, or ill, but who nonetheless faced life with optimism and vigor. Consider Laura Hillenbrand, who, despite an extremely weak body, wrote the best-seller *Seabiscuit*. Hillenbrand barely had enough physical energy to drag herself out of bed to write. But she was fueled by having a story she wanted to share. It was emotional energy that helped her succeed.

Unlike physical energy, which is finite and diminishes with age, emotional energy is unlimited and has nothing to do with genes or upbringing. So how do you get it? You can't simply tell yourself to be positive. You must take action. Here are six practical strategies that work.

1. Do something new.
Very little that's new occurs in our lives. The impact of this sameness

on our emotional energy is gradual, but huge: It's like a tire with a slow **leak** You don't notice it at first, but eventually you'll get a flat. It's up to you to plug the leak—even though there are always a dozen reasons to **stay stuck in** your dull routines of life. That's where Maura, 36, a waitress, found herself a year ago.

Fortunately, Maura had a **lifeline**—a group of women friends who meet regularly to discuss their lives. Their lively discussions **spurred** Maura to make small but nevertheless life-altering changes. She joined a gym in the next town. She changed her look with a short haircut and new black T-shirts. Eventually, Maura gathered the courage to quit her job and start her own business.

Here's a challenge: If it's something you wouldn't ordinarily do, do it. Try a dish you've never eaten. Listen to music you'd ordinarily **tune out**. You'll discover these small things add to your emotional energy.

2. Reclaim life's meaning.

So many of my patients tell me that their lives used to have meaning, but that somewhere along the line things went **stale**.

The first step in solving this meaning shortage is to **figure out** what you really care about, and then do something about it. **A case in point** is Ivy, 57, a pioneer in investment banking. "I mistakenly believed that all the money I made would mean something," she says. "But I feel lost, like a 22-year-old wondering what to do with her life." Ivy's solution? She started a program that shows **Wall Streeters** how to **donate** time and money to poor children. In the process, Ivy filled her life with meaning.

3. Put yourself in the fun zone.

Most of us grown-ups are seriously fun-**deprived**. High-energy people have the same day-to-day work as the rest of us, but they manage to find something enjoyable in every situation. A **real-estate broker** I know keeps herself amused on the job by mentally **redecorating** the houses she shows to clients. "I love imagining what even the most **run-down** house could look like with a little **tender** loving care," she says. "It's a challenge—and the **least** desirable properties are usually the most fun. "

We all **define** fun differently, of course, but I can guarantee this: If you put just a bit of it into your day, your energy will increase quickly.

4. Bid farewell to guilt and regret.

Everyone's past is filled with regrets that still cause pain. But from an emotional energy point of view, they are dead weights that keep us from moving forward. While they can't merely be willed away, I do recommend you remind yourself that whatever happened is in the past, and nothing can change that. Holding on to the memory only allows the damage to continue into the present.

5. Make up your mind.

Say you've been thinking about cutting your hair short. Will it look stylish—or too extreme? You endlessly think it over. Having the decision hanging over your head is a huge energy drain. Every time you can't decide, you burden yourself with alternatives. Quit thinking that you have to make the right decision; instead, make a choice and don't look back.

6. Give to get.

Emotional energy has a kind of magical quality: The more you give, the more you get back. This is the difference between emotional and physical energy. With the latter, you have to get it to be able to give it. With the former, however, you get it by giving it.

Start by asking everyone you meet, "How are you?" as if you really want to know, then listen to the reply. Be the one who hears. Most of us also need to smile more often. If you don't smile at the person you love first thing in the morning, you're sucking energy out of your relationship. Finally, help another person—and make the help real, concrete. Give a *massage* (按摩) to someone you love, or cook her dinner. Then, expand the circle to work. Try asking yourself what you'd do if your goal were to be helpful rather than efficient.

After all, if it's true that what goes around comes around, why not make sure that what's circulating around you is the good stuff?

文章词汇注释

▶▶▶ **fossil fuel** 矿物燃料

▶▶▶ **weary** ['wɪərɪ]
[释义] a. ①疲劳的，消沉的 ②使人疲劳的，令人厌烦的 v. (使) 疲劳，(使) 不耐烦
[同义] exhausted, worn out, tired
[同根] wear [wɪə] v. ①(使)疲乏，(使) 厌倦 ②面露，带有 ③穿破，磨损
wearing ['weərɪŋ] a. ①使人疲倦的 ②消耗性的，耗损的 ③穿戴（用）的

▶▶▶ **in truth** 的确，事实上
▶▶▶ **long for** 渴望，希望得到

▶▶▶ **exhaust** [ɪg'zɔ:st]
[释义] v. ①用尽，花光 ②使枯竭
n. ①（废气、废液等的）排出 ②排气装置 ③（排出的）废气
[同根] exhausting [ɪg'zɔ:stɪŋ] a. 使精疲力竭的，使疲惫不堪的
exhausted [ɪg'zɔ:stɪd] a. ①用完的，枯竭的 ②精疲力竭的
exhaustion [ɪg'zɔ:stʃən] n. ①耗尽，枯竭 ②筋疲力尽 ③竭尽，详尽

▶▶▶ **obligation** [ˌɒblɪ'geɪʃən]
[释义] n. ①（法律上或道义上的）义务，责任 ②施加义务（或责任）③合同，契约
[同义] responsibility, duty, requirement
[同根] oblige [ə'blaɪdʒ] v. ①强使，迫使 ②施恩惠于，帮…的忙 ③使感激
obligatory [ɒ'blɪgətərɪ] a. 有义务的，强制性的
[词组] lay/put under (an) obligation 施恩惠给，使负义务
under (an) obligation 处于负义务状态

▶▶▶ **encounter** [ɪn'kaʊntə]
[释义] v. ①与…邂逅，偶然遇见 ②遭

到，受到 n. ①邂逅，遭遇 ②冲突，交战
[词组] encounter with... 与…遭遇，遇到…

▶▶▶ **no wonder** 难怪，并不奇怪，不足为奇

▶▶▶ **fatigue** [fə'ti:g]
[释义] n. 疲劳，劳累 v. (使) 疲劳
[同义] tiredness, exhaustion

▶▶▶ **utter** ['ʌtə]
[释义] a. 完全的，彻底的，绝对的
v. 发出（声音），说，表露
[同义] complete, absolute
[反义] partial
[同根] utterance ['ʌtərəns] n. ①发声，吐露，表达 ②说话方式

▶▶▶ **disabled** [dɪs'eɪbəld]
[释义] a. 丧失能力的，残疾的

▶▶▶ **nonetheless** [ˌnʌnðə'les]
[释义] (=nevertheless) ad. 仍然，不过
conj. 然而，不过

▶▶▶ **optimism** ['ɒptɪmɪzəm]
[释义] n. 乐观，乐观主义
[同根] optimist ['ɒptɪmɪst] n. 乐天派，乐观者，乐观主义者
optimistic [ˌɒptɪ'mɪstɪk] a. 乐观的，乐观主义的
optimistical [ˌɒptɪ'mɪstɪkəl]
a. (=optimistic)
optimistically [ˌɒptɪ'mɪstɪkəlɪ] ad. 乐观地，乐天地

▶▶▶ **vigor** ['vɪgə]
[释义] n. [亦作 vigour] 活力，精力，体力，力量
[同义] energy, dynamism, strength

[同根] vigorous ['vɪgərəs] a. 精力旺盛的，有力的，健壮的

▶▶ fuel [fjʊəl]
[释义] v. ①激起，刺激，保持…的进行 ②加燃料，供以燃料 n. 燃料

▶▶ finite ['faɪnaɪt]
[释义] a. 有限的，有限制的
[同义] limited
[同根] infinite ['ɪnfɪnɪt] a. ①无限的，无穷的 ②极大的，巨大的

▶▶ diminish [dɪ'mɪnɪʃ]
[释义] v. ①减少，降低 ②削弱…的权势，贬低
[同义] cut, decrease, lessen, reduce
[反义] increase, raise
[同根] diminution [ˌdɪmɪ'nju:ʃən] n. 减少，缩小

▶▶ gene [dʒi:n]
[释义] n. (遗传)基因，(遗传)因子
[同根] genetic [dʒɪ'netɪk] a. 基因的，遗传的

▶▶ upbringing ['ʌpbrɪŋɪŋ]
[释义] n. 抚育，养育，教养，培养
[同义] rearing

▶▶ sameness ['seɪmnɪs]
[释义] n. ①同一(性)，相同(性) ②千篇一律，单调
[同义] likeness, similarity, resemblance
[反义] difference

▶▶ leak [li:k]
[释义] n. ①泄漏，透露 ②漏出物 ③漏洞，裂缝 v. ①漏，渗 ②泄漏，散布
[同根] leakage ['li:kɪdʒ] n. 漏，泄漏，渗漏
leaky ['li:kɪ] a. ①漏的 ②泄密的
[词组] leak away 浪费掉
leak out ①漏出 ②泄漏，透露

▶▶ be/stay stuck in... 受束缚于…，受

困于…，陷于…而不能自拔

▶▶ lifeline ['laɪflaɪn]
[释义] n. ①救生索 ②生命线，重要的交通线

▶▶ spur [spɜ:]
[释义] n. & v. 激励，鞭策，鼓舞，促进
[同义] provoke, urge, encourage
[词组] spur on 鞭策…，激励…
on the spur of the moment 一时冲动之下，不假思索地

▶▶ tune out ①关掉(收音机等)，停止收听(或收看) ②[俚]不注意，不理睬

▶▶ reclaim [rɪ'kleɪm]
[释义] v. & n. ①要求(或主张)收回，要求(或主张)恢复 ②改造，教化 ③回收利用(废物)

▶▶ stale [steɪl]
[释义] a. ①陈腐的，过时的 ②(空气等)污浊的 ③(食品等)不新鲜的 ④疲惫的，没劲的
[同义] out of date

▶▶ figure out ①想出，理解出 ②计算出，演算出

▶▶ a case in point 一个恰当的例子

▶▶ Wall Streeters (在华尔街及其周围金融区内工作的)华尔街大老板

▶▶ donate [dəʊ'neɪt]
[释义] v. 捐赠，赠予
[同义] contribute, offer
[同根] donation [dəʊ'neɪʃən] n. 捐赠品，捐款，贡献
donative ['dəʊnətɪv] a. 捐赠的，赠与的 n. 捐赠物，捐款
donator [dəʊ'neɪtə] n. 捐赠者
[词组] donate...to... 把…捐赠给…

▶▶ deprive [dɪ'praɪv]
[释义] v. 剥夺，使丧失

[同义] take away

[反义] provide

[同根] deprived [dɪ'praɪvd] a. (尤指儿童) 被剥夺的, 贫困的

deprival [dɪ'praɪvəl] n. 剥夺, 丧失

deprivation [ˌdeprɪ'veɪʃən] n. 剥夺

[词组] deprive sb of sth 剥夺某人的…, 使某人丧失…

▶▶ real-estate 房地产, 不动产

▶▶ broker ['brəʊkə]

[释义] n. ①经纪人, 代理人 ② (订立合同的) 中人

[同根] brokerage ['brəʊkərɪdʒ] n. 经纪业, (付给中间人的) 手续费, 佣金

▶▶ redecorate [ri:'dekəreɪt]

[释义] v. 重新装饰

[同根] decoration [ˌdekə'reɪʃən] n. 装饰

▶▶ run-down ['rʌn'daʊn]

[释义] a. ①失修的, 破败的 ② (钟、表等) 发条走完的, 电耗尽的 ③精疲力尽的, 衰弱的

▶▶ tender ['tendə]

[释义] a. ①亲切的, 温情的 ②嫩的, 柔软的 ③易感动的 ④微妙的, 棘手的 v. 使变嫩, 使变柔软

[同义] loving, caring, kind, gentle

[反义] rough

▶▶ least [li:st]

[释义] a. ① (little 的最高级) 最小的, 最少的 ②权力最小的, 最无足轻重的 n. 最少量, 最卑微者 ad. (little 的最高级) 最小, 最少

[词组] at (the) least ①至少 ②无论如何, 不管怎样, 反正

in the least 丝毫, 极少, 一点儿

least of all 尤其

not in the least 一点也不, 丝毫不

not the least 丝毫不, 全然不

▶▶ define [dɪ'faɪn]

[释义] v. ①解释, 给…下定义 ②定范围, 立界限

[同根] definition [ˌdefɪ'nɪʃən] n. 定义, 释义, 解释

definite ['defɪnɪt] a. ①明确的 ②一定的, 限定的 ③限制性的, 限定性的

definitive [dɪ'fɪnɪtɪv] a. ①确定的, 决定性的 ②限定的, 规定的

▶▶ bid farewell 说再见

▶▶ from...point of view 从…观点来看

▶▶ dead weight ①重负, 累赘 ② (静体的) 静止重量

▶▶ will away 通过意志力排除, 下决心驱除

▶▶ recommend [rekə'mend]

[释义] v. ①推荐, 建议 ②劝告, 忠告

[同义] suggest, advise, propose

[反义] oppose

[同根] recommendation [ˌrekəmen'deɪʃən] n. ①推荐 ②推荐信 ③劝告

recommendable [ˌrekə'mendəbl] a. ①可推荐的, 值得推荐的 ②可取的

▶▶ hold on to 保持, 坚持, 继续

▶▶ say 假定, 假如, 比如说

▶▶ stylish ['staɪlɪʃ]

[释义] a. 时髦的, 漂亮的, 新式的

[同义] fashionable

[同根] style [staɪl] n. ①流行式样, 时尚 ②样式, 类型 ③风格, 文体 ④方式, 方法

styling ['staɪlɪŋ] n. 式样, 款式

stylistic [staɪ'lɪstɪk] a. (文学或艺术) 风格 (上) 的, 文体 (上) 的, 语体 (上) 的

▶▶ hang over ①悬浮在…之上, 挂在…之上 ②靠近, 逼近, 笼罩 ③被延期

▶▶ drain [dreɪn]

[释义] n. ①消耗, 耗尽 ②排水沟

v. ①（使）逐渐消耗 ②排干积水

[同义] use up, exhaust, consume

[同根] drainage ['dreɪnɪdʒ] *n.* ①排水，排泄 ②排泄物 ③排泄设备

[词组] drain away 使排出，流出

　　 drain of 使逐渐消耗

▶▶ alternative [ɔːlˈtɜːnətɪv]

[释义] *n.* ①可供选择的办法（事物）②两者择一，取舍 *a.* 选择性的，二中择一的

[同根] alter ['ɔːltə] *v.* 改变

　　 alternate [ɔːlˈtɜːnɪt] *v.* 交替，改变 *a.* 交替的

　　 alternation [ˌɔːltɜːˈneɪʃən] *n.* 交替，轮流

▶▶ magical ['mædʒɪkəl]

[释义] *a.* ①有魔力的，神秘的 ②（似）巫术的，（似）魔术的

[同义] magic

[同根] magic ['mædʒɪk] *n.* ①魔法，巫术 ②魔术，戏法 ③魔力，魅力 *a.* ①（似）巫术的，（似）魔术的 ②有魔力的，神秘的

▶▶ suck [sʌk]

[释义] *v.* ①使耗尽，使枯竭 ②使卷入，吸引 ③吸食，吮吸 *n.* ①吸食，吮吸 ②吮吸力 ③（吮吸的）一口，一嘬

[同根] sucker ['sʌkə] *n.* ①吮吸者 ②涉世未深的人 ③［俚］寄生虫，吸血鬼

　　 sucking ['sʌkɪŋ] *a.* ①吸的，吮吸的 ②吃奶的，未断奶的 ③〈口〉非常年轻的，乳臭未干的

　　 suckle ['sʌkl] *v.* ①给…哺乳，给…喂奶 ②养育，使成长 ③吮吸，吸取

[词组] give suck to 给…喂奶，给…哺乳

　　 suck around 讨好地围着…转

　　 suck dry ①吸干，吮干 ②使耗尽，使枯竭

　　 suck in ①吸入，吸收，吸取 ②使卷入，把…吞没

▶▶ go around 满足人人的需要，人人能分到

▶▶ come around ①顺便来访 ②走弯路，绕道而来 ③再度降临（或发生）④（怒气、争论等）平息

▶▶ circulate ['sɜːkjʊleɪt]

[释义] *v.* ①（使）环行，环绕，（使）循环 ②发行，销售 ③流通

[同根] circulation [ˌsɜːkjʊˈleɪʃən] *n.* ①环流，循环 ②（书报等的）发行，发行量，（图书的）流通量 ③（货币等的）流通

　　 circulative ['sɜːkjʊleɪtɪv] *a.* ①循环的，促进循环的 ②流通的

　　 circulatory [sɜːkjʊˈleɪtərɪ] *a.*（血液等）循环的

Reading in Depth
Section A

　　The flood of women into the job market boosted economic growth and changed U.S. society in many ways. Many in-home jobs that used to be done primarily by women—ranging from family shopping to preparing meals to doing **voluntary** work—still need to be done by someone. Husbands and children now do some of these jobs, a situation that has changed the target market for many products. Or a working woman may face a **crushing** "poverty of time" and look for help elsewhere, creating opportunities for producers of frozen meals, child care centers, dry cleaners, financial services, **and the like**.

Although there is still a big wage gap between men and women, the income working women generate gives them new independence and buying power. For example, women now purchase about half of all cars. Not long ago, many car dealers **insulted** women shoppers by ignoring them or suggesting that they come back with their husbands. Now car companies have realized that women are potential customers. It's interesting that some leading Japanese car dealers were the first to really pay attention to women customers. In Japan, fewer women have jobs or buy cars—the Japanese society is still very much **male-oriented**. Perhaps it was the extreme contrast with Japanese society that **prompted** American firms to pay more attention to women buyers.

文章词汇注释

▶▶▶ **voluntary** ['vɒləntərɪ; (US) -terɪ]
[释义] *a.* ①自愿的，志愿的 ②非官办的 ③故意的，蓄意的 *n.* 自愿行动
[反义] involuntary
[同根] volunteer [vɒlən'tɪə] *n.* 志愿者，志愿兵 *v.* 自愿（做），自愿提供（或给予）*a.* 自愿参加的

▶▶▶ **crushing** ['krʌʃɪŋ]
[释义] *a.* ①压倒的，使人受不了的 ②压碎的，捣碎的
[同义] devastating, overwhelming
[反义] mild
[同根] crush [krʌʃ] *v.* ①压碎，压坏 ②弄皱，压皱 ③镇压，征服 ④榨，榨出

▶▶▶ **and the like** 等等，以及诸如此类

▶▶▶ **insult** [ɪn'sʌlt]

[释义] *v.* ①侮辱，辱骂 ②损害，危害 ③攻击，袭击
['ɪnsʌlt] *n.* ①侮辱，凌辱 ②损害，危害
[同根] insulting [ɪn'sʌltɪŋ] *a.* ①侮辱的，无礼的 ②损害人体的
[词组] add insult to injury ①在伤害之外又加以侮辱 ②雪上加霜，更糟的是

▶▶▶ **male-oriented** [meɪl'ɔːrɪentɪd]
[释义] *a.* 以男性为主的，男性导向的

▶▶▶ **prompt** [prɒmpt]
[释义] *v.* ①促使，怂恿 ②刺激，激起 ③提示 *a.* 敏捷的，及时的
[同义] encourage
[同根] promptive ['prɒmptɪv] *a.* 敦促的，激励的

Section B
Passage One

Reaching new peaks of **popularity** in North America is Iceberg Water, which is harvested from icebergs off the coast of Newfoundland, Canada.

Arthur von Wiesenberger, who carries the title Water Master, is one of the few water **critics** in North America. As a boy, he spent time in the larger cities of Italy, France and Switzerland, where bottled water is **consumed** daily. Even then, he kept a water journal, noting the brands he liked best. "My dog could tell the difference between bottled and **tap water**," he says.

But is plain tap water all that bad? Not at all. In fact, New York's **municipal** water for more than a century was called the **champagne** of tap water and until recently considered among the best in the world **in terms of** both taste and **purity**. Similarly, a magazine in England found that tap water from the Thames River tasted better than several leading brands of bottled water that were 400 times more expensive.

Nevertheless, soft-drink companies **view** bottled water **as** the next **battle-ground** for market share—this despite the fact that over 25 percent of bottled water comes from tap water: PepsiCo's Aquafina and Coca-Cola's Dasani are both purified tap water rather than spring water.

As diners **thirst for** leading brands, bottlers and **restaurateurs** *salivate* (垂涎) over the profits. A restaurant's typical **mark-up** on wine is 100 to 150 percent, whereas on bottled water it's often 300 to 500 percent. But since water is much cheaper than wine, and many of the fancier brands aren't available in stores, most diners don't notice or care.

As a result, some restaurants are **turning up** the pressure to sell bottled water. According to an article in *The Wall Street Journal*, some of the more shameless **tactics** include placing attractive bottles on the table for a **visual** sell, listing brands on the menu without prices, and pouring bottled water without even asking the diners if they want it.

Regardless of how it's sold, the popularity of bottled water **taps into** our desire for better health, our wish to appear **cultivated**, and even a longing for lost purity.

文章词汇注释

▶▶▶ **popularity** [ˌpɒpjuˈlærɪtɪ]
[释义] *n.* ①流行，普及，大众化 ②声望，讨人喜欢的特点
[反义] unpopularity
[同根] popular [ˈpɒpjulə] *a.* 通俗的，流行的，受欢迎的
popularize [ˈpɒpjuləraɪz] *v.* 普及，推广

▶▶▶ **critic** [ˈkrɪtɪk]
[释义] *n.* ①评论家，批评家，评论员 ②吹毛求疵的人，爱挑剔的人
[同义] analyst, reviewer
[同根] criticize [ˈkrɪtɪsaɪz] *v.* ①批评，批判，指责 ②评论，评价
criticism [ˈkrɪtɪsɪzəm] *n.* ①批评，批判，指责 ②评论，评论文章
critical [ˈkrɪtɪkəl] *a.* ①吹毛求疵的，爱挑剔的 ②批评的，评论的 ③关键性的，重大的

▶▶▶ **consume** [kənˈsjuːm]
[释义] *v.* ①消耗，耗尽 ②吃完，喝光 ③毁灭，挥霍
[同义] use, utilize
[反义] conserve
[同根] consumer [kənˈsjuːmə] *n.* ①消费者，用户 ②消耗者 ③毁灭者
consumption [kənˈsʌmpʃən] *n.* ①消费量，消耗量 ②消耗，消费

▶▶▶ **tap water** 自来水

▶▶▶ **municipal** [mju(ː)ˈnɪsɪpəl]
[释义] *a.* ①市（政）的，自治市的 ②地方性的，地方自治的 ③内政的，国内的
[同义] civic
[同根] municipality [mjuːˌnɪsɪˈpælɪtɪ] *n.* ①自治市 ②市政当局 ③（总称）市民

▶▶▶ **champagne** [ʃæmˈpeɪn]
[释义] *n.* 香槟酒，令人振奋（或极好）的东西

▶▶▶ **in terms of** ①就…而言 ②根据，按照

▶▶▶ **purity** [ˈpjuərɪtɪ]
[释义] *n.* ①纯净，洁净 ②纯洁，清白
[同义] cleanliness
[同根] pure [pjuə] *a.* ①纯洁的，不掺杂的 ②纯净的，无垢的 ③无瑕的，纯正的
purify [ˈpjuərɪfaɪ] *v.* ①使纯净，净化 ②提纯，精制 ③使纯洁，使纯粹

▶▶▶ **view...as...** 把…看作是…
▶▶▶ **battle-ground** *n.* 战场，斗争的领域
▶▶▶ **thirst for** 渴望，渴求

▶▶▶ **restaurateur** [restərəˈtɜː]
[释义] *n.* 餐馆老板，饭店主人

▶▶▶ **mark-up** [ˈmɑːkʌp]
[释义] *n.* ①涨价幅度 ②涨价，标高售价

▶▶▶ **turn up** ①开大，调高 ②改善，把…翻转过来 ③出现，重现 ④证明是，结果是

▶▶▶ **tactics** [ˈtæktɪks]
[释义] *n.* ①策略，手段 ②战术
[同义] strategy
[同根] tact [tækt] *n.* 圆通，乖巧，机敏，外交手腕
tactful [ˈtæktful] *a.* 圆通的，乖巧的，机敏的
tactical [ˈtæktɪkəl] *a.* ①战术的 ②有策略的，手段高明的

▶▶ **visual** [ˈvɪzjuəl]

[释义] a. ①视觉的，视力的 ②看得见的 n. ①（常用复数）（电视、电影等的）画面，图像 ②广告图画

[同根] vision [ˈvɪʒən] n. ①远见，洞察力 ②想象，幻想，幻影 ③视力，视觉
visible [ˈvɪzəbl] a. 看得见的
visionary [ˈvɪʒənərɪ] a. ①不切实际的，空幻的 ②爱幻想的

▶▶ **regardless of** 不管，不顾

▶▶ **tap into** ①（着手）利用 ②开发，发挥，开辟

▶▶ **cultivated** [ˈkʌltɪveɪtɪd]

[释义] a. ①有教养的 ②耕耘的，栽植的

[同义] educated, refined

[同根] cultivate [ˈkʌltɪveɪt] v. ①培养，养成 ②耕作，栽培 ③发展，建立
cultivation [ˌkʌltɪˈveɪʃən] n. ①培养，修养 ②耕作，栽培 ③发展，建立

选项词汇注释

▶▶ **message** [ˈmesɪdʒ]

[释义] n. ①信息，信，电报 ②正式公报，咨文 ③（故事等的）启示，教训 v. ①作为文电发出 ②通报，报告，报信

▶▶ **detect** [dɪˈtekt]

[释义] v. ①察觉，发现 ②查明，测出

[同根] detection [dɪˈtekʃən] n. 察觉，发现，侦查
detective [dɪˈtektɪv] n. ①侦探，私人侦探 ②发觉者，探测者 a. ①（关于）侦探的 ②侦查（用）的，探测（用）的
detectable [dɪˈtektəbl] a. 可察觉的，可查明的，可测出的

▶▶ **fine** [faɪn]

[释义] a. ①细微的，细微难察的 ②美好的，杰出的 ③精制的，精密的 ④健康的，舒适的

[同义] slight

▶▶ **intense** [ɪnˈtens]

[释义] a. ①激烈的，强烈，剧烈的 ②热切的，热情的

[同义] severe

[反义] moderate

[同根] intensify [ɪnˈtensɪfaɪ] v. 加剧，加强，增强，强化
intensive [ɪnˈtensɪv] a. ①加强的，集中的 ②深入细致的，密集的
intensity [ɪnˈtensɪtɪ] n. ①强烈，剧烈 ②强度，亮度

▶▶ **fashionable** [ˈfæʃənəbl]

[释义] a. ①流行的，时髦的 ②时髦人物的，受时髦人物欢迎的

[同义] stylish

[同根] fashion [ˈfæʃən] n. ①方式，样子 ②流行，时尚，时兴的样式，流行款式 ③种类 v. ①使成形，把…塑造成 ②使适应，使适合

Passage Two

As we have seen, the focus of **medical care** in our society has been **shifting from** curing disease **to** preventing disease—especially in terms of changing our many unhealthy behaviors, such as poor eating habits, smoking, and failure to exercise. The line of thought **involved in** this shift can be pursued further. Imagine a person who is about the right weight, but does not eat very *nutritious*（有营养的）foods, who feels OK but exercises only occasionally, who goes to work every day, but is not an outstanding worker, who drinks a few beers at home most nights but does not drive while drunk, and who has no chest pains or **abnormal** blood counts, but sleeps a lot and often feels tired. This person is not ill. He may not even be **at risk** for any particular disease. But we can imagine that this person could be a lot healthier.

The field of medicine has not traditionally **distinguished** between someone who is merely "not ill" and someone who is in excellent health and pays attention to the body's special needs. Both types have simply been called "well." In recent years, however, some health specialists have begun to **apply** the terms "well" and "wellness" only to those who are actively **striving** to maintain and improve their health. People who are well **are concerned with nutrition** and exercise, and they **make a point of monitoring** their body's condition. Most important, perhaps, people who are well **take** active **responsibility for** all matters **related to** their health. Even people who have a physical disease or *handicap*（缺陷）may be "well," **in this** new **sense,** if they **make an effort** to maintain the best possible health they can **in the face of** their physical limitations. "Wellness" may perhaps best be viewed not as a state that people can achieve, but as an **ideal** that people can strive for. People who are well are likely to be better able to resist disease and to fight disease when it strikes. And by focusing attention on healthy ways of living, the concept of wellness can **have a beneficial impact on** the ways in which people face the challenges of daily life.

文章词汇注释

▶▶▶ medical care 医疗保健

▶▶▶ shift from...to... 从…转移到…

▶▶▶ involved in... …所涉及的

▶▶▶ abnormal [æb'nɔ:məl]

[释义] *a.* ①不正常的，不规则的 ②变态的，畸形的

[同根] normal ['nɔ:məl] *a.* ①正常的 ②平常的 ③正规的，标准的 ④师范的 *n.* ①正常人 / 物 ②正常状态，通

常标准

abnormality [ˌæbnɔː'mælɪtɪ] n. ①变态，畸形 ②反常情况，变态特征

▶▶at risk 处境危险，遭受危险

▶▶distinguish [dɪ'stɪŋgwɪʃ]

[释义] v. ①区分，辨别，分清 ②使区别于其他物/人 ③认出，发现

[同根] distinguished [dɪ'stɪŋgwɪʃt] a. ①卓越的，杰出的 ②高贵的，地位高的，重要的

distinguishable [dɪ'stɪŋgwɪʃəbl] a. 可区别的，可辨识的

[词组] be distinguished as ①辨明为 ②称之为

be distinguished for 以…而著名

be distinguished from 不同于，与…加以区别

▶▶apply...to 把…应用于…

▶▶strive [straɪv]

[释义] v. ①力争，力求，努力，奋斗 ②斗争，反抗

[词组] strive for 争取，为…奋斗

strive against ①同…搏斗 ②反抗

strive with sb. in sth. 与某人就某事争论

strive together/with each other 互相争斗

▶▶be concerned with ①对…感兴趣，关心… ②关于 ③喜爱

▶▶nutrition [njuː'trɪʃən]

[释义] n. ①营养，滋养 ②营养物，滋养物

[同根] nutritionist [njuː'trɪʃənɪst] n. 营养学家

nutritious [njuː'trɪʃəs] a. 有营养成分的，营养的，滋养的

nutritional [njuː'trɪʃənel] a. 营养的，滋养的

malnutrition [ˌmælnjuː'trɪʃən] n. 营养不良

▶▶make a point of 重视，强调

▶▶monitor ['mɒnɪtə]

[释义] v. 监测，监控，密切注视

n. ①班长，监考员 ②监听器，监视器，监控器

[同根] monitorial [ˌmɒnɪ'tɔːrɪəl] a. ①班长的 ②告诫的，警告的 ③使用监听器（或监视器、监控器等）的

monitory ['mɒnɪtərɪ] a. 训诫的，警告的

▶▶take responsibility for 对…负责，承担…责任

▶▶(be) related to ①与…相关的 ②与…有亲属关系的

▶▶in this sense 从这个意义上来讲，从这个角度来看

▶▶make an effort 努力

▶▶in the face of 面对，面临

▶▶ideal [aɪ'dɪəl]

[释义] n. ①理想 ②终极目标 ③思想，观念 a. ①理想的，完美的 ②空想的，不切实际的

[同根] idealism [aɪ'dɪəlɪzm] n. ①理想主义 ②唯心主义，唯心论

idealist [aɪ'dɪəlɪst] n. 理想主义者，空想家

idealistic [aɪˌdɪə'lɪstɪk] a. ①理想主义（者）的 ②唯心主义（者）的

▶▶have a beneficial impact on 对…有有益的影响

四级词汇

选项词汇注释

▶▶▶ place stress on... 强调，把重点放在…上

▶▶▶ in a healthy physical condition 处于健康状态

▶▶▶ psychological well-being 心理健康

▶▶▶ to excess 过量，过度

▶▶▶ regular health checks 定期体检

▶▶▶ keeping fit 保持健康

▶▶▶ meet standards of 达到…的标准 / 水平

▶▶▶ keep a proper balance between... and... 保持…与…间的适当平衡

▶▶▶ advocate ['ædvəkɪt]

[释义] v. 主张，拥护，提倡 n. 拥护者，提倡者

[同义] support, promote, back

[反义] opponent

[同根] advocacy ['ædvəkəsɪ] n. 拥护，提倡

advocator ['ædvəkeɪtə] n. 拥护者，提倡者

▶▶▶ slim figure 苗条的身材

▶▶▶ experience...symptoms 经受 / 表现出…症状

Skimming and Scanning
Protect Your Privacy When Job-hunting Online

Identity theft and identity fraud are terms used to refer to all types of crime in which someone wrongfully obtains and uses another person's personal data in some way that involves fraud or deception, typically for economic gain.

The numbers associated with identity theft are beginning to add up fast these days. A recent General Accounting Office report estimates that as many as 750,000 Americans are victims of identity theft every year. And that number may be low, as many people choose not to report the crime even if they know they have been victimized.

Identity theft is "an absolute epidemic," states Robert Ellis Smith, a respected author and advocate of privacy. "It's certainly picked up in the last four or five years. It's worldwide. It affects everybody, and there's very little you can do to prevent it and, worst of all, you can't detect it until it's probably too late."

Unlike your fingerprints, which are unique to you and cannot be given to someone else for their use, your personal data, especially your social security number, your bank account or credit card number, your telephone calling card number, and other valuable identifying data, can be used, if they fall into the wrong hands, to personally profit at your expense. In the United States and Canada, for example, many people have reported that unauthorized persons have taken funds out of their bank or financial accounts, or, in the worst cases, taken over their identities altogether, running up vast debts and committing crimes while using the victims' names. In many cases, a victim's losses may include not only out-of-pocket financial losses, but substantial additional financial costs associated with trying to restore his reputation in the community and correcting erroneous information for which the criminal is **responsible**.

According to the **FBI**, identity theft is the number one fraud **committed** on the Internet. So how do job seekers protect themselves while continuing to **circulate** their **resumes** online? The key to a successful online job search is learning to manage the risks. Here are some tips for staying safe while **conducting** a job search on the Internet.

1. Check for a privacy policy.

If you are considering posting your resume online, make sure the job search site your are considering has a privacy policy, like CareerBuilder.com. The policy should **spell out** how your information will be used, stored and whether or not it will be shared. You may want to think twice about posting your resume on a site that **automatically** shares your information with others. You could be opening yourself up to unwanted calls from *solicitors* (推销员).

When **reviewing** the site's privacy policy, you'll be able to delete your resume just as easily as you posted it. You won't necessarily want your resume to remain out there on the Internet once you land a job. Remember, the longer your resume remains posted on a job board, the more **exposure**, both positive and not-so-positive, it will receive.

2. Take advantage of site features.

Lawful job search sites offer levels of privacy protection. Before posting your resume, carefully consider your job search **objective** and the level of risk you are willing to **assume**.

CareerBuilder.com, for example, offers three levels of privacy from which job seekers can choose. The first is **standard** posting. This **option** gives job seekers who post their resumes the most **visibility** to the broadest employer audience possible.

The second is *anonymous* (匿名的) posting. This allows job seekers the same visibility as those in the standard posting **category** without any of their contact information being **displayed**. Job seekers who wish to remain anonymous but want to share some other information may choose which pieces of contact information to display.

The third is private posting. This option allows a job seeker to post a resume without having it searched by employers. Private posting allows job seekers to quickly and easily apply for jobs that appear on CareerBuilder.com without retyping their information.

3. Safeguard your identity.

Career experts say that one of the ways job seekers can stay safe while using the Internet to search out jobs is to **conceal** their identities. Replace your name on your resume with a *generic*（泛指的）identifier, such as "**Intranet** Developer **Candidate**," or "Experienced Marketing Representative."

You should also consider **eliminating** the name and **location** of your current employer. Depending on your title, it may not be all that difficult to determine who you are once the name of your company is provided. Use a general description of the company such as "Major auto manufacturer," or "International packaged goods supplier."

If your job title is unique, consider using the generic **equivalent** instead of the exact title **assigned** by your employer.

4. Establish an email address for your search.

Another way to protect your privacy while seeking employment online is to open up an email account **specifically** for your online job search. This will safeguard your existing email box **in the event** someone you don't know **gets hold of** your email address and shares it with others.

Using an email address specifically for you job search also eliminates the possibility that you will receive unwelcome emails in your primary mailbox. When naming your new email address, be sure that it doesn't **contain references** to your name or other information that will **give away** your identity. The best solution is an email address that is **relevant to** the job you are seeking such as *salesmgr2004@provider.com*.

5. Protect your reference.

If your resume contains a section with the names and contact information of your references, take it out. **There's no sense** in safeguarding your information while sharing private contact information of your references.

6. Keep *confidential*（机密的）information confidential.

Do not, **under any circumstances**, share your social security, driver's license, and bank account numbers or other personal information, such as race or eye color. Honest employers do not need this information with an **initial** application. Don't provide this even if they say they need it in order to conduct a background check. This is one of the oldest tricks in the book—don't **fall for it**.

文章词汇注释

▶▶ **identity** [aɪˈdentɪtɪ]

[释义] n. ①身份，本身，身份证 (identity card 常略作 ID) ②同一人，同一物 ③相同，一致 ③相同处，一致处

[同根] identical [aɪˈdentɪkəl] a. ①同一的 ② (完全) 相同的，一模一样的
identify [aɪˈdentɪfaɪ] v. ①认为…等同于 ②认出，确定 ③使与…有关联
identification [aɪˌdentɪfɪˈkeɪʃən] n. ①认出，识别，鉴定，确认 ②有关联，认同，支持
identifier [aɪˈdentɪfaɪə] n. ①标识符 ②鉴别，识别 ③鉴定人
identifiable [aɪˈdentɪfaɪəbl] a. 可辨认的，可识别的，可证明是同一的

[词组] identity theft 身份盗窃

▶▶ **fraud** [frɔːd]

[释义] n. ①诈骗 ②欺骗（行为），骗人的东西 ③骗子，假货

[同义] deception, cheat, dishonesty, trickery; fake

[词组] expose a fraud 揭穿骗局

▶▶ **term** [tɜːm]

[释义] n. ① (特定意义的) 专门名词术语，措辞，说法 ②学期，任期 ③ [pl.] (契约、谈判等的) 条件，条款 ④ [pl.] 关系，交谊，地位

[词组] come to terms 妥协，达成协议，接受条件，对…采取将就态度
in terms of 依据…，从…方面来讲，就…来说
in the long term 从长远观点来看

▶▶ **refer to** ①谈及，涉及，指的是 ②参考，查阅

▶▶ **personal data** 个人资料

▶▶ **involve** [ɪnˈvɒlv]

[释义] v. ①涉及，包含，包括 ②使卷入，使陷入，拖累 ③使专注

[同义] contain, include, engage, absorb

[同根] involved [ɪnˈvɒlvd] a. 有关的，牵扯在内的，参与的，受影响的
involvement [ɪnˈvɒlvmənt] n. ①卷入，缠绕 ②复杂，混乱 ③牵连的事务，复杂的情况

[词组] be / become involved in 包含在…，与…有关，被卷入，专心地（做）
be / get involved with 涉及，给…缠住

▶▶ **deception** [dɪˈsepʃən]

[释义] n. ①欺骗，诓骗，蒙蔽 ②诡计

[同义] deceit

[同根] deceive [dɪˈsiːv] v. 欺骗，行骗
deceptive [dɪˈseptɪv] a. 骗人的，靠不住的，容易使人蒙蔽的

▶▶ **typically** [ˈtɪpɪkəlɪ]

[释义] ad. ①一般地，通常地 ②代表性地，典型地

[同根] type [taɪp] n. ①类型，种类 ②典型，模范 v. 打字，翻印
typical [ˈtɪpɪkəl] a. 典型的，象征性的

typicality [ˌtɪpɪ'kælɪtɪ] *n.* 典型性，代表性，特征

▶▶ **associated with** 与…有关的

▶▶ **estimate** ['estɪmeɪt]
[释义] *v. & n.* ①估计 ②估计…的价值，评价，判断
[同根] overestimate [ˌəuvə'estɪmeɪt] *v.* 过高估计
underestimate [ˌʌndə'estɪmeɪt] *v.* 低估，看轻
[词组] by estimate 据估计
make an estimate of 估计…，评价…

▶▶ **victimize** ['vɪktɪmaɪz]
[释义] *v.* 使受害，使牺牲，使受骗
[同根] victim ['vɪktɪm] *n.* 受害者，牺牲者，牺牲品

▶▶ **absolute** ['æbsəluːt]
[释义] *a.* ①纯粹的，完全的，绝对的 ②地道的，十足的 ③不受任何限制（或约束）的
[同义] complete, thorough, total, essential
[反义] relative
[同根] absolutely ['æbsəluːtlɪ] *ad.* ①完全地，非常 ②肯定地 ③绝对地

▶▶ **epidemic** [ˌepɪ'demɪk]
[释义] *n.* ①流行病，（风尚等的）流行 ②（流行病的）流行，传播 *a.* （疾病）流行性的 ②极为盛行的，流行极广的

▶▶ **advocate** ['ædvəkɪt]
[释义] *n.* ①提倡者，拥护者 ②辩护者，律师 *v.* 拥护，主张
[同义] supporter, promoter, backer
[同根] advocacy ['ædvəkəsɪ] *n.* ①拥护，提倡 ②辩护，辩护术
advocator ['ædvəkeɪtə] *n.* ①拥护者，提倡者 ②辩护者

▶▶ **privacy** ['praɪvəsɪ]
[释义] *n.* ①隐私，私生活 ②秘密，私下 ③隐居，独处
[同根] private ['praɪvɪt] *a.* ①私人的，私有的 ②秘密的
privatization [ˌpraɪvətaɪ'zeɪʃən] *n.* 私人化
privatize ['praɪvɪtaɪz] *v.* 使归私有，使私人化
privately [ˌpraɪvətaɪ'zeɪʃən] *ad.* ①私人地，私有地 ②秘密地

▶▶ **pick up** （从不动到动或慢速行驶后）增加（速度），加速

▶▶ **detect** [dɪ'tekt]
[释义] *v.* ①察觉，发觉，发现 ②查明，侦察出，测出
[同义] discover, locate, spy, recognize, perceive
[反义] conceal, hide
[同根] detection [dɪ'tekʃən] *n.* 察觉，发觉，侦察
detector [dɪ'tektə] *n.* 发现者，探测者，侦察器
detective [dɪ'tektɪv] *n.* 侦探，私人侦探 *a.* （关于）侦探的
detectable/ detectible [dɪ'tektəbl] *a.* 可察觉的，可查明的，可测出的

▶▶ **unique** [juː'niːk]
[释义] *a.* 唯一的，独特的，独一无二的
[同义] single, unparalleled, extraordinary
[反义] ordinary, common
[同根] uniqueness [juː'niːknɪs] *n.* 唯一，独特
uniquely [juː'niːklɪ] *ad.* 唯一地，独特地
[词组] be unique to 只有…才有的

▶▶ **social security number** 社会保险密码
▶▶ **bank account** 银行账户
▶▶ **credit card** 信用卡
▶▶ **fall into** ①落入，陷于（混乱，错误等）②开始，分成，属于

▶▶ **at one's expense** 归某人付费

▶▶ **unauthorized** [ˌʌn'ɔ:θəraɪzd]

[释义] a. 未经受权的，未经委托的，未经批准的

[同根] authorize ['ɔ:θəraɪz] v. ①授权，委托 ②批准，认可
authority [ɔ:'θɒrɪtɪ] n. ①权威，威信，权力 ②权威人士，当权者 ③ [pl.] 当局，官方
authorized ['ɔ:θəraɪzd] a. ①经授权的，经委托的 ②经认可的

▶▶ **account** [ə'kaʊnt]

[释义] n. ①户头，账户 ②解释 ③记述，报导，报告 ④理由，根据 v. ①解释，说明 ②报账 ③（数量）占 ④认为，把…归结于

[同根] accounting [ə'kaʊntɪŋ] n. ①会计，会计学 ②帐，记帐，清算帐目
accountant [ə'kaʊntənt] n. 会计（员），会计师
accountancy [ə'kaʊntənsɪ] n. 会计师之职，会计学

[词组] balance accounts with sb. 与某人结清账目

▶▶ **take over** 接收，接管

▶▶ **run up** 积欠（帐款或债务），（费用等）迅速增加

▶▶ **commit crimes** 犯罪

▶▶ **in many cases** 在许多情况下

▶▶ **out-of-pocket** ['aʊtəv'pɒkɪt]

[释义] a. 现款支付的，预算外开支的

▶▶ **substantial** [səb'stænʃəl]

[释义] a. ①可观的，大量的，重大的 ②结实的，牢固的 ③实质上的，大体上的

[同根] substance ['sʌbstəns] n. ①物质 ②实质，内容 ③主旨，要意
substantially [səb'stænʃ(ə)lɪ] ad. ①主要地，实质上地 ②重大地，

相当大地
additional [ə'dɪʃənl] a. ①另外的，附加的，额外的 ②补充的

[同义] extra, added, further

[同根] add [æd] v. ①增加，添加 ②计算…总和，加起来 ③补充说
addition [ə'dɪʃən] n. ①加，加法 ②增加物，增加
additionally [ə'dɪʃənlɪ] ad. 另外

▶▶ **restore** [rɪ'stɔ:]

[释义] v. ①恢复 ②使康复 ③使复原，修复，整修

[同义] reinstate, renew, renovate, repair

[同根] restoration [ˌrestə'reɪʃən] n. ①恢复 ②康复，复元 ③复原，修复，整修
restorative [rɪ'stɔ:rətɪv] a. 恢复的，有恢复作用的 n. 恢复药，滋补剂

▶▶ **reputation** [ˌrepjʊ'teɪʃən]

[释义] n. ①名声，名气 ②好名声，声望，声誉

[同根] disreputable [dɪs'repjʊtəbl] a. 声名狼藉的，破烂不堪的
repute [rɪ'pju:t] n. 名誉，名声 v. 被认为，称为

[词组] of reputation 有名望的
of no reputation 声名狼藉的
live up to one's reputation 不负盛名，名副其实
lose / ruin one's reputation 名誉扫地

▶▶ **erroneous** [ɪ'rəʊnjəs]

[释义] a. 错误的，不正确的

[同义] false, incorrect, untrue

[反义] correct, true

[同根] error ['erə] n. ①错误，谬误 ②过失，罪过 ③错误的想法

▶▶ **responsible** [rɪ'spɒnsəbl]

[释义] a. ①负有责任的，责任重大的 ②认真负责的

[同根] respond [rɪ'spɒnd] v. ①回答，

作答 ②(to) 响应，作出反应

response [rɪs'pɒns] n. ①回答，答复 ②响应，反应

responsible [rɪs'pɒnsəbl] a. ①有责任的，需承担责任的 ②有责任感的

responsibility [rɪsˌpɒnsə'bɪlɪtɪ] n. ①责任，负责的状态，责任心 ②职责

[词组] be responsible for 对…负责

hold sb. responsible for 使某人负…的责任

make oneself responsible for 负起…的责任

▶▶ FBI (Federal Bureau of Investigation) (美国) 联邦调查局

▶▶ commit [kə'mɪt]

[释义] v. ①犯(罪)，做(错事等) ②把…交托给 ③使做出保证，使承担义务

[同根] commitment [kə'mɪtmənt] n. ①承诺，许诺，保证，承担的义务 ②献身参与，介入 ③托付，交托 ④信奉，支持

committee [kə'mɪtɪ] n. 委员会

commission [kə'mɪʃən] n. ①委员会 ②授权，委托 ③委任状，任职令

[词组] commit oneself on 对…表态

commit oneself to 专心致志于…

▶▶ circulate ['sɜːkjʊleɪt]

[释义] v. ①散播，流传 ②发行，销售 ③(使) 环流，(使) 循环 ④流通

[同根] circulation [ˌsɜːkjʊ'leɪʃən] n. ①(书报等的) 发行，发行量，(图书的) 流通量 ②(货币等的) 流通

circulative ['sɜːkjʊleɪtɪv] a. ①循环的，促进循环的 ②流通的

circulatory ['sɜːkjʊ'leɪtərɪ] a. (血液等) 循环的

▶▶ resume ['rezjuːmeɪ]

[释义] n. ①(求职者的) 履历，简历 ②摘要，概略

[rɪ'zjuːm] v. (中断后) 再继续，重

新开始 ②恢复，重新得到 ③接着说

▶▶ conduct [kən'dʌkt]

[释义] v. ①实施，进行，处理，经营，②指挥 ③导 (电)

['kɒndʌkt] n. ①行为，品行 ②管理，实施，处理

[同义] manage

[同根] conduction [kən'dʌkʃən] n. ①引流，输送，传播 ②传导，导电，传导性

conductive [kən'dʌktɪv] a. 传导(性)的，有传导力的

conductor [kən'dʌktə] n. ①乐队指挥 ②向导 ③管理人，指挥者 ④(公共汽车) 售票员，列车员 ⑤导体

▶▶ spell out 详细解释，清楚地说明

▶▶ automatically [ˌɔːtə'mætɪklɪ]

[释义] ad. ①自动地，自动化地 ②机械地，无意识地

[反义] manually

[同根] automate ['ɔːtəmeɪt] v. ①使自动性 ②用自动化技术操作

automatic [ˌɔːtə'mætɪk] a. ①自动的 ②必然的，自然的 ③自发的

automation [ˌɔːtə'meɪʃən] n. ①自动化 (技术) ②自动操作

▶▶ review [rɪ'vjuː]

[释义] v. & n. ①细察，详检，审核 ②评论，回顾 ③复习

[同义] evaluate, survey, examine

[同根] view [vjuː] n. ①景色，风景 ②观点，见解 ③风景，眼界 v. 观看，认为

interview ['ɪntəvjuː] n. & v. ①采访，接见，会见 ②面试

preview ['priːvjuː] n. & v. 预习，预演，预映，预展

[词组] be under review 在检查中，在审查中

come under review ①开始受审查

②开始被考虑
in review ①回顾 ②检查中

▶▶▶ exposure [ɪks'pəʊzə]
[释义] n. ①暴露，显露 ②揭露，揭穿 ③陈列，展出
[同根] expose [ɪks'pəʊz] v. ①暴露，使遭受 ②使曝光 ③陈列，展出 ④揭露，揭发
exposition [ˌekspə'zɪʃən] n. ①阐述，评注，说明 ②博览会，展览会
expositive [ɪks'pɒzɪtɪv] a. 说明的，解释的，评注的
expository [ɪks'pɒzɪˌtərɪ] a. 说明的，解释的，评注的

▶▶▶ take advantage of 利用

▶▶▶ feature ['fi:tʃə]
[释义] n. ①特征，特色 ②面貌，相貌 ③特别吸引人的东西 ④（报纸，杂志的）特写 v. ①是…的特色，以…为特色 ②给…以显著地位 ③由…主演
[同义] characteristic, trait
[同根] -featured（用以构成复合形容词）有…特征的
featureless ['fi:tʃəlɪs] a. 无特色的，平凡的，平淡无味的
[词组] make a feature of 以…为特色，以…为号召
feature film 正片，故事片

▶▶▶ objective [əb'dʒektɪv]
[释义] n. ①目标，目的，任务 ②客观事实，实在事物 a. ①客观的，公正的 ②目标的
[同根] object ['ɒbdʒɪkt] n. ①物体 ②目标，对象 ③宾语
[əb'dʒekt] v. 反对，拒绝，抗议
objectivity [ˌɒbdʒek'tɪvətɪ] n. 客观性，客观现实
objectively [əb'dʒektɪvlɪ] ad. 客观地

▶▶▶ assume [ə'sju:m]
[释义] v. ①承担，担任 ②假定，设想 ③呈现，具有，采取
[同义] suppose, presume, suspect
[同根] assuming [ə'su:mɪŋ] conj. 假定，假如 a. 傲慢的，自负的
assumed [ə'sju:md] a. 假定的，假装的
assumption [ə'sʌmpʃən] n. ①假定，臆断 ②担任，承担
assumptive [ə'sʌmptɪv] a. ①被视为理所当然的 ②自负的

▶▶▶ standard ['stændəd]
[释义] n. 标准，水准 a. 标准的，模范的，普通的
[同义] criterion
[同根] standardize ['stændədaɪz] v. 使标准化，使符合标准
standardization [ˌstændədaɪ'zeɪʃən] n. 标准化
[词组] meet...standard 符合…的标准
below standard 不合格的，标准以下的
come up to the standard 达到标准
double standard 双重标准，不同标准（尤指性道德上男宽女严的标准）

▶▶▶ option ['ɒpʃən]
[释义] n. ①选择 ②可选择的东西 ③任选项 ④任意
[同根] optional ['ɒpʃənəl] a. 任选的，随意的，非强制的
optionally ['ɒpʃənəlɪ] ad. 随意地
[词组] have no option but to (do) 除了…以外没有别的办法
at one's option 随意

▶▶▶ visibility [ˌvɪzɪ'bɪlɪtɪ]
[释义] n. 可见度，可见性
[同根] visional ['vɪʒənəl] a. ①视力的，视觉的 ②幻觉的
visionary ['vɪʒənərɪ] a. 幻影的，幻想的 n. ①有眼力的人 ②空想家，梦

想者，好幻想的人

visible ['vɪzəbl] a. ①看得见的 ②明显的，显著的 n. 可见物

visionless ['vɪʒənlɪs] a. 无视觉的，瞎的

vision ['vɪʒən] n. ①看法，想象力，目光，眼力 ②看，看见，看见的事物 ③视力，视觉 ④幻想，想象 v. ①梦见，想象 ②显示

▶▶▶ category ['kætɪgərɪ]
[释义] n. ①种类，类，类别 ②范畴
[同根] categorize ['kætɪgəraɪz] v. 把…分类，将…归类

▶▶▶ display [dɪ'spleɪ]
[释义] n. & v. 展示，显露，表现，陈列
[同义] demonstration, exhibition, illustration, show
[词组] on display 在展览中，正在展出

▶▶▶ safeguard ['seɪf,gɑ:d]
[释义] v. ①保护，维护，捍卫 ②为…提供防护措施 ③保卫，护送 n. ①保护，预防措施 ②保护装置 ③护卫者，警卫员

▶▶▶ conceal [kən'si:l]
[释义] v. 隐藏，隐蔽，隐瞒
[同义] hide, disguise, veil
[反义] disclose, reveal
[同根] concealment [kən'si:lmənt] n. 隐匿，隐蔽，躲藏，躲避

▶▶▶ intranet ['ɪntrə'net]
[释义] n. 企业内部互联网

▶▶▶ candidate ['kændɪdɪt]
[释义] n. ①申请求职者 ②候选人 ③投考者

▶▶▶ eliminate [ɪ'lɪmɪneɪt]
[释义] v. ①排除，消除，根除 ②（比赛中）淘汰
[同义] discard, dispose of, exclude, reject
[同根] elimination [ɪ,lɪmɪ'neɪʃən] n. 排

除，消除，根除
eliminable [ɪ'lɪmɪnəbl] a. 可消除的，可消去的，可排除的

▶▶▶ location [ləʊ'keɪʃən]
[释义] n. ①位置，场所，地点 ②定位，安置 ③特定区域 ④外景拍摄场地
[同根] locate [ləʊ'keɪt] v. ①使…坐落于 ②找到，查明 ③指出…的位置，确定…的位置
locational [ləʊ'keɪʃənəl] a. 位置上的，地点上的

▶▶▶ equivalent [ɪ'kwɪvələnt]
[释义] n. 相等物，等价物，意义相同的词（或符号、表达法等）a. ①相当的，相等的，相同的 ②同等重要的
[同义] counterpart
[同根] equivalence [ɪ'kwɪvələns] n. 相等，等价，等效，（词语的）等义
[词组] be equivalent to ①相等于…，等（同）于 ②与…等效

▶▶▶ assign [ə'saɪn]
[释义] v. ①分配，指派，布置 ②确定，选定 ③把…归因于 (to, for)
[同义] allocate
[同根] assignment [ə'saɪnmənt] n. ①分配，分派 ②指定，规定 ③任务，课题，作业
assignee [,æsɪ'ni:] n. 受托者，代理人，受让人
assigner [ə'saɪnə] n. ①指定人 ②分配人

▶▶▶ establish [ɪs'tæblɪʃ]
[释义] v. ①建立，创立，开设 ②确立，确定，规定 ③证实，认可
[同义] fix, found, organize, prove, settle
[反义] destroy, ruin
[同根] establishment [ɪs'tæblɪʃmənt] n. ①建立，制定 ②（包括雇员、设备、场地、货物等在内的）企业，建立的机构（如军队、军事机构、行政机关、

学校、医院、教会）
established [ɪs'tæblɪʃt] a. ①已确立的，已制定的②确定的，证实的
[词组] establish sb. as... 任命（派）某人担任…

▶▶ specifically [spɪ'sɪfɪkəlɪ]
[释义] ad. 特定地，明确地
[同义] specially, particularly
[同根] specify ['spesɪfaɪ] v. 具体指定，详细说明
specified ['spesɪfaɪd] a. 规定的，指定的
specific [spɪ'sɪfɪk] a. ①明确的，具体的②特定的，特有的
specification [ˌspesɪfɪ'keɪʃən] n. ①详述 ②［常作～s］规格，工程设计（书），详细计划（书），说明书

▶▶ in the event (that) 假如，倘若
▶▶ get hold of 抓住，得到

▶▶ contain [kən'teɪn]
[释义] v. ①包含 ②容纳 ③抑制，克制
[同根] container [kən'teɪnə] n. ①容器②集装箱，货柜
containment [kən'teɪnmənt] n. ①控制，抑制②遏制，遏制政策

▶▶ reference ['refrəns]
[释义] n. ①参考，查阅 ②介绍人，推荐人③引文，参考书④提及
[同根] refer [rɪ'fɜ:] v. ①参考，查阅②提到，谈到，指称③询问，查询
referee [ˌrefə'ri:] n. ①（提供证明、推荐等文书的）证明人，介绍人②仲裁人，调停人③裁判员 v. ①当裁判②审阅，鉴定

▶▶ give away ①泄露，出卖 ②送掉，分发③放弃，让步，陷下

▶▶ be relevant to 与…有关的

▶▶ sense [sens]
[释义] n. ①意思，意义 ②感觉，知觉，见识 ③理解力，鉴赏力
[同根] sensation [sen'seɪʃən] n. ①知觉，感觉 ②引起轰动的人或事
sensible ['sensəbl] a. ①明智的，有判断力的 ②可感觉的，能注意到的
sensitive ['sensɪtɪv] a. ①敏感的，有感觉的 ②易受影响的 ③过敏的
senseless ['senslɪs] a. 无意识的，无感觉的，不省人事的
[词组] There's no sense in doing sth. 做某事毫无道理
in a sense 在某一方面，就某种意义来说
in no sense 决不（是）
make sense ①讲得通,有意义 ②（口）言之有理，是合情合理的
make sense of 理解，弄懂…的意思

▶▶ under any circumstances 在任何情况下

▶▶ initial [ɪ'nɪʃəl]
[释义] a. 开始的，最初的
[同义] beginning, primary
[同根] initiate [ɪ'nɪʃɪeɪt] v. ①开始，发动②使入门，启蒙③正式介绍，引进
initialize [ɪ'nɪʃəlaɪz] v. 预置（初始状态），初始化
initialization [ɪˌnɪʃəlaɪ'zeɪʃən] n. 预置，定初值，初始化
initially [ɪ'nɪʃəlɪ] ad. 最初，开头
[词组] take the initial step toward... 采取走向…的第一步

▶▶ fall for ①被骗②迷恋，爱上

选项词汇注释

▶▶ **minor offence** 轻微犯罪

▶▶ **overestimate** ['əʊvə'estɪmeɪt]

[释义] *v.* 评价过高 *n.* 估计的过高，评价的过高

[反义] underestimate

[同根] estimate ['estɪmeɪt] *n.* & *v.* 估计，估价，评估

▶▶ **recommend** [rekə'mend]

[释义] *v.* ①建议，推荐 ②劝告，忠告 ③使人喜欢，使诱人

[同义] advise, advocate, instruct, suggest

[同根] recommendation [ˌrekəmen'deɪʃən] *n.* 推荐，介绍（信），劝告，建议

recommendable [ˌrekə'mendəbl] *a.* 值得推荐的，可取的

recommendatory [ˌrekə'mendətərɪ] *a.* 推荐的，劝告的

▶▶ **submit** [səb'mɪt]

[释义] *v.* ①提交，呈递 ②（使）服从，（使）屈服 ③听从，忍受

[同义] present

[反义] withdraw

[同根] submission [səb'mɪʃən] *n.* 屈服，降服，服从

[词组] submit to ①提交给… ②服从于，屈从于

submit oneself to 甘受，服从

Reading in Depth
Section A

Years ago, doctors often said that pain was a **normal** part of life. **In particular**, when older patients **complained** of pain, they were told it was a natural part of **aging** and they would have to learn to **live with** it.

Times have changed. Today, we **take** pain **seriously**. Indeed, pain is now **considered** the fifth **vital** sign, as important as **blood pressure**, **temperature**, breathing rate and pulse in **determining** a person's **well-being**. We know that *chronic*（慢性的）pain can *disrupt*（扰乱）a person's life, causing problems that **range** from missed work to **depression**.

That's why a growing number of hospitals now depend upon physicians who **specialize** in pain medicine. Not only do we **evaluate** the cause of the pain, which can help us **treat** the pain better, but we also help provide **comprehensive therapy** for depression and other **psychological** and social **issues** related to chronic pain. Such comprehensive therapy often involves the work of social workers, *psychiatrists*（心理医生）and psychologists, as well as specialists in pain medicine.

This modern respect for pain **management** has led to **a wealth of innovative** treatments which are more **effective** and with fewer **side effects** than ever before. Decades ago, there were only a limited number of drugs **available**, and many of them caused **significant** side effects in older people, including **dizziness** and **fatigue**. This created a **double-edged sword**: the **medications** helped **relieve** the pain but caused other problems that could be worse than the pain itself.

文章词汇注释

▶▶ **normal** [ˈnɔ:məl]

[释义] a. ①正常的，通常的 ②正规的，规范的 ③师范的

[同义] usual, regular, ordinary

[反义] abnormal, unusual, extraordinary

[同根] norm [nɔ:m] n. ①标准，规范，准则 ②模范，典型
normalize [ˈnɔ:məlaɪz] v. (使) 正常化，(使) 标准化
normalization [ˌnɔ:məlaɪˈzeɪʃən] n. 正常化，标准化

▶▶ **in particular** 特别，尤其

▶▶ **complain** [kəmˈpleɪn]

[释义] v. (~ of/about) ①抱怨，发牢骚，诉苦 ②控告，抗议

[同根] complaint [kəmˈpleɪnt] n. ①抱怨，抗议，怨言 ②抱怨 (或抗议) 的缘由
complainant [kəmˈpleɪnənt] n. 诉苦者，抱怨者，抗议者，控告者

▶▶ **ageing** [ˈeɪdʒɪŋ]

[释义] n. ①变老，变 (陈) 旧 ②变陈，成熟

▶▶ **live with** ①容忍，忍受 (不愉快的事) ②和…住在一起，与…同居

▶▶ **take...seriously** 重视，认真对待，当真

▶▶ **consider** [kənˈsɪdə]

[释义] v. ①认为，把…看作 ②考虑，细想 ③体贴，考虑到，顾及

[同义] think, regard

[同根] consideration [kənˌsɪdəˈreɪʃən] n. ①体谅，考虑 ②需要考虑的事项
considerable [kənˈsɪdərəbl] a. ①值得考虑的 ②相当大的，相当可观的
considerate [kənˈsɪdərɪt] a. ①体贴的 ②考虑周到的
considering [kənˈsɪdərɪŋ] prep. 鉴于，考虑到

▶▶ **vital** [ˈvaɪtəl]

[释义] a. ①必不可少的，极其重要的 ② (有) 生命的 ②致命的，生死攸关的

[同根] vitality [vaɪˈtælɪtɪ] n. 生命力，活力

▶▶ **blood pressure** 血压

▶▶ **temperature** [ˈtemprɪtʃə(r)]

[释义] n. ①体温 ②温度 ②热度

▶▶ **determine** [dɪˈtɜ:mɪn]

[释义] v. ①确定，决定 ②下决心，决意 ③测定，查明

[同根] determined [dɪˈtɜ:mɪnd] a. ①已下决心的，决意的 ②坚决的，坚定的
determination [dɪˌtɜ:mɪˈneɪʃən]

n. ①决心，坚定 ②决定，决断

▶▶ **well-being** ['welbɪɪŋ]

[释义] *n.* 健康快乐，安宁，幸福

▶▶ **range** [reɪndʒ]

[释义] *v.* ①变化，变动 ②把…分类 ③延伸 ④排列 *n.* ①（变化等的）幅度，（影响等的）范围 ②排，行 ③山脉

[词组] a range of 一系列，一排
at long (short) range 在远（近）距离
out of one's range ①能力达不到的 ②知识以外的
within range of ①在…射程以内 ②在…范围以内

▶▶ **depression** [dɪ'preʃən]

[释义] *n.* ①抑郁，沮丧 ②不景气，萧条（期）

[反义] encouragement, inspiration

[同根] press [pres] *v.* ①压，按，推，挤压 ②（常与 on, upon 连用）迫使，进逼（与 for 连用）③敦促，力劝
depress [dɪ'pres] *v.* ①使沮丧，使消沉 ②使不景气，使萧条 ③削弱，抑制 ④减少，降低
depressant [dɪ'presənt] *n.* 抑制药，镇静剂
depressive [dɪ'presɪv] *a.* 令人沮丧的，令人抑郁的，压抑的 *n.* 抑郁症患者
depressed [dɪ'prest] *a.* 抑郁的，沮丧的，消沉的
depressing [dɪ'presɪŋ] *a.* 令人抑郁的，令人沮丧的

▶▶ **specialize** ['speʃə,laɪz]

[释义] *v.* ①专门研究 ②深入 ③使专用于

[同根] special ['speʃ(ə)l] *a.* 特殊的，特别的
specific [spɪ'sɪfɪk] *a.* ①详细而精确的，明确的 ②特殊的，特效的
specialization [,speʃəlaɪ'zeɪʃən]

n. 特殊化，专门化，专业化
specialist ['speʃəlɪst] *n.* ①专家 ②专科医生

[词组] specialize in 擅长于，专攻

▶▶ **evaluate** [ɪ'væljueɪt]

[释义] *v.* ①对…鉴定，对…评价 ②估…的值，定…的价

[同义] estimate

[同根] evaluation [ɪ,vælju'eɪʃən] *n.* 估算，评价
evaluative [ɪ'væljueɪtɪv] *a.* 可估价的，可评价的
evaluable [ɪ'væljuəbl] *a.* 可估值的，可评价的
evaluator [ɪ'væljueɪtə(r)] *n.* 估价者，评价者

▶▶ **treat** [triːt]

[释义] *v.* ①治疗 ②对待，视为 ③宴请，招待，款待 *n.* 宴请，款待

[同根] treatment ['triːtmənt] *n.* ①待遇，对待 ②处理 ③治疗
treated ['triːtɪd] *a.* 已处理过的，加工过的

[词组] treat... with... 用…治疗…
treat sb. to sth. 请某人吃 / 享受…

▶▶ **comprehensive** [,kɒmprɪ'hensɪv]

[释义] *a.* ①综合的，广泛的 ②理解的，有理解力的

[同根] comprehend [,kɒmprɪ'hend] *v.* ①理解，懂，领会 ②包含，包括
comprehension [,kɒmprɪ'henʃən] *n.* ①理解力 ②包含，含义，广泛性

▶▶ **therapy** ['θerəpɪ]

[释义] *n.* ①疗法，治疗 ②治疗力，治疗效果 ③理疗

▶▶ **psychological** [,saɪkə'lɒdʒɪkəl]

[释义] *a.* 心理的，心理学的

[同根] psychology [saɪ'kɒlədʒɪ] *n.* 心理学，心理状态

psychologist [psaɪˈkɒlədʒɪst] n. 心理学者

▶▶▶ issue [ˈɪsjuː]

[释义] n. ①问题，争议 ②流出，冒出 ③发行，出版 ④发行物，定期出版物的一期 v. ①发表，发布 ②流出，放出 ③发行（钞票等），出版（书等）

[词组] at/in issue 待解决的，争议中的
raise a issue 引起争论
take issue 对…持异议，不同意

▶▶▶ management [ˈmænɪdʒmənt]

[释义] n. ①处理，管理，经营 ②管理人员／部门

[同根] manage [ˈmænɪdʒ] v. ①处理，管理，经营 ②运用，使用 ③控制，操纵 ④设法做到，勉力完成
manager [ˈmænɪdʒə] n. 经理，管理人员
manageable [ˈmænɪdʒəbl] a. ①可管理的，易处理的 ②易驾驭的，驯服的 ③可使用的，易操纵的

▶▶▶ a wealth of 很多的

▶▶▶ innovative [ˈɪnəʊveɪtɪv]

[释义] a. 革新的，创新的，富有革新精神的

[同根] innovate [ˈɪnəʊveɪt] v. ①革新，创新，改革 ②创立，创始，引入
innovation [ˌɪnəʊˈveɪʃn] n. ①革新，创新，改革 ②新方法，新办法，新奇事物

▶▶▶ effective [ɪˈfektɪv]

[释义] a. ①有效的，能产生（预期）结果的 ②生效的，起作用的 ③给人深刻印象的，显著的 ④实际的，事实上的

[反义] ineffective

[同根] effect [ɪˈfekt] n. ①结果 ②效力，作用，影响 ③感受，印象 ④实行，生效，起作用

efficiency [ɪˈfɪʃənsɪ] n. 效率，功效
efficient [ɪˈfɪʃənt] a. ①效率高的，能干的，能胜任的 ②（直接）生效的
efficiently [ɪˈfɪʃəntlɪ] ad. ①效率高地 ②有能力地

[词组] be effective on 对…起作用
become effective 生效

▶▶▶ side effects ①（药物的）副作用 ②（事态发展的）意外情况，意外后果

▶▶▶ available [əˈveɪləbl]

[释义] a. ①可得到的，现成可使用的，在手边的，可利用的 ②可取得联系的

[同根] avail [əˈveɪl] v. 有用于，有助于 n.（一般用于否定句或疑问句中）效用，利益，帮助
availability [əˌveɪləˈbɪlɪtɪ] n. 利用（或获得）的可能性，有效性

[词组] make sth. available to/ for 使…可以享受某物，使…买得起某物

▶▶▶ significant [sɪɡˈnɪfɪkənt]

[释义] a. ①重大的，重要的 ②表示…的 (of) ③有意义的，意味深长的 ④相当数量的，值得注意的

[同义] marked, meaningful, vital, important

[反义] trivial, unimportant, insignificant

[同根] significance [sɪɡˈnɪfɪkəns] n. ①重要性，显著性 ②意义，含义 ③意思，意味
signify [ˈsɪɡnɪfaɪ] v. 表示…的意思，意味，预示

▶▶▶ dizziness [ˈdɪzɪnɪs]

[释义] n. 头昏眼花，糊涂

[同根] dizzy [ˈdɪzɪ] a. ①（指人）晕眩的，昏乱的 ②令人晕眩的 v. 使晕眩
dizzily [ˈdɪzɪlɪ] ad. 头昏眼花地，使人眼花地

▶▶ **fatigue** [fə'ti:g]

[**释义**] *n.* 疲乏，疲劳 *v.* ①使疲劳 ②使
心智衰弱

[**同义**] tiredness, exhaustion, weariness

▶▶ **double-edged sword** 双刃剑

▶▶ **medication** [ˌmedɪ'keɪʃən]

[**释义**] *n.* ①药物治疗，药物处理 ②药物

▶▶ **relieve** [rɪ'li:v]

[**释义**] *v.* ①缓解，减轻，解除 ②救济，
救援

[**同义**] ease, help, assist

[**反义**] intensify

[**同根**] relief [rɪ'li:f] *n.* ①缓解，减轻，
解除 ②宽心，宽慰 ③救济，解救

Section B
Passage One

I've been writing for most of my life. The book *Writing Without Teachers* introduced me to one **distinction** and one practice that has helped my writing **processes tremendously**. The distinction is between the **creative** mind and the **critical** mind. While you need to employ both to get to a finished result, they cannot work **in parallel** no matter how much we might like to think so.

Trying to criticize writing **on the fly** is possibly the single greatest **barrier** to writing that most of us **encounter**. If you are listening to that 5th grade English teacher correct your grammar while you are trying to **capture** a *fleeting*（稍纵即逝的）thought, the thought will die. If you capture the fleeting thought and simply share it with the world in **raw** form, no one is **likely to** understand. You must learn to create first and then criticize if you want to make writing the tool for thinking that it is.

The practice that can help you past your learned bad habits of trying to **edit** as you write is what Elbow calls "free writing." In free writing, the **objective** is to **get** words **down** on paper non-stop, usually for 15-20 minutes. No stopping, no going back, no criticizing. The goal is to get the words flowing. As the words begin to flow, the ideas will come from the shadows and let themselves be captured on your **notepad** or your screen.

Now you have **raw materials** that you can begin to work with using the critical mind that you've persuaded to sit on the side and watch quietly. Most likely, you will believe that this will take more time than you actually have and you will end up staring **blankly** at the pages as the **deadline draws near**.

Instead of staring at a blank screen start filling it with words no matter how bad. Halfway through you **available time**, stop and **rework** your raw writing into something closer to **finished product**. Move **back and forth** until you **run out of** time and the final result will most likely be far better than your **current** practices.

文章词汇注释

▶▶▶ **distinction** [dɪsˈtɪŋkʃən]

[释义] n. ①对比，不同，差别 ②区分，辨别 ③特征，特点，④荣誉，声望

[同根] distinct [dɪsˈtɪŋkt] a. ①有区别的，不同的 ②明显的，清楚的 ③明确的，确切的 ④显著的，难得的，极度的

distinctive [dɪsˈtɪŋktɪv] a. 特殊的，特别的，有特色的

distinguish [dɪsˈtɪŋgwɪʃ] v. ①区分，辨别 ②辨别出，认出，发现 ③（~ one-self）使杰出，使著名

▶▶▶ **process** [ˈprəusеs]

[释义] n. ①过程，进程 ②程序，步骤 ③（生产中的）工序，方法 v. ①对…进行加工 ②使接受处理（或检查等）

[同义] course, procedure, step, way, stage

[同根] proceed [prəˈsiːd] v. ①继续前进 ②进行，开展 ③行进，前进

procedure [prəˈsiːdʒə] n. ①程序，步骤 ②常规，传统做法

procession [prəˈseʃən, prəu-] n. ①（人等的）行列，队伍，列队行进 ②连续，一（长）排

processive [prəuˈsesɪv] a. 前进的，进行的，向前的

[词组] in process 在进行中

in process of time 随着时间的推移，渐渐

in (the) process of 在…进程中

▶▶▶ **tremendously** [trɪˈmendəslɪ]

[释义] ad. 极大地，非常地，惊人地

[同义] greatly

[同根] tremendous [trɪˈmendəs] a. ①巨大的 ②惊人的，精彩的，了不起的

▶▶▶ **creative** [kriːˈeɪtɪv]

[释义] a. ①有创造力的，创造性的 ②建设性的

[同义] innovative

[反义] conservative

[同根] create [krɪˈeɪt] v. ①生产，制造，创造 ②创作 ③创建，创设

creator [kriːˈeɪtə(r)] n. ①创造者，创作者 ② (the Creator) 造物主，上帝

creation [kriːˈeɪʃn] n. ①创造，创作 ②创建，创设 ③创造物

creativity [kriːeɪˈtɪvətɪ] n. 创造力，创造

▶▶▶ **critical** [ˈkrɪtɪkəl]

[释义] a. ①批评的，评判的 ②吹毛求疵的 ③决定性的，关键性的

[同根] critic [ˈkrɪtɪk] n. ①批评家，评论家 ②吹毛求疵者

critique [krɪˈtiːk] n. ①（关于文艺作品、哲学思想的）评论文章 ②评论

criticize [ˈkrɪtɪsaɪz] v. ①批评，评判，责备，非难 ②评论，评价

criticism [ˈkrɪtɪsɪzəm] n. ①批评，评判，责备，非难 ②评论文章

▶▶▶ **in parallel** 并行地，平行地

▶▶▶ **on the fly** ①在飞行中，未着地时 ②<口>匆忙地，在忙碌中，忙碌的

▶▶ **barrier** ['bærɪə(r)]

[释义] *n.* ①障碍，隔阂，壁垒 ②防碍的因素，障碍物

[同义] barricade, fortification, obstruction

[同根] bar [bɑ:(r)] *n.* ①条，棒（常用作栅栏，扣栓物）②酒吧间 ③障碍物 *v.* 禁止，阻挡，妨碍

barricade [,bærɪ'keɪd] *v.* 设路障 *n.* 路障

▶▶ **encounter** [ɪn'kauntə]

[释义] *v.* ①遭遇，遇到 ②意外遇见 ③迎（战、敌）*n.* ①遭遇，冲突 ②遭遇战，会战 ③偶然（短暂）的相见

[同义] meet, come across, confront

[词组] encounter with 遭遇…，遇到…

▶▶ **capture** ['kæptʃə]

[释义] *v.* 捕获，俘获，夺取 *n.* 捕获，战利品

▶▶ **raw** [rɔ:]

[释义] *a.* ①自然状态的，未经加工的 ②生的，未经蒸煮的 ③原始的，第一手的

[词组] in the raw 处在自然状态，不完善的，未加工的

▶▶ **be likely to** 可能的，有倾向的，看来要发生的

▶▶ **edit** ['edɪt]

[释义] *v.* ①编辑，编纂 ②剪辑（影片，录音）

[同根] edition [ɪ'dɪʃən] *n.* ①版本，版次 ②（书、报刊等的）一份，一期 ③复制，翻版

editor ['edɪtə] *n.* ①编者，编辑，校订者 ②社论撰写人

editorial [edɪ'tɔ:rɪəl] *a.* ①编辑的，编辑上的 ②社论性的 *n.* 社论

▶▶ **objective** [əb'dʒektɪv]

[释义] *n.* ①目标，目的 ②[语法] 宾格 *a.* ①客观的，如实的 ②目的的，目标的 ③[语法] 宾格的

[同根] object ['ɒbdʒɪkt] *n.* ①物体 ②目标，对象 ③宾语

objection [əb'dʒekʃ(ə)n] *n.* 反对（某人或某事）

▶▶ **get down** ①写下，记下 ②降下 ③吞下 ④使沮丧

▶▶ **notepad** ['nəutpæd]

[释义] *n.* 笔记本，记事本，记事手册

▶▶ **raw material** 原料

▶▶ **blankly** ['blæŋklɪ]

[释义] *ad.* ①没有表情地 ②空白地

[同根] blank [blæŋk] *a.* ①空白的 ②没有表情的 *n.* 空白，表格

▶▶ **deadline** ['dedlaɪn]

[释义] *n.* 最终期限

[词组] meet the deadline 在最后期限内做完某事

▶▶ **draw near** 接近，临近

▶▶ **available time** 可利用时间，有效时间

▶▶ **rework** ['ri:'wɜ:k]

[释义] *v.* 重做，改写，重写

▶▶ **finished product** 成品，产品

▶▶ **back and forth** 来回，往复

▶▶ **run out of** 用完

▶▶ **current** ['kʌrənt]

[释义] *a.* ①现在的，当前的 ②流行的，流传的 *n.* ①（空气、水等的）流，潮流 ②电流 ③趋势，倾向

[同义] present, happening

[同根] currency ['kʌrənsɪ] *n.* ①流传，流通 ②传播通货，货币

currently ['kʌrəntlɪ] *ad.* ①普遍地，通常地 ②现在，当前

[词组] against the current 逆流而行，不同流俗

go current 流行，通用，流传

go with the current 随波逐流

选项词汇注释

▶▶ in conflict with（与…）不一致

▶▶ constant ['kɒnstənt]
[释义] a. ①不变的，固定的 ②时常发生的，连续不断的 ③忠实的，忠心的 n. ①不变的事物 ②常数，恒量
[反义] inconstant
[同根] constancy ['kɒnstənsɪ] n. ①持久不变 ②忠实 ③永久性的事务
constantly ['kɒnstəntlɪ] ad. ①不断地 ②坚持不懈地

▶▶ ignore [ɪg'nɔ:]
[释义] v. ①忽视，不理，不顾 ②（因证据不足）驳回（诉讼）
[同根] ignorance ['ɪgnərəns] n. ①无知，愚昧 ②不知
ignorant ['ɪgnərənt] a. ①无知的，愚昧的 ②不知道的 ③由于无知产生的

▶▶ soundness ['saʊndnɪs]
[释义] n. ①正确，合理 ②完好无损

▶▶ chief [tʃi:f]
[释义] a. ①最重要的，主要的 ②等级最高的，为首的 n. ①首领，领袖，长官 ②酋长，族长
[同义] principal, central
[反义] subordinate, subservient
[同根] chiefly ['tʃi:flɪ] ad. ①首要，首要 ②主要地，大部分，多半

▶▶ logically ['lɒdʒɪkəlɪ]
[释义] ad. 逻辑上地，合乎逻辑地
[同根] logic ['lɒdʒɪk] n. 逻辑，逻辑学，逻辑性
logical ['lɒdʒɪkəl] a. ①逻辑的 ②合乎逻辑的，合理的

▶▶ appropriate [ə'prəʊprɪɪt]
[释义] a. 适合的，恰当的，相称的
[ə'prəʊprɪeɪt] v. ①挪用，占用 ②拨出（款项）
[同义] fitting, proper, suitable
[反义] inappropriate, unfit, unsuitable
[同根] appropriateness [ə'prəʊprɪɪtnɪs] n. 恰当，适当
appropriable [ə'prəʊprɪəbl] a. 可供专用的，可供私用的
appropriation [ə,prəʊprɪ'eɪʃən] n. ①拨付，拨款 ②占用，挪用
[词组] be appropriate to/for 适于…，合乎…

▶▶ overstress ['əʊvə'stres]
[释义] v. 过分强调，过分着重 n. ①过分的强调 ②压力过重
[同义] overstate, exaggerate
[反义] understate

▶▶ bring about 引起，致使，造成，达成

▶▶ refine [rɪ'faɪn]
[释义] v. ①[喻] 提炼，使变得完善，提炼 ②精炼，精制
[同根] refinement [rɪ'faɪnmənt] n. ①（感情、举止、语言的）优雅，有教养 ②提炼，精炼
refinery [rɪ'faɪnərɪ] n. 提炼厂，精炼厂

▶▶ come up with ①（针对问题、挑战等）提出，想出，提供 ②赶上

Passage Two

I don't ever want to talk about being a woman scientist again. There was a time in my life when people asked constantly for stories about what it's like to work in a field dominated by men. I was never very good at telling those stories because truthfully I never found them interesting. What I do find interesting is the origin of the universe, the shape of space-time and the nature of black holes.

At 19, when I began studying astrophysics, it did not bother me in the least to be the only woman in the classroom. But while earning my Ph.D. at MIT and then as a post-doctor doing space research, the issue started to bother me. My every achievement—jobs, research papers, awards—was viewed through the lens of gender（性别）politics. So were my failures. Sometimes, when I was pushed into an argument on left brain versus（相对于）right brain, or nature versus nurture（培育）, I would instantly fight fiercely on my behalf and all womankind.

Then one day a few years ago, out of my mouth came a sentence that would eventually become my reply to any and all provocations: I don't talk about that anymore. It took me 10 years to get back the confidence I had at 19 and to realize that I didn't want to deal with gender issues. Why should curing sexism be yet another terrible burden on every female scientist? After all, I don't study sociology or political theory.

Today I research and teach at Barnard, a women's college in New York City. Recently, someone asked me how many of the 45 students in my class were women. You cannot imagine my satisfaction at being able to answer, 45. I know some of my students worry how they will manage their scientific research and a desire for children. And I don't dismiss those concerns. Still, I don't tell them "war" stories. Instead, I have given them this: the visual of their physics professor heavily pregnant doing physics experiments. And in turn they have given me the image of 45 women driven by a love of science. And that's a sight worth talking about.

文章词汇注释

▶▶▶ **dominate** ['dɒmɪneɪt]
[释义] v. ①支配，控制 ②俯瞰，俯视 ③在…中占首要位置
[同义] control, rule
[同根] dominant ['dɒmɪnənt] a. ① 占优势的，统治的 ②（在数量等方面）占首位的，主要的 n. 占优势者
dominance ['dɒmɪnəns] n. 优势，统治或支配的地位，最高权力
domination [dɒmɪ'neɪʃən] n. 支配，统治，控制

▶▶▶ **origin** ['ɒrɪdʒɪn]
[释义] n. ①起源，由来 ② [常作复数] 出身，血统
[同义] source
[同根] originate [ə'rɪdʒɪneɪt] v. ① 发源，产生，引起 ②开创，发明
original [ə'rɪdʒənəl] a. ①起初的，原来的 ②独创的，新颖的，有独见解的 n. [the ~] 原作，原文，原件
originally [ə'rɪdʒənəlɪ] ad. 最初，原先

▶▶▶ **space-time** ['speɪs'taɪm]
[释义] n. 时空，时空关系

▶▶▶ **black hole** 黑洞

▶▶▶ **astrophysics** [æstrəʊ'fɪzɪks]
[释义] n. 天体物理学

▶▶▶ **not in the least** 绝不，一点也不

▶▶▶ **earn** [ɜːn]
[释义] v. ①获得，使得到 ②赚得，挣得 ③招致，惹起
[同根] earnings ['ɜːnɪŋz] n. ① 工资，收入 ②（由投资等）赚得的钱，收益，利润

▶▶▶ **achievement** [ə'tʃiːvmənt]

[释义] n. ①成就，成绩 ②达到，实现
[同义] accomplishment
[同根] achieve [ə'tʃiːv] v. ①（经努力）达到，得到 ②完成，实现

▶▶▶ **award** [ə'wɔːd]
[释义] n. ①奖，奖状，奖品 ②裁决，判决书 v. ①授予，给予 ②判给，判定
[同义] prize

▶▶▶ **view** [vjuː]
[释义] v. ①看待，考虑，估量 ②察看 ③看，观看 n. ①看法，见解 ②视力，视野 ③（从特定处看到的）景色 ④风景画
[同根] viewer ['vjuːə] n. ①电视观众 ②阅读器

▶▶▶ **lens** [lenz]
[释义] n. ①镜片，透镜 ②（照相机等的）镜头 ③（眼球的）晶状体

▶▶▶ **argument** ['ɑːgjumənt]
[释义] n. ①争论，辩论 ②论据，论点
[同根] argue ['ɑːgjuː] v. 争论，辩论
argumentative [ɑːgju'mentətɪv] a. 好辩的，争论的
argumentation [ɑːgjumen'teɪʃən] n. 争论，论证

▶▶▶ **instantly** ['ɪnstəntlɪ]
[释义] ad. 立即，马上 conj. 一…（就）
[同根] instant ['ɪnstənt] a. ①事先未准备（或考虑）的，即兴的，即时的 ②立即的，马上的 ③（食品）速溶的，方便的 n. ①瞬息 ②（某一）时刻 ③速溶饮料

▶▶▶ **fiercely** ['fɪəslɪ]
[释义] ad. ①猛烈地，凶猛地，残酷地，

强烈地 ②（口）极其地，非常，很

[同根] fierce [fɪəs] a. ①凶猛的，残酷的，好斗的 ②猛烈的，狂暴的 ③狂热的，强烈的

▶▶ on one's behalf ①为了某人的利益，为了某人 ②代表某人

▶▶ womankind ['wʊmənkaɪnd]

[释义] n. (总称) 妇女，女人们

▶▶ eventually [ɪ'ventjʊəlɪ]

[释义] ad. 最后，终于

[同义] finally, ultimately, in the end

[同根] eventual [ɪ'ventjʊəl] a. 最后的，结果的

▶▶ provocation [prɒvə'keɪʃən]

[释义] n. ①惹人恼火的事，激怒的原因 ②激怒，刺激

[同义] annoyance, irritation

[同根] provoke [prə'vəʊk] v. ①对…挑衅，激怒 ②激起，引起
provocative [prə'vɒkətɪv] a. ①挑衅的，煽动的 ②引起讨论的
provoking [prə'vəʊkɪŋ] a. 恼人的，挑动的

▶▶ confidence ['kɒnfɪdəns]

[释义] n. ①自信，狂妄 ②信任，信心 ③知心话，秘密

[同义] self-assurance, self-belief, self-reliance

[同根] confident ['kɒnfɪdənt] a. ①确信的，自信的 ②大胆的，过分自信的
confidential [kɒnfɪ'denʃəl] a. ①秘密的，机密的 ②表示信任的 ③易于信任他人的

▶▶ cure [kjʊə]

[释义] v. ①消除，改正 ②治愈，治疗 n. ①治愈，痊愈 ②对策

▶▶ sexism ['seksɪzəm]

[释义] n. ①（尤指对女性的）性别歧视，性别偏见 ②性别主义

[同根] sex [seks] n. 性别，男性或女性
sexual ['seksjʊəl] a. ①性的，性别的 ②关于两性的，两性之间的

▶▶ burden ['bɜːdn]

[释义] n. 负担，负荷 v. ①使负担，加负荷于 ②加重压于

[同义] load

[同根] burdensome ['bɜːdnsəm] a. 繁重的，烦人的，难以承担的

[词组] be burdened with... 被…所累
pass one's burden on sb. 把责任丢给某人

▶▶ desire for 渴望…

▶▶ dismiss [dɪs'mɪs]

[释义] v. ①拒绝考虑，不再考虑 ②解散，使（或让）离开 ③开除，解职 ④驳回，不受理

[同根] dismissal [dɪs'mɪsəl] n. ①不再考虑，不与理会 ②解散，遣散 ③开除，解职 ④驳回诉讼，撤回诉讼

▶▶ visual ['vɪzjʊəl]

[释义] n. （电影、电视等的）画面，图像 a. ①视觉的，视力的 ②看得见的，真实的 ③光学的

[同根] visually ['vɪzjʊəlɪ] ad. 在视觉上地，视力地
visualize ['vɪzjʊəlaɪz, 'vɪʒ-] v. ①使形象化，想像，设想 ②使成为看得见
visualization [ˌvɪzjʊəlaɪ'zeɪʃən, -ʒʊə-; -lɪ'z-] n. 直观化，可见性

▶▶ pregnant ['pregnənt]

[释义] a. 怀孕的

[同根] pregnancy ['pregnənsɪ] n. 怀孕

▶▶ in turn ①反过来，转而 ②依次，轮流地

选项词汇注释

▶▶ **be fed up with** ①对…极其厌倦 ②吃得过饱

▶▶ **gender discrimination** 性别歧视

▶▶ **attribute** [ə'trɪbjuːt]
[释义] v. 把…归因于 (to)…，认为是…的属性 n. ①属性，特质 ②标志，象征
[同义] ascribe
[同根] attribution [ˌætrɪ'bjuːʃən] n. 归因，归属
attributable [ə'trɪbjutəbl] a. 可归（因）于…的
attributive [ə'trɪbjutɪv] a. ①归属的，属性的 ②定语的
[词组] attribute sth. to... 把…归功于…，认为某事物是…的属性

▶▶ **bear** [beə]
[释义] v. (bore, borne, bearing) ①承担，负担 ②忍受，容忍 ③具有，显示 ④经得起（考验等）⑤写有，刻有 ⑥生（孩子），结（果实）n. 熊
[同根] bearing ['beərɪŋ] n. ①举止，风度 ②关系，关联 ③意义，意思 ④方面
bearable ['beərəbl] a. 可忍受的，支持得住的
[词组] bear fruit 结果实，奏效，有成效
bear out 证实
bear in mind 铭记，记在心里
be borne in on/upon sb. 被某人认识到
have a bearing on/upon 关系到…，影响到…

▶▶ **accusation** [ækju(ː)'zeɪʃən]
[释义] n. ①指责，控告，指控 ②（被控告的）罪名
[同根] accuse [ə'kjuːz] v. ①指控，控告，指责 ②归咎于

▶▶ **stereotyped** ['sterɪəutaɪpt]
[释义] a. 已成陈规的，老一套的
[同根] stereotype ['stɪərɪəutaɪp] n. 成见，陈规，刻板模式 v. 使一成不变，使变得刻板

▶▶ **misconception** ['mɪskən'sepʃən]
[释义] n. 误解，错误想法，错误印象
[同义] misunderstanding, mistaken belief
[同根] concept ['kɒnsept] n. 概念，观念，思想
conception [kən'sepʃən] n. 思想，观念，概念
conceptual [kən'septʃuəl, -tjuəl] a. 概念的

▶▶ **performance** [pə'fɔːməns]
[释义] n. ①行为，行动 ②履行，执行，实现 ③演出，演奏 ④功绩，成绩
[同根] performer [pə'fɔːmə(r)] n. 执行者，表演者，演奏者
perform [pə'fɔːm] v. ①履行，执行，进行 ②表演 ③表现，操作
[词组] perform one's duties 尽责任
perform a play 演一出戏
perform in the role of 扮演…角色

▶▶ **pursue** [pə'sjuː]
[释义] v. ①从事，忙于 ②追随，跟随 ③追求，寻求 ④追赶，追捕
[同义] follow, carry on
[同根] pursuer [pə'sjuːə(r)] n. ①追随者，追求者 ②从事者，研究者
pursuit [pə'sjuːt] n. ①追赶，追逐 ②追求，寻求 ③从事，爱好
[词组] pursue after 追赶，追随

▶▶ **academic** [ˌækə'demɪk]
[释义] a. ①学术的 ②教学的，教务的 ③学院的，大学的 ④纯理论的，学

究式的，不切实际的

[同根] academy [ə'kædəmɪ] *n.* ①（高
等）专科院校，研究院，学院 ②学会，
学术团体，学院

academician [ə,kædə'mɪʃən]
n. 学会会员，院士，学者

[词组] the academic world 学术界

▶▶▶ **balance** ['bæləns]

[释义] *n.* ①平衡，均衡 ②天平，秤
③（布局、比例等的）协调，和谐，
对称 ④镇静，沉着 *v.* ①使平衡，使
均衡 ②使协调 ③权衡，斟酌

[同根] balanced ['bælənst] *a.* ①平衡
的，均衡的 ②协调的，和谐的

[词组] on balance 总的说来
keep one's balance ①保持身体平衡
②保持镇静
lose/off one's balance ①失去平衡，
有跌落、倾覆的危险 ②惊慌失措

Skimming and Scanning
Universities Branch Out

As never before in their long story, universities have become instruments of national competition as well as instruments of peace. They are the place of the scientific discoveries that move economies forward, and the primary means of educating the talent required to obtain and maintain competitive advantages. But at the same time, the opening of national borders to the flow of goods, services, information and especially people has made universities a powerful force for global integration, mutual understanding and geopolitical stability.

In response to the same forces that have driven the world economy, universities have become more self-consciously global: seeking students from around the world who represent the entire range of cultures and values, sending their own students abroad to prepare them for global careers, offering courses of study that address the challenges of an interconnected world and collaborative research programs to advance science for the benefit of all humanity.

Of the forces shaping higher education none is more sweeping than the movement across borders. Over the past three decades the number of students leaving home each year to study abroad has grown at an annual rate of 3.9 percent, from 800,000 in 1975 to 2.5 million in 2004. Most travel from one developed nation to another, but the flow from developing to developed countries is growing rapidly. The reverse flow, from developed to developing countries, is on the rise, too. Today foreign students earn 30 percent of the doctoral degrees awarded in the United States and 38 percent of those in the United Kingdom. And the number crossing borders for undergraduate study is growing as well, to 8 percent of the undergraduates at America's best institutions and 10 percent of all undergraduates in the U.K. In the United

States, 20 percent of the newly hired professors in science and engineering are foreign-born, and in China many newly hired faculty membersat the top research universities received their graduate education abroad.

Universities are also encouraging students to spend some of their undergraduate years in another country. In Europe, more than 140,000 students participate in the Erasmus program each year, taking courses for credit in one of 2, 200 participating institutions across the continent. And in the United States, institutions are helping place students in summer internships (实习) abroad to prepare them for global careers. Yale and Harvard have led the way, offering every undergraduate at least one international study or internship opportunity and providing the financial resources to make it possible.

Globalization is also reshaping the way research is done. One new trend involves sourcing portions of a research program to another country. Yale professor and Howard Hughes Medical Institute investigator Tian Xu directs a research center focused on the genetics of human disease at Shanghai's Fudan University, in collaboration with faculty colleagues from both schools. The Shanghai center has 95 employees and graduate students working in a 4,300-square-meter laboratory facility. Yale faculty, postdoctors and graduate students visit regularly and attend videoconference seminars with scientists from both campuses. The arrangement benefits both countries; Xu's Yale lab is more productive, thanks to the lower costs of conducting research in china, and Chinese graduate sdudents, postdoctors and faculty get on-the-job training from a world-class scientist and his U.S. team.

As a result of its strength in science, the United States has consistently led the world in the commercialization of major new technologies, from the mainframe computer and integrated circuit of the 1960s to the internet infrastructure (基础设施) and applications software of the 1990s. The link between university-based science and industrial application is often indirect but sometimes highly visible: Silicon Valley was intentionally created by Stanford University, and Route 128 outside Boston has long housed companies spun off from MIT and Harvard. Around the world, governments have encouraged copying of his model, perhaps most successfully in Cambridge, England, where Microsoft and scores of other leading software and biotechnology companies have set up shop around the university.

For all its success, the United States remains deeply **hesitant** about **sustaining** the research university model. Most politicians recognize the link between investment in science and national economic strength, but support for research funding has been **unsteady**. The **budget** of the National Institutes of Health doubled between 1998 and 2003, but has risen more slowly than **inflations** since then. Support for the physical sciences and engineering barely **kept pace with** inflation during that same period. The attempt to **make up** lost ground is welcome, but the nation would be better served by steady, **predictable** increases in science funding **at the rate of long-term** GDP growth, which is **on the order of** inflation plus 3 percent per year.

American politicians have great difficulty recognizing that **admitting** more foreign students can greatly **promote** the **national interest** by increasing international understanding. **Adjusted** for inflation, public funding for international exchanges and foreign-language study is well below the levels of 40 years ago. **In the wake of** September 11, changes in the **visa process** caused a **dramatic** decline in the number of foreign students seeking admission to U.S. Universities, and a **corresponding surge** in **enrollments** in Australia, Singapore and the U.K. Objections from Americans university and business leaders led to improvements in the process and a **reversal** of the decline, but the United States is still seen by many as unwelcoming to international students.

Most Americans recognize that universities **contribute to** the nation's well-being through their scientific research, but many fear that foreign students threaten American competitiveness by taking their knowledge and skills back home. They fail to grasp that welcoming foreign students to the United States has two important positive effects: first, the very best of them stay in the States and—like **immigrants** throughout history—strengthen the nation; and second, foreign students who study in the United States become **ambassadors** for many of its most *cherished*（珍视）values when they return home. Or at least they understand them better. In America as elsewhere, few instruments of foreign policy are as **effective** in promoting peace and stability as welcoming international university students.

文章词汇注释

▶▶ **branch out** ①扩大活动范围，扩充 ②长出枝条

▶▶ **instrument** ['ɪnstrʊmənt]
[释义] *n.* ①工具，器具 ②手段，重要因素 ③仪器，仪表
[同义] apparatus, appliance, device
[同根] instrumental [ˌɪnstru'mentl] *a.* ①器具的，机械的 ②有帮助的，起作用的

▶▶ **competition** [kɒmpɪ'tɪʃən]
[释义] *n.* ①竞争 ②比赛，竞赛，赛会
[同根] compete [kəm'piːt] *v.* ①竞争，对抗 ②比赛 ③（事物）媲美，比得上
competitive [kəm'petɪtɪv] *a.* ①竞争的，好竞争的 ②有竞争力的
competitiveness [kəm'petɪtɪvnɪs] *n.* 竞争力，竞争性
competence ['kɒmpətəns] *n.* ①能力，称职
competent ['kɒmpɪtənt] *n.* ①有能力的，能胜任的 ②合格的，合适的

▶▶ **primary** ['praɪmərɪ]
[释义] *a.* ①主要的，首要的 ②最初的，初等的 *n.* ①最初的东西 ②初选，预选
[同根] primarily ['praɪmərɪlɪ] *ad.* ①最初，首先，原来 ②主要地，根本上
primitive ['prɪmɪtɪv] *a.* 原始的，远古的
prime [praɪm] *n.* ①最佳部分，最完美的状态 ②第一部分，最初部分，青春 *a.* ①主要的，最重要的 ②最好的，第一流的 ③根本的

▶▶ **talent** ['tælənt]
[释义] *n.* ①有才能的人 ②天资，天才，

才干
[同义] genius
[同根] talentless ['tæləntlɪs] *a.* 没有天赋的，无才能的
talented ['tæləntɪd] *a.* 天才的，有才干的

▶▶ **maintain** [meɪn'teɪn]
[释义] *v.* ①保持，维持 ②坚持，维护，主张 ③保养，维修 ④赡养，供给
[同义] keep, retain, sustain
[同根] maintenance ['meɪntɪnəns] *n.* ①维护，保持 ②维修 ③生活费用 ④扶养
maintainable [men'teɪnəbl] *a.* ①可维持的 ②主张的
maintainer [men'teɪnə] *n.* 养护工，维护人员
[词组] maintain oneself 自立
maintain one's family 养家

▶▶ **global** ['gləʊbəl]
[释义] *a.* ①全球的，世界的 ②球形的，球面的 ③普遍的，全面的
[同义] worldwide, international
[同根] globe [gləʊb] *n.* ①地球，世界 ②球体，地球仪
globalize ['gləʊbəlaɪz] *v.* 使全球化
globalization [ˌgləʊbəlaɪ'zeɪʃən] *n.* 全球化，全球性

▶▶ **integration** [ˌɪntɪ'greɪʃən]
[释义] *n.* 结合，和而为一，整和，融合
[同义] incorporation, combination, assimilation
[反义] break-up, decay
[同根] integrate ['ɪntɪgreɪt] *v.* ①使成整体，使完整 ②使结合，使合并，使一体化
integral ['ɪntɪgrəl] *a.* ①构成整体所

需要的 ②完整的，整体的
integrity [ɪnˈtegrɪtɪ] n. ①正直，诚实 ②完整，完全，完善
disintegrate [dɪsˈɪntɪɡreɪt] v. 瓦解，（使）分解，（使）碎裂

▶▶ **mutual** [ˈmjuːtʃʊəl]
[释义] a. ①相互的，彼此的 ②共同的，共有的 ③亲密的
[同根] mutualise/mutualize [ˈmjuːtʃʊəlaɪz] v. ①（使）交互作用 ②使互利化
mutuality [ˌmjuːtjuˈælɪtɪ] n. ①相互关系 ②感情共鸣
mutualism [ˈmjuːtʃʊəlɪzəm] n. ①互助论 ②互利共生

▶▶ **geopolitical** [ˌdʒɪ(ː)əupəˈlɪtɪkəl]
[释义] a. 地理政治论的，地缘政治学的

▶▶▶ **stability** [stəˈbɪlɪtɪ]
[释义] n. ①稳定性 ②永久（性），耐久（度）③坚定，坚决
[同根] stabilize [ˈsteɪbɪlaɪz] v. ①使稳定，保持…的稳定，使稳固 ②平抑价格
stable [ˈsteɪbl] a. ①稳定的，稳固的 ②持久的 ③坚定的 ④平稳的 n. 马厩
stably [ˈsteɪblɪ] ad. ①稳定地，稳固地 ②固定地，持久地 ③坚定地，不动摇地

▶▶▶ **in response to** 作为对…的反应，作为对…的答复

▶▶ **self-consciously** [selfˈkɒnʃəslɪ]
[释义] ad. 自觉地，有意识地
[同义] intentionally, knowingly, on purpose
[反义] unintentionally
[同根] conscious [ˈkɒnʃəs] a. ①意识到的，感到的 ②神志清醒的 ③有意的，存心的
consciousness [ˈkɒnʃəsnɪs] n. ①感觉，知觉，自觉 ②意识，观念

unconscious [ʌnˈkɒnʃəs] a. 失去知觉的，无意识的
subconscious [ˈsʌbˈkɒnʃəs] a. 下意识的

▶▶ **address** [əˈdres]
[释义] v. ①对付，处理 ②向…致辞，演说 ③给…写信，对…说话 ④称呼 n. ①地址 ②致辞，演讲，说话的技巧 ③举止，谈吐
[同根] addressee [ˌædreˈsiː] n. 收信人，收件人
addresser [əˈdresə(r)] n. 发信人，发件人，发言人
[词组] closing address 闭幕词
inadequate address 地址不全（无法投寄）
address oneself to ①向…讲话，论述 ②致力于，着手

▶▶ **challenge** [ˈtʃælɪndʒ]
[释义] n. ①挑战，要求决斗 ②要求，需要 ③怀疑 v. ①向…挑战 ②刺激，激励 ③对…怀疑，对…质询
[同根] challenging [ˈtʃælɪndʒɪŋ] a. ①挑战性的 ②令人深思的 ③有迷惑力的
challenger [ˈtʃælɪndʒə] n. 挑战者

▶▶ **interconnected** [ˌɪntə(ː)kəˈnektɪd]
[释义] a. 互相联系的，相互连接的
[同根] connect [kəˈnekt] v. ①连接，把…联系起来 ②联想，联系
interconnect [ˌɪntə(ː)kəˈnekt] v. （使）互相联系/连接
connectible [kəˈnektəbl] a. 可联结的

▶▶ **collaborative** [kəˈlæbəreɪtɪv]
[释义] a. 合作的，协作的，协力完成的
[同根] collaborate [kəˈlæbəreɪt] v. 合作
collaborator [kəˈlæbəreɪtə(r)] n. 合作者
collaboratively [kəˈlæbəreɪtɪvlɪ]

ad. 合作地，协作地

▶▶ **for the benefit of** 为…的利益

▶▶ **humanity** [hju(ː)'mænɪtɪ]

[释义] *n.* ①人类 ②人性 ③仁慈，人道 ④ (*pl.*) 人文学科

[同根] human ['hjuːmən] *n.* 人，人类 *a.* ①人的，人类的 ②人性的
humanly ['hjuːmənlɪ] *ad.* 像人一样地，用人力地
humane [hjuː'meɪn] *a.* 仁慈的
humanely [ˌɪnhju(ː)'meɪnlɪ] *ad.* 有人情味地，慈悲地
inhuman [ɪn'hjuːmən] *a.* 残忍的，无情的 *n.* 残忍，残忍的行为

▶▶ **sweeping** ['swiːpɪŋ]

[释义] *a.* ①势不可挡的 ②规模大的，广阔的 ③打扫的，清扫的

[同根] sweep [swiːp] *v. & n.* ①快速移动，猛力推进 ②扫，拂，清扫，清除
sweeper ['swiːpə] *n.* 打扫者，清洁工

[词组] sweep up 扫掉，清扫
sweep along 冲走，掠过
sweep away 扫清，迅速消灭，冲走
sweep out 扫掉，清除

▶▶ **annual** ['ænjuəl]

[释义] *a.* ①年度的，每年的 ②一年一次的 *n.* ①年报，年鉴 ②一年一度的事

[同根] annually ['ænjuəlɪ] *ad.* 一年一次地，年度地

▶▶ **reverse** [rɪ'vɜːs]

[释义] *n.* ①相反，反面，背面 ②倒退 ③失败，挫折 *v.* ①颠倒，翻转，(使)倒退 ②改变…的次序或地位 ③废除，取消 *a.* 相反的，颠倒的

[同根] reversal [rɪ'vɜːsəl] *n.* 反转，倒退，废弃
reversible [rɪ'vɜːsəbl] *a.* 可反转，倒退的，两面都可用的
reversibly [rɪ'vɜːsəblɪ] *ad.* 可反转、倒退、废弃地

▶▶ **on the rise** 在增长，在上涨

▶▶ **award** [ə'wɔːd]

[释义] *v.* ①授予，给予 ②判给，判定 *n.* ①奖，奖状，奖品 ②裁决，判决书

[同义] accord, give, present, distribute

[同根] awarder [ə'wɔːdə] *n.* 授奖者
awardee [əwɔː'diː] *n.* 受奖者

▶▶ **institution** [ˌɪnstɪ'tjuːʃən]

[释义] *n.* ①院校，(教育、慈善等)公共机构 ②设立，制定 ③制度，习俗

[同根] institute ['ɪnstɪtjuːt] *n.* ①学院，协会 ②学院，研究院 ③原则，规则 *v.* ①设立，制定 ②开创，实行
institutional [ˌɪnstɪ'tjuːʃənəl] *a.* ①学会、协会、教育等公共机构的，社会慈善事业性质的 ②设立的，规定的，制度上的

▶▶ **faculty** ['fækəltɪ]

[释义] *n.* ① (大学的) 院、系，大学或学院的) 全体教职员 ②才能，本领，能力

▶▶ **encourage** [ɪn'kʌrɪdʒ]

[释义] *v.* ①激发，鼓励，劝告，促进 ②赞助，支持

[反义] discourage

[同根] encouragement [ɪn'kʌrɪdʒmənt] *n.* 鼓励，促进
encouraging [ɪn'kʌrɪdʒɪŋ] *a.* 鼓励的，赞助的，促进的

▶▶ **participate in** 参加，参与，分享

▶▶ **credit** ['kredɪt]

[释义] *n.* ①学分 ②相信，信任 ③信誉，声望 ④信用，信贷，贷方 ⑤荣誉，赞许 *v.* ①信任，相信 ②把…归于 (to)，认为…有 (某种优点或成绩)(with)

[同根] discredit [dɪs'kredɪt] *v.* ①使不

相信，证明…是假的 ②不信，怀疑 ③使丢脸，诽谤 n. ①失去名誉，丢面子 ②玷辱名誉的人或事 ③怀疑，不相信

creditor ['kredɪtə] n. 债主，债权人

credibility [,kredɪ'bɪlɪtɪ] n. 可信性，可靠性

credible ['kredəbl] a. 值得赞扬的，可信的

credulous ['kredjʊləs] a. 轻信的，易受骗的

▶▶ resource [rɪ'sɔ:s]

[释义] n. ① [pl.] 资财，储备力量 ②资源 ③谋略，对策，应付方法

[同根] resourceful [rɪ'sɔ:sfʊl] a. ①资源丰富的 ②足智多谋的

[词组] be full of resource(s) 富有机智
leave sb. to his own resources ①让某人独自解决困难 ②不给某人以任何协助

▶▶ trend [trend]

[释义] n. ①趋势，趋向 ②（海岸、河流、山脉等）走向，方向 ③时髦，时尚

[同义] direction, drift, movement, tendency

[同根] trendy ['trendɪ] a. 流行的 n. 新潮人物，穿着时髦的人
trendily ['trendɪlɪ] ad. 时髦地

▶▶ involve [ɪn'vɒlv]

[释义] v. ①涉及，包含，包括 ②使卷入，使陷入，拖累 ③使专注

[同义] contain, include, engage, absorb

[同根] involved [ɪn'vɒlvd] a. 有关的，牵扯在内的，参与的，受影响的
involvement [ɪn'vɒlvmənt] n. ①卷入，缠绕 ②复杂，混乱 ③牵连的事务，复杂的情况

[词组] be /become involved in 包含在…，与…有关,被卷入,专心地（做）
be/get involved with 涉及，给…缠住

▶▶ source [sɔ:s]

[释义] v. 发起，向…提供消息 n. ①源，来源，根源，原因 ②消息来源，提供消息者 ③出处，原始资料

[同义] supply; beginning, derivation, origin, root

[词组] at source 在源头，在始发地
draw from a good source 据可靠消息
take its source at ①发源于 ②出自，起于
trace to its source 追本溯源

▶▶ portion ['pɔ:ʃən]

[释义] n. 部分，一份 v. 分配，把…的一份分给某人

▶▶ investigator [ɪn'vestɪgeɪtə(r)]

[释义] n. 调查者，审查者

[同根] investigate [ɪn'vestɪgeɪt] v. 调查，调查研究
investigation [ɪn,vestɪ'geɪʃən] n. 调查，研究
investigative [ɪn'vestɪgeɪtɪv] a. 研究的，调查研究的

▶▶ focus on 集中在…上

▶▶ genetics [dʒɪ'netɪk]

[释义] n. ①遗传现象，遗传性 ②遗传学

[同根] gene [dʒi:n] n. 遗传因子，遗传基因
genetic [dʒɪ'netɪk] a. ①创始的，起源的 ②演变的，发展的 ③遗传学的
genetically [dʒɪ'netɪk] ad. 基因上，遗传地

▶▶ in collaboration with ①与…协作/合作 ②与…勾结

▶▶ videoconference [,vɪdɪəʊ'kɒnfərəns]

[释义] n. 视频会议

[同根] confer [kən'fɜ:] v. ①协商，交换意见 ②授予（称号、学位等）③赠与，把…赠与

conferee [ˌkɒnfə'ri:] *n.* ①参加会议者 ②被授予（荣誉）称号的人

conference ['kɒnfərəns] *n.* 协商会，讨论会

▶▶ **seminar** ['seminɑ:]

[释义] *n.* ①专家讨论会 ②研究班的专题讨论会 ③研究班

▶▶ **thanks to** 由于，多亏了…

▶▶ **conduct research** 搞研究，进行研究

▶▶ **on-the-job** ['ɒnðə'dʒɒb]

[释义] *a.* 在职的

▶▶ **world-class** *a.* 世界级的，国际水平的

▶▶ **consistently** [kən'sɪstəntlɪ]

[释义] *ad.* 一向，一贯地，始终如一地

[同义] constantly, always

[反义] inconsistently

[同根] consistent [kən'sɪstənt] *a.* ①一贯的，始终如一的 ②连续的，持续的 ③(with sth.) 和…一致的，相符的

inconsistently [ˌɪnkən'sɪstəntlɪ] *ad.* 不一致地

▶▶ **commercialization** [kəˌmɜ:ʃəlaɪ'zeɪʃn]

[释义] *n.* 商品化，商业化

[同根] commerce ['kɒmə(:)s] *n.* ①商业，贸易 ②交往，社交 ③（思想等）交流

commercial [kə'mɜ:ʃəl] *a.* ①商业的，商务的 ②商品化的 ③质量一般

commercialize [kə'mɜ:ʃəlaɪz] *v.* ①使商业化 ②使商品化 ③为追求利润而降低质量 ④在…发展商业

commercialism [kə'mɜ:ʃəlɪz(ə)m] *n.* ①商业主义 / 精神 / 行为 ②重商主义

▶▶ **mainframe** ['meɪnfreɪm]

[释义] *n.* ①[计] 主机 ②大型机

[同根] frame [freɪm] *n.* ①结构，框架 ②画面，背景 ③体格 *v.* 构成，设计

▶▶ **integrated circuit** 集成电路

▶▶ **applications software** 应用软件

▶▶ **intentionally** [ɪn'tenʃənlɪ]

[释义] *ad.* 有意地，故意地

[同义] deliberately, on purpose

[同根] intend [ɪn'tend] *v.* ①想要，打算 ②意指，意思是

intent [ɪn'tent] *n.* ①意图，目的 ②意思，含义

intention [ɪn'tenʃən] *n.* ①意图，目的 ②意思，含义

▶▶ **spin off** ①派生出 ②通过离心力从旋转体中抛出

▶▶ **biotechnology** [ˌbaɪəʊtek'nɒlədʒɪ]

[释义] *n.* 生物工艺学，生物技术

[同根] technology [tek'nɒlədʒɪ] *n.* ①工业技术 ②技术应用 ③应用科学

technologize [tek'nɒlədʒaɪz] *v.* ①使技术化，使工艺化 ②技术化，工艺化

▶▶ **hesitant** ['hezɪtənt]

[释义] *a.* 犹豫不决，犹豫的，吞吞吐吐的

[同根] hesitate ['hezɪteɪt] *v.* 犹豫，踌躇

hesitation [ˌhezɪ'teɪʃən] *n.* 犹豫，踌躇

▶▶ **sustain** [səs'teɪn]

[释义] *v.* ①保持 ②维持，持续 ③支撑，撑住 ④支持，给…以力量

[同根] sustainable [sə'steɪnəbl] *a.* ①支撑得住，能承受的 ②可持续的

sustained [səs'teɪnd] *a.* ①持续的，持久的 ②经久不衰的，一直保持高水平的

▶▶ **unsteady** ['ʌn'stedɪ]

[释义] *a.* ①不稳定的，不安定的 ②不稳固的，摇摆的 ③反复无常的 *v.* 使不稳定，动摇

[同义] unreliable, changeable, variable

[同根] steady ['stedɪ] a. ①稳步的
②稳固的 ③沉稳的，可靠的 v. ①使
平稳，稳住 ②稳定下来 ad. 稳步地，
持续地，稳固地

steadily ['stedɪlɪ] ad. ①有规则地
②稳固地，不动摇地

steadiness ['stedɪnɪs] n. 稳定性，坚
定性

▶▶ budget ['bʌdʒɪt]

[释义] n. ①预算，预算拨款 v. ①编制
预算 ②把编入预算 ③使按照预算，
在预算中拨款给

[同根] budgetary ['bʌdʒɪtərɪ] a. 预算的
budgeteer [ˌbʌdʒɪ'tɪə(r)] n. 预算编制
者，按预算办事的人

▶▶ inflation [ɪn'fleɪʃən]

[释义] n. ①通货膨胀 ②胀大，夸张

[同根] inflate [ɪn'fleɪt] v. ①使膨胀，打
气 ②使通货膨胀

inflationary [ɪn'fleɪʃənərɪ] a. 通货膨
胀的，有通货膨胀倾向的

▶▶ keep pace with 跟上，与…同步，
并驾齐驱

▶▶ make up ①弥补，补偿 ②虚构，捏造
③组成 ④调停，和解 ⑤化妆，打扮

▶▶ predictable [prɪ'dɪktəbl]

[释义] a. 可预言的，可预测的

[同根] predict [prɪ'dɪkt] v.（常 与 that
连用）预言，预测，预示

predictive [prɪ'dɪktɪv] a. 预言性的，
前兆的

prediction [prɪ'dɪkʃən] n. 预言，预料

▶▶ at the rate of 以…速度

▶▶ long-term [lɒŋtɜːm]

[释义] a. 长期的

[反义] short-term

▶▶ on the order of 大约，与…相似的，
属于…一类的

▶▶ admit [əd'mɪt]

[释义] v. ①接纳，让…进入 ②承认
③使获得（某种地位或特权）

[反义] deny, refuse

[同根] admission [əd'mɪʃən] n. ① 承
认 ②允许进入

[词组] admit sb. to/ into 接纳某人进
入…，吸收某人参加…

▶▶ promote [prə'məut]

[释义] v. ①促进 ②提升，提拔，晋升
为 ③推销（商品）

[同根] promotion [prə'məuʃən]
n. ①促进，发扬 ②提升，提拔，晋升
promotee [prəməu'ti:] n. ①被提升
者 ②获晋级者
promoter [prə'məutə] n. 促进者，
助长者
promotive [prəu'məutɪv] a. 促进的，
提升的

▶▶ national interest 国家利益

▶▶ adjust [ə'dʒʌst]

[释义] v. ①调整，调准，校正 ②整理，
安排 ③使适合，符合

[同义] change, alter, modify

[同根] adjustment [ə'dʒʌstmənt]
n. ①调整，调节 ②调节器

▶▶ in the wake of ①在…后，紧跟着…
②随着…而来，作为…的结果 ③仿效

▶▶ visa process 签证手续/程序

▶▶ dramatic [drə'mætɪk]

[释义] a. ①突然的，引人注目的，给
人深刻印象的 ②戏剧般的，戏剧性
的 ③戏剧的，有关戏剧的

[同根] drama ['drɑːmə] n.（在舞台上
演的）戏剧，戏剧艺术
dramatize ['dræmətaɪz] v. ①戏剧性
描述，使引人注目 ②改编成剧本，
使戏剧化
dramatization [ˌdræmətaɪ'zeɪʃən]

n. 戏剧化，改编成戏剧
dramatist ['dræmətɪst] *n.* 剧作家
dramatically [drə'mætɪkəlɪ] *ad.* 显
著地，引人注目地，戏剧性地

▶▶ **corresponding** [,kɒrɪ'spɒndɪŋ]
[释义] *a.* ①相应的 ②符合的，一致的
[同根] correspond [,kɒrɪ'spɒnd]
v. ①相符合，相称 (to, with) ②相当，
相类似 (to) ③通信 (with)
correspondent [,kɒrɪ'spɒndənt] *n.* 通
信者，通讯员，记者 *a.* 符合的，一
致的
correspondence [,kɒrɪ'spɒndəns]
n. ①符合，一致 ②相当，类似 ③通
信 (联系)，信函

▶▶ **surge** [sɜːdʒ]
[释义] *n. & v.* ①激增，急剧上升 ②巨
浪，波涛 ③ (浪涛等) 汹涌，澎湃
[同义] mount, rush
[同根] surgent ['sɜːdʒənt] *a.* 澎湃的，
汹涌的

▶▶ **enrollment** [ɪn'rəʊlmənt]
[释义] *n.* ①登记，注册，入学，入伍
②登记 / 注册等人数
[同根] enroll [ɪn'rəʊl] *v.* ①招收 ②登
记，加入，入学 ③招募 ④记录，记下

▶▶ **reversal** [rɪ'vɜːsəl]
[释义] *n.* 反转，倒退，废弃
[同根] reverse [rɪ'vɜːs] *n.* ①相反，反
面，背面 ②倒退 ③失败，挫折
v. ①颠倒，翻转，(使) 倒退 ②改变…
的次序或地位 ③废除，取消 *a.* 相反
的，颠倒的
reversible [rɪ'vɜːsəbl] *a.* 可反转、倒
退、废弃的，两面都可用的

▶▶ **contribute to** ①有助于，促成 ②作
出贡献 ③捐款，捐献

▶▶ **immigrant** ['ɪmɪɡrənt]
[释义] *n.* (外来) 移民,侨民 *a.* 移入的,

迁入的
[反义] emigrant
[同根] immigrate ['ɪmɪɡreɪt] *v.* (从外
国) 移入，作为移民定居
immigration [,ɪmɪ'ɡreɪʃən]
n. ① < 美 > [总称] (外来的) 移民
②移居
emigrate ['emɪɡreɪt] *v.* 自本国移居
他国
emigrant ['emɪɡrənt] *n.* 移居外国
者，移民
emigration [,emɪ'ɡreɪʃən] *n.* 移民出
境，侨居，[总称] 移民
migrate [maɪ'ɡreɪt, 'maɪɡreɪt]
v. ①移居，迁移 ② (动物的) 迁徙
migrant ['maɪɡrənt] *n.* 移居者，候
鸟 *a.* 迁移的，移居的
migration [maɪ'ɡreɪʃən] *n.* ①迁移，
移居 ②移民群，移栖群

▶▶ **ambassador** [æm'bæsədə]
[释义] *n.* ① (喻) 使者，代表 ②大使
[同根] ambassadress [æm'bæsədrɪs]
n. 大使夫人，女大使
ambassadorship [æm'bæsədəʃɪp]
n. 大使的职位
embassy ['embəsɪ] *n.* 大使馆

▶▶ **effective** [ɪ'fektɪv]
[释义] *a.* ①有效的，能产生 (预期)
结果的，起作用的 ②给人深刻印象
的，显著的 ③实际的，事实上的
[反义] ineffective
[同根] effect [ɪ'fekt] *n.* ①结果 ②效
力，作用，影响 ③感受，印象 ④实行，
生效，起作用
efficiency [ɪ'fɪʃənsɪ] *n.* 效率，功效
efficient [ɪ'fɪʃənt] *a.* ①效率高的，能
干的，能胜任的 ② (直接) 生效的
[词组] be effective on 对…起作用
become effective 生效

选项词汇注释

▶▶ **oriented** [ˈɔːrɪentɪd]
[释义] a. ①以…为导向的，以…为目的的 ②对…感兴趣的，重视…的
[同根] orient [ˈɔːrɪent] v. ① (to, toward) 使朝向，以…为方向 ②使适应，使熟悉情况（或环境等）n. (the O-)东方，亚洲（尤指远东），东半球
orientate [ˈɔːrɪenteɪt] v. 向东，朝向
orientation [ˌɔː(ː)rɪenˈteɪʃ ən] n. ①方向，方位 ②熟悉，适应
oriental [ˌɔː(ː)rɪˈentl] n. 东方人（尤指中国 / 日本人）a. 东方的，东方人的，东方文化的
orientalize [ˌɒrɪˈentəlaɪz] v. （使）东方化

▶▶ **popularize** [ˈpɒpjuləraɪz]
[释义] v. 普及，推广
[同根] popular [ˈpɒpjulə] a: 通俗的，流行的，受欢迎的
popularly [ˈpɒpjulələ] ad. 一般地，流行地，通俗地，大众地
popularity [ˌpɒpjuˈlærɪtɪ] n. ①普及，流行，大众化 ②讨人喜欢的特点，声望

▶▶ **a series of** 一系列的，一连串的

▶▶ **various** [ˈveərɪəs]
[释义] a. 不同的，各种各样的，多方面的
[同根] vary [ˈveərɪ] v. 改变，变化

varied [ˈveərɪd] a. 各式各样的，有变化的
variety [vəˈraɪətɪ] n. ①变化，多样性 ②品种，种类
variable [ˈveərɪəbl] a. 可变的，不定的，易变的
variation [ˌveərɪˈeɪ ʃ ne] n. 变更，变化，变异，变种
variability [ˌveərɪəˈbɪlɪtɪ] n. ①多样性，变化 ②变化性，可变性

▶▶ **illustrate** [ˈɪləstreɪt]
[释义] v. ①举例或以图表等说明 ②加插图于
[同义] clarify, demonstrate, explain
[同根] illustration [ˌɪləsˈtreɪʃən] n. ①举例或以图表等说明，例证 ②图表，插图

▶▶ **establish** [ɪsˈtæblɪ ʃ]
[释义] v. ①建立，设立，创立，开设 ②确立，制定，规定 ③证实，认可
[同义] fix, found, organize, settle
[同根] establishment [ɪsˈtæblɪ ʃ mənt] n. ①建立，确立，制定 ②（包括雇员、设备、场地、货物等在内的）企业，建立的机构（如军队、军事机构、行政机关、学校、医院、教会）
[词组] establish sb. as... 任命（派）某人担任…

▶▶ **branch campus** 分校

Reading in Depth
Section A

As war spreads to many corners of the globe, Children sadly have been drawn into the center of **conflicts**. In Afghanistan, Bosnia, and Colombia, however, groups of children have been taking part in peace education projects. The children, after learning to **resolve** conflicts, **took on** the **role** of **peacemakers**. The Children's Movement for Peace in Colombia was even *nominated*（提名）for the Nobel Peace Prize in 1998. Groups of children acting as peacemakers studied human rights and poverty issues in Colombia, eventually forming a group with five other schools in Bogota known as The Schools of Peace.

The classroom offers opportunities for children to replace angry, **violent behaviors** with **cooperative**, peaceful ones. It is in the classroom that caring and respect for each person **empowers** children to **take a step forward** toward becoming peacemakers. **Fortunately**, educators have access to many online resources that are especially useful when helping children along the path to peace. The Young Peacemakers Club, started in 1992, provides a Website with resources for teachers and information on starting a Kindness **Campaign**. The World Centers of **Compassion** for Children International **call attention to** children's rights and how to help the victims of war. Starting a Peacemakers' Club is a **praiseworthy venture** for a class and one that could spread to other classrooms and ideally affect the culture of the entire school.

文章词汇注释

▶▶▶ conflict ['kɒnflɪkt]
[释义] n. ①冲突 ②斗争, 战斗 ③纠纷, 争执, 争论, 抵触 v. 冲突, 争执, 抵触
[同义] clash, struggle
[同根] conflicting [kən'flɪktɪŋ] a. 相冲突的, 不一致的, 相矛盾的
[词组] come into conflict with 和…冲突 in conflict with 同…相冲突 / 有抵触 / 有矛盾

▶▶▶ resolve [rɪ'zɒlv]
[释义] v. ①解决, 解答 ②决心, 决定 ③(使)分解, 溶解 n. ①决心 ②坚决, 刚毅
[同义] solve, settle, put an end to; determine, make up one's mind
[同根] resolution [,rezə'lu:ʃən] n. ①决心, 决定, 决议 ②坚决, 刚毅 ③解决 resolute ['rezəlu:t] a. 坚决的, 刚毅的 resolutely ['rezəlu:tlɪ] ad. 毅然地,

坚决地

resolvable [rɪ'zɒlvəbl] a. ①可决定的 ②可解决的 ③可分解的，可溶解的

[词组] resolve to do 决心做，决定做

resolve on / upon (doing) sth 决心做，决定做

▶▶▶ take on ①承担（工作、责任等）②雇用，聘用 ③开始显现，变得有

▶▶▶ role [rəʊl]

[释义] n. 角色，任务，作用

[词组] play an important role in 在…中起重要作用

play the leading role 起主要作用，起带头作用

play the role of(sb.) （在剧中）扮演（某人）角色

▶▶▶ peacemaker ['piːsmeɪkə(r)]

[释义] n. ①制造和平的人 ②调解人，和事佬

[反义] peacebreaker ['piːs,breɪkə(r)] n. 破坏和平的人，扰乱治安者，肇事者

▶▶▶ violent ['vaɪələnt]

[释义] a. ①暴力的，暴力引起的 ②猛烈的，激烈的

[同义] aggressive, cruel, fierce, furious

[反义] friendly, peaceful

[同根] violence ['vaɪələns] n. ①暴力，暴行 ②猛烈，强烈

violently ['vaɪələntlɪ] ad. 猛烈地，激烈地，极端地

▶▶▶ behavior [bɪ'heɪvjə]

[释义] n. ①举止，行为，品行 ②（待人的）态度

[同义] action, conduct, manner

[同根] behave [bɪ'heɪv] v. ①行为，举止 ②工作，运转，开动

behavioral [bɪ'heɪvjər(ə)l] a. 行为的，动作的

▶▶▶ cooperative [kəʊ'ɒprətɪv]

[释义] a. ①合作的，协作的 ②有合作意向，乐意合作的 n. 合作社，合作商店（或企业等）

[同义] supportive, helpful, shared, accommodating, collaborative

[同根] operate ['ɒpəreɪt] v. 操作，运转，开动

cooperate [kəʊ'ɒpəreɪt] v. ①合作，协作 ②共同起作用

cooperation [kəʊ,ɒpə'reɪʃən] n. 合作，协作，配合

cooperatively [kəʊ'ɒprətɪvlɪ] ad. 合作地，协作地

▶▶▶ empower [ɪm'paʊə]

[释义] (=impower) v. ①使能够，许可 ②授权给

[同根] power ['paʊə(r)] n. ①体能，智能，能力 ②权力 ③有权力的人，强国

powered ['paʊəd] a. ①装有动力的 ②产生动力的 ③用动力推动的

▶▶▶ take a step forward 向前进

▶▶▶ fortunately ['fɔːtʃənətlɪ]

[释义] ad. 幸运地，幸亏

[同根] fortune ['fɔːtʃən] n. ①运气，命运 ②财富，大量财产

fortunate ['fɔːtʃənɪt] a. ①幸运的，侥幸的 ②吉利的 n. 幸运儿

unfortunate [ʌn'fɔːtʃənɪt] a. 不幸的，不吉利的

misfortune [mɪs'fɔːtʃən] n. 不幸，灾祸

▶▶▶ access ['ækses]

[释义] n. ①使用权，接近权 ②通道，入口 ③进入，接近 v. ①接近 ②存取

[同根] accession [æk'seʃən] n. ①就职 ②添加（物)，增加（物）③正式加入，正式接受

accessional [æk'seʃənəl] a. 附加的，

添加的，增加的

accessible [əkˈsesəbl] a. ①可 / 易接近的，易相处的 ②可 / 易得到的，可 / 易使用的 ③易受影响的 ④可理解的

[词组] have/gain/get/obtain access to ①得以使用 ②得以接近 / 进入

be of easy/difficult access 容易 / 难接近

give access to 接见，准许出入

▶▶ **campaign** [kæmˈpeɪn]

[释义] n. ①运动，（政治或商业性）活动 ②战役 v. 参加活动，从事活动

[同义] movement, drive, battle

[词组] enter upon a campaign 发动运动，走上征途

on campaign 出征，从军

▶▶ **compassion** [kəmˈpæʃən]

[释义] n. & v. 同情，怜悯

[同义] sympathy

[同根] passion [ˈpæʃne] n. ①激情，热情 ②（与理智相对）强烈感情 ③强烈的情欲，热恋对象

passionate [ˈpæʃənɪt] a. 热情的，感情强烈的

passionful [ˈpæʃənful] a. 充满热情的

compassionate [kəmˈpæʃənɪt] a. ①富于同情心的 ②照顾性的

[词组] have/take compassion on 怜悯，同情

in/with compassion 怜悯地

▶▶ **call attention to...** 唤起对…的注意

▶▶ **praiseworthy** [ˈpreɪzˌwɜːðɪ]

[释义] a. 值得赞扬的，可嘉许的

[同义] commendable, admirable

▶▶ **venture** [ˈventʃə]

[释义] n. ①（冒险）事业 ②冒险行动，冒险 ③投机活动，（为赢利而投资其中的）企业 v. ①使有风险，冒…险 ②以…作赌注 ③敢于

[同义] enterprise, endeavor, undertaking; risk

[同根] venturesome [ˈventʃəsəm] a. ①冒险的，危险的 ②好冒险的，大胆的

[词组] at a venture 冒险地，胡乱地，随便地

joint venture 合资企业

Section B
Passage One

By almost **any measure**, there is a **boom** in Internet-based **instruction**. In just a few years, 34 percent of American universities have begun offering some form of distance learning (DL), and among the larger schools, it's closer to 90 percent. If you doubt the **popularity** of the trend, you probably haven't heard of the University of Phoenix. It enrolls 90,000 students, a **statistic** used to support its **claim** to be the largest private university in the country.

While the kinds of instruction offered in these programs will differ,

DL usually **signifies** a course in which the instructions post **syllabi**, reading **assignments**, and **schedules** on Websites, and students **send in** their assignments by e-mail. **Generally speaking**, face-to-face **communication** with an instructor is **minimized** or **eliminated** altogether.

The attraction for students might at first seem obvious. **Primarily**, there's the **convenience** promised by courses on the Net: you can do the work, as they say, in your **pajamas**. But **figures indicate** that the reduced effort results in a reduced **commitment** to the course. While **dropout** rates for all freshmen at American universities is around 20 percent, the rate for online students is 35 percent. Students themselves seem to understand the weaknesses **inherent** in the **setup**. In a **survey** conducted for eCornell, the DL division of Cornell University, less than a third of the **respondents** expected the quality of the online course to be as good as the classroom course.

Clearly, from the schools' **perspective**, there's a lot of money to be saved. Although some of the more **ambitious** programs require new investments in **servers** and networks to support collaborative software, most DL courses can run on existing or minimally **upgraded** systems. The more students who enroll in a course but don't come to campus, the more the school saves on keeping the lights on in the classrooms, paying doorkeepers, and maintaining parking lots. And, while there's **evidence** that instructors must work harder to run a DL course for **a variety of** reasons, they won't be paid any more, and might well be paid less.

文章词汇注释

▶▶▶ **by any measure** 不管用什么标准衡量

▶▶▶ **boom** [bu:m]
[释义] *n.* ①迅速发展，（营业额等的）激增，（经济等的）繁荣 ②隆隆声
v. ①激增，繁荣，迅速发展 ②发出隆隆声
[同义] thrive, flourish, advance
[反义] slump
[同根] booming ['bu:mɪŋ] *a.* ①激增的，兴旺发达的 ②隆隆作响的

boomy ['bu:mɪ] *a.* ①经济繁荣的，景气的 ②隆隆作响的

▶▶▶ **instruction** [ɪn'strʌkʃən]
[释义] *n.* ①教育，讲授，教学 ②教诲，教导 ③用法说明
[同义] teaching, education, tutoring; command direction
[同根] instruct [ɪn'strʌkt] *v.* ①教，讲授，训练，指导 ②命令，指示
instructor [ɪn'strʌktə] *n.* 教员，教练，指导者

instructive [ɪn'strʌktɪv] *a.* 有启发的，有教育意义的

instructively [ɪn'strʌktɪvlɪ] *ad.* 启发地，有益地

[词组] give instructions to do sth. 指挥／命令（做某事）

ask for instruction 请示

give instruction in 讲授

▶▶ **popularity** [ˌpɒpjʊ'lærɪtɪ]

[释义] *n.* ①普及，流行，大众化 ②声望，讨人喜欢的特点

[反义] unpopularity

[同根] popular ['pɒpjʊlə] *a.* 通俗的，流行的，受欢迎的

popularly ['pɒpjʊləlɪ] *ad.* 流行地，通俗地，大众地

popularize ['pɒpjʊləraɪz] *v.* 普及，推广

▶▶ **statistic** [stə'tɪstɪk]

[释义] *n.* 统计数字，统计量

[同根] statistics [stə'tɪstɪks] *n.* ①统计，统计资料 ②统计学

statistical [stə'tɪstɪkəl] *a.* 统计的，统计学的

statistician [ˌstætɪs'tɪʃən] *n.* 统计员，统计学家

statistically [stə'tɪstɪkəlɪ] *ad.* 据统计，统计地

▶▶ **claim** [kleɪm]

[释义] *n.* ①主张，声称，断言 ②要求，索赔 ③权利，要求权 *v.* ①声称，断言 ②对（头衔等）提出要求，索取 ③要求，需要

[同义] assertion, statement, declaration

[同根] claimable [kleɪməbl] *a.* 可要求的，可索取，可索赔的

[词组] have a claim on/to 对…有要求权

make a claim for 对（赔偿等）提出要求…

▶▶ **signify** ['sɪgnɪfaɪ]

[释义] *v.* ①表示，表明 ②表示…的意思，意味着，预示

[同义] mean, count

[同根] sign [saɪn] *n.* ①标记，符号，手势 ②指示牌 ③足迹，痕迹 ④征兆，迹象 *v.* ①签名（于），署名（于），签署 ②做手势，示意

signal ['sɪgnl] *n.* 信号 *v.* 发信号，用信号通知

significance [sɪg'nɪfɪkəns] *n.* 意义，重要性

significant [sɪg'nɪfɪkənt] *a.* 有意义的，重大的，重要的

▶▶ **syllabi** ['sɪləbaɪ]

[释义] *n.* syllabus 的复数

[同根] syllabus ['sɪləbəs] *n.* 课程提纲

▶▶ **assignment** [ə'saɪnmənt]

[释义] *n.* ①（指定的）作业，（分派的）任务 ②分配，指派

[同义] task, job, allocation

[同根] assign [ə'saɪn] *v.* ①分配，布置 ②指派，选派 ③指定（时间、地点等）

▶▶ **schedule** ['ʃedjuːl; 'skedʒuːl]

[释义] *n.* ①计划（表），日程安排（表） ②时间表，时刻表 ③明细表，一览表 *v.* ①将…列表，为…作目录 ②将…列入计划表

[同根] scheduled ['ʃedjuːld] *a.* 预定的，预先安排的，按时刻表的

scheduling ['ʃedjuːlɪŋ] *n.* 列入计划表，安排，调度

[词组] ahead of schedule 提前

behind schedule ①落后于计划或进度 ②迟于预定时间

on schedule 按时间表，准时

▶▶ **send in** 上交，呈报，递送

▶▶ **generally speaking** 总的来说，一般而言

▶▶ **communication** [kəˌmjuːnɪ'keɪʃn]

[释义] n. ①交流 ②通讯，交际 ③传达

[同根] communicate [kə'mju:nɪkeɪt]
v. ①传达，传送 ②通讯，交际 ③传染
communicative [kə'mju:nɪkətɪv]
a. ①健谈的 ②通讯的，交际的
communicatory [kə'mju:nɪkətərɪ]
a. ①通信的，交际的 ②供通信用的

[词组] be in communication with 与…通讯，与…保持联系

▶▶▶ minimize ['mɪnɪmaɪz]

[释义] v. ①将…减到最少 ②对…作最低估计，小看

[反义] maximize; emphasize

[同根] minimum ['mɪnɪməm] n. ①最小量 ②最低极限 a. 最小的，最低的
minimal ['mɪnɪməl] a. 最小的，最小限度的
minimally ['mɪnɪməlɪ] ad. 最小地，最小限度地

▶▶▶ eliminate [ɪ'lɪmɪneɪt]

[释义] v. ①消除，排除，根除 ②（比赛中）淘汰

[同义] discard, dispose of, exclude, eradicate, abolish

[同根] elimination [ɪ,lɪmɪ'neɪʃən] n. 排除，消除，根除
eliminable [ɪ'lɪmɪnəbl] a. 可消除的，可消去的，可排除的

▶▶▶ primarily ['praɪmərɪlɪ]

[释义] ad. ①首先，起初 ②主要地，根本上

[同根] prime [praɪm] n. ①最佳部分，最完美的状态 ②第一部分，最初部分，青春 a. ①主要的，最重要的 ②最好的，第一流的 ③根本的
primary ['praɪmərɪ] a. ①第一的，基本的，主要的 ②初步的，初级的
primitive ['prɪmɪtɪv] a. 原始的，远古的
primitively ['prɪmɪtɪvlɪ] ad. 最初地，

自学而成地

▶▶▶ convenience [kən'vi:njəns]

[释义] n. ①便利 ②有益 ③方便的用具、安排等

[同根] convenient [kən'vi:njənt] a. 便利的，方便的
inconvenient [,ɪnkən'vi:njənt]
a. ①不便的 ②有困难的
inconvenience [,ɪnkən'vi:njəns]
n. 麻烦，不方便之处

[词组] at one's convenience 在方便时
at your earliest convenience 在你方便时尽早
for the convenience of 为…方便起见
marriage of convenience 基于利害关系的婚姻，权宜结婚

▶▶▶ pajamas [pə'dʒɑ:məz]

[释义] n. 睡衣

▶▶▶ figure ['fɪgə]

[释义] n. ①数字 ②人物 ③体形，轮廓 ④图形 v. 认为，考虑，估计

▶▶▶ indicate ['ɪndɪkeɪt]

[释义] v. ①指出，显示 ②象征，暗示 ③简要地说明

[同义] show, suggest, reveal, denote, imply

[同根] indication [,ɪndɪ'keɪʃən] n. 迹象，表明，指示
indicative [ɪn'dɪkətɪv] a. (～ of) 指示的，表明的，可表示的
indicator ['ɪndɪkeɪtə] n. 指示物，指示者，指标

▶▶▶ commitment [kə'mɪtmənt]

[释义] n. ①承诺，许诺，保证，承担的义务 ②献身参与，介入 ③托付，交托 ④信奉，支持

[同根] commit [kə'mɪt] v. ①使承担义务，使做出保证 ②把…托付给，把…提交 ③犯（罪），做（错事、坏事、

傻事等）

committed [kə'mɪtɪd] *a.* ①受委托的，承担义务的 ②忠诚的，忠于…的

▶▶ dropout 辍学学生，中途退学

▶▶ inherent [ɪn'hɪərənt]

[释义] *a.* 内在的，固有的，生来就有的

[同义] internal，natural，existing，instinctive

[反义] acquired

[同根] inherit [ɪn'herɪt] *v.* ①继承…②遗传而得（性格、特征等）③（从前人、前任等）接过，得到 ④成为财产的继承人

inheritable [ɪn'herɪtəbl] *a.* ①可继承的 ②可遗传的

▶▶ setup [set'ʌp]

[释义] *n.* ①（事物的）安排，计划，方案 ②姿势，姿态 ③装配，装置

▶▶ survey [sɜ:'veɪ]

[释义] *n.* 调查，检验，调查报告，民意测验 *v.* ①调查（收入、民意等），勘定，检验 ②测量，测绘

[同义] investigation，research，inquiry

[同根] surveyor [sɜ:'veɪə] *n.* 测量员，检查员

▶▶ respondent [rɪs'pɒndənt]

[释义] *n.* ①回答者，响应者 ②（论文）答辩人

[同根] respond [rɪs'pɒnd] *v.* ①回答，作答 ②作出反应

response [rɪs'pɒns] *n.* ①回答，答复 ②响应，反应

responsible [rɪs'pɒnsəbl] *a.* ①有责任的，应负责的 ②责任重大的 ③可靠的，可依赖的

responsive [rɪs'pɒnsɪv] *a.* ①回答的，应答的，响应的

responsibility [rɪs,pɒnsə'bɪlɪtɪ] *n.* 责

任，责任感，职责

▶▶ perspective [pə'spektɪv]

[释义] *n.* ①（观察问题的）视角，观点，看法 ②透视画法，透视图 ③远景，前途 *a.* 透视的，透视画法的

[同义] viewpoint，attitude，opinion

[同根] perspectivity [pɜ:spek'tɪvɪtɪ] *n.* 透视（性），明晰度

perspectively [pə'spektɪvlɪ] *ad.* 依透视画法

[词组] from ... perspective 从…角度看（问题）

in perspective ①合乎透视法 ②关系恰当的

out of perspective 不按透视法的，（位置或比例）不成比例的

▶▶ ambitious [æm'bɪʃəs]

[释义] *a.* ①有雄心的，有抱负的 ②由野心、雄心引起的 ③费劲的，要求过高的 ④过分矫饰的，炫耀的

[同义] aspiring

[同根] ambition [æm'bɪʃən] *n.* 野心，雄心

ambitiously [æm'bɪʃəslɪ] *ad.* 雄心勃勃地

▶▶ server ['sɜ:və]

[释义] *n.* 服务器，服务者，服役者

▶▶ upgrade ['ʌpgreɪd]

[释义] *v.* 提升，使升级 *n.* 升级，上升

[反义] degrade

[同根] grade [greɪd] *n.* ①等级，级别，年级 ②分数，成绩 *v.* 分等，分类，评分

degrade [dɪ'greɪd] *v.* ①（使）降级②（使）堕落

degrading [dɪ'greɪdɪŋ] *a.* 有辱人格的，可耻的

degradation [,degrə'deɪʃən] *n.* 降级，降格，退化

degradable [dɪ'greɪdəbl] *a.* 可降解的

[词组] on the upgrade 有进步，有进展

▶▶ evidence ['evɪdəns]

[释义] n. ①证据，根据，论据 ②迹象，痕迹，征兆 ③证人，证词 ④明白，明显 v. 表明，证明，显示

[同义] proof, indication, sign, prove

[同根] evident ['evɪdənt] a. 显然的，明显的
evidently [evɪ'dentlɪ] ad. ①明显地，显然 ②根据现有证据

[词组] bear/show evidence of 表明，证明
in evidence ①显而易见的，明显的 ②作为证据

▶▶ a variety of 多种多样的

选项词汇注释

▶▶ striking ['straɪkɪŋ]

[释义] a. ①显著的，鲜明的，引人注目的 ②打击的 ③罢工的

[同义] outstanding, remarkable, noticeable, prominent

[同根] strike [straɪk] v. ①侵袭 ②罢工 ③撞击，冲击 n. ①罢工 ②打击，殴打

[词组] be on strike 举行罢工
be struck on（常用于否定句）非常喜爱
be struck with(by) ①为…所袭击 ②为…所感动

▶▶ boast [bəust]

[释义] v. 自夸，以有…而自豪 n. ①自吹自擂 ②足以自豪的事物

[同根] boastful ['bəustful] a. 自负的，喜夸耀的，自夸的
boaster ['bəustə] n. 自夸的人

[词组] make a boast of sth. 夸耀某事
boast about/of 自夸，自吹自擂
boast oneself of 自负，自夸

▶▶ characterize ['kærɪktəraɪz]

[释义] v. ①成为…的特征，以…为特征 ②描绘…的特征，刻画…的性格

[同根] character ['kærəktə] n. ①（事物的）性质，特性，（人的）品质，性格 ②（小说、戏剧等的）人物，角色 ③（书写或印刷）符号，（汉）字

characteristic [ˌkærəktə'rɪstɪk] a. 独有的，典型的 n. 特性，特征

characterization [ˌkærɪktəraɪ'zeɪʃən] n. ①（对人、物）特性描述 ②人物塑造，性格描写

[词组] be characterized by ... …的特点在于，…的特点是
be characterized as ... 被描绘为…，被称为…

▶▶ flexibility [ˌfleksə'bɪlɪtɪ]

[释义] n. ①灵活性，弹性 ②适应性 ③机动性

[同义] adjustability, elasticity, bendability, variableness

[反义] inflexibility, rigidity

[同根] flexible ['fleksəbl] a. ①灵活的，可通融的 ②有弹性的，柔韧的
flexibly ['fleksəblɪ] ad. 灵活地，有弹性地，易曲地

▶▶ diversity [daɪ'vɜːsɪtɪ]

[释义] n. 差异，多样性

[同义] variety, difference

[同根] diverse [daɪ'vɜːs] a. 不同的，多样的
diversify [daɪ'vɜːsɪfaɪ] v. 使不同，使多样化
diversified [daɪ'vɜːsɪfaɪd] a. 多变化

的，各种的

diversification [daɪvɜːsɪfɪ'keɪʃən] n. 变化，多样化

▶▶ casual ['kæʒjuəl]

[释义] a. ①非正式的，随便的 ②偶然的，碰巧的 ③临时的，不定期的

[同根] casually ['kæʒjuəlɪ] ad. 偶然地，随便地，临时地

casualness ['kæʒjuəlnɪs] n. 随便，不拘礼节

casualty ['kæʒjuəltɪ] n. ①严重的意外，事故，横祸 ②死伤（者），受害者 ③ [pl.] [军] 伤亡（人数）

▶▶ boarding expenses 寄宿费

▶▶ required courses 必修课程

▶▶ account for ①解释，说明 ②（在数量或比例上）占

▶▶ evaluation system 评估体系

▶▶ mechanism ['mekənɪzəm]

[释义] n. ①办法，途径 ②机制，机理 ③机械装置

[同根] machine [mə'ʃiːn] n. 机器，机械

mechanic [mɪ'kænɪk] n. 技工，机修工，机械师

mechanical [mɪ'kænɪkl] a. 机械的，机械制的，机械似的

mechanically [mɪ'kænɪkəlɪ] ad. 机械地

▶▶ ensure [ɪn'ʃuə]

[释义] v. ①保证，担保，保证得到 ②使安全

[同义] guarantee, insure, protect, defend

[同根] insure [ɪn'ʃuə] v. ①给…保险 ②保证，确保

insurance [ɪn'ʃuərəns] n. ①保险，保险单，保险费 ②预防措施，安全保证

assure [ə'ʃuə] v. 有信心地说，使确信

assurance [ə'ʃuərəns] n. ①保证，表示保证（或鼓励、安慰）的话 ②把握，信心 ③（人寿）保险

▶▶ enthusiasm [ɪn'θjuːzɪæzəm]

[释义] n. 热心，热情，巨大兴趣 (for, about)

[同义] passion, warmth, zeal

[同根] enthuse [ɪn'θjuːz] v. （使）热心

enthusiastic [ɪn,θjuːzɪ'æstɪk] a. 满腔热情的，极感兴趣的

enthusiastically [ɪn,θjuːzɪ'æstɪklɪ] ad. 热心地，热情地

enthusiast [ɪn'θjuːzɪæst] n. 热心家，狂热者

[词组] enthusiasm for 对…的热情

lack of enthusiasm 缺乏热情

arouse the enthusiasm of 激发…的积极性

be in enthusiasm 怀有热情

▶▶ for the purpose of 为了…的目的，为了…起见

▶▶ build up one's reputation 提高名气

▶▶ cut down on 减少…，缩减…

▶▶ teaching facilities 教学设施

Passage Two

In this age of Internet chat, **videogames** and reality television, there is no shortage of **mindless** activities to keep a child occupied. Yet, despite the competition, my 8-year-old daughter Rebecca wants to spend her **leisure** time writing short stories. She wants to **enter** one of her stories **into** a writing **contest**, a competition she won last year.

As a writer I know about winning contest, and about losing them. I know what it is like to work hard on a story **only to** receive a **rejection slip** from the publisher. I also know the **pressures** of trying to **live up to** a reputation created by **previous** victories. **What if** she doesn't win the contest again? That's the strange thing about being a parent. So many of our own **past scars and dashed hopes** can **surface**.

A **revelation** came last week when I asked her, "Don't you want to win again?" "No," she replied, "I just want to tell the story of an angel going to first grade."

I had just spent weeks correcting her stories as she **spontaneously** told them. Telling myself that I was **merely** an experienced writer guiding the young writer across the hall, I offered suggestions for characters, conflicts and endings for her tales. The story about a fearful angel starting first trade was quickly "guided" by me into the tale of a little girl with a wild imagination taking her fist music lesson. I had turned her contest into my contest without even realizing it.

Staying back and giving kids space to grow is not as easy as it looks. Because I know very little about farm animals who use tools or angels who go to first grade, I had to accept the fact that I was *co-opting*（借用）my daughter's experience.

While **stepping back** was difficult for me, it was certainly a good first step that I will quickly follow with more steps, putting myself far enough away to give her room but close enough to help if asked. **All the while** I will be reminding myself that children need room to experiment, grow and find their own voices.

文章词汇注释

▶▶▶ videogame [ˈvɪdɪəʊgeɪm]
[释义] *n.* 电视游戏，电子游戏

▶▶▶ mindless [ˈmaɪndlɪs]

[释义] *a.* ①不用脑子的，没头脑的
②愚笨无知的，粗心大意的
[同根] mindful [ˈmaɪndfʊl] *a.* [通常用作表语] 注意…的，留心…的，不忘…

的 (of)

▶▶ leisure ['leʒə;'liːʒə]

[释义] n. ①悠闲，安逸 ②空闲，闲暇

[同义] ease, freedom, rest

[同根] leisured ['leʒəd] a. 有许多闲暇
的，有闲的
leisurely ['leʒəlɪ] ad. 从容的，不匆
忙的

[词组] at leisure 空闲的，闲暇中的
at one's leisure 在空闲之时

▶▶ enter into ①参加，开始从事，进
②成为…的一部分，成为…的一方

▶▶ contest ['kɒntest]

[释义] n. ①比赛，竞争 ②斗争，争夺
[kən'test] v. ①争夺 ②对…提出质
疑，争论

[同义] game, contend, struggle,
tournament

[同根] contestant [kən'testənt] n. 竞争
者，争论者
contestation [,kɒntes'teɪʃ ən] n. ①争
论，论战 ②（争执中的）主张，见解

▶▶ only to 不料竟会…，结果却…

▶▶ rejection slip n. 退稿附条

▶▶ pressure ['preʃ ə(r)]

[释义] n. ①压，压力，电压 ②压迫，
强制，紧迫

[同义] stress, strain

[反义] relaxation, relief, ease

[同根] press [pres] v. ①（常与 on,
upon 连用）迫使，进逼（与 for 连用）
②压，按，推，挤压，榨取 ③敦促，
力劝
pressing ['presɪŋ] a. 紧迫的，紧张的

[词组] under pressure 被迫，在强制下

▶▶ live up to ①不辜负，符合 ②遵守，
实践（诺言等）③与…相配

▶▶ previous ['priːvɪəs]

[释义] a. 以前的，先前的

[同根] previously ['priːvɪəslɪ] ad. 先前，
以前

▶▶ what if... 如果…将会怎样，假使…
该怎么办？

▶▶ past scars and dashed hopes 过去的
创伤和破灭的希望

▶▶ surface ['sɜːfɪs]

[释义] v. ①浮现，出现，公开化 ②升
到地面 / 水面 n. 表面，外表 a. 表面
的，肤浅的

[词组] come to the surface 显露出来
on the surface 表面上，外表上

▶▶ revelation [,revɪ'leɪʃ ən]

[释义] n. ①惊人的新发现 ②揭露，暴
露，透露

[同根] reveal [rɪ'viːl] v. ①揭示，暴露，
泄露，透露 ②使显露，展现，显示
revelatory ['revɪlətərɪ] a. 揭示性的，
揭露性的，展示的
revealing [rɪ'viːlɪŋ] a. ①暴露部分身
体的，袒胸露肩的 ②有启迪作用的

▶▶ spontaneously [spɒn'teɪnjəslɪ]

[释义] ad. 自发地，自然地，本能地，
不由自主地

[同义] automatically, inherently,
instinctively, naturally

[反义] compulsorily

[同根] spontaneity [,spɒntə'niːɪtɪ]
n. ①自发性 ②自发动作
spontaneous [spɒn'teɪnjəs] a. ①自
发的 ②无意识的 ③自然的

▶▶ merely ['mɪəlɪ]

[释义] ad. 仅仅，只，不过

[同义] only, just, simply

▶▶ step back ①后退，后退一步 ②回
想，回顾

▶▶ all the while ad. 一直，始终

选项词汇注释

▶▶ **draw on** ①利用，吸收，动用 ②接近，靠近 ③招来，招致

▶▶ **distraction** [dɪs'trækʃən]

[释义] n. ①分心的事 ②娱乐，消遣 ③注意力分散，分心

[同义] interruption, disruption, disturbance

[同根] distract [dɪs'trækt] v. ①转移（注意力），分散（思想）②使转变 ③扰乱

distractive [dɪs'træktɪv] a. ①分散注意力的 ②使人困惑的

distracted [dɪs'træktɪd] a. ①思想不集中的 ②混乱的，困惑的

▶▶ **frustration** [frʌs'treɪʃən]

[释义] n. 挫败，挫折，使人失望的事

[同义] defeat, disturbance, annoyance

[反义] satisfaction, success

[同根] frustrate [frʌs'treɪt] v. ①挫败，阻挠 ②使灰心，使沮丧

▶▶ **constantly** ['kɒnstəntlɪ]

[释义] ad. ①经常地，不变地 ②坚持不懈地

[同义] continuously, always, all the time, frequently

[同根] constancy ['kɒnstənsɪ] n. ①坚定不移，始终如一 ②恒久不变的状态或性质

constant ['kɒnstənt] a. ①不变的，持续的 ②始终如一的 n. 常数，恒量

▶▶ **reject** [rɪ'dʒekt]

[释义] v. ①驳回，拒绝 ②抵制 ③丢弃 ④呕出 n. ①被拒之人，被弃之物 ②不合格品 ③落选者，不及格者

[同义] discard, eliminate, deny, decline

[反义] accept

[同根] rejection [rɪ'dʒekʃən] n. ①拒绝，退回，剔除 ②摈弃，厌弃 ③剔除物，呕出物

▶▶ **keep an eye on** 注意，密切注视，照看

Skimming and Scanning
Media Selection for Advertisements

After determining the target audience for a product or service, advertising agencies must select the appropriate media for the advertisement. We discuss here the major types of media used in advertising. We focus our attention on seven types of advertising: television, newspapers, radio, magazines, out-of-home, Internet, and direct mail.

Television

Television is an attractive medium for advertising because it delivers mass audiences to advertisers. When you consider that nearly three out of four Americans have seen the game show *Who Wants to Be a Millionaire*? you can understand the power of television to communicate with a large audience. When advertisers create a brand, for example, they want to impress consumers with the brand and its image. Television provides an ideal vehicle for this type of communication. But television is an expensive medium, and not all advertisers can afford to use it.

Television's influence on advertising is fourfold. First, narrowcasting means that television channels are seen by an increasingly narrow segment of the audience. The Golf Channel, for instance, is watched by people who play golf. Home and Garden Television is seen by those interested in household improvement projects. Thus, audiences are smaller and more *homogeneous* (具有共同特点的) than they have been in the past. Second, there is an increase in the number of television channels available to viewers, and thus, advertisers. This has also resulted in an increase in the sheer number of advertisements to which audiences are exposed. Third, digital recording devices allow audience members more control over which commercials they watch. Fourth, control over programming is being passed from the networks

to local cable operators and satellite programmers.

Newspapers

After television, the medium attracting the next largest annual ad **revenue** is newspapers. *The New York Times*, which reaches a national audience, **accounts for** $1 billion in ad revenue **annually**, It has **increased** its national **circulation by** 40% and is now available for home delivery in 168 cities. Locally, newspapers are the largest advertising medium.

Newspapers are a less expensive advertising medium than television and provide a way for advertisers to **communicate** a longer, more detailed message to their audience than they can through television. **Given** new production techniques, advertisements can be printed in newspapers in about 48 hours, meaning newspapers are also a quick way of getting the message **out**. Newspapers are often the most important form of news for a local community, and they develop a high degree of loyalty from local readers.

Radio

Advertising on radio continues to grow. Radio is often used **in conjunction with** outdoor **bill-boards** and the Internet to reach even more customers than television. Advertisers are likely to use radio because it is a less expensive medium than television, which means advertisers can afford to repeat their ads often. Internet companies are also turning to radio advertising. Radio provides a way for advertisers to communicate with audience members at all times of the day. Consumers listen to radio on their way to school or work, at work, on the way home, and in the evening hours.

Two major changes—satellite and Internet radio—will force radio advertisers to **adapt** their methods. Both of these radio forms allow listeners to **tune in** stations that are more distant than the local stations they could receive in the past. As a result, radio will increasingly attract target audiences who live many miles apart.

Magazines

Newsweeklies, women's titles, and business magazines have all seen increases in advertising because they attract the **high-end** market. Magazines **are popular with** advertisers because of the narrow market that they deliver.

A broadcast medium such as network television attracts all types of audience members, but magazine audiences are more homogeneous. If you read Sports *Illustrated*, for example, you **have much in common with** the magazine's other readers. Advertisers **see** magazines **as** an efficient way of reaching target audience members.

Advertisers using the print media—magazines and newspapers—will need to adapt to two main changes. First, the Internet will bring larger audiences to local newspapers. These audiences will be more **diverse** and geographically **dispersed** than in the past. Second, advertisers will have to understand how to use an increasing number of magazines for their target audiences. Although some magazines will maintain national audiences, a large number of magazines will entertain narrower audiences.

Out-of-home advertising

Out-of-home advertising, also called place-based advertising, has become an increasingly effective way of reaching consumers, who are more active than ever before. Many consumers today do not sit at home and watch television. Using billboards, **newsstands**, and bus shelters for advertising is an effective way of reaching these **on-the-go** consumers. More consumers travel longer distances to and from work, which also makes out-of-home advertising effective, technology has changed the nature of the billboard business, making it a more effective medium than in the past. Using **digital** printing, billboard companies can print a billboard in 2 hours, compared with 6 days **previously**. This allows advertisers more variety in the types of messages they create because they can change their messages more quickly.

Internet

As consumers become more comfortable with online shopping, advertisers will seek to reach this market. As consumers get more of their news and information from the Internet, the ability of television and radio to get the word out to consumers will decrease. The challenge to Internet advertisers is to create ads that audience members remember.

Internet advertising will play a more **prominent** role in organizations' advertising in the near future. Internet audiences tend to be quite homogeneous, but small. Advertisers will have to **adjust** their methods to reach these audiences and will have to adapt their **persuasive strategies** to the online medium as well.

Direct mail

A final advertising medium is direct mail, which uses **mailings** to consumers to communicate a **client**'s message. Direct mail includes **newsletters**, postcards and special **promotions**. Direct mail is an effective way to build relationships with consumers. For many businesses, direct mail is the most effective from of advertising.

文章词汇注释

▶▶ **agency** [ˈeɪdʒənsɪ]
[释义]] n. ①社，机构，（政府等的）专业行政部门 ②公众服务机构 ③代理行，经销处
[同根] agent [ˈeɪdʒənt] n. ①代理人，代理商 ②执法官，政府特工人员

▶▶ **appropriate** [əˈprəuprɪɪt]
[释义] a. 适当的，恰当的，相称的 [əˈprəuprɪeɪt] v. 拨给，拨出，挪用
[同义] suitable
[同根] appropriation [əˌprəuprɪˈeɪʃ ən] n. ①拨付，拨发，拨款 ②占用，挪用
appropriable [əˈprəuprɪəbl] a. 可供专用的，可供私用的
appropriately [əˈprəuprɪɪtlɪ] ad. 适当地
[词组] be appropriate to/for 适于，合乎

▶▶ **out-of-home** 一种方便离家在外的人获取信息的广告形式（OOH），如利用广告牌等

▶▶ **medium** [ˈmiːdjəm]
[释义] n. ①媒质，媒介物，传导体 ②中间（物），中庸，适中 ③手段，方法 a. 中间的，适中的，中等的

▶▶ **deliver** [dɪˈlɪvə]
[释义] v. ①交出，引渡 ②运送，投递，传递 ③发表，讲，宣布 ④排出，放出
[同根] delivery [dɪˈlɪvərɪ] n. ①递送，运送，传送 ②讲演，表演
deliverer [dɪˈlɪvərə] n. 递送人
[词组] deliver (oneself) of 讲，表达

▶▶ **brand** [brænd]
[释义] n. ①商标，（商品的）牌子 ②（独特的）一种，（自成一格的）一类
[同根] brand-new [brændˈnjuː] a. 全新的，崭新的

▶▶ **vehicle** [ˈviːɪkl]
[释义] n. ①工具，手段 ②交通工具，车辆，运载器

▶▶ **fourfold** [ˈfɔːfəuld]
[释义] a. ①有四部分的，四重的 ②四倍的 ad. 四倍地，四重地

▶▶ **narrowcasting** [ˈnærəuˈkɑːstɪŋ]
[释义] n. ①（为少量特定听众）小范围播送的（有线）电视节目 ②小范围播送；电缆电视播送

▶▶ **segment** [ˈsegmənt]
[释义] n. ①部分，部门 ②片断，环节 v. 分割，切割

[同义] division，fraction，subdivision

[同根] segmentation [ˌsegmən'teɪʃən] *n.* 分割，切断

▶▶ **available** [ə'veɪləbl]

[释义] *a.* ①可利用的，可获得的 ②在手边的 ③可取得联系的，有空的

[同义] convenient，obtainable，ready，handy

[反义] unavailable

[同根] avail [ə'veɪl] *v.* 有用于，有助于 *n.* (一般用于否定句或疑问句中) 效用，利益，帮助
availability [əˌveɪlə'bɪlɪti] *n.* 利用 (或获得) 的可能性，有效性

▶▶ **sheer** [ʃɪə]

[释义] *a.* ①绝对的，全然的，纯粹的 ② (织物) 透明的 ③陡峭的 *ad.* ①完全，全然 ②峻峭地

[同义] absolute

▶▶ **expose** [ɪks'pəʊz]

[释义] *v.* ①使面临，使接触 ②使暴露，揭露，揭示 ③使遭受，招致

[同根] exposure [ɪks'pəʊʒə] *n.* ①暴露，揭露，揭穿 ②曝晒 ③曝光

[词组] expose to 使暴露于，使接触，使遭受

▶▶ **commercial** [kə'mɜːʃəl]

[释义] *n.* 商业广告 *a.* ①商业的 ②商品的，商品化的

[同根] commerce ['kɒmə(ː)s] *n.* 商业，贸易
commercialize [kə'mɜːʃəlaɪz] *v.* 使商业化，使商品化

▶▶ **revenue** ['revɪnjuː]

[释义] *n.* 财政收入，税收

[同义] earnings，income

▶▶ **account for** ① (在数量或比例上) 占 ②解释，说明

▶▶ **annually** *ad.* ①年度地，每年地 ②一年一次地 ③全年地

[同根] annual *a.* ①每年的，年度的 ②一年一次的，一年一度的庆典 ③全年的 *n.* ①年报，年刊，年鉴

▶▶ **increase by** 增加了… (具体数字)

▶▶ **circulation** [ˌsɜːkju'leɪʃən]

[释义] *n.* ① (书报等的) 发行量，发行，(图书的) 流通量 ② (货币等的) 流通

[同根] circulate ['sɜːkjuleɪt] *v.* ①发行，销售 ② (使) 环行,(使) 环流,(使) 循环 ③流通
circulative ['sɜːkjuleɪtɪv] *a.* ①循环的，促进循环的 ②流通的
circulatory [sɜːkju'leɪtərɪ] *a.* (血液等) 循环的

▶▶ **communicate** [kə'mjuːnɪkeɪt]

[释义] *v.* ①传达，传送 ②通讯，交际，联络，通信

[同义] convey

[同根] communication [kəˌmjuːnɪ'keɪʃn] *n.* ①交流，交际 ②通信，通讯 ③传达，传播 ④信息
communicatee [kəˌmjuːnɪkə'tiː] *n.* 交流对象
communicative [kə'mjuːnɪkətɪv] *a.* ①乐意说的，爱说话的，不讳言的 ②通信的，交际的

▶▶ **given** *prep.* 考虑到 *a.* ①规定的，特定的 ②有癖好的，有倾向的 ③已知的，假设的

▶▶ **get...out** 使…传播出去，使…泄露

▶▶ **loyalty** ['lɔɪəltɪ]

[释义] *n.* ①忠诚，忠心 ②忠诚的行为

[同义] devotion, allegiance

[反义] disloyalty

[同根] loyal ['lɔɪəl] *a.* 忠诚的，忠心的
loyally ['lɔɪəlɪ] *ad.* 忠诚地

▶▶ **in conjunction with** 与…共同 (或协力)，连同

▶▶ **bill-board** [ˈbɪːbɔːd]

[释义] *n.* (户外) 告示牌，广告牌，招贴板，电视（或广告）节目开始时的插播 *v.* 宣传

▶▶ **adapt** [əˈdæpt]

[释义] *v.* ①使适应，使适合 ②改编，改写

[同义] adjust, alter, modify

[同根] adaptation [ˌædæpˈteɪʃən] *n.* ①适应，适合 ②改编，改写本
adaptable [əˈdæptəbl] *a.* ①能适应新环境的 ②可改编的

[词组] adapt...to... 使…适应…

▶▶ **tune in** ①（指收音机、电视机等）调整频率等以接收某一节目 ②与…建立无线电联系 ③使协调，使和谐

▶▶ **newsweekly** [ˈnjuːzˌwiːklɪ]

[释义] *n.* 周报，周刊

▶▶ **high-end** *a.* 深受老练的、识货的顾客喜爱的，有品位的，老练的；高端的

▶▶ **be popular with** 受…喜欢的，讨…欢心的

▶▶ **have much in common with** 与…有很多相同之处

▶▶ **see...as** 把…看作

▶▶ **diverse** [daɪˈvɜːs]

[释义] *a.* 不同的，多变化的

[同义] different, distinct, various

[反义] same, similar

[同根] diversity [daɪˈvɜːsɪtɪ] *n.* 差异，各式各样
diversify [daɪˈvɜːsɪfaɪ] *v.* 使不同，使多样化
divert [dɪˈvɜːt] *v.* ①使转向，使改道 ②转移，转移…的注意力 ③使娱乐，使消遣

▶▶ **disperse** [dɪsˈpɜːs]

[释义] *v.* ①（使）分散 ②（使）消散，驱散

[同义] distribute, scatter, spread

[同根] dispersion [dɪsˈpɜːʃən] *n.* 散布，驱散，传播，分散
dispersal [dɪsˈpɜːsəl] *n.* ①分散，疏散，散布，传播 ②消散
dispersive [dɪsˈpɜːsɪv] *a.* （趋向）分散的

▶▶ **newsstand** [ˈnjuːzstænd]

[释义] *n.* 报摊，报刊柜，报刊出售处

▶▶ **on-the-go** ①［口］在进行活动，不停工作的，忙碌的 ②刚要动身

▶▶ **digital** [ˈdɪdʒɪtl]

[释义] *a.* 数字的，数字显示的

▶▶ **previously** [ˈpriːvɪəslɪ]

[释义] *ad.* 先前，以前

[同义] before, earlier, formerly

[同根] previous [ˈpriːvɪəs] *a.* 在前的，早先的

▶▶ **prominent** [ˈprɒmɪnənt]

[释义] *a.* ①突出的，显著的 ②卓越的，杰出的 ②突起的

[同义] important, outstanding, celebrated, distinguished, eminent, famous

[反义] anonymous

[同根] prominence [ˈprɒmɪnəns] *n.* ①显著 ②突出 ③突出物
prominently [ˈprɒmɪnəntlɪ] *ad.* 卓越地，显眼

▶▶ **adjust** [əˈdʒʌst]

[释义] *v.* ①调整，调准，校正 ②整理，安排 ③使适合，符合

[同义] change, alter

[同根] adjustment [əˈdʒʌstmənt] *n.* ①调整，调节 ②调节器

▶▶ **persuasive** [pəˈsweɪsɪv]

[释义] *a.* 有说服力的，令人信服的

[同根] persuade [pəˈsweɪd] *v.* ①说服，

124

劝服 ②（使）相信

persuasion [pɜ:'sweɪʒən] *n.* ①说服，劝说 ②信念，信仰

persuadable [pə'sweɪdəbl] *a.* 可以说服的，容易说服的

▶▶ **strategy** ['strætɪdʒɪ]

[释义] *n.* 策略，战略，对策

[同根] strategic [strə'ti:dʒɪk] *a.* 战略（上）的 ②关键的

strategics [strə'ti:dʒɪks] *n.* 兵法

▶▶ **mailing** ['meɪlɪŋ]

[释义] *n.* 邮件；邮寄，邮递；（同时寄出的或由一名邮递员投递的）一批邮件

▶▶ **client** ['klaɪənt]

[释义] *n.* ①顾客，客户 ②委托人

[同义] customer，patron

▶▶ **newsletter** ['nju:zˌletə(r)]

[释义] *n.* 时事通讯，时事分析

▶▶ **promotion** [prə'məʊʃən]

[释义] *n.* ①（商品等的）推销运动，宣传，促销 ②提升，晋升 ③促进，发扬

[同根] promote [prə'məʊt] *v.* ①提升，晋升 ②促进，发扬

promotive [prəʊ'məʊtɪv] *a.* 提升的，促进的

promotee [prəməʊ'ti:] *n.* ①被提升者 ②获晋级者

promoter [prə'məʊtə] *n.* 促进者，助长者

选项词汇注释

▶▶ **in that**（在这一点上）因为，由于

▶▶ **appeal to** ①投合…的心意，引起…的兴趣 ②向…呼吁（请求）

▶▶ **build up one's reputation** 提高某人的声誉

▶▶ **affordable** [ə'fɔ:dəbl]

[释义] *a.* ①花费得起的，担负得起的 ②经受得住的

[同根] afford [ə'fɔ:d] *v.* ①担负得起费用，花费得起 ②经受得住 ③抽得出（时间）④给与，提供

▶▶ **access** ['ækses]

[释义] *n.* ①接近（或进入）的机会，享用的机会 ②接近，进入 ③入口，通道 *v.* ① [计] 存取，访问 ②接近，使用

[同根] accessible [ək'sesəbl] *a.* ①可（或易）得到的，易相处的 ②可（或易）接近（进入）的

▶▶ **convey** [kən'veɪ]

[释义] *v.* ①表达，传达 ②运送，输送 ③传播，传送

[同义] deliver，put into words，transport

[词组] convey...to... 把…送 / 转到…

▶▶ **revolutionize** [ˌrevə'lu:ʃənaɪz]

[释义] *v.* ①使发生革命性变化 ②向…灌输革命思想

[同根] revolve [rɪ'vɒlv] *v.* ①旋转 ②考虑 ③（与 around 连用）以…为中心

revolution [ˌrevə'lu:ʃən] *n.* 突破性进展，大变革

revolutionary ['revə'lu:ʃənərɪ] *a.* 大变革的，突破性的，完全创新的

▶▶ **update** [ʌp'deɪt]

[释义] *v.* ①更新，刷新…的内容，使现代化 ②为…提供最新消息 *n.* ①新的消息，新的情况 ②（最）新版,(最)新型

Reading in Depth
Section A

Some years ago I was offered a writing assignment that would require three months of travel through Europe. I had been abroad a couple of times, but I could hardly claim to know my way around the continent. Moreover, my knowledge of foreign languages was limited to a little college French.

I hesitated. How would I, unable to speak the language, totally unfamiliar with local geography or transportation systems, set up interviews and do research? It seemed impossible, and with considerable regret I sat down to write a letter begging off. Halfway through, a thought ran through my mind: *you can't learn if you don't try*. So I accepted the assignment.

There were some bad moments. But by the time I had finished the trip I was an experienced traveler. And ever since, I have never hesitated to head for even the most remote of places, without guides or even advanced bookings, confident that somehow I will manage.

The point is that the new, the different, is almost by definition scary. But each time you try something, you learn, and as the learning piles up, the world opens to you.

I've learned to ski at 40, and flown up the Rhine River in a balloon. And I know I'll go on doing such things. It's not because I'm braver or more daring than others. I'm not. But I'll accept anxiety as another name for challenge and I believe I can accomplish wonders.

文章词汇注释

▶▶▶ **claim** [kleɪm]
[释义] v. ①声称，断言 ②（对头衔、财产、名声等）提出要求 ③认领，声称有 n. ①声称，主张 ②要求，认领，索赔
[词组] lay claim to 对…提出所有权要求，自以为

▶▶▶ **be limited to...** 局限于…
▶▶▶ **set up** 安排，组织

▶▶▶ **beg off** ①恳求免除某种义务（或约束等）②为…说情
▶▶▶ **run through** ①回响，萦绕于 ②（使）流过 ③（使）穿透，（使）刺穿 ④贯穿，普遍存在于
▶▶▶ **ever since** 从那时起直至今日，此后一直
▶▶▶ **head for** ①（使）朝…行进，（使）走向 ②注定（…）要遭受

▶▶ **booking** [ˈbʊkɪŋ]

[释义] *n.* ①（座位、票等的）预订 ②预订票的出售 ③预约，（讲演、演出等的）约定

[同根] book [bʊk] *v.* ①预订，预雇，预约 ②接受…的预订，为…预订 ③为…预先安排时间，将…列入时间表

▶▶ **somehow** [ˈsʌmhaʊ]

[释义] *ad.* ①由于某种未知的原因，不知怎的 ②以某种方式，用某种方法，从某种角度

▶▶ **by definition** 按定义，按释义，按本质

▶▶ **scary** [ˈskeərɪ]

[释义] *a.* ①引起惊慌的，吓人的 ②易受惊的；胆怯的 ③惊恐的

[同根] scare [skeə] *v.* ①使惊恐，使害怕 ②吓走，吓跑 ③受惊吓 *n.* 惊恐，恐慌，恐惧

▶▶ **pile up** ①积累，积聚，（把…）堆积起来 ②（使船）搁浅，（汽车、飞机等）撞毁

▶▶ **daring** [ˈdeərɪŋ]

[释义] *a.* 大胆的，勇敢的，鲁莽的 *n.* 大胆，勇敢，胆量，冒险精神

[同义] brave, courageous, bold; bravery, courage, boldness

▶▶ **accomplish** [əˈkʌmplɪʃ]

[释义] *v.* ①成就，达到（目的），完成（任务），实现（计划、诺言等）②做到，做成，走完（距离等），度完（时间）

[同根] accomplishment [əˈkʌmplɪʃmənt] *n.* ①成就，成绩 ②［常作~s］造诣，技能 ③完成，实现 accomplished [əˈkʌmplɪʃt] *a.* ①完成了的，已实现的 ②熟练的，有造诣、才艺的

Section B
Passage One

Global warming may or may not be the great environmental crisis of the 21st century, but—**regardless of** whether it is or isn't—we won't do much about it. We will argue over it and may even, as a nation, make some fairly **solemn-sounding commitments** to avoid it. But the more **dramatic** and meaningful these commitments seem, the less likely they are to be **observed**.

Al Gore calls global warming an "**inconvenient** truth," as if **merely** recognizing it could **put us on a path to a solution**. But the real truth is that we don't know enough to **relieve** global warming, and—without major technological **breakthroughs**—we can't do much about it.

From 2003 to 2050, the world's population is **projected** to grow from 6.4 billon to 9.1 billion, a 42% increase. If energy use per person and technology remain the same, total energy use and greenhouse gas **emissions** (mainly, CO_2) will be 42% higher in 2050. But that's too low, because societies that grow richer use more energy. We need economic growth unless we **condemn** the world's poor to their present poverty and **freeze** everyone else's living standards. With **modest** growth, energy use and greenhouse emissions more than double by 2050.

No government will **adopt rigid restrictions** on economic growth and personal freedom (limits on electricity usage, driving and travel) that might **cut back** global warming. Still, politicians want to show they're "doing something." Consider the *Kyoto Protocol*（京都议定书）. It allowed countries that joined to punish those that didn't. But it hasn't reduced CO_2 emissions(up about 25% since 1990), and many *signatories*（签字国）didn't adopt **tough** enough policies to **hit** their 2008-2012 targets.

The practical conclusion is that if global warming is a **potential** disaster, the only solution is new technology. Only an **aggressive** research and development program might find ways of breaking our dependence on **fossil fuels** or dealing with it.

The trouble with the global warming debate is that it has become a moral problem when it's really an engineering one. The inconvenient truth is that if we don't solve the engineering problem, we're helpless.

文章词汇注释

▶▶▶ **regardless of** 不管，不顾

▶▶▶ **solemn-sounding** *a.*（听起来）庄严的，（听起来）严肃的，冠冕堂皇的

▶▶▶ **commitment** [kə'mɪtmənt]

[释义] *n.* ①承诺，许诺，保证，承担的义务 ②献身参与，介入 ③托付，交托 ④信奉，支持

[同根] commit [kə'mɪt] *v.* ①使承担义务，使做出保证 ②把…托付给，把…提交 ③犯（罪），做（错事、坏事、傻事等）

committed [kə'mɪtɪd] *a.* ①受委托的，承担义务的 ②忠诚的，忠于…的

▶▶▶ **dramatic** [drə'mætɪk]

[释义] *a.* ①引人注目的，突然的 ②戏剧性的，戏剧般的 ③戏剧的，剧本的

[同根] drama ['drɑːmə] *n.*（在舞台上演的）戏剧，戏剧艺术

dramatize ['dræmətaɪz] *v.* ①戏剧性描述，使引人注目 ②改编成剧本，使戏剧化

dramatization [ˌdræmətaɪ'zeɪʃən;-ɪ'z-] *n.* 戏剧化，改编成戏剧

dramatist ['dræmətɪst] *n.* 剧作家

▶▶▶ **observe** [əb'zɜːv]

[释义] ①遵守，奉行（规章、习俗等） ②观察，监视 ③看到，注意到，觉察到

▶▶▶ **inconvenient** [ˌɪnkən'viːnjənt]

[释义] *a.* ①令人感到麻烦的，令人为难的，不方便的 ②不适宜的

[同根] convenient [kən'vi:njənt] a. 便利的，方便的

inconvenient [ˌɪnkən'vi:njəns] n. 麻烦，不方便之处

convenience [kən'vi:njəns] n. ①便利 ②有益 ③方便的用具、安排等

▶▶ merely ['mɪəlɪ]

[释义] ad. 仅仅，只，不过

[同根] mere [mɪə] a. 只不过的，仅仅的

▶▶ put...on a path to a solution 使…找到解决问题的办法

▶▶ relieve [rɪ'li:v]

[释义] v. ①缓解，减轻，解除 ②救济，救援 ③接替

[反义] intensify

[同根] relief [rɪ'li:f] n. ①缓解，减轻，解除 ②宽心，宽慰 ③救济，解救

▶▶ breakthrough ['breɪk'θru:]

[释义] n. 突破

▶▶ project [prə'dʒekt]

[释义] v. ①根据现有资料）预测（结果）；推断 ②打算，计划 ③发射，投掷 ②投射，放映

['prɒdʒekt] n. ①工程,项目 ②计划,方案

[同义] predict; design, plan, program, scheme

[同根] projection [prə'dʒekʃən] n. ①设计，规划 ②发射 ③投射，投影

projector [prə'dʒektə] n. 放映机，投影机

projecting [prəu'dʒektɪŋ] a. 突出的，凸出的

[词组] project sth. onto the screen 把…投射到屏幕上

▶▶ emission [ɪ'mɪʃən]

[释义] n. ①（光、热、电波、声音、液体、气味等的）发出，散发 ②发出物，散发物

[同根] emit [ɪ'mɪt] v. 发出，散发（光、热、电、声音、液体、气味等），发射

▶▶ condemn [kən'dem]

[释义] v. ①谴责 ②宣告（某人）有罪 ③判（某人）刑 ④证明（某人）有罪

[同根] condemned [kən'demd] a. 被判罪的，受谴责的

condemnation [ˌkɒndem'neɪʃən] n. ①定罪，判罪；宣告有罪 ②谴责，非难，指责

▶▶ freeze [fri:z]

[释义] v. ①稳定，冻结 ②结冰，凝固，冻僵 ③变僵硬，变刻板，变得冷淡

[词组] freeze in 使冻住

freeze (on) to（口）紧紧抓住，依附于

freeze over（使）被冰覆盖

▶▶ modest ['mɒdɪst]

[释义] a. ①适中的，适度的 ②谦虚的，谦让的 ③端庄的，正派的 ④朴素的，朴实无华的

[同义] moderate, reasonable, humble, ordinary

[同根] modesty ['mɒdɪstɪ] n. ①适中，适度 ②谦虚，谦让 ③端庄，正派 ④朴素，朴实

▶▶ adopt [ə'dɒpt]

[释义] v. ①采用，采纳，采取 ②收养

[同义] take on, implement, approve

[同根] adopted [ə'dɒptɪd] a. ①被收养的 ②被采用的

adoption [ə'dɒpʃən] n. ①采用，采纳 ②收养

adoptive [ə'dɒptɪv] a. ①收养关系的 ②采用的

adopter [ə'dɒptə] n. ①养父母 ②采纳者，接受器

adoptee [ə'dɒpti:] n. 被收养者，被立嗣者

▶▶▶ **rigid** ['rɪdʒɪd]

[释义] *a.* ①严格的 ②刚硬的，刚性的 ③坚固的，僵硬的

[同义] strict

[同根] rigour ['rɪgə] *n.* ①严格，严厉 ②艰苦，严酷 ③严密，精确

rigorous ['rɪgərəs] *a.* ①严密的，缜密的 ②严格的，严厉的

▶▶▶ **restriction** [rɪs'trɪkʃən]

[释义] *n.* ①限制，限制，规定 ②约束因素

[同义] limit, constraint

[同根] restrict [rɪs'trɪkt] *v.* 限制，约束，限定

restricted [rɪs'trɪkt] *a.* ①受限制的，被限制的，有限的 ②不对公众开放的

restrictive [rɪs'trɪktɪv] *a.* 限制（性）的，约束（性）的

▶▶▶ **cut back** 减少，削减，缩减

▶▶▶ **tough** [tʌf]

[释义] *a.* ①强硬的，顽固的 ②激烈的，紧张的 ③强壮的，坚强的 ④困难的，艰苦的

[同义] rough, harsh, hard, difficult

[同根] toughness ['tʌfnɪs] *n.* 韧性，坚韧，刚性，健壮性

toughly ['tʌflɪ] *ad.* ①坚强地 ②固执地

▶▶▶ **hit** [hɪt]

[释义] *v.* ①达到，到达 ②打，击，打击 ③碰撞，使碰撞 ④袭击，使遭受

▶▶▶ **potential** [pə'tenʃəl]

[释义] *a.* 潜在的，可能的 *n.* ①潜能，潜力 ②潜在性，可能性

[同根] potentiality [pə,tenʃɪ'ælɪtɪ] *n.* ①可能性 ② [*pl.*] 潜能，潜力

potentially [pə'tenʃəlɪ] *ad.* 潜在地，可能地

▶▶▶ **aggressive** [ə'gresɪv]

[释义] *a.* ①积极进取的，攻击性的 ②侵略的，侵犯的，挑衅的 ③放肆的，过分自信的

[同根] aggress [ə'gres] *v.* 侵犯，侵略，挑衅

aggression [ə'greʃən] *n.* ①侵犯，侵略，挑衅 ②侵犯行为，侵略行为

aggressively [ə'gresɪvlɪ] *ad.* 侵略地，侵犯地

▶▶▶ **fossil fuel** 矿物燃料

选项词汇注释

▶▶▶ **be unaware of** 不清楚，不知道，没意识到

▶▶▶ **contribute to** 有助于

▶▶▶ **moral issue** 道德问题

▶▶▶ **ultimate** ['ʌltɪmɪt]

[释义] *a.* ①最后的，最终的 ②极点的，终极的 *n.* ①最终的事物，基本事实 ②终点，结局

[同义] last

[同根] ultimately ['ʌltɪmətlɪ] *ad.* 最后，终于

▶▶▶ **lie in** ①在于 ②待产 ③睡懒觉

Passage Two

Someday a stranger will read your e-mail without your permission or scan the Website you've visited. Or perhaps someone will casually glance through your credit card purchases or cell phone bills to find out your shopping preferences or calling habits.

In fact, it's likely some of these things have already happened to you. Who would watch you without your permission? It might be a spouse, a girlfriend, a marketing company, a boss, a cop or a criminal. Whoever it is, they will see you in a way you never intended to be seen—the 21st century equivalent of being caught naked.

Psychologists tell us boundaries are healthy, that it's important to reveal yourself to friends, family and lovers in stages, at appropriate times. But few boundaries remain. The digital bread *crumbs*（碎屑）you leave everywhere make it easy for strangers to reconstruct who you are, where you are and what you like. In some cases, a simple Google search can reveal what you think. Like it or not, increasingly we live in a world where you simply cannot keep a secret.

The key question is: Does that matter?

For many Americans, the answer apparently is "no."

When opinion polls ask Americans about privacy, most say they are concerned about losing it. A survey found an overwhelming pessimism about privacy, with 60 percent of respondents saying they feel their privacy is "slipping away, and that bothers me."

But people say one thing and do another. Only a tiny fraction of Americans change any behaviors in an effort to preserve their privacy. Few people turn down a discount at *tollbooths*（收费站）to avoid using the EZ-Pass system that can track automobile movements. And few turn down supermarket loyalty cards. Privacy economist Alessandro Acquisti has run a series of tests that reveal people will surrender personal information like Social Security numbers just to get their hands on a pitiful 50-cents-off *coupon*（优惠券）.

But privacy does matter—at least sometimes. It's like health: When you have it, you don't notice it. Only when it's gone do you wish you'd done more to protect it.

文章词汇注释

▶▶ **scan** [skæn]

[释义] *n.* ①浏览，粗略一看 ②细看，审视 ③扫描 *v.* ①扫描 ②细看，反复查看，审视 ③粗略地看，浏览，快读

▶▶ **casually** ['kæʒjʊəlɪ]

[释义] *ad.* 偶然地，随便地，临时地

[同根] casual ['kæʒjʊəl] *a.* ①偶然的，碰巧的 ②非正式的，随便的 ③临时的，不定期的

▶▶ **glance** [glɑ:ns]

[释义] *v.* ①看一眼，瞥 ②闪烁，闪耀，擦过，③掠过，简略提及 *n.* ①一瞥，扫视 ②闪光，闪烁 ③擦过，掠过

[词组] glance at / down / over / through 看一眼，瞥，扫视

glance one's eye down/over/through sth 匆匆或草草看某物一眼

glance off 擦过，掠过

at first glance/sight 乍一看，最初看到时

▶▶ **spouse** [spauz]

[释义] *n.* 配偶（指夫或妻）

▶▶ **marketing** ['mɑ:kɪtɪŋ]

[释义] *n.* ①销售，营销 ②（市场上的）交易，买卖 ③销售学

▶▶ **equivalent** [ɪ'kwɪvələnt]

[释义] *n.* 对应词，相等物，等价物 *a.* ①相等的，相同的，相当的 ②等价的，等值的，等效的

[同根] equivalence [ɪ'kwɪvələns] *n.* （数量、力量、意义、重要性等的）相等，等价，等效

▶▶ **naked** ['neɪkɪd]

[释义] *a.* ①裸露的，光秃的 ②衣不蔽体的，赤贫的 ③暴露的，显露的 ④无保护的，赤手空拳的

▶▶ **boundary** ['baundərɪ]

[释义] *n.* 界限，分界线，边界

[同义] border, bound, division

[同根] bound [baund] *n.* [常作复数] 边界，界限，界线，限制，范围 *a.* (bind 的过去式和过去分词) ①被束缚的 ②受束缚的 ③一定的，必然的，注定了的 *v.* ①跳，跃，弹回 ②限制，定…的界限，成为…界限 ③ (for, to) 准备到…去，正在到…去 boundless ['baundlɪs] *a.* 无限的，无边无际的

▶▶ **reveal** [rɪ'vi:l]

[释义] *v.* ①暴露，透露 ②揭示，揭露 ③展现，显示

[同义] expose, disclose, unfold

[同根] revelation [ˌrevɪ'leɪʃən] *n.* 揭示，揭露，暴露，泄露

▶▶ **reconstruct** ['ri:kən'strʌkt]

[释义] *v.* ①重建，改建，改组，（根据证据或想像）重现（存在过的或发生过的事物）②（按原样）修复

[同根] construct [kən'strʌkt] *v.* ①制造，建造，构造 ②创立 construction [kən'strʌkʃən] *n.* ①建设，修筑 ②建筑物，构造物 constructive [kən'strʌktɪv] *a.* ①建设性的，起改进或提高作用的，有帮助的 ②结构上的

▶▶ **like it or not** 不管你喜欢不喜欢

▶▶ **poll** [pəul]

[释义] *n.* ①民意测验 ②[常用复数] 政治选举，大选 *v.* ①对…进行民意测验 ②投票 ③得票，获（某特定数

目的）选票

[同义] questionnaire，survey

▶▶ **privacy** ['praɪvəsɪ]

[释义] n. ①隐私，私生活 ②秘密，私下 ③隐居，独处，清净

[同义] intimacy，secrecy

[反义] publicity

[同根] private ['praɪvɪt] a. ①私人的，私有的 ②秘密的 n. 士兵，列兵

privately ['praɪvɪtlɪ] ad. ①私人地，私有地 ②秘密地

[词组] in privacy 隐避的，秘密地

in the privacy of one's thoughts 在内心深处

in strict privacy 完全私下的

live in privacy 过隐居生活

▶▶ **survey** [sɜ:'veɪ; 'sɜ:veɪ]

[释义] n. ①调查，调查报告，民意测验 ②勘查，测勘 ③概括论述 v. ①调查（收入、民意等）勘定，检验 ②测量，测绘

[同义] investigation，review，study，examination

[词组] make a survey of ①测量，勘察 ②对…作全面的调查 / 观察

▶▶ **overwhelming** [ˌəʊvə'welmɪŋ]

[释义] a. 压倒性的，势不可挡的，莫大的

[同根] overwhelm ['əʊvə'welm] v. ①征服，制服 ②压倒，淹没 ③使受不了，使不知所措

overwhelmingly [ˌəʊvə'welmɪŋlɪ] ad. 势不可挡地，压倒性地

▶▶ **pessimism** ['pesɪmɪzm]

[释义] n. ①悲观情绪，悲观 ②悲观主义

[反义] optimism

[同根] pessimistic [ˌpesɪ'mɪstɪk] a. ①悲观的 ②悲观主义的

pessimist ['pesɪmɪst] n. ①悲观者 ②悲观主义者

▶▶ **respondent** [rɪs'pɒndənt]

[释义] n. ①（民意测验等的）调查对象 ②回答者，相应者 ③反映，反射 a. ①回答的，应答的，反射的 ②（对外部刺激）反应，反射

[同根] respond [rɪs'pɒnd] v. ①回答，作答 ②响应，作出反应

response [rɪs'pɒns] n. ①回答，答复 ②响应，反应

respondence [rɪs'pɒndəns] n. ①回答，答复 ②反应，响应

responsible [rɪs'pɒnsəbl] a. ①有责任的，应负责任的 ②有责任感的 ③作为原由的

responsibility [rɪsˌpɒnsə'bɪlɪtɪ] n. ①责任，负责的状态 ②责任心 ③职责，义务

▶▶ **slip away** 悄然逝去，不知不觉地失掉

▶▶ **fraction** ['frækʃən]

[释义] n. ①一部分，小部分，片段 ②些微，一点儿 ③割 ④分数，小数 v. 把…分成几部分，使分开

[同根] fractional ['frækʃənl] a. ①部分的，局部的，碎片的 ②少量的，短暂的 ③分数的，小数的

[词组] a fraction of 一小部分

a fraction of a second 转瞬间，顷刻

▶▶ **in an effort to do** 想干…

▶▶ **preserve** [prɪ'zɜ:v]

[释义] v. ①保存，保留 ②保持，保守 ③保护，保养 ④保藏、加工食品 n. ①[pl.]（用腌制等方法）加工成的食品 ②动植物保护区 ③防护用品

[同义] guard

[反义] destroy，ruin

[同根] preserved [prɪ'zɜ:vd] a. ①保护好的，保养好的 ②保存好的，保留好的

preservation [ˌprezə'veɪʃən] n. ①保

护，保养 ②保持，保守 ③保存，保留 ④保藏，（食品的）耐藏加工
preservative [prɪˈzɜːvətɪv] a. ①有保护能力的，保护性的 ②有保存能力的 ③有助于保藏的 n. 防腐剂，保护剂
[词组] preserve sth. from... 保护…不受…

▶▶ **turn down** ①拒绝 ②使颠倒 ③关小 ④（金融）低落，下降

▶▶ **discount** [ˈdɪskaunt]
[释义] n. 折扣 v. 打折扣

▶▶ **track** [træk]
[释义] v. 追踪，跟踪 n. 足迹，踪迹，（飞机、轮船等的）航迹，车辙
[同义] trace，trail
[词组] on the right/ wrong track 循着正确/错误的路线，正确/错误地
track down 跟踪找到，追捕到，追查

到，搜寻到

▶▶ **surrender** [səˈrendə]
[释义] v. ①交出，放弃，让出 ②使投降，使自首 ③使沉溺于 n. ①投降，自首 ②放弃，交出
[同义] give up
[反义] resist

▶▶ **get one's hands on** 把…弄到手

▶▶ **pitiful** [ˈpɪtɪful]
[释义] a. ①可怜的，令人同情的 ②可鄙的
[同根] pity [ˈpɪtɪ] n. ①同情，怜悯，可怜 ②可惜，遗憾，遗憾的事，可惜（或遗憾）的原因 v. 同情，怜悯，可怜
pitiless [ˈpɪtɪlɪs] a. 无情的

选项词汇注释

▶▶ **try every means** 想方设法，竭尽全力
▶▶ **look into** ①调查，观察 ②朝…里面看 ③浏览（书籍等）
▶▶ **be frank with** 坦诚相待
▶▶ **on the spot** ①当场，在现场 ②立刻 ③处于困难境地

▶▶ **faithful** [ˈfeɪθful]
[释义] a. ①忠诚的，忠实的，守信的 ②尽职的，认真的
[同义] loyal
[反义] faithless，disloyal，unfaithful
[同根] faith [feɪθ] n. ①信任，信念，信赖 ②信仰上帝，宗教信仰
faithfulness [ˈfeɪθfulnɪs] n. 忠诚
faithless [ˈfeɪθlɪs] a. 背信弃义的，不忠的，不忠实的

▶▶ **dispute** [dɪsˈpjuːt]
[释义] n. 争端，争论，辩论，纠纷 v. ①对表示异议，反对 ②争论，辩论
[同义] arguement
[词组] in / under dispute 在争论中，处于争议中

▶▶ **evolve** [ɪˈvɒlv]
[释义] v. （使）进化，（使）发展，（使）进展
[同义] develop，grow，advance
[同根] evolution [ˌiːvəˈluːʃən，ˌevə-] n. ①进化，演变 ②进展，发展
evolutionary [ˌiːvəˈluːʃənərɪ] a. 进化的
evolutionism [ˌiːvəˈluːʃənɪzəm] n. 进化论
evolutionist [ˌiːvəˈluːʃənɪst] n. 进化论者

▶▶▶ **trace** [treɪs]

[释义] *n.* 痕迹，踪迹，足迹，遗迹
　　v. 追踪，跟踪

[同义] track，trail

[词组] trace back to 追溯到，追究到，
　　追查到
　　trace out 探寻踪迹

▶▶▶ **be curious about sth.** 对（某事物）
感到好奇

▶▶▶ **identity** [aɪˈdentɪtɪ]

[释义] *n.* ①身份 ②个性，特性 ③同
　　一性

[同根] identical [aɪˈdentɪkəl] *a.* 同一
　　的，同样的
　　identify [aɪˈdentɪfaɪ] *v.* 识别，鉴别，
　　确定
　　identification [aɪˌdentɪfɪˈkeɪʃən]
　　n. ①鉴定，验明，认出 ②身份证明

▶▶▶ **with regard to** 关于，至于，在…方面

▶▶▶ **disclose** [dɪsˈkləuz]

[释义] *v.* ①泄露，揭露，透露 ②使显露

[同义] reveal，uncover

[反义] conceal，hide

[同根] disclosure [dɪsˈkləuʒə] *n.* ① 揭
　　发，泄露，透露，公开 ②揭发的事实

▶▶▶ **transaction** [trænˈzækʃən]

[释义] *n.* ①（一笔）交易，业务 ②办理，
　　处理

[同义] business

[同根] transact [trænˈzækt,-ˈsækt]
　　v. 办理，交易，处理，商议

▶▶▶ **electronic devices** 电子设备

▶▶▶ **make every effort** 尽一切努力

▶▶▶ **cherish** [ˈtʃeriʃ]

[释义] *v.* ①珍爱，珍视 ②爱护，抚育
　　③抱有，怀有（希望、想法、感情等）

[同义] treasure，value

[反义] ignore，neglect

Skimming and Scanning
That's enough, kids

It was a lovely day at the park and Stella Bianchi was enjoying the sunshine with her two children when a young boy, aged about four, approached her two-year-old son and pushed him to the ground.

"I'd watched him for a little while and my son was the fourth or fifth child he'd shoved." she says, "I went over to them, picked up my son, turned to the boy and said, firmly, 'No, we don't push.' What happened next was unexpected.

"The boy's mother ran toward me from across the park." Stella says. "I thought she was coming over to apologize, but instead she started shouting at me for 'disciplining her child'. All I did was let him know his behavior was unacceptable. Was I supposed to sit back while her kid did whatever he wanted, hurting other children in the process?"

Getting your own children to play nice is difficult enough. Dealing with other people's children has become a minefield.

In my house, jumping on the sofa is not allowed. In my sister's house it's encouraged. For her, it's about kids being kids: "If you can't do it at three, when can you do it?"

Each of these philosophies is valid and, it has to be said, my son loves visiting his aunt's house. But I find myself saying "no" a lot when her kids are over at mine. That's OK between sisters but becomes dangerous territory when you're talking to the children of friends or acquaintances.

"Kids aren't all raised the same." agrees Professor Naomi White of Monash University. "But there's still an idea that they're the property of the parents. We see our children as an extension of ourselves, so if you're saying that my child is behaving inappropriately, then that's somehow a criticism of me."

In those circumstances, it's difficult to know whether to approach the child directly or the parent first. There are two schools of thought.

"I'd go to the first." says Andrew Fuller, author of *Tricky Kids,* "Usually a quiet reminder that 'we don't do that here' is enough. Kids have finely tuned antennae for how to behave in different settings."

He points out that bringing it up with the parent first may make them feel neglectful, which could cause problems. Of course, approaching the child first can bring its own headaches, too.

This is why White recommends that you approach the parents first. "Raise your concerns with the parents if they're there and ask them to deal with it." she says.

Asked how to approach a parent in this situation, psychologist Meredith Fuller answers: "Explain your needs as well as stressing the importance of the friendship. Preface your remarks with something like: 'I know you'll think I'm silly but in my house I don't want...'"

When it comes to situations where you're caring for another child, White is straightforward: "Common sense must prevail. If things don't go well, then have a chat."

There're a couple of new grey areas. Physical punishment, once accepted from any adult, is no longer appropriate. "Now you can't do it without feeling uneasy about it." White says.

Men might also feel uneasy about dealing with other people's children. "Men feel nervous," White says. "A new set of considerations has come to the fore as part of the debate about how we handle children."

For Andrew Fuller, the child-centric nature of our society has affected everyone. "The rules are different now from when today's parents were growing up," he says. "Adults are scared of saying, 'Don't swear' or asking a child to stand up on a bus. They're worried that there will be conflict if they point these things out---either from older children, or their parents."

He sees it as a loss of the sense of common public good and public courtesy, and says that adults suffer from it as much as children.

Meredith Fuller agrees, "A code of conduct is hard to create when you're living in a world in which everyone is exhausted from overwork and lack of sleep, and a world in which nice people are perceived to finish last."

"It's about what I'm doing and what I need," Andrew Fuller says. "The days when a kid came home from school and said, 'I got into trouble.' and dad said, 'you probably **deserved** it', are over. Now the parents are **charging up to** the school to **have a go at** teachers."

This jumping to our children's defense is part of what **fuels** the "walking on eggshells" feeling that surrounds our dealings with other people's children. You know that if you **remonstrate** with the child, you're going to have to deal with the parent. It's admirable to **be protective of** our kids, but is it good?

"Children have to learn to **negotiate** the world on their own, within reasonable **boundaries**," White says. "I suspect that it's only certain sectors of the population doing the running to the school—better-educated parents are probably more likely to be too **involved**."

White believes our **notions** of a more child-centered society should be challenged. "Today we have a situation where, in many families, both parents work, so the amount of time children get from parents has **diminished**," she says.

"Also, sometimes when we talked about being children-centred, it's a way of talking about treating our children like **commodities**. We're centred on them but in ways that **reflect** positively on us. We treat them as objects whose appearance and achievements are something we can be proud of, rather than serve the best interests of the children."

One way over-worked, **under-resourced** parents show **commitment** to their children is to **leap to their defence**. Back at the park, Bianchi's *intervention*（干预）**on her son's behalf** ended in an **undignified** exchange of **insulting** words with the other boy's mother.

As Bianchi approached the park bench where she'd been sitting, other mums came up to her and congratulated her on **taking a stand**. "Apparently the boy had a longstanding reputation for bad behavior and his mum for even worse behavior if he was challenged."

Andrew Fuller doesn't believe that we should be afraid of dealing with other people's kids. "Look at kids that aren't your own as a **potential** minefield," he says. He recommends that we don't stay silent over inappropriate behavior, particularly with regular visitors.

文章词汇注释

▶▶▶ **shove** [∫ʌv]

[释义] v.① (使劲) 推，挤，撞 ②强使

[同义] push, ram, thrust

[词组] shove along 推着走

shove around ①推来推去 ②使唤来唤去

shove in 推进

shove off ①把船撑开 ②[美俚] 乘船离开 ③分别，走掉

shove on 推着往前走

shove one's clothes on [口] 穿上衣服

shove publicity 指挥宣传

▶▶▶ **discipline** ['dɪsɪplɪn]

[释义] v.① 惩罚，惩戒 ②训练，操练 ③使有纪律

n.①纪律，风纪，行为准则 ②（智力，道德的）训练，训导，③学科

[同义] v.① penalize, punish ② drill, exercise, practice, train

[同根] disciplined ['dɪsɪplɪnd] n. 受过训练的，遵守纪律的

disciplinary ['dɪsɪplɪnərɪ] a.①训练的 ②有关纪律的 ③学科的

[词组] academic discipline ①学科 ②学习纪律

active discipline ①自觉纪律 ②积极训练

character discipline 性格锻炼

classroom discipline 课室秩序

compulsory discipline 必修学科

financial discipline 财务纪律

▶▶▶ **sit back** ①不采取行动 ②休息一下

▶▶▶ **minefield** ['maɪnfi:ld]

[释义] n. 布雷区，充满隐伏危险的事物

▶▶▶ **valid** ['vælɪd]

[释义] a.①（指论据、理由等）正确的，有根据的 ②（法律上）有效的

[反义] false, invalid

[同根] validate ['vælɪdeɪt] v. 使生效，证实

validity [və'lɪdɪtɪ] n.①（法律上）有效，合法 ②合逻辑，正确

[词组] valid evidence 确凿的证据

be valid for two weeks 有效期两周

▶▶▶ **extension** [ɪks'ten∫ən]

[释义] n.①延伸、延长、(扩大，附加) 部分 ②延长，扩张 ③（电话）分机

[反义] ① & ② intension , contraction

[同根] extend [ɪk'stend] v.①延长，延期 ②伸，伸展，拉开 ③扩大，扩充，扩展

extensive [ɪk'stensɪv] a.①广阔的，广泛的 ②全面的，彻底的，大量的

extent [ɪk'stent] n.①范围，广度，长度 ②程度，限度

[词组] extension to …的延长、扩建部分

▶▶▶ **inappropriately** [ˌɪnə'prəʊprɪɪtlɪ]

[释义] ad. 不适当的，不相宜的，不相称的

[反义] properly, suitably

[同根] appropriate [ə'prəʊprɪɪt] a. 适合的，恰当的，相称的

[ə'prəʊprɪeɪt] v.①挪用，占用 ②拨出（款项）

appropriable [ə'prəʊprɪəbl] a. 可供专用的，可供私用的

appropriateness [ə'prəʊprɪɪtnɪs] n. 恰当，适当

appropriation [əˌprəʊprɪ'eɪ∫ən] n.①拨付，拨发，拨款 ②占用，挪用

▶▶▶ **in those circumstances** 在那种情况下

▶▶▶ **approach** [ə'prəʊt∫]

[释义] v. ①靠近，接近，与…打交道 ②探讨，看待，处理
n. ①靠近，接近 ②探讨，态度，方法
[同义] v. access, advance, come near
n. way, method, means
[反义] v. leave, part, separate
[同根] approachable [əˈprəʊtʃəb(ə)l] a. ①可接近的 ②易接近的，随和的
[词组] at the approach of… 在…快到的时候
be approaching (to)… 与…差不多，大致相等
make an approach to… 对…进行探讨
approach sb. on/about sth. 和某人接洽/商量/交涉某事
approach to… ①接近 ②近似，约等于

▶ school [sku:l]
[释义] n. ①学派，流派 ②（鱼及水族动物）群，队
[词组] a school of thought 有类似观点的一批人，学派
one of the old school 老派人物，保守人物

▶ reminder [rɪˈmaɪndə]
[释义] n. ①提醒者，令人回忆的东西，纪念品 ②提示、暗示，信号，通知
[同根] remind [rɪˈmaɪnd] v. 使想起/记起，提醒 (of, that, how)

▶ tune [tju:n; (US) tu:n]
[释义] v. ①调整（收音机的波长或周率等），收听，为（乐器）调音 ②使和谐，使一致，调整，调节 n. ①曲调，旋律 ②调和，和谐 ③声调，语调
[同根] tunefulness [ˈtju:nfʊlnɪs] n. 曲调优美，音律和谐
tuneful [ˈtju:nfʊl] a. 悦耳动听的，曲调优美的
tuneless [ˈtju:nlɪs] a. 不成调的，不和谐的，不悦耳的

[词组] dance to sb.'s tune 跟着某人的指挥棒转，唯某人之命是从
in tune (with) 合调，合谐，和睦
keep...in tune 使…保持正常状态
out of tune 不合调，走调
put in tune 校准…音调
tune in 收听…，收看…，调准收音机的波长，调准电视机的频道，调谐，调入

▶ antennae [ænˈtenə]
[释义] n. [常用复] 直觉 (pl. antennas)，[无] 天线（英国一般用 aerial），(pl. -nae [-nɪ:]) [动] 触角，触须

▶ neglectful [nɪˈglektfʊl]
[释义] a. 疏忽的，不受注意的
[同根] neglect [nɪˈglekt] v.&n. 忽视，疏忽，漏做
negligent [ˈneglɪdʒənt] a. 疏忽的，粗心大意的
negligence [ˈneglɪdʒəns] n. 疏忽
negligible [ˈneglɪdʒəbl] a. 可忽略不计的
[词组] to be neglectful of one's duty 玩忽职守

▶ preface [ˈprefɪs]
[释义] vt. ①开始，导致 ②给…作序，作为…的开端 n. 序，绪言、前言，引语，开端
[同根] prefatory [ˈprefətərɪ] a. 前言的，序文的
[词组] preface with /by doing sth. 以某事为开场白，在讲主要问题之前先讲某事

▶ straightforward [streɪtˈfɔ:wəd]
[释义] a. ①坦白的，坦诚的 ②易懂的，直截了当的，简单明 ad. ①坦率地，直接地
[同义] frank

▶ common sense 常识（尤指判断力）

▶▶ **prevail** [prɪ'veɪl]

[释义] v. ①胜过，压倒，占优势 (over, against)，成功，奏效 ②流行，盛行，风行，普及，传开

[同义] reign, rule, predominate, triumph

[同根] prevailing [prɪ'veɪlɪŋ] a. ①流行的，盛行的 ②优势的，主要的，有力的

prevalence ['prevələns] n. 流行，盛行，普及，广泛

prevalent ['prevələnt] a. 普遍的，流行的，盛行的

[词组] prevailing trends 流行趋势

prevailing wind 盛行风

▶▶ **grey area** [英] 灰色地区（指就业率低但又没有贫困到能申请政府特别救济的地区）

▶▶ **come to the fore** ①涌现出来，惹人注意 ②走到前面来 ③发作

▶▶ **child-centric** 以孩子为中心的

▶▶ **be scared of** 害怕…

▶▶ **swear** [sweə]

[释义] v. ①诅咒，咒骂 ②宣誓，发誓 ③保证说，肯定地说

[同义] ① curse ② promise

[同根] swearword ['sweəwɜːd] n. 诅咒，骂人的话

[词组] be sworn in (to office) 宣誓就职

swear against 指控（某人）并起誓所控属实

swear by ①以（…名义）起誓，以（人格）担保 ② [口] 非常信赖，肯定，确定

swear for 保证，担保

swear on 凭…起誓

swear sb. to sth. 使某人发誓做某事

swear to sth. 保证某事，肯定某事

▶▶ **courtesy** ['kɜːtɪsɪ]

[释义] n. ①礼貌，礼节，亲切 ②恩惠，允许 ③礼貌的行为，殷勤的举动

[同义] politeness

[反义] discourtesy

[同根] courteous ['kɜːtjəs] a. 有礼貌的，谦恭的

[词组] by courtesy ①按惯例，礼貌上，[美] 情面上 ②为表示礼貌起见，承蒙好意

by courtesy of ①经…同意，承…好意赠送 ②由…提供，经由…的途径

stand at the courtesy of 有赖于…的宽容或好意

▶▶ **code of conduct** ①行动守则 ②管理法典

▶▶ **perceive** [pə'siːv]

[释义] v. ①认为，理解，领悟 ②察觉，感知，感到，认识到

[同义] ① view, think ② sense, discover, realize

[同根] perception [pə'sepʃən] n. ①感知，感觉 ②认识，看法，洞察力

perceptive [pə'septɪv] a. 有感知能力的，有洞察力的，理解的

▶▶ **deserve** [dɪ'zɜːv]

[释义] v. 应得，值得，应受

[同根] deserved [dɪ'zɜːvd] a. 应得的，理所当然的

deserving [dɪ'zɜːvɪŋ] a. ①有功的，该受奖赏的 ②值得的，该得的 (of)

[词组] deserve ill of 有罪于

deserve well of 有功于

▶▶ **charge up to** ①把…归咎于 ②把…记入帐册

▶▶ **have a go at** ①批评，攻击 ②企图，尝试（做某事）

▶▶ **fuel** [fjuəl]

[释义] v. ①激起，刺激，推动 ②加燃料，给…加油 n. 燃料

[词组] add fuel to the flames/fire 火上加油

fuel up ①加燃料 ③填肚子，吃喝

▶▶ remonstrate [rɪ'mɒnstreɪt]
[释义] v. ①忠告，规劝，劝诫 (with, on, upon) ②抗议 (against)
[同根] remonstration [ˌrɪmɒns'treɪʃ(ə)n] n. ①忠告，规劝，劝诫 ②抗议

▶▶ be protective of... 给予…保护的，对…保护的

▶▶ negotiate [nɪ'gəʊʃɪeɪt]
[释义] v. ①成功地应付 ②（与某人）商议，谈判，磋商，买卖②让渡（支票、债券等）
[同根] negotiation [nɪˌgəʊʃɪ'eɪʃ(ə)n] n. ①谈判，协商 ②（票据的）转让，流通
negotiable [nɪ'gəʊʃjəbl] a. 可通过谈判解决的

▶▶ boundary ['baʊndərɪ]
[释义] n. ①界线，范围②边界，境界，分界线
[同义] border, bound, division
[同根] bound [baʊnd] n.（常作复数）边界，界限，界线，限制，范围 a. (bind 的过去式和过去分词)①被束缚的 ②受束缚的 ③一定的，必然的，注定了的
v. ①跳，跃，弹回 ②限制，定…的界限，成为…界限
boundless ['baʊndlɪs] a. 无限的，无边无际的

▶▶ involve [ɪn'vɒlv]
[释义] v. ①影响，涉及，与…直接有关 ②包含，包括，需要 ③专心于，忙于
[同义] include, encompass, contain, embrace
[同根] involved [ɪn'vɒlvd] a. ①有关的 ②混乱的，复杂的
involvement [ɪn'vɒlvmənt] n. ①卷入，

牵连 (in, with) ②复杂，混乱 ③牵涉到的事务，复杂的情况
involuntary [ɪn'vɒləntərɪ; (US) -terɪ] a. 无意的，不由自主的，不自觉的
[词组] be involved in ①与…关系密切的 ②与…有牵连的

▶▶ notion ['nəʊʃ(ə)n]
[释义] n. ①概念，观念，感知，理念 ②看法，见解
[同义] belief, idea, opinion, thought, view
[同根] notional ['nəʊʃənəl] a. 概念的，感知的

▶▶ diminish [dɪ'mɪnɪʃ]
[释义] v. 减少，缩小，降低
[同义] curtail, cut, decrease, lessen, reduce
[反义] increase, raise
[同根] diminished [dɪ'mɪnɪʃt] a. 减少了的，缩小了的
diminishable [dɪ'mɪnɪʃəbl] a. 可减少的，可缩减的，可降低的
diminishingly [dɪ'mɪnɪʃɪŋlɪ] ad. 逐渐减小地

▶▶ commodity [kə'mɒdɪtɪ]
[释义] n. ①商品，货物②农产品，矿产品③有用的东西，用品
[同义] article, product, goods
[同根] commerce ['kɒmə(ː)s] n. 商业
commercial [kə'mɜːʃ(ə)l] a. 商业的，商务的 n.（广播、电视的）商业广告
commercialize [kə'mɜːʃəlaɪz] v. 使商业化
commercialism [kə'mɜːʃə'lɪzəm] n. 商业主义，重商主义，商业精神
[词组] a commodity of brown paper 廉价处理的次品，不值钱的货，无用的东西

▶▶ reflect [rɪ'flekt]
[释义] v. ①深思，考虑，反省 (on) ②反射（光，热，声等）③反映，表明

[同义] ① consider, contemplate, meditate, ponder, deliberate

[同根] reflective [rɪ'flektɪv] a. ①反射的，反照的，反映的 ②思考的，沉思的

reflection [rɪ'flekʃən] n. ①映像 ②反射，反照，反响 ③深思，考虑，反省

▶▶ under-resourced 财力不足的

▶▶ commitment [kə'mɪtmənt]

[释义] n. ①责任，义务 ②承诺，约定，约束 ③托付，交托

[同义] promise

[同根] commit [kə'mɪt] v. ①犯（罪），做（错事等）②把…交托给 ③使做出保证

committee [kə'mɪtɪ] n. 委员会

▶▶ leap to one's defence 迅速保护，保卫…

▶▶ on one's behalf 以某人的名义，为了某人，代表某人

▶▶ undignified [ʌn'dɪgnɪfaɪd]

[释义] a. 无尊严的，不庄重的，不体面的

[反义] dignified, self-esteemed

[同根] dignity ['dɪgnɪtɪ] n. 尊严，高贵
dignify ['dɪgnɪfaɪ] v. 使显得有价值或可尊敬，使显赫，使高贵

▶▶ insulting [ɪn'sʌltɪŋ]

[释义] a. ①侮辱的，污蔑的，无礼的 ②损害人体的

[同义] ① offensive, abusive, rude

[反义] ① polite

[同根] insult ['ɪnsʌlt] n. ①侮辱 ②损伤
v. ①侮辱，辱骂 ②损害，危害 ③攻击，袭击

▶▶ take a stand 对…采取某种立场

▶▶ potential [pə'tenʃəl]

[释义] a. 潜在的，可能的 n. ①潜力，潜能 ②潜在性，可能性

[同义] a. underlying, latent, possible, probable, likely, would-be
n. capability, ability, possibility

Reading in Depth
Section A

A bookless life is an incomplete life. Books influence the depth and breadth of life. They **meet** the natural **desire for** freedom, for expression, for creativity and beauty of life. Learners, therefore, must have books, and the right type of book, for the satisfaction of their need. Readers turn naturally to books because their curiosity **concerning all manners of** things, their eagerness to share in the experiences of others and their need to escape from their own limited environment lead them to find in books **food for the mind and the spirit**. Through their reading they find a deeper significance to life as books **acquaint** them **with** life in the world as it was and it is now. They are presented with a **diversity** of human experiences and come to respect other ways of thought and living. And while establishing their own relationships and responses to life, the readers often find that the characters in their stories are **going through** similar **adjustments**, which help to **clarify** and give **significance** to their own.

Books provide **abundant** material for readers' imagination to grow. Imagination is a valuable quality and a **motivating** power, and **stimulates** achievement. While enriching their imagination, books widen their **outlook**, develop a fact-finding attitude and train them to use leisure properly. The social and educational significance of the readers' books cannot be **overestimated** in an academic library.

文章词汇注释

▶▶▶ **meet … desire for…** 满足…的愿望

▶▶▶ **concerning** 关于

▶▶▶ **all manners of** 各种各样的

▶▶▶ **food for the mind and the spirit** 精神食粮

▶▶▶ **acquaint sb. with sth.** 使某人了解 / 认识某事物

▶▶▶ **diversity** [daɪˈvɜːsɪtɪ]
[释义] n. 多样性，差异，不同点
[同义] variety, multiplicity
[反义] uniformity
[同根] divert [dɪˈvɜːt] v. ①使转向，使（河流等）改道，转移…的注意力 ②使得到消遣，给…娱乐
diversion [daɪˈvɜːʃən] n. ①转移，转向，偏离 ②消遣，娱乐
diverse [daɪˈvɜːs] a. 不同的，多种多样的，多变化的
diversify [daɪˈvɜːsɪfaɪ] v. 使不同，使多样化
divergent [daɪˈvɜːdʒənt] a. ①有分歧的，不同的，偏离的 ②分叉的，叉开的
diversely [daɪˈvɜːslɪ] ad. 不同地，各色各样地
[词组] a diversity of 各种各样的

▶▶▶ **go through** ①经历，经受 ②仔细检查 ③用完 ④通过 ⑤参加

▶▶▶ **adjustment** [əˈdʒʌstmənt]
[释义] n. ①调整，调节 ②调节装置
[同义] ① adaption, accommodation
[同根] adjust [əˈdʒʌst] v. ①调整，调节 ②使适合于（新环境等）
[词组] make adjustment to 适应

▶▶▶ **clarify** [ˈklærɪfaɪ]
[释义] v. ①澄清，阐明 ②使（头脑等）变清楚 ③净化
[同义] explain, make clear, simplify
[同根] clarification [ˌklærɪfɪˈkeɪʃən] n. 澄清，阐明，净化

▶▶▶ **significance** [sɪɡˈnɪfɪkəns]
[释义] n. ①意义，含义 ②重要性，重大
[同义] ① meaning ② importance
[同根] signify [ˈsɪɡnɪfaɪ] v. 表示…的意思，意味，预示
significant [sɪɡˈnɪfɪkənt] a. ①意味深长的 ②重要的 ③相当数量的 ④显著的
signature [ˈsɪɡnɪtʃə] n. 签名，署名

▶▶▶ **abundant** [əˈbʌndənt]
[释义] a. 丰富的，大量的，充裕的

[同义] plentiful, rich, fertile

[反义] scarce

[同根] abundance [ə'bʌndəns] n. 丰富，充裕，大量

[词组] be abundant in/ with 有丰富…的，有大量…的

▶▶ motivate ['məutɪveɪt]

[释义] v. ①（使）有动机，推动 ②激起（行动），激发…的积极性，促成

[同根] motivation [,məutɪ'veɪʃən] n. ①提供动机，激发积极性②动力，诱因，刺激

motivator ['məutɪveɪtə(r)] n. 激起行为（或行动）的人（或事物），促进因素，激发因素

motivational [,məutɪ'veɪʃənəl] a. 动机的，有关动机的

motivated ['məutɪveɪtɪd] a. 有目的的，有动机的

[词组] motivate sb. to do sth. 促使某人做某事

▶▶ stimulate ['stɪmjuleɪt]

[释义] v. ①刺激，激励 ②促使，引起

[同义] incite, excite, stir, inspire, motivate

[反义] discourage

[同根] stimulating ['stɪmjuleɪtɪŋ] a. 刺激的，有刺激性的

stimulus ['stɪmjuləs] n. ①刺激物，促进因素 ②刺激，刺激

stimuli ['stɪmjuləɪ] n. stimulus 的复数

stimulant ['stɪmjulənt] n. ①刺激物 ②兴奋剂

stimulation [,stɪmju'leɪʃən] n. 激励，鼓舞，刺激

▶▶ outlook ['autluk]

[释义] n. ①观点，视野，态度 ②景色，景致 ③前景，前途

[同义] ① view, prospect ③ expectation

[词组] be on the outlook for ①注视着，在瞭望 ②寻找着，物色中

▶▶ overestimate ['əuvə'estɪmeɪt]

[释义] v. 评价过高 n. 估计过高，评价过高

[反义] underestimate

[同根] estimate ['estɪmeɪt] v. 估计，评价，判断 n. ①估计，估计数 ②看法，评价，判断

estimation [estɪ'meɪʃən] n. 估计，评价，判断

Section B
Passage one

If you're a male and you're reading this, congratulations: you're a survivor. According to statistics, you're more than twice as likely to die of skin cancer than a woman, and nine times more likely to die of AIDS. Assuming you make it to the end of your natural term, about 78 years for men in Australia, you'll die on average five years before a woman.

There're many reasons for this—typically, men take more risks than women and are more likely to drink and smoke—but perhaps more importantly, men don't go to the doctor.

"Men aren't seeing doctors as often as they should," says Dr. Gullotta.

"This is particularly so for the over-40s, when diseases tend to strike."

Gullotta say a healthy man should visit the doctor every year or two. For those over 45, it should be at least once a year.

Two months ago Gullotta saw a 50-year-old man who had delayed doing anything about his smoker's cough for a year.

"When I finally saw him it had already spread and he has since died from lung cancer," he says. "Earlier detection and treatment may not have cured him but it would have **prolonged** his life."

According to a recent survey, 95% of women aged between 15 and early 40s see a doctor once a year, **compared to** 70% of men in the same age group.

"A lot of men think they're *invincible* (不可战胜的)," Gullatta says. "They only come in when a friend **drops dead** on the golf course and they think, 'Geez, if it could happen to him…'

Then there's the **ostrich** approach. "Some men are scared of what might be there and would rather not know," says Dr.Ross Cartmill.

"Most men get their cars serviced more regularly than they service their bodies," Garmill says. He believes most diseases that commonly affect men could be **addressed** by preventive **check-ups**.

Regular check-us for men would inevitably **lace strain on** the public purse, Cartmill says. "But prevention is cheaper **in the long run** than having to treat the disease. Besides, the ultimate cost is far greater: it's called **premature** death."

文章词汇注释

▶▶▶ **assume** [ə'sjuːm; (US) ə'suːm]

[释义] v. ①假定，设想 ②采取，采纳 ③装出，佯作 ④承担，接受

[同义] ① suppose, presume ② adopt ③ put on ④ take on

[同根] assumption [ə'sʌmpʃən] n. ①假定，臆断 ②担任，承担

[词组] assume this to be true 假定这是真的

assume that 假定

assume office 就职

assume the reins of government 执政，开始掌权

assume a leading position 担任领导职务

assume responsibility 负责，承担责任

assume a new aspect 呈现新的面貌

assume airs of 摆…架子

assume great airs 神气活现，装作要人的模样，摆架子

▶▶ make it ① [口] 达到预定目标 ②及时抵达，走完路程 ③（病痛等）好转

▶▶ prolong [prə'lɒŋ]
[释义] v. 延长，拖延
[同义] drag out, extend, lengthen, stretch
[反义] shorten
[同根] prolongation [ˌprəʊlɒŋ'geɪʃən] n. ①延长，拖延 ②延长部分

▶▶ compared to 与…相比
▶▶ drops dead 倒毙，暴死

▶▶ Geez [gɪː'ez]
[释义] 哎呀！（用以表达稍微的惊讶、喜悦、不满或是恼怒）

▶▶ ostrich ['ɒstrɪtʃ]
[释义] n. 鸵鸟，鸵鸟般的人，不正视不利现实的人 v. 采取自欺态度
[同根] ostrichism ['ɒstrɪtʃɪzəm] n. 不正视现实，自我陶醉
ostrichlike ['ɒstrɪtʃlaɪk] a. 鸵鸟般的，自欺的

▶▶ address [ə'dres]
[释义] v. ①处理，解决，专注于，致力于 ②对…发表演说，向…作

（正式）讲话 ③对…说话，写信给… n. ①演说，讲话 ②地址，住址

[同根] addresser [ə'dresə(r)] n. ①发信人，发件人 ②发言人
addressee [ˌædre'siː] n. 受信人，收件人

[词组] address oneself to ① 对 … 说，跟…谈 ②与…通信（用于正式场合）③着手，从事于
form of address（在口头上或书面上对具有某种地位的人的）称呼
pay one's addresses to 追求（某女），向（某女）求婚

▶▶ check-up 检查，体格检查
▶▶ lace strain on 收紧，勒紧
▶▶ in the long run 长远看，从最终结果来看

▶▶ premature ['premətʃʊə; (US) priː-mə'tʊər]
[释义] a. ①过早的，提前的 ②不成熟的，早熟的 ③仓促的
[同根] mature [mə'tjʊə; (US) mə'tʊər] a. 成熟的，理智的 v. （使）成熟
maturity [mə'tjʊərɪtɪ] n. ①成熟，完备 ②（票据）到期
prematurely [priːmə'tʊərlɪ] ad. ①过早地 ③早熟地

Passage Two

High-quality customer service is **preached** by many, but actually keeping customers happy is easier said than done.

Shoppers seldom complain to the manager or owner of a **retail store**, but instead will **alert** their friends, relatives, co-workers, strangers and anyone who will listen.

Store managers are often the last to hear complaints, and often find out only when their regular customers decide to **frequent** their competitors, according to a study **jointly** conducted by Verde Group and Wharton School.

"Storytelling hurts retailers and entertains consumers," said Paula Courtney, President of the Verde Group. "The store loses the customer, but the shopper must also find a **replacement**."

On average, every unhappy customer will complain to at least four others, and will no longer visit the specific store. For every dissatisfied customer, a store will lose up to three more due to negative reviews. The resulting "snowball effect" can be **disastrous** to retailers.

According to the research, shopper who purchased clothing encountered the most problems. **Ranked** second and third were grocery and electronics customers.

The most common complaints include filled parking lots, **cluttered** shelves over loaded racks, **out-of-stock** items, long check-out lines, and rude salespeople.

During peak shopping hours, some retailers solved the parking problems by getting *moonlighting*（业余兼职的）local police to work as parking attendants. Some hired flag wavers to direct customers to empty parking spaces. This guidance **eliminated** the need for customers to circle the parking lot endlessly, and avoided **confrontation** between those eyeing the same parking space.

Retailers can relieve the headaches by redesigning store **layouts**, pre-stocking sales items, hiring speedy and experienced cashiers, and **having sales representatives on hand** to answer question.

Most importantly, salespeople should be **diplomatic** and polite with angry customers.

"Retailers who're **responsive** and friendly are more likely to **smooth over** issues than those who aren't so friendly," said Professor Stephen Hoch. "Maybe something as simple as a greeter at the store entrance would help."

Customers can also improve future shopping experiences by **filing** complaints to the retailer, instead of complaining to the rest of the world. Retailers are **hard-pressed** to improve when they have no idea what is wrong.

文章词汇注释

▶▶ **preach** [pri:tʃ]

[释义] v. ①鼓吹，宣传 ②讲（道），说（教）③讲（学）劝告，告诫

[同根] preacher [ˈpri:tʃə(r)] n. 布道者，传教士，说教者，鼓吹者

preachment [ˈpri:tʃmənt] n. [贬]（冗长的）讲道，说教

[词组] practise what one preaches 躬行实践，身体力行

preach at/to sb. 对某人谆谆告诫

preach down 贬损，当众谴责

preach up 赞扬，吹捧

▶▶ **retail store** 零售店

▶▶ **alert** [əˈlɜ:t]

[释义] v. ①警告 ②向…报警，使警惕 n. ①警觉（状态），戒备（状态）②警报 a. ①留神的，注意的 ②警觉的，警惕的

[同义] v. alarm a. watchful, attentive

[同根] alertness [əˈlɜ:tnɪs] n. 警戒，机敏

alertly [əˈlɜ:tlɪ] ad. 提高警觉地，留意地

[词组] on(the)alert 警戒着，随时准备着，密切注意着

▶▶ **frequent** [ˈfri:kwənt]

[释义] v. ①常去，时常出入于 ②与…时常交往 a. 时常发生的，频繁的

[同义] v. haunt

[同根] frequency [ˈfri:kwənsɪ] n. 频率，周率，发生次数

▶▶ **jointly** [ˈdʒɔɪntlɪ]

[释义] ad. 共同地，联合地，连带地

[同根] joint [dʒɔɪnt] a. ①联合的，共同的 ②接合的，连接的 ③共有的，共享的 n. ①接头，接缝 ②关节，节 v. 连接，接合

▶▶ **replacement** [rɪˈpleɪsmənt]

[释义] n. 代替，替换

[同根] replace [ri:ˈpleɪs] v. 取代，代替

displace [dɪsˈpleɪs] v. ①移动…的位置 ②取代（某人的）位置

displacement [dɪsˈpleɪsmənt] n. 移位，取代，撤换

▶▶ **disastrous** [dɪˈza:strəs]

[释义] a. ①灾难性的，悲惨的 ②很糟的

[同根] disaster [dɪˈza:stə] n. ①灾难，天灾，灾祸 ②彻底的失败

disastrously [dɪˈza:strəslɪ] ad. 悲惨地

▶▶ **rank** [ræŋk]

[释义] v. ①排列，把…分等级 ②把…排列整齐 n. ①排，列，行 ②军衔，地位 ③显贵，高地位 ④ (pl.) 士兵

[同义] v. ① class, grade, categorize ② position n. grade, position, status

[词组] be ranked number one 排名第一

rank sb/sth in order 给…按顺序排名

rank... as... 把…归类为…，把…分等级

▶▶ **clutter** [ˈklʌtə]

[释义] v. 弄乱，乱七八糟地堆满（up, with）n. ①喧嚣，喧闹 ②混乱，零乱 ③（房屋等）拥挤杂乱的一团

[同义] disorder, jumble

[词组] be cluttered (up) with... 堵满了…的

in a clutter 乱七八糟

▶▶ **out-of-stock** 已脱销的

▶▶ **eliminate** [ɪˈlɪmɪneɪt]

[释义] v. ①消除，排除，清除 ②淘汰，不加考虑

[同义] discard, dispose of, exclude, reject,

get rid of, throw out

[反义] add

[同根] elimination [ɪˌlɪmɪˈneɪʃən] n. ①排除，除去，消除 ②忽视，略去

[词组] eliminate the false and retain the true 去伪存真

eliminate errors 消除错误

eliminate the need of 使不需要

eliminate the possibility of 排除…的可能性，使…不可能

eliminate the risk/problem 消除风险/问题

▶▶ **confrontation** [ˌkɒnfrʌnˈteɪʃən]

[释义] n. 对抗，对峙，对质，面对

[同义] encounter, opposition

[同根] confront [kənˈfrʌnt] v. ①（困难等）临头 ②（使）面对，（使）面临 ③勇敢地面对危险等，正视，对抗

confrontationist [ˌkɒnfrʌnˈteɪʃənɪst] n. 主张在国际关系中持对抗态度的人，对抗主义者

▶▶ **layout** [ˈleɪaʊt]

[释义] n. ①布局，规划，设计 ②版面设计 ③规划图，设计图

[同根] lay [leɪ] v. ①放，搁 ②设置，布置 ③铺，砌 ④生（蛋），产（卵） a. ①世俗的 ②外行的，非专业的

layer [ˈleɪə] n. 层，地层，阶层

layman [ˈleɪmən] n. 门外汉

layoff [ˈleɪɒf] n. ①暂时解雇 ②暂时解雇期

▶▶ **have...on hand** ①把…放在手头，…在附近 ②即将发生 ③…在场

▶▶ **sales representatives** 商品经销代理，营业代表

▶▶ **diplomatic** [ˌdɪpləˈmætɪk]

[释义] a. ①外交的，与外交有关的 ②有外交手腕的，老练的，策略的

[同根] diplomat [ˈdɪpləmæt] n. 外交官，外交家

diplomacy [dɪˈpləʊməsɪ] n. ①外交 ②外交手腕

diplomatically [ˌdɪpləˈmætɪkəlɪ] ad. 在外交上地，经外交途径地

▶▶ **responsive** [rɪsˈpɒnsɪv]

[释义] a. ①反应热烈的或良好的，赞同的，支持的 ②回答，应答的，响应的

[同根] respond [rɪsˈpɒnd] v. ①回答，作答 ②作出反应

response [rɪsˈpɒns] n. ①回答，答复 ②响应，反应

responsible [rɪsˈpɒnsəbl] a. ①有责任的，应负责的 ②责任重大的 ③可靠的，可依赖的

responsibility [rɪsˌpɒnsəˈbɪlɪtɪ] n. 责任，责任感，职责

▶▶ **smooth over** ①消除，解决（障碍等） ②把…弄平；使平息/稳定下来 ③遮盖，掩饰

▶▶ **file** [faɪl]

[释义] v. ① 提出（申请、诉讼等），呈请把…备档 ② 把（文件等）归档 ③ 列队行进 n. 文件，档案，文件夹

[同根] filer [ˈfaɪlə] n. 档案管理员，文件装钉员，锉磨工人

[词组] on file 存档，归档

in file 成纵队，依次，鱼贯地

file for ①申请 ②报名参加竞选

file in 鱼贯而入

file out 鱼贯而出

file a complaint/lawsuit/petition (against sb) 对…提出控告/诉讼/请愿

▶▶ **hard-pressed** 处境艰难的，被紧迫追赶的，被催逼的

Skimming and Scanning
How Do You See Diversity?

As a manager, Tiffany is responsible for interviewing applicants for some of the positions with her company. During one interview, she noticed that the **candidate** never made direct eye contact. She was puzzled and **somewhat** disappointed because she liked the individual **otherwise**.

He had a perfect **resume** and gave good responses to her questions, but the fact that he never looked her in the eye said "**untrustworthy**," so she decided to offer the job to her second choice.

"It wasn't until I attended a **diversity workshop** that I realized the person we **passed over** was the perfect person," Tiffany **confesses**. What she hadn't known at the time of the interview was that the candidate's "different" behavior was simply a cultural misunderstanding. He was an Asian-American raised in a household where respect for those **in authority** was shown by *averting* (避开) your eyes.

"I was just **thrown off** by the lack of eye contact; not realizing it was cultural," Tiffany says. "I **missed out**, but will not miss that opportunity again."

Many of us have had similar **encounters** with behaviors we **perceive** as different. As the world becomes smaller and our workplaces more diverse, it is becoming **essential** to expand our understanding of others and to reexamine some of our false **assumptions**.

Hire Advantage

At a time when hiring qualified people is becoming more difficult, employers who can eliminate **invalid** *biases* (偏爱) from the process have a **distinct** advantage. My company, Mindsets LLC, helps organizations and individuals see their own **blind spots**. A **real estate recruiter** we worked with **illustrates** the positive difference such training can make.

"During my Mindsets coaching session, I was taught how to recruit a diversified workforce. I recruited people from different cultures and skill sets. The agents were able to utilize their full potential and experiences to build up the company. When the real estate market began to change, it was because we had a diverse agent pool that we were able to stay in the real estate market much longer than others in the same profession."

Blinded by Gender

Dale is an account executive who attended one of my workshops on supervising a diverse workforce. "Through one of the sessions, I discovered my personal bias," he recalls. "I learned I had not been looking at a person as a whole person, and being open to differences." In his case, the blindness was not about culture but rather gender.

"I had a management position open in my department; and the two finalists were a man and a woman. Had I not attended this workshop, I would have automatically assumed the man was the best candidate because the position required quite a bit of extensive travel. My reasoning would have been that even though both candidates were great and could have been successful in the position, I assumed the woman would have wanted to be home with her children and not travel." Dale's assumptions are another example of the well-intentioned but incorrect thinking that limits an organization's ability to tap into the full potential of a diverse workforce.

"I learned from the class that instead of imposing my gender biases into the situation, I needed to present the full range of duties, responsibilities and expectations to all candidates and allow them to make an informed decision." Dale credits the workshop, "because it helped me make decisions based on fairness."

Year of the Know-It-All

Doug is another supervisor who attended one of my workshops. He recalls a major lesson learned from his own employee.

"One of my most embarrassing moments was when I had a Chinese-American employee put in a request to take time off to celebrate Chinese New Year. In my ignorance, I assumed he had his dates wrong, as the first of January had just passed. When I advised him of this, I gave him a long talking-to about turning in requests early with the proper dates.

"He patiently waited, then when I was done, he said he would like

Chinese New Year did not begin January first, and that Chinese New Year, which **is tied to** the **lunar** cycle, is one of the most **celebrated** holidays on the Chinese calendar. **Needless to say**, I felt very embarrassed in assuming he had his dates mixed up. But I learned a great deal about assumptions, and that the **timing** of holidays varies considerably from culture to culture.

"Attending the diversity workshop helped me realize how much I could learn by simply asking questions and creating dialogues with my employees, rather than making assumptions and trying to be a **know-it-all**," Doug admits. "The biggest thing I took away from the workshop is learning how to be more 'inclusive' to differences."

A better Bottom Line

An open mind about diversity not only improves organizations internally, it is **profitable** as well. These **comments** from a customer service representative show how an inclusive attitude can improve sales." Most of my customers speak English as a second language. One of the best things my company has done is to **contract** with a language service that offers translations over the phone. It wasn't until my boss received Mindsets' training that she was able to understand how important inclusiveness was to customer service. As a result, our customer base has increased."

Once we start to see people as individuals, and **discard** the **stereotypes**, we can move positively toward inclusiveness for everyone. Diversity is about coming together and taking advantage of our differences and similarities. It is about building better communities and organizations that enhance us as individuals and **reinforce** our shared humanity.

When we begin to question our assumptions and challenge what we think we have learned from our past, from the media, peers, family, friends, etc, we begin to realize that some of our conclusions are **flawed** or contrary to our **fundamental** values. We need to train ourselves to think differently, shift our **mindsets** and realize that diversity opens doors for all of us, creating opportunities in organizations and communities that benefit everyone.

文章词汇注释

▶▶ **candidate** ['kændɪdət; (US) 'kændɪdeɪt]

[释义] n. ①应试者，应聘者 ②候选人

[同根] candid ['kændɪd] a. 忠实的，率直的，坦诚的

candidateship ['kændɪdeɪtəʃɪp] n. 候选（人）资格/身份

▶▶ **somewhat** ['sʌm(h)wɒt]

[释义] ad. 稍微，有些

[同义] rather, fairly, to some extent, a bit

[同根] somehow ['sʌmhaʊ] ad. ①不知怎么地，反正 ②以某种方式，设法地

[词组] more than somewhat (正式)非常，极其

▶▶ **otherwise** ['ʌðəwaɪz]

[释义] ad. ①要不然，否则 ②用不同的方式，另外 ③在其他方面 conj. 否则，不然

[词组] and otherwise 等等

or otherwise 或相反

otherwise from 不同于

otherwise than 与…不同，除…之外

▶▶ **resume** ['rezjuːmeɪ]

[释义] n. ①（求职者的）履历，简历 ②摘要，概略

[rɪ'zjuːm] v. ①（中断后）再继续，重新开始 ②恢复，重新得到 ③接着说

▶▶ **untrustworthy** [ʌn'trʌstwɜːθɪ]

[释义] a. 不值得信赖的，靠不住的

[反义] trustworthy

▶▶ **diversity** [daɪ'vɜːsɪtɪ]

[释义] n. 多样性，歧异，不同

[同义] variety, diverseness

[同根] diverse [daɪ'vɜːs] a. 不同的，多种多样的，多变化的

diversify [daɪ'vɜːsɪfaɪ] v. 使不同，使多样化

divert [daɪ'vɜːt] v. ①使转向，使（河流等）改道，转移…的注意力 ②使得到消遣，给…娱乐 ③盗用，贪污

diversion [daɪ'vɜːʃən; (US) daɪ'vɜːʒən] n. ①转移，转向 ②消遣，娱乐

divergent [daɪ'vɜːdʒənt] a. ①分叉的，叉开的 ②有分歧的，偏离的

[词组] a great diversity of 各种各样的

▶▶ **workshop** ['wɜːkʃɒp]

[释义] n. ①研习会，讨论会 ②车间，工场

▶▶ **pass over** 忽略，不加注意，忽视

▶▶ **confess** [kən'fes]

[释义] v. ①承认，供认，坦白，②忏悔（罪恶等）

[同义] ① admit, declare, profess, affirm, assert, aknowledge

[反义] ① deny, conceal

[同根] confession [kən'feʃən] n. 忏悔，认错，招供

[词组] confess to (doing) sth 承认做过某事

confess to murder/ crime/robbery 承认犯谋杀罪 / 犯罪 / 犯抢劫罪

▶▶ **in authority** 持有权力的地位

▶▶ **throw off** ①使犯错误，产生错觉，使分心、转移或误导 ②扔出，摆脱 ③发出，射出

▶▶ **miss out** ①错失机会 ②漏掉，遗漏

▶▶ **encounter** [ɪn'kaʊntə]

[释义] n. ①相会，相遇 ②遭遇，会战 v. ①偶遇，邂逅 ②遭到，突遇

[同义] n. ① battle, combat

v. ② meet with, confront, face

[同根] count [kaʊnt] v. ①数数，计算

②计入，包括

counter ['kaʊntə] n. ①柜台 ②筹码 a. ①相反的，对立的 ②反对的，敌意的 v. 反击，反驳，反对

[词组] encounter with 遭遇…，遇到…

▶▶ perceive [pə'siːv]

[释义] v. ①察觉，感知 ②感到，认识到

[同义] sense, discover, realize

[反义] ignore

[同根] perception [pə'sepʃən] n. ①感知，感觉 ②认识，看法，洞察力
perceptive [pə'septɪv] a. 有感知能力的，有洞察力的，理解的

[词组] perceive sth as sth 把…理解 / 认为是…

▶▶ essential [ɪ'senʃəl]

[释义] a. ①必要的，本质的，实质的 ②提炼的，精华的 n. [pl.] 本质，实质，要素，要点

[同义] a. ① basic, fundamental, important, necessary, needed, required, vital

[同根] essence ['esəns] n. ①基本，本质，要素 ②香精
essentially [ɪ'senʃəli] ad. 本质上，本来，根本

▶▶ assumption [ə'sʌmpʃən]

[释义] n. ①设想，假定 ②担任，承当 ③假装，作态

[同根] assume [ə'sjuːm] v. ①假定，设想 ②担任，承担，③呈现，具有，采取
assuming [ə'suːmɪŋ] conj. 假定，假如 a. 傲慢的，自负的
assumed [ə'sjuːmd] a. 假定的，假装的
assumptive [ə'sʌmptɪv] a. ①被视为理所当然的 ②自负的

▶▶ invalid [ɪn'vælɪd]

[释义] a. ①无适当根据的，无道理的 ②无用的，法律上不承认的，无效

的 ③病弱的，伤残的 n. 病弱者，伤残者，久病者

[反义] a. ① sound ② valid

[同根] valid ['vælɪd] a. ①（法律上）有效的 ②（指论据、理由等）正确的，有根据的
validate ['vælɪdeɪt] v. 使生效，证实
validity [və'lɪdɪti] n. ①（法律上）有效，合法 ②合逻辑，正确

[词组] be invalided out (of) 因病被解除…职务

▶▶ distinct [dɪs'tɪŋkt]

[释义] a. ①清楚的，明显的，确实的 ②不同的，个别的

[同义] ① clear, clear-cut, definite, evident ② different, diverse, divergent

[反义] ① ambiguous, vague

[同根] distinction [dɪs'tɪŋkʃən] n. ①区分，不同，特征 ②卓越，著名，优良 ③荣誉（称号），殊勋，奖赏
distinctive [dɪs'tɪŋktɪv] a. 特殊的，有特色的，区别性的
distinguish [dɪs'tɪŋgwɪʃ] v. ①区分，辨别 ②辨别出，认出，发现 ③使区别于它物 ④ (~ oneself) 使杰出，使著名
distinguished [dɪs'tɪŋgwɪʃt] a. ①卓越的，杰出的 ②高贵的，地位高的

[词组] distinct from 与…有所区别

▶▶ blind spot ①盲点，盲区 ②（礼堂里）观众视听不清的区域 ③（公路等）驾驶员难于辨认的区域 ④缺乏理解的领域，敏感的领域

▶▶ real estate 不动产，房地产

▶▶ recruiter [rɪ'kruːtə(r)]

[释义] n. 征兵人员，招聘人员

[同根] recruit [rɪ'kruːt] vt. ①征募（新兵），吸收（新成员）②充实，补充 n. 新兵，新手，新成员

illustrate ['ɪləstreɪt]

[释义] v. ①（用图或例子）说明，表明，阐明 ②给…作插图说明

[同义] ① clarify, demonstrate, explain, portray, exemplify

[同根] illustrated ['ɪləstreɪtɪd] n. 有插画的报章杂志 a. 有插图的
illustration [ˌɪləs'treɪʃən] n. ①说明，图解，图示 ②例证，实证
illustrative ['ɪləstreɪtɪv] a. 起说明作用的，作为例证的

[词组] be illustrated with/by… 以…说明之

session ['seʃən]

[释义] n. ①从事某项活动的一段时间 ②会议，会期 ③上课时间

agent ['eɪdʒənt]

[释义] n. ①代理人，代理商，经纪人 ②执法官，政府特工人员

[同根] agency ['eɪdʒənsɪ] n. ①（政府等的）专业行政部门，社，机构 ②公众服务机构 ③代理行，经销处

utilize ['ju:tɪlaɪz]

[释义] v. 利用，应用

[同义] use, employ

[同根] utility [ju:'tɪlɪtɪ] n. ①实用，效用 ②公用事业 a. 实用的，有多种用途的
utilitarian [ju:ˌtɪlɪ'teərɪən] a. 实用的，功利的，功利主义的

pool [pu:l]

[释义] n. ①集中使用的资金、物资、服务等，集合基金成员，垄断性联营 ②池塘，游泳池 ③水洼，小水坑 v. ①集中（钱、力量等）②共同承担 ③（使）形成池塘

[同根] dirty pool [美俚] 不正直/不道德的行为，欺骗的伎俩

supervise ['sju:pəvaɪz]

[释义] v. 监督，管理，指导

[同义] administer, direct, govern, head, lead, regulate

[同根] supervision [ˌsju:pə'vɪʒən] n. 监督，管理
supervisor ['sju:pəvaɪzə] n. 监督人，管理人，检查员
supervisee [sju:pəvaɪ'zi:] n. 被监督者，被管理者，被指导者

bias ['baɪəs]

[释义] n. ①偏见，偏爱，偏袒 v. 使存偏见，影响…以至产生偏差

[同义] prejudice

[同根] biased ['baɪəst] a. 有偏见的，偏袒一方的

gender ['dʒendə]

[释义] n. 性别

[同义] sex

finalist ['faɪnəlɪst]

[释义] n. 参加决赛的选手

assume [ə'sju:m; (US) ə'su:m]

[释义] v. ①假定，设想 ②承担，接受 ③装出，佯作

[同义] ① presume,presuppose ② take on ③ put on

[同根] assumption [ə'sʌmpʃən] n. ①假定，臆断 ②担任，承担
assumed [ə'sju:md] a. 假定的，假装的

well-intentioned ['welɪn'tenʃənd]

[释义] a. 好心的，出于善意的

tap into the full potential 充分发挥/挖掘全部潜力

impose [ɪm'pəuz]

[释义] v. ①把…强加于 ②征（税）③利用，占便宜

[同义] ① place,put,set,force ② levy,tax

[反义] ① free,liberate

[同根] imposition [ˌɪmpə'zɪʃən] n. 强

加，（税等的）征收，（惩罚等的）施加

imposing [ɪmˈpəʊzɪŋ] a. 壮丽的，雄伟的，使人印象深刻的

[词组] impose a ban/tax/fine 实施禁令 / 征收税款 / 征收罚款

impose a burden/strain (on/upon) 增加负担 / 压力

impose sth on sb 将（想法、信仰等）强加给某人

▶▶▶ **informed** [ɪnˈfɔːmd]

[释义] a. ①见多识广的，消息灵通的 ②有学识的，受过教育的

[词组] be informed of 听说，接到…的通知

be rightly informed 得到正确的知识 / 情报

be wrongly informed 得到错误的知识 / 情报

keep ... informed 随时向…报告情况

an informed mind 见识广博的人

informed public opinion 明达的舆论

a well-informed man 消息灵通的人

▶▶▶ **credit** [ˈkredɪt]

[释义] v. ①赞扬，赞同 ②信任，相信 n. ①荣誉，赞扬 ②信赖，声望，威信 ③信任，信用 ④学分 ⑤赊购 ⑥（银行）存款，债权

[同义] n. ① honor ② belief, faith, trust, conviction

[反义] n.& v. ② discredit, distrust

[同根] creditor [ˈkredɪtə] n. 债主，债权人

credibility [kredɪˈbɪlɪtɪ] n. 可信性，可靠性

credible [ˈkredɪbəl] a. 可靠的，可信的

credulous [ˈkredjʊləs; (US) ˈkredʒələs] a. 轻信的，易受骗的

[词组] a man of high credit 很有名望的人

add to one's credit 增加荣誉

be a credit to 使…感到光荣，给…争光

credit card 信用卡，签帐卡

do sb. credit 为某人增光，证明某人具有某种才能或品质

get/take credit for 因…而得到好评

give credit to ①相信，信任 ②称赞，赞扬

give sb. credit for sth. ①为…赞扬某人 ②认为某人具有（某种品德、才能等）

have the credit of 有…的好名声

lose credit with sb. 失去某人的信任，在某人眼中失去威信

on credit 赊（购）

place credit in 相信

credit sb./sth. with 认为某人 / 某事具有…；把…归因于某人 / 某事

▶▶▶ **put in** ①提出，提交 ②放进，插入，进入 ③使就职 ④种植 ⑤进港

▶▶▶ **talking-to** [口] 责备，斥责

▶▶▶ **turn in** ①上交，交还 ②检举，陈述 ③完成

▶▶▶ **be tied to** 与…密切相关

▶▶▶ **lunar** [ˈljuːnə]

[释义] a. ①阴历的，按月球运转而量度的 ②月的，月球的；似月的 ③因月球作用而引起的

[词组] lunar cycle 月运周期

lunar calendar 阴历

▶▶▶ **celebrated** [ˈselɪbreɪtɪd]

[释义] a. 著名的，声誉卓著的

[同根] celebrate [ˈselɪbreɪt] v. ①颂扬，赞美，歌颂 ②庆祝

celebration [ˌselɪˈbreɪʃən] n. 庆祝，庆祝会，典礼

celebrity [sɪˈlebrɪtɪ] n. ①名誉，声誉 ②名人，名流

▶▶▶ **needless to say** 不用说，不出意料

▶▶▶ **timing** [ˈtaɪmɪŋ]

[释义] n. ①时间的选择，时机的选择

②计时，定时，安排时间，[体] 速度的控制，校准

▶▶▶ **know-it-all** ['nəʊɪtɔ:l]

[释义] *a.&n.* 自称无所不知的（人）

[同根] know-all ['nəʊ'ɔ:l] *n.* [口] 自称无所不知的人，知识里手

know-nothing ['nəʊˌnʌθɪŋ] *n.* ①无知的人 ②不可知论者

▶▶▶ **inclusive** [ɪn'klu:sɪv]

[释义] *a.* ①包括的,包含的 ②一切（项目）开支包括在内的

[反义] exclusive

[同根] include [ɪn'klu:d] *v.* 包括,包含,把…计算在内

inclusion [ɪn'klu:ʒən] *n.* 包括, 包含

[词组] Wednesday to Friday inclusive 包括星期三到星期五在内

inclusive of... 包括…, 包含…

▶▶▶ **profitable** ['prɒfɪtəbl]

[释义] *a.* 有益的, 有利可图的

[同义] gainful, lucrative, commercial, beneficial, rewarding, helpful

[反义] unhelpful

[同根] profit ['prɒfɪt] *n.* ①利润 ②益处 *v.* 获益, 有益于

profiteer [ˌprɒfɪ'tɪə] *n.* 暴发户, 发横财的人, 投机商 *v.* 牟取暴利, 投机倒把

▶▶▶ **comment** ['kɒment]

[释义] *v.& n.* 评论, 评价

[同义] *v.& n.* remark, mention

[同根] commentary ['kɒməntərɪ] (US) 'kɒmənterɪ] *n.* ①（对书籍等的）评语, 评注, 评论 ②实况报道

commentate ['kɒmənteɪt] *v.* 作实况报道, 评述

commentator ['kɒmənteɪtə] *n.* ①注释者, 解说者 ②实况转播评论员, 新闻广播员

[词组] ask for comment 征求意见

make comments on/upon sth. 评论某事

offer comments 提意见

No comment 无可奉告

without comment 不必多说

comment on/upon 评论…, 对…提意见

▶▶▶ **contract** [kən'trækt]

[释义] *v.* ①订立（合同）②缔结, 结成 ③与…订婚结交（朋友等）④缩小, 紧缩

['kɒntrækt] *n.* ①契约, 合同, 承包（合同）②婚约

[同义] *n.* ① agreement, treaty, alliance *v.* bargain, compress

[词组] make a contract with 与…签定合同

contract oneself out of ①约定使自己不受…的约束 ②退出（契约,协议等）

▶▶▶ **discard** [dɪs'kɑ:d]

[释义] *v.&n.* 丢弃, 抛弃

[同义] dispose of, get rid of, reject, throw away

[词组] into the discard 成为无用之物, 被遗忘

throw sth. into the discard [美] 放弃某事

▶▶▶ **stereotype** ['stɪərɪəʊtaɪp]

[释义] *n.* ①陈词滥调, 老一套, 模式化的形象, 思想, 人物 ②铅版 *v.* 套用老套, 使定型, 使固定

[同根] stereo ['stɪərɪəʊ] *n.* ①立体声, 立体声系统 ②铅板 *a.* 立体声的

stereotyped ['stɪərɪəʊtaɪpt] *a.*（常作贬义）模式化的, 已成陈规, 老一套的

[词组] stereotype of 模式化的

break through the stereotypes 破除陈规

▶▶▶ **reinforce** [ˌri:ɪn'fɔ:s]

[释义] *v.* 加强, 增援, 补充

[同义] fortify, intensify, strengthen

[同根] enforce [ɪn'fɔːs] v. ①实施，使生效 ②强迫，迫使，强加

reinforcement [ˌriːɪn'fɔːsmənt] n. ①加强，增强，补充 ②[pl.] 援军

▶▶ **flawed** [flɔːɪd]

[释义] a. ①有缺陷的 ②有裂纹的，有瑕疵的

[同根] flaw [flɔː] n. ①裂纹 ②缺点，瑕疵 v. 使破裂，使有缺陷，使无效

flawless ['flɔːlɪs] a. 无瑕疵的，无缺点的，无裂缝的

▶▶ **fundamental** [fʌndə'mentəl]

[释义] a. ①基础的，基本的，重要的 ②起始的，主要的 n. (pl.) 基本原则（原理），根本法则（规律），纲要

[同义] a. ① basic, elementary, essential, primary, radical, vital

[同根] fund [fʌnd] n. ① [pl.] 资金，存款，公债 ②基金，专款，储备 v. 为…提供资金，资助

fundament ['fʌndəmənt] n. 基础，基本原理

fundamentally [fʌndə'mentəlɪ] ad. 基础地，根本地

▶▶ **mindset** ['maɪndset]

[释义] n. 精神状态，思想倾向

Reading in Depth
Section A

Every year in the first week of my English class, some students inform me that writing is too hard. They never write, unless assignments require it. They find the writing process painful and difficult.

How awful to be able to speak in a language but not to write in it—especially English, with its rich vocabulary. Being able to speak but not write is like living in an **enormous** *mansion*（豪宅）and never leaving one small room. When I meet students who think they can't write, I know as a teacher my **mission** is to show them the rest of the rooms. My task is to build **fluency** while providing the opportunity **inherent** in any writing activity to **enhance** the moral and emotional development of my students. One great way to do this is by having students write in a **journal** in class every day.

Writing ability is like strength training. Writing needs to be done daily, just like exercise; just as muscles grow stronger with exercise, writing skills improve quickly with writing practice. I often see a rise in student confidence and performance after only a few weeks of journal writing.

Expressing oneself in writing is one of the most important skills I teach to strengthen the whole student. When my students practice journal writing, they are practicing for their future academic, political, and emotional lives. They build skills so that some day they might write a great novel, a piece of

sorely needed **legislation**, or the perfect love letter. Every day that they write in their journals puts them a step **closer** to fluency, **eloquence**, and **command** of language.

文章词汇注释

▶▶▶ **enormous** [ɪˈnɔːməs]

[释义] *a.* ①巨大的，极大的，庞大的 ②穷凶极恶的

[同义] ① huge, immense, vast

[同根] enormously [ɪˈnɔːməslɪ] *ad.* 极大地，巨大地

enormity [ɪˈnɔːmətɪ] *n.* ①巨大，庞大 ②穷凶极恶，残暴

▶▶▶ **mission** [ˈmɪʃən]

[释义] *n.* ①个人或集团担负的特殊任务，使命 ②使团，代表团

[同根] missioner [ˈmɪʃənə(r)] *n.* 教区传教士

[词组] mission in life 天职

▶▶▶ **fluency** [ˈfluːənsɪ]

[释义] *n.* 流畅，流利，流畅的写作或演说

[同根] fluent [ˈfluːənt] *a.* 流利的，流畅的

[词组] fluency of speech 口齿流利

with fluency 流畅地，滔滔不绝

▶▶▶ **inherent** [ɪnˈhɪərənt]

[释义] *a.* 内在的，固有的，生来就有的

[同义] existing, instinctive, internal, natural

[反义] acquired

[同根] inhere [ɪnˈhɪə] *v.* 生来即存在，本质上即属于

inherence [ɪnˈhɪərəns] *n.* （性质等的）内在，固有，天赋

nherently [ɪnˈhɪərəntlɪ] *ad.* 天性地，

固有地

[词组] be inherent in 为…所固有，是…的固有性质

▶▶▶ **enhance** [ɪnˈhɑːns]

[释义] *v.* 提高（质量、价值、吸引力等），增强，增进，增加

[同义] better, improve, uplift, strengthen

[同根] enhanced [ɪnˈhɑːnst] *a.* 增强的，提高的，放大的

enhancement [ɪnˈhɑːnsmənt] *n.* 增进，增加，提高

[词组] enhance sb's status, reputation and position 提高某人的身分、声望和地位

▶▶▶ **journal** [ˈdʒɜːn(ə)l]

[释义] *n.* ①日志，日记 ②杂志，期刊

[同根] journalism [ˈdʒɜːnəlɪz(ə)m] *n.* 新闻业，新闻工作

journalist [ˈdʒɜːnəlɪst] *n.* 新闻工作者，新闻记者

▶▶▶ **sorely** [ˈsɔːlɪ]

[释义] *ad.* ①极度地，非常 ②痛苦地，悲伤地 ③严厉地，狂暴地

[同义] ① extremely, very much ② painfully

[同根] sore [sɒ:sɒə] *a.* 疼痛的，痛心的，剧烈的 *n.* 痛的地方，痛处

[词组] be sorely needed 迫切需要

▶▶▶ **legislation** [ledʒɪsˈleɪʃən]

[释义] *n.* ①法律，法规 ②立法，制定法律

[同义] ① regulation, statute ② lawmaking

[同根] legislate ['ledʒɪsleɪt] v. 立法，
制定法律

legislative ['ledʒɪslətɪv] a. 立法的，
有立法权力和职责的 n. 立法机关

legislature ['ledʒɪsleɪtʃə] n. 立法机构

legitimate [lɪ'dʒɪtɪmət] a. ①合法的，
法律认可的 ②合乎逻辑的 v. 使合法

legitimize [lɪ'dʒɪtɪmaɪz] v. ①使合法，
使可接受 ②给（孩子）合法地位

legitimacy [lɪ'dʒɪtɪməsɪ] n. ①合法
（性），正统（性）

▶▶ eloquence ['eləkwəns]

[释义] n. ①雄辩，口才 ②说服力

[同义] ① fluency, smoothness

[同根] eloquent ['eləkwənt] a. ①雄辩
的，有说服力的 ②意味深长的

▶▶ command [kə'mɑ:nd]

[释义] n. ①使用或控制某事物的能力，
掌握 ②控制，指挥，命令 v. ①支配，
控制，指挥，管辖 ②命令，指示

[同义] v. ① control ② order, direct, instruct

[反义] n. ② compliance, obedience,
submission

[同根] commanding [kə'mɑ:ndɪŋ]
a. ①指挥的 ②有权威的

commandment [kə'mɑ:n(d)mənt]
n. 戒律

[词组] at command 掌握，可自由使用

at/ by sb.'s command 听某人支配

have a good command of 能自由应
用…

take command of 开始担任…指挥

have … at one's command 能充分掌握

Section B
Passage One

The January fashion show, called FutureFashion, **exemplified** how far green design has come. Organized by the New York-based nonprofit Earth Pledge, the show **inspired** many top designers to work with **sustainable fabrics** for the first time. Several have since made **pledges** to include **organic** fabrics in their lines.

The designers who **undertake** green fashion still face many challenges. Scott Hahn, cofounder with Gregory of Rogan and Loomstate, which uses all-organic cotton, says high-quality sustainable materials can still be **tough** to find. "Most designers with existing labels are finding there aren't **comparable** fabrics that can just replace what you're doing and what your customers are used to," he says. For example, organic cotton and non-organic cotton are **virtually indistinguishable** once **woven** into a dress. But some popular **synthetics**, like **stretch nylon**, still have few **eco-friendly equivalents**.

Those who do make the **switch** are finding they have more support. Last year the **influential** trade show Designers & Agents stopped **charging** its participation fee for young green *entrepreneurs*（企业家）who attend its two springtime shows in Los Angeles and New York and gave special recognition to designers whose collections are at least 25% sustainable. It now **counts** more than 50 green designers, up from fewer than a dozen two years ago. This week Wal-Mart **is set to** announce a major **initiative** aimed at helping cotton farmers go organic: it will buy *transitional*（过渡型的）cotton at higher prices, thus helping to expand the supply of a key sustainable material. "**Mainstream** is about to occur." says Hahn.

Some *analysts*（分析师）are less sure. Among consumers, only 18% are even aware that **ecofashion** exists, up from 6% four years ago. Natalie Hormilla, a fashion writer, is an example of the **unconverted** consumer, when asked if she owned any sustainable clothes, she replied: "Not that I'm aware of." Like most consumers, she finds little time to shop, and when she does, she's **on the hunt for** "**cute** stuff that isn't too expensive." By her own admission, green just isn't yet on her mind. But—thanks to the combined efforts of designers, retailers and suppliers—one day it will be.

文章词汇注释

▶▶▶ **exemplify** [ɪɡ'zemplɪfaɪ]
[释义] *v.* ①举例证明／说明，示范 ②作…的范例／榜样
[同义] demonstrate, illustrate, show
[同根] exemplification [ɪɡ,zemplɪfɪ'keɪʃən] *n.* ①举例说明，示范 ②例子，范例

▶▶▶ **inspire** [ɪn'spaɪə]
[释义] *v.* ①激起灵感，启示 ②鼓舞，激发，激励
[同义] encourage, excite, stimulate
[同根] inspiring [ɪn'spaɪərɪŋ] *a.* 鼓舞人心的，启发灵感的
inspired [ɪn'spaɪəd] *a.* 在灵感支配下（写）的，凭灵感的
inspiration [ɪnspə'reɪʃən] *n.* ①灵感，启示，妙计 ②鼓舞人心的人（或事物）
[词组] inspire confidence/hope/enthu-siasm/distrust in sb. 激发某人的信心／希望／热情／疑虑

▶▶▶ **sustainable** [sə'steɪnəbl]
[释义] *a.* ①可持续的，对环境无害的，能保持的，能维持的 ②支撑得住的，能承受的
[同根] sustain [səs'teɪn] *v.* ①支撑，承受（压力或重量），承担（费用等）②支援，救济 ③支持 ④保持
sustained [səs'teɪnd] *a.* 持久的，维持的
sustaining [səs'teɪnɪŋ] *a.* 用以支撑（或支持，保持、维持、供养等）的
sustainment [səs'teɪnmənt] *n.* 支持，维持

▶▶▶ **fabric** ['fæbrɪk]
[释义] *n.* ①织物 ②结构，构造，建筑物

[同义] ① textile, cloth, material

[同根] fabricate ['fæbrɪkeɪt] v. ① 建造，制造 ②捏造，编造(谎言、借口等)
fabrication [ˌfæbrɪ'keɪʃ en] n. ①捏造的东西②建造，制造

▶▶ pledge [pledʒ]

[释义] n. ①保证，誓言 ②抵押，抵押品 v. ①保证，使发誓②抵押，典当

[同义] n. ① assurance, guarantee, oath, promise

[同根] pledgee [ple'dʒiː] n. [律] 接受抵押/典押人

[词组] make a pledge 发誓，宣誓
hold sth. in pledge 以某物作抵押，以某物为担保
redeem one's pledge ①履行信约 ②赎回抵押品
under pledge 已作出保证，在作出保证的情况下
pledge oneself 保证，宣誓

▶▶ organic [ɔː'gænɪk]

[释义] a. ①有机的，不用化学物质的，有机体的 ②器官的，组织的

[同根] organ ['ɔːgən] n. ①器官 ②机构，机关
organism ['ɔːgənɪzəm] n. ①生物体，有机体 ②机体，有机组织

▶▶ undertake [ˌʌndə'teɪk]

[释义] v. ①开始，着手，承担，接受 ②许诺，保证 ③采取

[同义] ① to set about, pursue ② pledge or commit (oneself) to, promise

[同根] undertaking [ˌʌndə'teɪkɪŋ] n. ①事业，企业，任务 ②承诺，保证

▶▶ tough [tʌf]

[释义] a. ①困难的，费力的 ②坚韧的，不屈不挠的，坚强的 ③强壮的，耐劳苦的 ④倔强的(精神)，固执的，[口] 强硬的(政策等)

[同义] ① difficult, hard, hardy ② firm

③ strong, sturdy

[反义] tender

[词组] get tough [美俚] 强硬起来，行动勇敢
tough it out 忍耐过去
a tough guy [美] 无赖
a tough job 棘手的工作
a tough customer 难伺候的客人
a tough criminal 怗恶不悛的罪犯
have a tough time of it 日子不好过

▶▶ comparable ['kɒmpərəbl]

[释义] a. 可相比的 (with)，比得上的，类似的 (to)

[反义] incomparable

[同根] compare [kəm'peə] v. ①比较，对照 ②比喻，比作 ③比得上，相比
comparison [kəm'pærɪsn] n. ① 比较，对照 ②相拟，比拟
comparative [kəm'pærətɪv] a. 比较的，比较上的，相当的 n. 比较级
comparatively [kəm'pærətɪvlɪ] ad. 比较地

▶▶ virtually ['vɜːtjʊəlɪ]

[释义] ad. 事实上，实际上，差不多

[同义] actually, in fact, practically

[同根] virtual ['vɜːtjʊəl;-tʃʊəl] a. ①(用于名词前) 几乎 ②实际上起作用的，事实上生效的③ [计] 虚拟的

▶▶ indistinguishable [ˌɪndɪs'tɪŋgwɪʃ əbl]

[释义] a. ①无差别的，难分辨的 ②不易察觉的 ③难以理解的

[反义] distinguishable

[同根] distinguish [dɪ'stɪŋgwɪʃ] v. ①使具有特色，使有区别 ②区分，辨别 ③看清，发现，听出
distinguished [dɪ'stɪŋgwɪʃt] a. 卓越的，杰出的，著名的
distinct [dɪ'stɪŋkt] a. ①个别的，不同的，单独的 ②清晰的，清楚的
distinction [dɪ'stɪŋkʃən] n. ①区别，

特征 ②卓越，著名，优良 ③荣誉（称
号），殊勋，奖赏

distinctly [dɪ'stɪŋktlɪ] ad. 清楚地，
显然

distinctive [dɪ'stɪŋktɪv] a. 特殊的，
区别性的，有特色的

distinctively [dɪ'stɪŋktɪvlɪ] ad. 特殊
地，特别地

▶▶▶ weave [wi:v]

[释义] v. ①织，编，编结 ②编排，编
成（故事、小说等）③使迂回前进

[同义] intertwine, lace

[词组] weave thread into cloth 把线织
成布

weave a story 编一个故事

get weaving on… 干劲十足地开始（一
项事业）

weave one's way through a crowd 在
人群中迂回穿行

▶▶▶ synthetic [sɪn'θetɪk]

[释义] n. 化学合成物，合成纤维 a.①综
合的 ②合成的，人工制造的

[同根] synthesize ['sɪnθɪsaɪz] v. ① 综
合 ②合成

synthesis ['sɪnθɪsɪs] n.①综合②合成

synthetically [sɪn'θetɪkəlɪ] ad. ① 综
合地 ②合成地，人工制造地

▶▶▶ stretch nylon 弹性尼龙

▶▶▶ eco-friendly 对生态环境友好的，不
妨害生态环境的

▶▶▶ equivalent [ɪ'kwɪvələnt]

[释义] n. ①相等物，等价物 ②等值
（量、价等）a. 相等的，相当的，等
价的

[同义] n. ② the same, similarity a. same,
identical, equal

[同根] equal ['i:kw(ə)l] a. ①相等的，
相同的，均等的 ②平等的 ③胜任的，
合适的 n. 相等物，匹敌者 v. ①等于
②比得上，敌得过

equate [ɪ'kweɪt] v. 等同，使相等

equivalence [ɪ'kwɪvələns] n. 等 效，
等值，等量，相当

[词组] be equivalent to 与…相当，与…
相等

▶▶▶ switch [swɪtʃ]

[释义] n. ①改变，转换 ②开关 v. ①转
变，改变 ②接通或切断电流

[同义] v. ① change, exchange, substitute,
replace n. ① button, control, knob
② change, exchange, substitution,
replacement

[同根] switchboard ['swɪtʃ,bɔ:d] n. 电
话交换台、总机或配电板（工作人员）

[词组] switch jobs/positions 改变工作 /
职位

switch one's attention 注意

switch with sb 和某人调换上班时间，
调班

switch on/off （用开关）开启/关闭(电
灯、收音机等)

switch off 不再注意；失去兴趣

switch over ① （方法、产品等）完
全改变，完全转变 ②转换（广播电
台或电视频道）

switch to 转换，改变到

▶▶▶ influential [,ɪnflu'enʃəl]

[释义] a. 有影响的，有势力的

[同义] powerful, important, significant,
dominant, prominent

[反义] unimportant

[同根] influence ['ɪnfluəns] n.①影响，
势力，有影响的人（或事）②势力，
权利 v. 影响，改变

▶▶▶ charge [tʃɑ:dʒ]

[释义] v.①收（费），要（价）②控告，
指责(with), 把…归咎于 (to, on, upon)
③命令，使负责 ④装 （满），使饱含，
装料，充气 / 电，注入（油）n. ①控
诉，指控 ②费用，价钱，索价 ③责

任，管理

[同义] v. ② blame, accuse, attack

[词组] in/ take charge of… 负责…，经管…，在…掌管之下

make a charge against… 指控…

on a (the) charge of 因…罪，因…嫌疑

under the charge of 在…看管 / 负责之下

charge … with… 控告(某人)犯(某罪)

▶▶▶ count [kaʊnt]

[释义] v. ①把（某人 / 某物）计算在内 ②数，计算 ③有价值，有重要意义 n. ①计数，计算

[词组] be counted as 被算作…，被认为…

count against（被）认为对…不利

count for much/nothing/little 很有 / 没有 / 很少价值

count on/ upon 指望，依赖

count out ①逐一数出 ②不包括

▶▶▶ be set for sth/to do sth 准备好某事 / 做某事

▶▶▶ initiative [ɪˈnɪʃɪətɪv]

[释义] n. ①为解决困难而采取的行动 ②首创精神，进取心 ②主动权，主动性 a. 起始的，初步的，创始的

[同根] initial [ɪˈnɪʃəl] a. 开始的，最初的，词首的 n. ①首字母 ②(pl.) 姓名 / 组织机构的开头字母

initially [ɪˈnɪʃəlɪ] ad. 最初，开头，首先

initiate [ɪˈnɪʃɪeɪt] v. ①开始，实施，

创始，发起 ②介绍（接纳）某人加入（某团体），传授基本要领（秘密知识）

initiation [ɪnɪʃɪˈeɪʃən] n. ①开始，创始 ②入会，加入组织 ③指引，传授

[词组] have the initiative 掌握主动权，有优先权

on one's own initiative 主动地

take the initiative 带头，倡导，争取主动，发起

▶▶▶ mainstream [ˈmeɪnstriːm]

[释义] n. 主流

▶▶▶ ecofashion [ˌiːkəʊˈfæʃən]

[释义] n. 环保时尚，生态时尚

▶▶▶ unconverted [ˈʌnkənˈvɜːtɪd]

[释义] a. ①不变的，无变化的 ②未改变信仰的（尤指未改信基督教的）

[同根] convert [kənˈvɜːt] v. 使转变，使转换 ②使改变信仰(态度、观点等) n. 皈依者

conversion [kənˈvɜːʃən] n. ①转变，变换 ②改变信仰，皈依

convertible [kənˈvɜːtəbl] a. 可改变的，可转换形式（或用途）的

▶▶▶ on the hunt for 在搜寻…

▶▶▶ cute [kjuːt]

[释义] a. ①逗人喜爱的，漂亮的 ②聪明的，伶俐的，娇小可爱的 ③故作风雅的

Passage Two

Scientists have **devised** a way to determine **roughly** where a person has lived using a *strand*（缕）of hair, a technique that could help **track** the movements of criminal suspects or **unidentified** murder victims.

The method relies on measuring how chemical **variations** in drinking water **show up** in people's hair.

"You're what you eat and drink, and that's recorded in you hair," said Thure Cerling, a geologist at the University of Utah.

While U.S diet is relatively identical, water supplies vary. The differences result from weather patterns. The chemical composition of rainfall changes slightly as raid clouds move.

Most hydrogen and oxygen atoms in water are stable, but traces of both elements are also present as heavier *isotopes* (同位素). The heaviest raid falls first. As a result, storms that form over the Pacific deliver heavier water to California than to Utah.

Similar patterns exist throughout the U.S. By measuring the proportion of heavier hydrogen and oxygen isotopes along a strand of hair, scientists can construct a geographic timeline. Each inch of hair corresponds to about two months.

Cerling's team collected tap water samples from 600 cities and constructed a mop of the regional differences. They checked the accuracy of the map by testing 200 hair samples collected from 65 barber shops.

They were able to accurately place the hair samples in broad regions roughly corresponding to the movement of rain systems.

"It's not good for *pinpointing* (精确定位)," Cerling said. "It's good for eliminating many possibilities."

Todd Park, a local detective, said the method has helped him learn more about an unidentified woman whose skeleton was found near Great Salt Lake.

The woman was 5 feet tall. Police recovered 26 bones, a T-shirt and several strands of hair.

When Park heard about the research, he gave the hair samples to the researchers. Chemical testing showed that over the two years before her death, she moved about every two months.

She stayed in the Northwest, although the test could not be more specific than somewhere between eastern Oregon and western Wyoming.

"It's still a substantial area," Park said "But it narrows it way down for me."

文章词汇注释

▶▶▶ **devise** [dɪ'vaɪz]

[释义] v. ①设计，想出 ②创造，发明 ③图谋，策划

[同义] ① & ② conceive, design, invent

[同根] device [dɪ'vaɪs] n. ①装置，设备，设计，图案 ②策略 ③发明物

▶▶▶ **roughly** ['rʌflɪ]

[释义] ad. ①大概，大约 ②粗暴地，粗暴地

[同义] ① almost, nearly, about, approximately, around

[反义] ① accurately

[同根] rough [rʌf] n. ①草样，草图 ②粗制品 ③粗人 a. ①表面粗糙的，崎岖不平的 ②粗暴的，粗野的 ③约略的，概略的 ④艰难的，困难的

roughen ['rʌfən] v. (使某物) 变得粗糙或不平整

roughness ['rʌfnɪs] n. 粗糙，粗暴，粗糙程度

▶▶▶ **track** [træk]

[释义] v. 追踪，跟踪 n. 足迹，踪迹，(飞机、轮船等的) 航迹，车辙

[同义] trace, trail

[词组] on the right track 循着正确的路线，正确地

on the wrong track 循着错误的路线，错误地

track down 跟踪找到，追捕到，追查到，搜寻到

▶▶▶ **unidentified** ['ʌnaɪ'dentɪfaɪd]

[释义] a. ①未经确认的，身分不明的 ②未透露姓名的

[同根] identify [aɪ'dentɪfaɪ] v. 认明，识别，认同，鉴定

identification [aɪ'dentɪfɪ'keɪʃən]

n. ①认明，确认，识别 ②身份证明

identity [aɪ'dentɪtɪ] n. ①身份，本体 ②个性，特性 ③相同处，同一性

identical [aɪ'dentɪkəl] a. 完全相同的，同一的

identically [aɪ'dentɪkəlɪ] ad. 同一地，相等地

▶▶▶ **variation** [veərɪ'eɪʃən]

[释义] n. ①变异，变种 ②变化，变动

[同义] ① adaptation, modification, transformation ② alteration, change

[同根] vary ['veərɪ] v. ①有变化，相异 ②改变，变更

variety [və'raɪɪtɪ] n. ①多样性，变化性 ②品种，变种 ③种类

variability [ˌveərɪə'bɪlɪtɪ] n. ①多样性，变化 ②变化性，可变性

various ['veərɪəs] a. ①不同的，各种各样的 ②多个的

variable ['veərɪəbəl] a. 可变的，可变的，易变的 n. (pl.) 可变的事物，可变的量

variant ['veərɪənt] n. 变体，变种，变型

▶▶▶ **show up** ①暴露或揭示…的真实特征或本质 ②露面，到达 ③清楚可见的

▶▶▶ **composition** [kɒmpə'zɪʃən]

[释义] n. ①成分，合成 ②作文，乐曲 ③结构，构图

[同根] compose [kəm'pəuz] v. ①组成，构成 ②创作，作曲 ③使安定，使平静

composer [kəm'pəuzə] n. 作曲家，创造者

component [kəm'pəunənt] n. 组成部

份，成分，元件 *a.* 组成的，合成的
composite ['kɒmpəzɪt] *a.* 混合成的，综合成的 *n.* 合成物，复合材料

▶▶▶ **stable** ['steɪbl]
[释义] *a.* 稳定的，坚固的
[同义] established, firm, secure, settled, sound, steadfast, steady
[反义] instable
[同根] stability [stə'bɪlɪtɪ] *n.* 稳定，稳固
stabilize ['steɪbɪlaɪz] *v.* 使稳定、坚固、不动摇

▶▶▶ **deliver** [dɪ'lɪvə]
[释义] *v.* ①释放，排出，放出 ②传递，投递，运送 ③发表，讲，宣布
[同根] delivery [dɪ'lɪvərɪ] *n.* ① 递送，运送，传送 ②讲演，表演
delivererer [dɪ'lɪvərə] *n.* 递送人
[词组] deliver (oneself) of 讲，表达
deliver up/over to 交出，移交

▶▶▶ **construct** [kən'strʌkt]
[释义] *v.* ①建造，构筑，组成，构成 ②制造，编造 ③对…进行构思，按句法组合
['kɒnstrʌkt] *n.* ①建造物，构成物 ②观念，概念
[同义] create,make
[同根] construction [kən'strʌkʃən] *n.* 建筑，建筑物
constructive [kən'strʌktɪv] *a.* 建设性的
constructor [kən'strʌktə] *n.* 建造者，施工者

▶▶▶ **timeline** ['taɪmlaɪn]
[释义] *n.* ①活动时间表 ②年代记，年表 ③大事记，年代表

▶▶▶ **correspond** [ˌkɒrɪ'spɒnd]
[释义] *v.* ①与…相关，相应 ②与…一致，符合，相类似 ③通信
[同义] ② agree, harmonize, resemble

③ write
[同根] correspondent [ˌkɒrɪ'spɒndənt] *n.* 通信者，通讯员，记者 *a.* 符合的，一致的
corresponding [ˌkɒrɪ'spɒndɪŋ] *a.* ①相应的 ②符合的，一致的
correspondence [ˌkɒrɪ'spɒndəns] *n.* ①符合，一致 ②相当，类似 ③通信（联系），信函
[词组] correspond to 与…符合/一致相称
correspond with 与…通信

▶▶▶ **tap water** 自来水

▶▶▶ **eliminate** [ɪ'lɪmɪneɪt]
[释义] *v.* ①消除，排除，清除 ②淘汰，不加考虑
[同义] discard, dispose of, exclude, reject, get rid of, throw out
[反义] add
[同根] elimination [ɪˌlɪmɪ'neɪʃən] *n.* ①排除，除去，消除 ②忽视，略去
[词组] eliminate the false and retain the true 去伪存真
eliminate errors 消除错误
eliminate the need of 使不需要
eliminate the possibility of 排除…的可能性，使…不可能
eliminate the risk/problem 消除风险/问题

▶▶▶ **skeleton** ['skelɪtən]
[释义] *n.* ①骨骼，骸骨 ②骨瘦如柴的人或动物 ③（建筑物的）骨架，框架 ④梗概，提要，轮廓 *a.* ①骨骼的，骨骼般的 ②梗概的，提要的，轮廓的 ③骨瘦如柴的
[词组] be reduced to a skeleton 瘦得皮包骨
be worn to a skeleton 瘦得象骷髅
family skeleton (=skeleton in the cupboard, skeleton in the family closet) 家丑，见不得人的事

walking skeleton 骨瘦如柴的人

skeleton at the feast/banquet 扫兴的东西 / 家伙

▶▶▶ **substantial** [səbˈstænʃəl]

[释义] *a.* ①有重大价值的，重要的 ②主要的，实质性的，实体的 ③数目大的，可观的 ④充裕的，充足的

[同根] substance [ˈsʌbstəns] *n.* ①实质，本旨 ②物质，物

substantive [ˈsʌbstəntɪv] *a.* 实质的，重要的

substantially [səbˈstænʃ(ə)lɪ] *ad.* 充分地，实质地

[词组] substantial things 实际存在的东西

a man of substantial build 体格结实的人

a substantial victory 巨大的胜利

a substantial argument 重要的论证

a substantial meal 丰盛的一餐

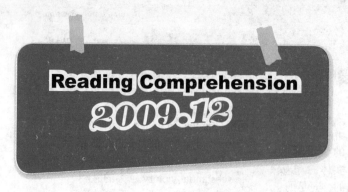

Skimming and Scanning
Colleges taking another look at value of merit-based aid

Good grades and high test scores still matter — a lot — to many colleges as they award financial aid.

But with low-income students projected to make up an ever-larger share of the college-bound population in coming years, some schools are re-examining whether that aid, typically known as merit aid, is the most effective use of precious institutional dollars.

George Washington University in Washington, D.C., for example, said last week that it would cut the value of its average merit scholarships by about one-third and reduce the number of recipients (接受者), pouring the savings, about $2.5 million, into need-based aid. Allegheny College in Meadville, Pa., made a similar decision three years ago.

Now, Hamilton College in Clinton, N.Y., says it will phase out merit scholarships altogether. No current merit-aid recipients will lose their scholarships, but need-based aid alone will be awarded beginning with students entering in fall 2008.

Not all colleges offer merit aid; generally, the more selective a school, the less likely it is to do so. Harvard and Princeton, for example, offer generous need-based packages, but plenty of families who don't meet need eligibility (资格) have been willing to pay whatever they must for a big-name school.

For small regional colleges that struggle just to fill seats, merit aid can be an important revenue-builder because many recipients still pay enough tuition dollars over and above the scholarship amount to keep the institution running.

But for rankings-conscious schools in between, merit aid has served primarily as a tool to recruit top students and to improve their academic profiles. "They're trying to buy students," says Skidmore College economist

Sandy Baum.

Studies show merit aid also tends to benefit **disproportionately** students who could afford to **enroll** without it.

"As we **look to the future**, we see a more **pressing** need to invest in need-based aid," says Monica Inzer, dean of admission and financial aid at Hamilton, which has offered merit scholarships for 10 years. During that time, it rose in *US News & World Report*'s ranking of the best **liberal arts** colleges, from 25 to 17.

Merit aid, which benefited about 75 students a year, or about 4% of its student body, **at a cost of** about $1 million a year, "served us well," Inzer says, but "to be **discounting** the price for families that don't need financial aid doesn't feel right anymore."

Need-based aid remains by far the largest share of all student aid, which includes state, federal and institutional **grants**. But merit aid, offered primarily by schools and states, is growing faster, both **overall** and at the institutional level.

Between 1995-96 and 2003-04, institutional merit aid alone increased 212%, compared with 47% for need-based grants. At least 15 states also offer merit aid, typically in a **bid** to enroll top students in the state's public institutions.

But in recent years, a growing *chorus*（异口同声）of critics has begun pressuring schools to **drop the practice**. Recent decisions by Hamilton and others may be "a sign that people are starting to realize that there's this **destructive** competition going on," says Baum, co-author of a recent College Report that raises concerns about the role of institutional aid not based on need.

David Laird, president of the 17-member Minnesota Private College Council, says many of his schools would like to reduce their merit aid but fear that in doing so, they would **lose** top students **to** their competitors.

"No one can take **unilateral** action," says Laird, who is exploring whether to seek an **exemption** from federal **antitrust** laws so member colleges can discuss how they could jointly reduce merit aid. "This is a **merry-go-round** that's going very fast, and none of the institutions believe they can **sustain** the risks of trying to **break away** by themselves."

A **complicating** factor is that merit aid has become so popular with middle-income families, who don't **qualify** for need-based aid, that many have come to depend on it. And, as tuitions continue to increase, the line between merit and need blurs.

That's one reason Allegheny College doesn't plan to drop merit aid entirely.

"We still believe in rewarding superior achievements and know that these top-notch students truly value the scholarship," says Scott Friedhoff, Allegheny's vice president for enrollment.

Emory University in Atlanta, which boasts a $4.7 billion *endowment* (捐赠), meanwhile, is taking another approach. This year, it announced it would eliminate loans for needy students and cap them for middle-income families. At the same time, it said it would expand its 28-year-old merit program.

"Yeah, we're playing the merit game," acknowledges Tom Lancaster, associate dean for undergraduate education. But it has its strong points, too, he says. "The fact of the matter is, it's not just about the lowest-income people. It is the average American middle-class family who is being priced out of the market."

A few words about merit-based aid:

Merit-based aid is aid offered to students who achieve excellence in a given area, and is generally known as academic, athletic and artistic merit scholarships.

Academic merit scholarships are based on students' grades, GPA and overall academic performance during high school. They are typically meant for students going straight to college right after high school. However, there are scholarships for current college students with exceptional grades as well. These merit scholarships usually help students pay tuition bills, and they can be renewed each year as long as the recipients continue to qualify. In some cases, students may need to be recommended by their school or a teacher as part of the qualification process.

Athletic merit scholarships are meant for students that *excel* (突出) in sports of any kind, from football to track and field events. Recommendation for these scholarships is required, since exceptional athletic performance has to be recognized by a coach or a *referee* (裁判). Applicants need to send in a tape containing their best performance.

Artistic merit scholarships require that applicants excel in a given artistic area. This generally includes any creative field such as art, design, fashion, music, dance or writing. Applying for artistic merit scholarships usually requires that students **submit** a *portfolio* (选择) of some sort, whether that includes a collection of artwork, a recording of a **musical performance** or a video of them dancing.

文章词汇注释

▶▶ **financial aid** 财政援助

▶▶ **project** [prə'dʒekt]
[释义] *v.* ①突出，使凸出 ②发射，投掷，投（影）③设计，计划
['prɒdʒekt] *n.* 方案，规划，项目，工程
[同义] *v.* ① stand out, stick out ② throw, launch, cast ③ plan, devise *n.* scheme, plan, assignment, task
[同根] projection [prə'dʒekʃən] *n.* ①设计，规划，计划 ②投影图 ③凸出，凸出部 ④发射，投掷
projector [prə'dʒektə] *n.* 投影机，幻灯机，放映机
[词组] advanced project ①尖端研究计划 ②已提出的计划 ③远景规划
project oneself ①突出自己，表现自己 ②设想自己处身于 (into)
project sth. onto sb. ①设想某人怀有和自己一样的想法或感情

▶▶ **make up** ①构成，组成 ②和解，和好 ③化妆，化装 ④捏造，虚构 ⑤弥补

▶▶ **merit** ['merɪt]
[释义] *n.* ①值得称赞或奖励的品质，价值，长处，优点 [pl.] 功绩，功劳
v. 应获得（某事物，值得）
[同义] *n.* ① virtue, value, goodness, excellence
[反义] *n.* ① demerit, fault, defect

[词组] according to one's merits 按价值，按资质
have the merits [律] 在诉讼中处于有利的地位
make a merit of (=take merit to oneself for) 以某事居功自夸
on one's merits 按其本身条件(或情况)
stand on one's own merits 靠实力

▶▶ **precious** ['preʃəs]
[释义] *a.* 珍贵的，宝贵的
[同义] priceless, special, valuable
[反义] valueless
[词组] precious seconds/minutes/hours/time 宝贵时间
precious resources 宝贵资源
precious gem/stone/jewel 宝石
be precious to 对…来说是宝贵的

▶▶ **institutional** [ˌɪnstɪ'tjuːʃənəl]
[释义] *a.* ①学会、协会、教育等公共机构的，社会慈善事业性质的 ②设立的，规定的，制度上的
[同根] institute ['ɪnstɪtjuːt] *v.* ①建立，创立，制定 ②实行，开始 *n.* ①学院，(大专) 学校 ②学会，协会
institution [ɪnstɪ'tjuːʃn] *n.* ①创立，制定 ②风俗，习惯 ③（教育，慈善，宗教等的）公共社会机构

▶▶ **cut...by...** 把…减少…

▶▶ **scholarship** ['skɒləʃɪp]

[释义] *n.* ①奖学金 ②学问，学术成就 ③获得奖学金的资格

[同根] scholar [ˈskɒlə] *n.* ①学生，学习者 ②（尤指人文学科的学生）学者 ③奖学金获得者

▶▶▶ pour... into... 把…大量投入…

▶▶▶ phase out 逐渐淘汰，逐渐退出，逐步停止

▶▶▶ package [ˈpækɪdʒ]

[释义] *n.* ①一揽子计划（或交易等）②包裹，小盒 ③包装袋 *v.* ①包裹，把…打包 ②包装（商品）③把…组合成一体

[同根] pack [pæk] *n.* 包裹，背包 *v.* 包装，捆扎，塞满，压紧

packaging [ˈpækɪdʒɪŋ] *n.* ①包装，打包 ②包装物，包装术，包装业

[词组] financial aid package 大学助学金（包括奖学金，贷款和校内工读自给）

package deal 一揽子交易

package tour 包办旅游

package store 瓶装酒小卖店

aid package 援助计划

▶▶▶ need [ni:d]

[释义] *n.* ①贫穷，不幸，逆境 ②缺乏，需要

[同根] needy [ˈni:dɪ] *a.* 贫困的，非常贫穷的，缺乏生活必需品的

[词组] at one's need 在紧急时，在困难时，在危险时

be/stand in need of ... 需要…

crying need 迫切的需要

If need be/were/require 如果必要的话

in need 在危难中，在危急中

in case/time of need 在紧急的时候

▶▶▶ big-name 著名，知名人士，众所周知的事情

▶▶▶ fill seat 招满学生

▶▶▶ revenue [ˈrevɪnju:]

[释义] *n.* ①收入，（尤指）岁入 ②国家的税收 ③ (*pl.*) 收入总额 ④（个人或国家的）税务所，税务局

[同义] income, profit, returns, takings

▶▶▶ ranking [ˈræŋkɪŋ]

[释义] *n.* ①等级，排名，顺序 ②等级评定 *a.* 第一流的，出类拔萃的，首席的，高级的

[同根] rank [ræŋk] *v.* ①排列，把…分等级 ②把…排列整齐 *n.* ①排，列，行 ②军衔，地位 ③显贵，高地位 ④ (*pl.*) 士兵

[词组] persons of rank 达官显贵

ranked first in the class 在班上名列前茅

pull rank 弄权，利用某人的高级职位谋求利益

▶▶▶ primarily [ˈpraɪmərɪlɪ]

[释义] *ad.* ①主要地，首要地 ②最初，原来

[同义] ① above all, chiefly, mainly, principally

[同根] primary [ˈpraɪmərɪ] *a.* ①最初的，原始的 ②初级的 ③主要的，首要的

prime [praɪm] *n.* ①最佳部分，最完美的状态，（某人的）鼎盛期 ②第一部分，最初部分 *a.* ①主要的 ②最佳的 ③最初的

primitive [ˈprɪmɪtɪv] *a.* ①原始的 ②粗糙的 ③纯朴的 *n.* 原始人

▶▶▶ profile [ˈprəʊfaɪl]

[释义] *n.* ①形象，外观，外形，轮廓 ②剖面，侧面 ③传略，人物简介，概况 *v.* ①给…画侧面像，描…的轮廓 ②写…的传略或概况

▶▶▶ disproportionately [ˌdɪsprəˈpɔ:ʃənɪtlɪ]

[释义] *ad.* ①不成比例地 ②不均衡地，不相称地

[同根] proportion [prəˈpɔ:ʃən] *n.* ①比

例 ②均衡，匀称 ③份额

proportional [prə'pɔːʃ[nəl] *a.* 成比例的，均衡的，与…相称的 (to)

proportionate [prə'pɔːʃ[ineɪt] *a.* 相称的，成比例的，均衡的 *v.* ①使相称，使成适当比例，使均衡 ②使适应

▶▶ **enroll** [ɪn'rəʊl]

[释义] *v.* ①（使）入学，入伍，入会 ②吸收（成员），招收 ③登记，注册

[同根] enrollment [ɪn'rəʊlmənt] *n.* ①登记，注册 ②入伍，入会，入学

▶▶ **look to the future** 考虑未来

▶▶ **pressing** ['presɪŋ]

[释义] *a.* ①（工作、要求等）急迫的，紧急的，迫切的 ②（邀请等）恳切的

[同根] press [pres] *v.* ①压，按 ②紧握，紧抱 ③压，榨取 ④催促，迫使 *n.* ①新闻界，报界 ②压，按 ③印刷业，出版社

impressive [ɪm'presɪv] *a.* 给人深刻印象的（尤指因巨大、壮观或重要），令人难以忘记的

impressionable [ɪm'preʃənəbəl] *a.* 易受影响的，敏感的

▶▶ **liberal arts** 大学文科

▶▶ **at a cost of** 以…的代价，花…

[同根] at all costs/at any cost/cost what it may 不惜任何代价，无论如何

at the cost of 以…为代价，丧失…，牺牲…

free of cost 免费

labour cost 人工成本

cost of living 生活费用

to one's cost 付出了代价才…，吃亏后才…

cost sb. dear/dearly 使某人花很多钱，使人付出很高的代价

▶▶ **discount** [dɪs'kaʊnt]

[释义] *v.* ①减少 ②打去（若干）折扣，打折扣买／卖 ③不全信，怀疑地看待 ④不重视，低估，贬低 ['dɪskaʊnt] *n.* ①折扣 ②不全信

[同根] discountable [dɪs'kaʊntəbl] *a.* ①不可全信的 ②可享受折扣的

[词组] at a discount ①打折扣，不值钱的 ②不受重视的

with some discount ①打折扣 ②以保留态度

▶▶ **grant** [grɑːnt]

[释义] *n.* ①补助金，助学金 ②授予物，拨款 ③财产转让 *v.* ①准予，准许 ②赠予，提供 ③承认，认可

[同义] *v.* ① allow, permit, consent ② award, allot, deal out, donate, give, give out,present

[词组] granted/granting that… 假定，就算…

take… for granted ①认为…理所当然 ②（因视作当然）对…不予重视

a grant in aid (of) 补助金，助学金

▶▶ **overall** ['əʊvərɔːl]

[释义] *a.* 总的，全部的，全面的 *ad.* ①总共 ②大体上，一般地 *n.* [*pl.*] 工装裤，长罩衣

[同义] *a.* total, whole

[词组] overall impression 总体印象

overall situation 总的形势，全局

overall utilization 综合利用

▶▶ **bid** [bɪd]

[释义] *n.* ①（做、获得、实现某事物的）企图，努力 ②出价，投标 *v.* ①投标，出价 ②企图，努力

[同义] *n.& v.* ① attempt. try, effort, end-eavor ② offer

[词组] make a bid for ①为…投标，为…出价 ②努力争取…

bid for ①为…投标，为…出价 ②努力争取…

bid up 哄抬，抬高出价数

▶▶ drop the practice 停止这种做法

▶▶ destructive [dɪsˈtrʌktɪv]

[释义] a. ①破坏（性）的，毁灭（性）的 ②消极的，非建设性的

[同义] devastating, damaging

[反义] constructive

[同根] destruct [dɪˈstrʌkt] v. ①破坏 ②自毁 n. 故意有计划的破坏 a. 破坏的
destruction [dɪsˈtrʌkʃən] n. ①破坏，消灭 ②破坏物，毁灭的原因或手段

▶▶ lose...to... 丧失某事物（由某事物或某人获得）

[同根] be lost in 全神贯注于…；沉湎于…
be lost to 不再属于…所有，对…无动于衷
be lost without sth. [口] 缺少某物就无法有效地工作 / 愉快地生活
lose oneself in ①在…迷路 ②全神贯注于…之中

▶▶ unilateral[ˈjuːnɪˈlætərəl]

[释义] a. 单方面，单边的，片面的

[同根] unilateralism [ˈjuːnɪˈlætərəlɪzm] n. 单边主义
bilateral [baɪˈlætərəl] a. 有两面的，双边的
multilateral [ˈmʌltɪˈlætərəl] a. 多边的，多国参加的

▶▶ exemption [ɪgˈzempʃən]

[释义] n. ①解除，免除，豁免 ②免税，免税额

[同根] exempt [ɪgˈzempt] a. 被免除（义务、责任等）的，被豁免的 v. 免除，豁免 (from) n. 被免除（义务，责任）的人，免税人

▶▶ antitrust [ˌæntɪˈtrʌst]

[释义] a. 反托拉斯的，反垄断的

▶▶ merry-go-round n. ①旋转木马 ②忙

得团团转，一连串的繁忙活动

▶▶ sustain [səsˈteɪn]

[释义] v. ①经受住，忍受 ②支撑，撑住 ③保持，使持续，供养

[同义] ① stand, bear, tolerate, endure ② support ③ keep up, maintain, suffer

[同根] sustainable [səˈsteɪnəbl] a. ①可持续性的 ②能承受的

▶▶ break away 突然离开，突然改变，脱离，放弃

▶▶ complicate [ˈkɒmplɪkeɪt]

[释义] v. （使）复杂化

[反义] simplify

[同根] complicated [ˈkɒmplɪkeɪtɪd] a. 复杂的，难解的
complication [ˌkɒmplɪˈkeɪʃən] n. ①复杂化 ② [医] 并发症

▶▶ qualify [ˈkwɒlɪfaɪ]

[释义] v. ① （使）具有资格，(使)合适，证明…合格 ②准予，授予…权力

[同根] qualification [kwɒlɪfɪˈkeɪʃən] n. ①资格，资历，[pl.] 考试合格证书 ②限制，条件 ③授权，批准，赋予资格
qualified [ˈkwɒlɪfaɪd] a. ①有资格的，合适的，胜任的 ②有限度的，有条件的，有保留的

[词组] qualify as ①取得…资格 ②把（某人）说成
qualify for 有…资格 / 有…权，应得，使合格，使能担任，使适合于
qualify to do sth. 使有资格做某事

▶▶ blur [blɜː]

[释义] v. ①变得模糊，使模糊不清 ②弄污，涂污 n. ①污点，污迹 ②模糊，模糊的东西

[同根] blurring [ˈblɜːrɪŋ] n. 模糊，斑点甚多，（图像的）混乱 a. 模糊的，不清楚的

blurry ['blɜːrɪ] a. 模糊的，不清楚的

▶▶▶ **superior** [suːˈpɪərɪə; sjuː-]

[释义] a. ①（在质量等方面）较好的，优秀的 ②上级的，（在职位等方面）较高的 ③有优越感的，高傲的
n. ①上级，领导 ②长辈 ③优越者，优胜者

[反义] inferior

[同根] super ['sjuːpə] a. ①上等的，极好的 ②特大的 adv. 非常，过分地
n. 特级品
superiority [suːpɪərɪˈɒrɪtɪ] n. 优势，优等，上等

[词组] be superior to ①胜过，比…好 ②不为…所动（屈服）

▶▶▶ **top-notch** 拔尖的

▶▶▶ **boast** [bəust]

[释义] v. 夸，自夸，夸口 n. 大话，自夸的话

[同义] brag

[同根] boastful ['bəustful] a. 自夸的，自负的
boaster ['bəustə] n. 自夸的人

[词组] make a boast of sth. 夸耀某事
without boasting 不是自夸（用于插入语）
boast about/ of 自夸，自吹自擂

▶▶▶ **approach** [əˈprəutʃ]

[释义] n. ①（处理问题的）方式，方法，态度 ②接近，靠近 ③途径，通路
v. ①接近，靠近 ②（着手）处理，（开始）对付

[同义] n. ① way, method, means, manner, mode

[同根] approachable [əˈprəutʃəbəl]
a. ①可接近的 ②平易近人的，亲切的

[词组] at the approach of... 在…快到的时候
make an approach to... 对…进行探讨
make approaches to sb. 设法接近某

人，想博得某人的好感
approach sb. on/about sth. 和某人接洽 / 商量 / 交涉某事
approach to... ①接近，近似，约等于 ②（做某事）的方法（途径）

▶▶▶ **cap** [kæp]

[释义] 覆盖

[词组] cap in hand 尊敬地 / 卑躬地，谦逊地

▶▶▶ **acknowledge** [əkˈnɒlɪdʒ]

[释义] v. ①承认 ②告知收到（信件、礼物等）③表示感谢

[同义] ① admit, accept ② reply, respond, answer ③ greet, salute

[反义] ① deny ② & ③ ignore

[同根] acknowledgement [əkˈnɒlɪdʒmənt]
n. ①承认，确认 ②感谢，鸣谢 ③（表示收到某物的）回信，收条

[词组] be acknowledged as 被公认为是…
acknowledge receipt of 签收…

▶▶▶ **price out of the market** 定价过高以致无人问津

▶▶▶ **exceptional** [ɪkˈsepʃənl]

[释义] a. ①格外的，异常的，优越的 ②例外的，特殊的

[同义] ① extraordinary, notable, outstanding, remarkable, unusual

[反义] common, ordinary

[同根] except [ɪkˈsept] v. ①把…除外，不计 ②反对，表示异议 prep. 除…之外
exception [ɪkˈsepʃən] n. ①例外，除外的人（或物）②反对，异议，抗辩

▶▶▶ **recommend** [rekəˈmend]

[释义] v. ①推荐，介绍 ②劝告，建议

[同义] advise, counsel, suggest, propose, urge, commend

[反义] oppose

[同根] recommendation [ˌrekəmen'deɪʃən] *n.* ①推荐，介绍，推荐信 ②劝告，建议

recommendable [ˌrekə'mendəbl] *a.* 值得推荐的，可取的

recommendatory [ˌrekə'mendətərɪ] *a.* ①推荐的 ②引起重视的 ③劝告的

[词组] recommend doing sth 建议做… recommend sth to sb 向某人推荐某物

▶▶ **track and field events** [体] 田径，田径运动

▶▶ **contain** [kən'teɪn]

[释义] *v.* ①包含，容纳 ②控制，遏制（感情等）

[同义] ① comprise, consist of, include, involve ② control, hold, restrain

[同根] container [kən'teɪnə] *n.* 容器，集装箱

containment [kən'teɪnmənt] *n.* 遏制，遏制政策

[词组] be contained between / within 含于…间，夹在…之间

contain oneself 自制

▶▶ **submit** [səb'mɪt]

[释义] *v.* ①提交，呈递 ②（使）服从，（使）屈服 ③听从，忍受

[同义] present

[反义] withdraw

[同根] submission [səb'mɪʃən] *n.* 屈服，降服，服从

[词组] submit to ①提交给… ②服从于，屈从于

submit oneself to 甘受，服从

▶▶ **musical performance** 演奏（会）

Reading in Depth
Section A

In families with two working parents, fathers may have more impact on a child's language development than mothers, a new study suggests.

Researchers **recruited** 92 families from 11 child care centers before their children were a year old, interviewing each to establish income, level of education and child care arrangements. Overall, it was a group of well-educated middle class families, with married parents both living in the home.

When the children were two, the researchers **videotaped** them at home in **free-play sessions** with both parents, recording all of their speech. The study will appear in the November **issue** of the Journal of *Applied Developmental Psychology*.

The scientists measured the total number of *utterances*（话语）of the parents, the number of different words they used, the **complexity** of their sentences and other **aspects** of their speech. On average, fathers spoke less than mothers did, but they did not differ in the length of utterances or proportion of questions asked.

Finally, the researchers analyzed the children's speech at the age of 3, using a standardized language test. The only **predictors** of high scores on the test were the mother's level of education, the quality of child care and the number of different words the father used.

The researchers are **unsure** why the father's speech, and not the mothers', had an effect.

"It's well **established** that the mother's language does have an impact," said Nadya Pancsofar, the lead author of the study. It could be that the high-functioning mothers in the study had already had a strong influence on their children's speech development. Ms. Pancsofar said, "or it may be that mothers are **contributing** in a way we did not measure in the study."

文章词汇注释

▶▶▶ recruit [rɪ'kruːt]

[释义] v. ①吸收（新成员），征募（新兵）②充实，补充 ③使恢复 n. 新兵，新手，新成员

[同义] v. ① draft, enlist, enroll, sign up

[同根] recruitment [rɪ'kruːtmənt] n. 征募新兵，补充

▶▶▶ videotape ['vɪdɪəuteɪp]

[释义] v. 把…录在录像磁带上 n. 录像带

▶▶▶ free-play ①自由游戏 ②空转

▶▶▶ session ['seʃən]

[释义] n. ① 从事某项活动的一段时间 ②会议，会期 ③上课时间

▶▶▶ issue ['ɪʃuː; 'ɪsjuː]

[释义] n. ①（报刊等）期、号 ②问题，争论，争论点 ③（水、血等）流出，放出 ④河口，出口 v. ①（报刊等）发行，发布，颁布 ②排出，（使）流出 ③分配

[同义] n. ① copy ② subject, theme, topic v. ① distribute, publish

[词组] at issue 在争论中；不一致，有分歧；待裁决的

bring an issue to a close 把问题解决

die without issue 死时无子嗣

in issue 在争论中；结果，结局

make an issue of sth. 使某事成为有争论的问题

raise a new issue 提出新论点

take issue against 反对

issue from 从…流出 / 冒出 / 传出

▶▶▶ complexity [kəm'pleksɪtɪ]

[释义] n. ①复杂（性），错综（性）②错综复杂的事物，

[同义] complication

[反义] simplicity

[同根] complex ['kɒmpleks] a. ①由部件组成的，组合的 ②复杂的，难懂的 n. ①综合体，集合体 ② [心] 情结

complexion [kəm'plekʃən] n. ①肤色，气色，面色 ②外观，形势，局面

▶▶▶ aspect ['æspekt]

[释义] n. ①（问题等的）方面，情况，状况 ②样子，外表，面貌，神态

▶▶ **predictor** [prɪ'dɪktə]

[释义] *n.* 起预报作用的事物，预言者

[同根] predict [prɪ'dɪkt] *v.* 预言，预测

prediction [prɪ'dɪkʃən] *n.* 预言，预报，被预言的事物

predictable [prɪ'dɪktəbəl] *a.* 可预言的

predictive [prɪ'dɪktɪv] *a.* 预言性的，成为前兆的

▶▶ **unsure** ['ʌn'ʃuə]

[释义] *a.* ①不肯定的，不确定的，不确知的 ②缺乏信心的，没有把握的

▶▶ **establish** [ɪs'tæblɪʃ]

[释义] *v.* ①证实，确定，确立，使被接受，使得到承认 ②建立，设立 ③制定，规定

[同义] ① demonstrate, prove ② found, organize, set, settle

[反义] demolish destroy ruin

[同根] established [ɪs'tæblɪʃt] *a.* ①确定的，证实的 ②已确立的，已建立的，已制定的

establishment [ɪs'tæblɪʃmənt] *n.* ①建立，确立，制定 ②建立的机构（如军队、军事机构、行政机关、学校、医院、教会）

the Establishment 当权派（通常为守旧派）

[词组] establish sb. as… 任命 / 派某人担任…

▶▶ **contributing** [kən'trɪbjuːtɪŋ]

[释义] *a.* 起作用的，有贡献的

[同根] contribute [kən'trɪbjuːt] *v.* ①捐助，捐赠 ②投稿 ③贡献，对…做出贡献

contribution [kɒn'trɪbjuːʃən] *n.* ①贡献 ②捐款 ③投稿

contributor [kən'trɪbjuːtə] *n.* 捐助者，投稿者

contributive [kən'trɪbjuːtɪv] *a.* 有助的，促成的

contributory [kəntrɪ'bjuːtərɪ; (US) kən-trɪ'bjuːtɔːrɪ] *a.* ①贡献的 ②促成的，起一份

Section B
Passage One

Throughout this long, **tense** election, everyone has focused on the **presidential candidates** and how they'll change America. Rightly so. But selfishly, I'm more **fascinated** by Michelle Obama and what she might be able to do, not just for this country, but for me as an African-American woman. As the **potential** First Lady, she would have the world's attention. And that means that for the first time people will have a chance to get up close and personal with the type of African-American woman they so rarely see.

Usually, the lives of black women go largely unexamined. The **prevailing** theory seems to be that we're all **hot-tempered** single mothers who can't keep a man. Even in the world of **make-believe**, black women still can't escape the **stereotype** of being **eye-rolling**, **oversexed** females raised by our never-married, *alcoholic*（酗酒的）mothers.

These images have helped define the way all black women are viewed, including Michelle Obama. Before she ever gets the chance to **commit** to a cause, **charity** or **foundation** as First Lady, her most urgent and perhaps most complicated duty may be simply to be herself.

It won't be easy. Because few **mainstream publications** have done in-depth **features** on regular African-American women, little is known about who we are, what we think and what we face on a regular basis. **For better or worse**, Michelle will represent us all.

Just as she will have her critics, she will also have millions of fans who usually have little interest in the First Lady. Many African-American blogs have written about what they'd like to see Michelle bring to the White House—mainly showing the world that a black woman can support her man and raise a strong black family. Michelle will have to work to please everyone—an impossible task. But for many African-American women like me, just a little of her *poise*（沉着）, confidence and intelligence will **go a long way** in changing an image that's been around for far too long.

文章词汇注释

▶▶▶ **tense** [tens]

[释义] *a.* ①紧张的 ②拉紧的 *v.* ①（使）紧张 ②（使）拉紧

[同义] *a.* rigid, strained, tight

[同根] tension ['tenʃən] *n.* ①紧张（状态），不安 ②拉紧，压力，张力 *v.* 拉紧，使紧张

intense [ɪn'tens] *a.* ①强烈的，剧烈的，激烈的 ②热切的，热情的

intensive [ɪn'tensɪv] *a.* 加强的，集中的，深入细致的，密集的

intension [ɪn'tenʃən] *n.* 紧张，强烈，加强

intensity [ɪn'tensɪtɪ] *n.* ①（思想、感情、活动等的）强烈,剧烈 ②（电、热、光、声等的）强度，烈度

intensify [ɪn'tensɪfaɪ] *v.* （使）增强，

（使）变尖锐

intensification [ɪnˌtensɪfɪ'keɪʃən] *n.* 强烈，加强，增强

▶▶▶ **presidential candidates** 总统候选人

▶▶▶ **fascinate** ['fæsɪneɪt]

[释义] *v.* ①迷住，吸引，使着迷 ②使呆住，使不动

[同义] attract, charm

[同根] fascinating ['fæsɪneɪtɪŋ] *a.* 迷人的，吸引人的，使人神魂颠倒的

fascinated ['fæsɪneɪtɪd] *a.* 被迷住的，被吸引住的，极感兴趣的

fascination [ˌfæsɪ'neɪʃən] *n.* 感染力，魅力，迷恋，入迷

▶▶▶ **potential** [pə'tenʃəl]

[释义] *a.* 可能的，潜在的 *n.* ①潜能，

潜力 ②潜在性，可能性

[同义] *a.* possible, hidden, underlying
n. ability, capability

[同根] potentially [pə'tenʃəlɪ] *ad.* 潜在地，可能地

potentiality [pə,tenʃɪ'ælɪtɪ] *n.* ① 可能性 ② (*pl.*) 潜能，潜力

▶▶ prevailing [prɪ'veɪlɪŋ]

[释义] *a.* ①盛行的，流行的 ②优势的，主要的，有力的

[同义] ① current, existing, popular, general, widespread ② main, dominant, principal, fundamental

[同根] prevail [prɪ'veɪl] *v.* ①流行，盛行 ②战胜

prevalence ['prevələns] *n.* 流行，盛行，普及，广泛

prevalent ['prevələnt] *a.* 普遍的，流行的，盛行的

[词组] prevailing trends 流行趋势
prevailing wind 盛行风

▶▶ hot-tempered 性急的，易怒的，暴躁的

▶▶ make-believe ['meɪkbɪ,li:v]

[释义] *n.* ①虚假，伪装 ②虚伪（的人）
a. 虚假的，虚伪的

▶▶ stereotype ['stɪərɪəutaɪp]

[释义] *n.* ①模式化的形象，思想，人物等，陈词滥调，老一套 ②铅版 *v.* 套用老套，使定型，使固定

[同根] stereo ['sterɪəu] *n.* ①立体声，立体声系统 ②铅板 *a.* 立体声的

stereotyped ['sterɪəutaɪpt] *a.* （常作贬义）模式化的，已成陈规的，老一套的

[词组] stereotype of 模式化的
break through the stereotypes 破除陈规

▶▶ eye-rolling 眼睛骨碌碌转动着

▶▶ oversexed [,əuvə'sekst]

[释义] *a.* 性欲过剩的，纵欲的

▶▶ commit [kə'mɪt]

[释义] *v.* ①致力，献身（于某事物）②犯（罪），做（错事、坏事等）③承诺，使承担义务，使做出保证

[同根] commitment [kə'mɪtmənt] *n.* ①承诺，许诺，保证，承担的义务 ②献身参与，介入 ③托付，交托 ④信奉，支持

commission [kə'mɪʃən] *n.* ①委员会 ②授权，委托 ③委任状，任职令

committee [kə'mɪtɪ] *n.* 委员会

[词组] commit oneself to 专心致志于，委身于

commit oneself on 对…表态

▶▶ charity ['tʃærɪtɪ]

[释义] *n.* ①慈善事业，慈善团体 ②施舍，施舍物 ③慈悲，慈善

[同根] charitable ['tʃærɪtəbl] *a.* ①慈善的，施舍慷慨的 ②仁爱的，慈悲的

charitarian [,tʃærɪ'teərɪən] *n.* 慈善家

▶▶ foundation [faun'deɪʃən]

[释义] *n.* ①基金会，机构 ②创立，设立 ③基础，根据

[同义] ① charity, institution ② establishment ③ base, groundwork

[同根] found [faund] *v.* ①建立，建造，创立 ②把…建立在

founder ['faundə] *n.* 奠基者，创立者，缔造者

foundational [faun'deɪʃənəl] *a.* 基本的，基础的

[词组] lay the foundations 打地基
solid/firm foundation 坚实的基础
lay/provide the foundation for/of 为…打下基础

be without foundation/have no foundation 没有根据

shock/ rock sth to its foundations 从根本上动摇某物，动摇某物的基础

▶▶ mainstream publication 主流出版物

▶▶ feature ['fiːtʃə]

[释义] n. ①特写 ②特征，特色 ③ [pl.] 面貌，相貌 ④正片，故事片 v. ①描绘，画…特征 ②是…的特色 ③以…为特色

[同义] n. ② characteristic, trait, quality, property

[同根] featured ['fiːtʃəd] a. 被给以显著地位的，被作为号召物的

[词组] make a feature of ①以…为特色 ②以…为号召 ③给…以显要位置

▶▶ for better or worse 不论如何，不论好坏

▶▶ go a long way ① 对…非常有效，对…大有帮助 ②足够，充分，可以维持很久 ③可以购买很多东西（指钱）④（人）有成就，有前途

Passage Two

When next year's **crop** of high-school graduates arrive at Oxford University in the fall of 2009, they'll be joined by a new face: Andrew Hamilton, the 55-year-old *provost*（教务长）of Yale, who'll become Oxford's **vice-chancellor**—a position equivalent to university president in America.

Hamilton isn't the only educator crossing the Atlantic. Schools in France, Egypt, Singapore, etc. have also recently made **top-level hires** from abro*ad*. Higher education has become a big and competitive business nowadays, and like so many businesses, it's gone global. Yet the **talent** flow isn't **universal**. High-level **personnel** tend to head in only one direction: outward from America.

The chief reason is that American schools don't tend to seriously consider looking abro*ad*. For example, when the **board** of the University of Colorado searched for a new president, it wanted a leader familiar with the state government, a major source of the university's budget. "We didn't **do** any **global consideration**," says Patricia Hayes, the board's chair. The board **ultimately** picked Bruce Benson, a 69-year-old Colorado businessman and political *activist*（活动家）who is likely to do well in the main task of modern university presidents: **fund-raising**. Fund-raising is a **distinctively** American thing, since U.S. schools rely heavily on **donations**. The fund-raising ability is largely a product of experience and necessity.

Many European universities, meanwhile, are still mostly dependent on government funding. But government support has failed to **keep pace with** rising student numbers. The decline in government support has made fund-raising an increasingly necessary ability among **administrators**, and has hiring committees hungry for Americans.

In the past few years, **prominent** schools around the world have joined the trend. In 2003, when Cambridge University **appointed** Alison Richard, another former Yale provost, as its vice-chancellor, the university publicly **stressed** that in her **previous** job she had *overseen*（监督）"a major strengthening of Yale's financial position."

Of course, fund-raising isn't the only skill **outsiders** offer. The globalization of education means more universities will be **seeking** heads with international experience of some kind to promote international programs and attract a global **student body**. Foreigners can offer a fresh **perspective** on established practices.

文章词汇注释

▶▶ **crop** [krɒp]
[释义] n. ①一批，大量 ②农作物，产量 ③平头，短发 v. 收割，修剪，种植
[词组] a high-yielding crop 高产作物
a crop of question 大量问题

▶▶ **vice-chancellor** ['vaɪs'tʃɑːnsələ]
[释义] n. 大学副校长，副大法官

▶▶ **top-level** 最高阶层的

▶▶ **hire** ['haɪə]
[释义] n. ①被雇佣的人 ②租金，工钱 ③租用，雇用 v. ①出钱雇人作某事 ②租入，租用，暂时租借（房屋等），雇用 ③租出，使受雇
[词组] for/on hire 供出租，供雇用

▶▶ **talent** ['tælənt]
[释义] n. ①有才能的人 ②天资，天才，才干
[同义] genius
[同根] talentless ['tæləntlɪs] a. 没有天赋的，无才能的
talented ['tæləntɪd] a. 有天才的，有才干的
[词组] hide one's talents in a napkin 埋没自己的才能
literary talent 文学才能
natural talent 自然禀赋
special talent 特殊才能/人才

▶▶ **universal** [ˌjuːnɪ'vɜːsəl]
[释义] a. ①全世界的，宇宙的 ②全体的，普遍的 ③万能的，通用的
[同义] ① worldwide ② widespread, entire, complete ③ general, common
[同根] universe ['juːnɪvɜːs] n. ①宇宙，天地万物 ②星河，银河系
university [ˌjuːnɪ'vɜːsɪtɪ] n.（综合）大学

▶▶ **personnel** [ˌpɜːsə'nel]
[释义] n. ①全体人员，职员 ②人事部门

[同义] ② personnel department, personnel office, staff office

[同根] personal ['pɜːsənəl] a. ①个人的，私人的 ②本人的，亲自的 ③身体的

impersonal [ɪm'pɜːsənəl] a. ①冷淡的，没有人情味的 ②与个人无关的

personage ['pɜːsənɪdʒ] n. ①人，个人 ②要人，名人

personality [pɜːsə'nælɪtɪ] ① 个性，人格 ②富于个性 ③名人

personify [pɜː'sɒnɪfaɪ] v. ①是…的典型，表现 ②拟人，使人格化

personification [pə(:)ˌsɒnɪfɪ'keɪ ʃən] n. ①拟人化 ②化身，象征

▶▶ board [bɔːd]

[释义] n. ①董事会，委员会 ②木板，板 ③伙食 v. 登上（飞机、火车、轮船等）

[同根] aboard [ə'bɔːd] ad. & prep. ①登上（船、飞机、车等）②在（船、飞机、车等）上

boardroom ['bɔːdruːm] n. （公司董事会的）会议室

boarding ['bɔːdɪŋ] n. ①寄膳宿 ②木板

[词组] above board 在桌面上，公开的，诚实的

on board 在火车上，在船上

board of directors 董事会

boarding school 寄宿学校

▶▶ do global consideration 进行全球性的考虑

▶▶ ultimately ['ʌltɪmətlɪ]

[释义] ad. 最后，最终

[同义] last, finally, in the end

[同根] ultimate ['ʌltɪmət] a. ①最后的，最终的 ②极点的，绝顶的 ③基本的，首要的

ultimatum [ʌltɪ'meɪtəm] n. 最后通牒

▶▶ fund-raising n. 筹款，募款 a. 筹款的

▶▶ distinctively [dɪs'tɪŋktɪvlɪ]

[释义] ad. 明显不同地，特别地，突出地

[同义] uniquely, characteristically

[反义] commonly

[同根] distinct [dɪs'tɪŋkt] a. ①独特的，截然不同的 ②清楚的，明白的 ③清晰的，明显的

distinctive [dɪs'tɪŋktɪv] a. 明显不同的，独特的

distinction [dɪs'tɪŋkʃən] n. ①区分，分清 ②差别 ③特点，特性 ④显赫，声望

distinguish [dɪs'tɪŋgwɪʃ] v. ①区分，分清 ②辨别出，看清 ③使杰出，使著名

▶▶ donation [dəʊ'neɪʃən]

[释义] n. ①捐款，赠品 ②捐赠，捐献

[同根] donate [dəʊ'neɪt] v. 捐赠，捐献，赠给

donator [dəʊ'neɪtə] n. 捐赠者

[词组] make a donation 捐赠

▶▶ keep pace with 跟得上，与…并驾齐驱

▶▶ administrator [əd'mɪnɪstreɪtə]

[释义] n. ①管理人员，行政人员 ②行政官员

[同义] manager, supervisor

[同根] administer [əd'mɪnɪstə] v. ①掌管，管理 ②执行，处理

administrate [əd'mɪnɪstreɪt] v. ①掌管，管理 ②执行，处理

administration [ədmɪnɪs'treɪʃən] n. ①管理，行政 ②管理部门 ③官员任期

administrative [æd'mɪnɪstrətɪv] a. 行政的，管理的，政府的

▶▶ prominent ['prɒmɪnənt]

185

[释义] a. ①著名的，杰出的 ②突出的，显著的

[同义] ① celebrated, distinguished, eminent, renowned, outstanding ② major, leading, foremost

[反义] ① notorious

[同根] prominence ['prɒmɪnəns] n. ①显著，杰出 ②突出部分，突出物 prominently ['prɒmɪnəntlɪ] ad. 卓越地，显眼

[词组] play a prominent role 起重要作用 a prominent place/position 突出的（显著的，显眼的）位置

▶▶ appoint [ə'pɔɪnt]

[释义] v. ①任命，委派 ②约定，指定（时间，地点）③下令

[同义] ① assign, nominate

[同根] appointment [ə'pɔɪntmənt] n. ①约会 ②任命，委派 appointed [ə'pɔɪntɪd] a. ①任命的 ②约定的，指定的 ③装饰的，布置陈设的

[词组] appoint sb. to a post 指派某人任某职 appoint a time for... 约定…时间

▶▶ stress [stres]

[释义] v. 着重，强调 n. ①压力，紧张 ②重点，强调

[同义] v. emphasis n. ① strain, pressure, tension ② focus

[同根] stressful [stresful] a. 压力重的，紧张的

[词组] under/driven by the stress of 为…所迫，为…所驱使，处境紧张 / 困难 in the stress of the moment 一时紧张 lay /place/put stress on 把重点放在…上，在…上用力

▶▶ previous ['pri:vɪəs]

[释义] a. 以前的，在先的

[同义] preceding, earlier, prior

[反义] succeeding, following, subsequent

[词组] previous offences/convictions 前科 a bit previous 有点儿操之过急的 previous to sth 在某时间（事物）以前

▶▶ outsider [,aut'saɪdə]

[释义] n. 外人（被某党派、社团或某一群人排除在外的人），局外人，获胜机会很少者

▶▶ seek [si:k]

[释义] v. ①找寻，寻求 ②调查 ③设法，企图，试图 ④征求，请求

[同义] ① hunt, look for, pursue, quest ② explore, search

[词组] be not far to seek ①在近处 ②很简单，不难找到 ③显而易见 seek after/for ①寻求，探索 ②追求 ③寻找 seek out ①找出，搜出 ②挑出 seek through 找遍

▶▶ student body 学生（总称）

▶▶ perspective [pə'spektɪv]

[释义] n. ①观点，看法 ②前景，展望 ③（对事物的）正确判断，洞察力，视角 ④透视画法，透视图

[同义] ① view, outlook

[同根] prospect ['prɒspekt] n. 景色，前景，前途，期望 [prəs'pekt] v. 寻找，勘探

[词组] in perspective 合乎透视法，比例正确 out of perspective 不按透视法的 / 地，不成比例的 / 地 in the right perspective 正确地、客观地、全面地（观察事物） in the wrong perspective 片面地、错误地（观察事物）

41. A word processor is much better than a typewriter in that it enables you to enter and _____ your text more easily.

A) register   B) edit

C) propose   D) discharge

▶▶▶ **word processor** 文字处理机，文字处理程序

▶▶▶ **propose** [prə'pəʊz]

[释义] v. ①提议，建议 ②推荐，提（名）③打算 ④求（婚）

[同义] suggest, put forward

[反义] deny, oppose

[同根] proposal [prə'pəʊzəl] n. ①（建议等的）提出 ②提议，建议 ③求婚
proposition [ˌprɒpə'zɪʃən] n. ①主张，建议 ②陈述 ③命题
propositional [ˌprɒpə'zɪʃənəl] a. ①建议的 ②提议的

[词组] propose sb. for ①提名某人（任某职）②推荐某人
propose to sb. 向某人求婚

42. We don't know why so many people in that region like to wear dresses of such _____ colors.

A) low   B) humble

C) mild   D) dull

▶▶▶ **humble** ['hʌmbl]

[释义] a. ①低下的，卑微的 ②谦逊的，虚心的 ③微不足道，无特别之处的
v. ①降低…地位 ②使谦逊，低声下气，羞辱

[同义] low, modest, unimportant, insignificant

[同根] humbleness ['hʌmblnɪs] n. ①谦逊 ②粗鄙 ③卑贱

[词组] humble sb's pride ①压某人的气焰 ②使某人丢脸

▶▶▶ **mild** [maɪld]

[释义] a. ①（性情的）温和的 ②（天气）温和的 ③（疾病、惩罚等）轻微的，不强烈的

[同义] gentle, moderate, tender, soft

[反义] fierce, severe

[同根] milden ['maɪldn] v.（使）变温和，（使）变暖和，（使）和缓
mildly ['maɪldlɪ] ad. ①温和地 ③适度地，稍微

▶▶▶ **dull** [dʌl]

[释义] a. ①单调的 ②愚钝的 v. ①使迟钝 ②使阴暗 ③缓和 ④减少

[同根] dullhead ['dʌlhed] n. 傻瓜，笨蛋
dullish ['dʌlɪʃ] a. ①迟钝的 ②有点沉闷的 ③无趣味的

43. The news has just _____ that the president is going to visit China next month.

A) come down   B) come up

C) come out   D) come about

▶▶▶ **come down** ①下来 ②落下，塌下 ③减价，跌价

▶▶▶ **come up** ①被提及，被讨论 ②发生，出现 ③接近，前来

▶▶▶ **come about** 发生

44. The _____ that exists among nations could certainly be lessened if misunderstanding and mistrust were removed.

A) tension   B) strain

C) stress   D) intensity

▶▶▶ **tension** ['tenʃən]

[释义] n. ①紧张局势 / 关系 / 状况 ②矛盾，对立 ③（情绪）紧张，烦躁 ④拉伸，张力 v. ①拉紧，绷紧 ②使紧张

[同根] tense [tens] a. ①神经紧张的，担心的 ②令人紧张的 ③绷紧的 v. 使（肌肉）拉紧 n. 时态

▶▶▶ **strain** [streɪn]

[释义] n. ①压力，重压之下产生的问题 ②压力，张力 ③劳损，拉伤 v. ①损伤，拉伤 ②尽力，竭力 ③过度使用 ④用力推 / 拉

[同义] extend, pull, stretch

[反义] relax

[同根] strained [streɪnd] a. ①勉强的，不自然的 ②紧张的

45. The other day, Mum and I went to St. James's Hospital, and they did lots and lots of tests on me, most of them _____ and frightening.

A) cheerful   B) horrible

C) hostile   D) friendly

▶▶▶ **horrible** ['hɒrəbl]

[释义] a. ①恐怖的，令人震惊的 ②极坏的，讨厌的，可恶的

[同义] dreadful, frightful, terrible, fearful

[同根] horror ['hɒrə] n. ①恐惧，震惊 ②厌恶

horrify ['hɒrɪfaɪ] v. ①使恐惧，惊吓 ②使极度厌恶

horrified ['hɒrɪfaɪd] a. ①非常讨厌的 ②很不友善的

▶▶▶ **hostile** ['hɒstaɪl]

[释义] a. ①敌意的，敌对的 ②强烈反对的

[同义] unfriendly, unkind

[同根] hostility [hɒs'tɪlɪtɪ] n. ①敌意，对抗 ②愤怒，反抗

46. In the Mediterranean, seaweed is so abundant and so easily harvested that it is never of great _____.

A) fare   B) payment

C) worth   D) expense

▶▶▶ **harvest** ['hɑːvɪst]

[释义] v. ①收获 ②获得 ③收割 n. ①收获 ②结果

[同义] crop, collect, outcome

▶▶▶ **payment** ['peɪmənt]

[释义] n. ①付款，支付 ②款项，款额 ③报答，报偿

[同根] pay [peɪ] v. ①支付，交纳 ②付清（账单、债务）③生利，有…收益 ④做，致（意 / 敬）n. 薪水，工资

payable ['peɪəbl] a. ①可付的 ②应付的

payout ['peɪaʊt] n. 支出

[词组] payment on account 分期偿还

payment on terms 定期付款

47. The writer was so _____ in her work that she didn't notice him enter the room.

A) absorbed   B) abandoned

C) focused   D) centered

▶▶▶ **absorbed** [əb'sɔːbd]

[释义] a. 全神贯注的，专心致志的，被…吸引住的

[同根] absorb [əb'sɔːb] v. ①使（精神）贯注 ②吸收 ③使吞并，并入

absorbing [əb'sɔːbɪŋ] a. 吸引人的，引人入胜的，精彩的

absorption [əb'sɔ:pʃən] n. ①吸收
②全神贯注，专注 ③并吞，兼并
[词组] be absorbed in 全神贯注于…

▶▶ abandoned [ə'bændənd]
[释义] a. ①被抛弃的 ②自甘堕落的
③没有约束的 ④放荡的
[同根] abandon [ə'bændən] v. ①离开，
丢弃 ②放弃 n. 放任，放纵
abandonee [ə,bændə'ni:] n. 被遗弃者
abandoner [ə'bændənə] n. 遗弃者

▶▶ focused ['fəukəst]
[释义] a. ①集中的 ②聚焦的
[同根] focus ['fəukəs] v. ①使集中
②调节（镜头、眼睛等的）焦距，
使聚焦 n. ①（兴趣活动等的）中心
②焦点 ③焦距，聚光点

48. Actually, information technology can
_____ the gap between the poor and
the rich.
A) link   B) break
C) ally   D) bridge

▶▶ ally [ə'laɪ;'ælaɪ]
[释义] v. ①（使）结盟，（使）联姻
②使…发生联系 ③联合，结盟
n. ①同盟者/国 ②助手，支持者
[同义] associate, connect
[同根] allied [ə'laɪd;'ælaɪd] a. 联合的，
同盟的
alliance [ə'laɪəns] n. 联盟，联合，
结盟
[词组] ally oneself with/to ①与…联合
②与…结婚
be allied to ①与…有关联 ②与…类似

▶▶ bridge [brɪdʒ]
[释义] v. ①把…连接（或弥合）起来
②架桥于 n. ①桥 ②桥牌
[同义] overpass
[词组] bridge the gap between...and... 弥
合…和…之间的鸿沟

49. Some research workers completely
_____ all those facts as though they
never existed.
A) ignore   B) leave
C) refuse   D) miss

▶▶ refuse [rɪ'fju:z]
[释义] v. ①拒绝，拒绝接受，拒绝给
予 ②不肯，不愿
[同义] deny, reject, rubbish
[同根] refusal [rɪ'fju:zəl] n. 拒绝，推却

50. Computer power now allows
automatic searches of fingerprint files
to match a print at a crime _____.
A) stage   B) scene
C) location   D) occasion

▶▶ stage [steɪdʒ]
[释义] n. ①舞台 ②阶段，时期，步骤
v. ①上演 ②展现，呈现 ③举行，举办
[词组] set the stage for 为…做准备，
使…可能，促成
at this stage 眼下

▶▶ scene [si:n]
[释义] n. ①现场，出事地点 ②场面，
情景 ③（戏剧）场景，布景 ④景色，
风景
[同义] setting, landscape
[同根] scenery ['si:nərɪ] n. 风景，景色
scenic ['si:nɪk] a. ①布景的，舞台上
的 ②景色优美的 ③戏剧性的 n. 风景
照片
[词组] make the scene ①露面 ②到场参
与某项活动
on the scene 出现，到场，在场

▶▶ location [ləu'keɪʃən]
[释义] n. ①位置，场所，地点 ②定位，
特定区域 ③外景拍摄场地
[同根] locate [ləu'keɪt] v. ①把…设置
在，使…坐落于 ②找到，查明 ③指
出…的位置，确定…的位置

locational [ləu'keɪʃənəl] a. 位置上的，地点上的

locative ['lɒkətɪv] a. 表示位置的

51.The most basic reason why dialects should be preserved is that language helps to _____ a culture.

A) retain   B) relate

C) remark   D) review

▶▶▶ **retain** [rɪ'teɪn]

[释义] v. 保留，保持，保存

[同义] keep, maintain, preserve, save

[反义] abandon

[同根] retainable [rɪ'teɪnəbl] a. 能保持的，可保留的

▶▶▶ **relate** [rɪ'leɪt]

[释义] v. ①叙述，讲述 ②使互相关联，证明…之间的必然联系

[同根] relative ['relətɪv] a. ①有关系的 ②相对的 ③比较而言的 n. ①亲戚 ②相关物

relation [rɪ'leɪʃən] n. ①关系 ②叙述，故事 ③亲戚

related [rɪ'leɪtɪd] a. ①叙述的，讲述的 ②有关系的

[词组] relate to 涉及

relate with 使符合，使关联

▶▶▶ **review** [rɪ'vju:]

[释义] v. ①回顾 ②复习 ③审查 ④写评论 n. ①回顾 ②复习 ③评论

[词组] be under review 在检查中，在审查中

52.Companies are struggling to find the right _____ between supply and demand, but it is no easy task.

A) equation   B) formula

C) balance   D) pattern

▶▶▶ **equation** [ɪ'kweɪʃən]

[释义] n. ①平衡，等同 ②等式，方程式

[同根] equate [ɪ'kweɪt] v. ①使相等，使均衡 ②等同，视为平等

[词组] the equation of/between supply and demand 供求关系的平衡

▶▶▶ **formula** ['fɔ:mjulə]

[释义] n. ①公式，方程式 ②惯例，常规 ③（礼节中）客套语 ④准则，方案 a. ①根据公式的 ②俗套的

▶▶▶ **balance** ['bæləns]

[释义] n. ①平衡，均衡 ②天平，秤 ③（布局、比例等的）协调，和谐 对称 ④镇静，沉着 v. ①使平衡，使均衡 ②使协调 ③权衡，斟酌

[同根] balanced ['bælənst] a. ①平衡的，均衡的 ②协调的，和谐的

[词组] on balance 总的说来

keep one's balance ①保持身体平衡 ②保持镇静

lose/off one's balance ①失去平衡，有跌落、倾覆的危险 ②惊慌失措

53.Mass advertising helped to _____ the emphasis from the production of goods to their consumption.

A) vary   B) shift

C) lay   D) moderate

▶▶▶ **vary** ['veərɪ]

[释义] v. ①改变，变更 ②使多样化

[同义] alter, change, modify, transform

[同根] varied ['veərɪd] a. ①杂色的 ②各式各样的

various ['veərɪəs] a. ①不同的，各种各样的 ②多方面的，多样的

variable ['veərɪəbl] a. 可变的，不定的，易变的 n. [数] 变数，变量

variety [və'raɪətɪ] n. ①变化 ②多样性 ③品种，种类

variation [,veərɪ'eɪʃən] n. ①变更，变化 ②变异，变种

[词组] vary from...to... 在…到…之间变

动，从…到…不等
vary with 随…而变化

▶▶ **lay** [leɪ]

[释义] v. ①搁，放下 ②把…放下，使休息 ③产卵 ④铺放，覆盖

[同义] place, settle, arrange, position

[同根] layer ['leɪə] n. ①层，阶层，层次 ②放置者，铺设者 ③产卵鸡
layman ['leɪmən] n. 外行，门外汉
layoff ['leɪ,ɔːf] n. ①临时解雇（期）②失业期 ③停工

[词组] lay off ①解雇 ②停止
lay out ①布置，安排 ②设计建筑等
lay emphasis on... 强调…

▶▶ **moderate** ['mɒdəreɪt]

[释义] v. ①缓和 ②减轻 ③节制 ④调节
['mɒdərɪt] n. 温和派，稳健派
a. ①有节制的 ②温和的 ③中等的，平庸的，普通的

[同根] moderation [,mɒdə'reɪʃən] n. ①温和，中庸 ②缓和，减轻 ③适度，节制

54.Because of his excellent administration, people lived in peace and _____, and all previously neglected matters were taken care of.
A) conviction   B) contest
C) consent   D) content

▶▶ **previously** ['priːvɪəslɪ]

[释义] ad. 先前，以前

[同根] previous ['priːvɪəs] a. 在前的，早先的

▶▶ **conviction** [kən'vɪkʃən]

[释义] n. ①说服，信服 ②确信，深信 ③判罪，定罪

[同根] convict ['kɒnvɪkt] v. ①证明…有罪，宣判…有罪 ②使深感有罪，使服罪
convictive [kən'vɪktɪv] a. ①有说服

力的，令人信服的 ②能定罪的

▶▶ **contest** ['kɒntest]

[释义] n. ①比赛，竞争 ②斗争，争夺
[kən'test] v. ①争夺 ②对…提出质疑，争论

[同义] game, contend, struggle, tournament

[同根] contestant [kən'testənt] n. 竞争者，争论者
contestation [,kɒnte'steɪʃən] n. ①争论，论战 ②（争执中的）主张，见解

▶▶ **consent** [kən'sent]

[释义] n. & v. (to sth.) 同意，应允，赞成

[同根] consensus [kən'sensəs] n. 意见一致，一致同意，多数人的意见

[词组] by common/mutual consent 经一致 / 双方同意
carry the consent of sb. 得到某人的允许
withhold one's consent 不答应，拒绝答应

55.I know you've got a smooth tongue, so don't talk me _____ buying it.
A) away   B) down
C) out   D) into

▶▶ smooth tongue 油嘴滑舌
▶▶ talk sb.into doing 说服某人做某事

56.Showing some sense of humor can be a(n) _____ way to deal with some stressful situation.
A) effective   B) efficient
C) favorable   D) favorite

▶▶ sense of humor 幽默感

▶▶ **stressful** ['stresful]

[释义] a. 压力重的，紧张的

[同根] stress [stres] v. ①强调，把重点放在 ②加压力于，使紧张 ③重读
n. ①紧迫，紧张，重压 ②强调，重

要性③重音，重读

stressed ['strest] a. ①焦虑不安，心力交瘁的　②重读的

▶▶ **effective** [ɪ'fektɪv]

[释义] a. ①能产生（预期）结果的，有效的 ②生效的，起作用的 ③给人深刻印象的，显著的 ④实际的，事实上的

[反义] ineffective

[同根] effect [ɪ'fekt] n. ①结果 ②效力，作用，影响 ③感受，印象 ④实行，生效，起作用

efficiency [ɪ'fɪʃənsɪ] n. 效率，功效

efficient [ɪ'fɪʃənt] a. ①效率高的，能干的，能胜任的 ②（直接）生效的

efficiently [ɪ'fɪʃəntlɪ] ad. ①效率高地 ②有能力地

[词组] be effective on 对…起作用

become effective 生效

▶▶ **favorable** ['feɪvərəbl]

[释义] a. ①表示同意的，赞扬的 ②赢得赞扬的 ③有利的，起促进作用的

[同根] favor ['feɪvə] v. ①支持，赞成 ②偏爱 ③赐予 n. ①好感，喜爱 ②恩惠

favored ['feɪvəd] a. ①受到优待的，受惠的 ②有天赋的 ③有利的

favorably ['feɪvərəblɪ] ad. ①顺利地 ②好意地 ③亲切地

57. The situation described in the report _____ terrible, but it may not happen.

A) inclines　　　B) maintains

C) sounds　　　D) remains

▶▶ **incline** [ɪn'klaɪn]

[释义] v. ①（性格上）倾向，赞同 ②趋向，趋势 ③（使）倾斜，弯腰，点头 ④近于

[同根] inclined [ɪn'klaɪnd] a. 倾向…的，有…意向的

inclination [ˌɪnklɪ'neɪʃən] n. ①（性

格上）倾向，爱好 ②趋向，趋势 ③倾斜，弯腰

[词组] incline to/towards sth. ①倾向于某事 ②赞同某事

incline to do sth. 倾向于做某事

58. The company is trying every means to _____ the wholesale price of its products.

A) pull down　　　B) put down

C) set down　　　D) bring down

▶▶ try every means 千方百计，想方设法

▶▶ wholesale price 批发价

▶▶ **pull down** ①毁坏，拆毁（如旧建筑物），摧毁 ②使某人虚弱

▶▶ **set down** ①放下 ②使下车 ③登记

▶▶ **bring down** ①降低 ②击落 ③打倒

59. The mayor _____ the police officer a medal of honor for his heroic deed in rescuing the earthquake victims.

A) rewarded　　　B) awarded

C) credited　　　D) prized

▶▶ **prize** [praɪz]

[释义] v. ①重视，珍视 ②估价，评价 n. ①奖赏，奖金，奖品 ②赠品

[同义] cherish, value, appreciate, esteem

60. The native Canadians lived in _____ with nature, for they respected nature as a provider of life.

A) coordination　　　B) acquaintance

C) contact　　　D) harmony

▶▶ **coordination** [kəʊˌɔːdɪ'neɪʃən]

[释义] n. 协作，协调，配合

[同义] regulation, organization, arrangement

[同根] coordinate [kəʊ'ɔːdɪneɪt] v. ①使协调，使相配合 ②搭配，协调 ③使（身体各部位）动作协调

▶▶ **harmony** ['hɑ:mənɪ]

[释义] *n.* ①和谐，协调 ②融洽，和睦 ③（内心）平静

[反义] conflict, discord, disharmony

[同根] harmonize ['hɑ:mənaɪz] *v.* ①使融洽，使和谐 ②相一致，和谐 (with)

[词组] be in/out of harmony with 与…（不）协调一致
live in harmony 和睦相处

61. Many people are asking whether traditional research universities in fact have any future _____.

A) at all　　　　　B) so far
C) in all　　　　　D) on end

▶▶ **at all** ①（用于肯定、疑问、条件句）究竟，在任何程度上，从任何方面考虑 ②（用于否定）丝毫，一点，根本

▶▶ **so far** ①迄今为止 ②就此程度来说

▶▶ **on end** ①非常 ②无限 ③连续地 ④竖着

62.I was impressed _____ the efficiency of the work done in the company.

A) in　　　　　　B) about
C) with　　　　　D) for

▶▶ **be impressed by/with** 使对…留有深刻的印象

63. Now in Britain, wines take up four times as much _____ in the storehouse as both beer and spirits.

A) block　　　　　B) land
C) patch　　　　　D) space

▶▶ **take up space** 占据空间

▶▶ **patch** [pætʃ]

[释义] *n.* ①小块土地 ②小块，碎片 ③补丁，补块 *v.* 修补，拼凑

[词组] patch up ①修补 ②匆忙处理 ③平息，解决（纠纷等）

64. His hand shook a little as he _____ the key in the lock.

A) squeezed　　　　B) inserted
C) stuffed　　　　　D) pierced

▶▶ **pierce** [pɪəs]

[释义] *v.* ①刺穿，戳入 ②（光、声音等）透进，响彻 ③识破，看穿

[同义] penetrate, puncture, stab

[同根] pierced ['pɪəst] *a.* 有空的
piercing ['pɪəsɪŋ] *a.* ①尖厉的，刺耳的 ②锐利的，有洞察力的 ③刺骨的，彻骨寒冷的 ④尖锐的

65. For professional athletes, _____ to the Olympics means that they have a chance to enter the history books.

A) access　　　　　B) attachment
C) appeal　　　　　D) approach

▶▶ **professional athlete** 职业运动员

▶▶ **attachment** [ə'tætʃmənt]

[释义] *n.* ①附着，附件 ② (to/for) 情感，爱慕，忠诚

[反义] detachment

[同根] attach [ə'tætʃ] *v.* ①系，贴，装，连接 ②使依附，使附着 ③使成为一部分，使附属
attached [ə'tætʃt] *a.* ①附属的 ②连接的

▶▶ **appeal** [ə'pi:l]

[释义] *n.* ①请求，呼吁 ②上诉 ③吸引力 *v.* ①呼吁，恳求 ②诉诸，求助 ③有感染力，有吸引力

[同根] appealing [ə'pi:lɪŋ] *a.* ①有感染力的，有吸引力的 ②恳求的
appealingly [ə'pi:lɪŋlɪ] *ad.* ①上诉地 ②恳求地

[词组] appeal to ①向…呼吁 ②投合…

的心意 ③引起…的兴趣 ④诉诸
appeal to sb. for 为…向某人呼吁
make an appeal to sb. ①向某人提出
呼吁 ②引起某人兴趣

66. In the long _____ , the new information technologies may fundamentally alter our way of life.

A) view   B) distance
C) jump   D) run

▶▶▶ **alter** [ˈɔːltə]
[释义] v. 改变，改动
[同义] adapt, change, convert, modify
[同根] alternative [ɔːlˈtɜːnətɪv] a. 选择性的，随便一个的，二者择一的
alteration [ˌɔːltəˈreɪʃn] n. ①变更
②改造

67. All the arrangements should be completed _____ your departure.

A) prior to   B) superior to
C) contrary to   D) parallel to

▶▶▶ **prior to** 在…之前
▶▶▶ **superior to** 胜过，比…好
▶▶▶ **contrary to** 与…相反
▶▶▶ **parallel to** 与…平行，与…并联

68. We need to create education standards that prepare our next generation who will be _____ with an even more competitive market.

A) tackled   B) encountered
C) dealt   D) confronted

▶▶▶ **tackle** [ˈtækl]
[释义] v. ①应付，处理 ②抓住，揪住，擒抱
[同义] deal with, dispose, transact
[词组] tackle sb.about/on/over sth. 为某事与某人交涉，与某人坦率地谈谈某事

▶▶▶ **encounter** [ɪnˈkauntə]
[释义] v. ①偶然遇见，与…邂逅 ②遭到，受到 n. ①偶然的相见，邂逅，遭遇 ②冲突，交战
[词组] encounter with... 与…遭遇，遇到…

▶▶▶ **confront** [kənˈfrʌnt]
[释义] v. ①使面对 ②迎面遇到，面临，遭遇 ③勇敢面对，正视
[同义] encounter, face, oppose
[同根] confrontation [ˌkɒnfrʌnˈteɪʃn] n. ①对质，比较 ②对抗，冲突
[词组] be confronted with/by 面临，面对，碰上

69. In the late seventies, the amount of fixed assets required to produce one vehicle in Japan was _____ equivalent to that in the United States.

A) rudely   B) roughly
C) readily   D) coarsely

▶▶▶ **fixed assets** 固定资产

▶▶▶ **rudely** [ruːdlɪ]
[释义] ad. 粗暴地，无礼地
[同义] crudely, uncivilly
[反义] politely, gracefully
[同根] rude [ruːd] a. ①原始的 ②粗制的 ③粗略的 ④无礼的，粗鲁的
rudeness [ˈruːdnɪs] n. 粗蛮，无礼

▶▶▶ **roughly** [ˈrʌflɪ]
[释义] ad. ①大约，概略地 ②粗暴地，粗鲁地 ③粗糙地
[同义] coarsely, toughly, crudely, cruelly
[同根] rough [rʌf] a. ①粗糙的 ②粗略的 ③粗野的
roughness [ˈrʌfnɪs] n. ①粗糙，粗糙之处，不平滑 ②粗鲁 ③粗略
roughen [ˈrʌfən] v. 变粗

▶▶▶ **readily** [ˈredɪlɪ]

[释义] ad. ①乐意地，欣然 ②容易地

[反义] reluctantly

[同根] ready ['redɪ] a. ①有准备的
②甘心的 ③现成的 ④迅速的

▶▶ **coarsely** [kɔːslɪ]

[释义] ad. ①质地粗糙地 ②粗俗地，低
级地

[同义] crudely, roughly

[反义] refinedly, politely

[同根] coarse [kɔːs] a. ①粗的，粗糙
的 ②供做粗活用的，普通的 ③质量
差的 ④粗鄙的

> 70.Many people believe we are heading
> for environmental disaster _____
> we radically change the way we live.
> A) but   B) although
> C) unless   D) lest

▶▶ **head for** ①朝…行进 ②出发，动身，
前往

▶▶ **disaster** [dɪˈzɑːstə]

[释义] n. ①天灾，灾难 ②不幸，祸患

[同义] casualty, misfortune, tragedy

[同根] disastrous [dɪˈzɑːstrəs] a. ①损
失惨重的，灾难性的 ②悲伤的

▶▶ **radically** [ˈrædɪkəlɪ]

[释义] ad. ①完全地，根本上 ②以激进
的方式

[同根] radical [ˈrædɪkəl] a. ①根本的
②基本的 ③激进的 n. 激进分子
radicalize [ˈrædɪkəlaɪz] v. ①使激进
②成为激进主义者
radicalism [ˈrædɪkəlɪzəm] n. 激进主义

Answer Key									
41.B	42.D	43.C	44.A	45.B	46.C	47.A	48.D	49.A	50.B
51.A	52.A	53.B	54.D	55.D	56.A	57.C	58.D	59.B	60.D
61.A	62.C	63.D	64.B	65.A	66.D	67.A	68.D	69.B	70.C

41. Some people believe that since oil is scarce, the _____ of the motor industry is uncertain.

A) terminal   B) benefit

C) fate   D) estimate

▶▶▶ **scarce** [skeəs]

[释义] *a.* ①缺乏的，不足的 ②稀有的，难得的

[同义] rare, sparse

[反义] plentiful

[同根] scarcely ['skeəslɪ] *ad.* ①刚刚，才 ②几乎不，简直没有

scarcity ['skeəsɪtɪ] *n.* ①缺乏，不足 ②罕见，难得

▶▶▶ **motor industry** 汽车制造业

▶▶▶ **terminal** ['tɜ:mɪnl]

[释义] *n.* ①末端，终点 ②（陆、海、空运输路线的）终点（站）③终端，接线端 *a.* ①末端的，终点的 ②期末的 ③末期的，不治的

[同根] terminate ['tɜ:mɪneɪt] *v.* 停止，结束，终止

termination [ˌtɜ:mɪ'neɪʃən] *n.* ①结束，终止 ②结果，结局

▶▶▶ **fate** [feɪt]

[释义] *n.* 命运，运气，宿命

[同义] destiny, fortune, lot

[同根] fated ['feɪtɪd] *a.* 宿命的，命中注定的

fatal ['feɪtəl] *a.* ①致命的，毁灭性的 ②重大的，决定性的 ③命中注定的

[词组] as sure as fate 千真万确地

go to one's fate 自取灭亡

share the same fate 遭受同样的命运

42. To speed up the _____ of letters, the Post Office introduced automatic sorting.

A) treatment   B) delivery

C) transmission   D) departure

▶▶▶ **speed up** 加速，加快

▶▶▶ **introduce** [ˌɪntrə'dju:s]

[释义] *v.* ①引进，引入 ②介绍，引荐 ③插入，纳入

[同根] introduction [ˌɪntrə'dʌkʃən] *n.* ①介绍，引见 ②引进，传入 ③导言，绪论 ④采用

introductive [ˌɪntrə'dʌktɪv]

(= introductory [ˌɪntrə'dʌktərɪ])

a. ①引言的，导论的 ②介绍的，引导的

[词组] introduce into ①把…引入，传入 ②把…列入 ③插入

▶▶▶ **automatic sorting** 自动分类，自动分拣

43. These overseas students show great _____ for learning a new language.

A) enthusiasm   B) authority

C) convention   D) faith

▶▶▶ **authority** [ɔ:'θɒrɪtɪ]

[释义] *n.* ① [*pl.*] 官方，当局 ②当权者，行政管理单位权 ③权力，管辖权 ④学术权威，威信 ⑤权威，权威的典据

[同根] authorize/ise ['ɔ:θəraɪz] v. ①授权 ②批准，认可，核定
authorized ['ɔ:θəraɪzd] a. 经授权的，权威认可的，审定的
authoritative [ɔ:'θɒrɪtetɪv] a. ①权威性的，可信的 ②官方的，当局的 ③专断的，命令式的

[词组] by/on the authority of ①得到…许可 ②根据…所授的权力

44. The defense lawyer was questioning the old man who was one of the _____ of the murder committed last month.

A) observers   B) witnesses
C) audiences   D) viewers

▶▶ **defense lawyer** 辩护律师

▶▶ **observer** [əb'zɜ:və]

[释义] n. ①观察者 ②观察员 ③遵守者，奉行者

[同根] observe [əb'zɜ:v] v. ①观察，注意到 ②遵守，奉行 ③评述，评论
observation [,əbzɜ:'veɪʃən] n. ①注意，觉察 ②观察，观测 ③言论
observatory [əb'zɜ:vətərɪ] a. ①天文台，观象台 ②气象台 ③瞭望台
observing [əb'zɜ:vɪŋ] a. ①观察力敏锐的 ②注意观察的

45. Politically these nations tend to be _____, with very high birth rates but poor education and very low levels of literacy.

A) unstable   B) reluctant
C) rational   D) unsteady

▶▶ **low levels of literacy** 文化水平低

▶▶ **reluctant** [rɪ'lʌktənt]

[释义] a. 勉强的，不情愿的

[反义] willing, eager, ready

[同根] reluctance [rɪ'lʌktəns] n. 不情愿，勉强

reluctantly [rɪ'lʌktəntlɪ] ad. 不情愿地，勉强地

▶▶ **rational** ['ræʃnl]

[释义] a. ①理性的，理智的 ②基于理性的，合理的 ③神志健全的

[同义] logical, reasonable, sensible

[反义] absurd, crazy, irrational, illogical

[同根] ration ['ræʃən] v. 配给，分发 n. 定量，配给量
rationalize ['ræʃənəlaɪz] v. ①使合理化 ②合理地解释，自圆其说
rationality [,ræʃə'nælɪtɪ] n. 合理性，合理意见
rationalization [,ræʃənəlaɪ'zeɪʃən] n. 合理化，理性化

▶▶ **unsteady** [ʌn'stedɪ]

[释义] a. ①不安定的 ②反复无常的 v. 使不稳定，动摇

[同义] unreliable, changeable, variable

[同根] steady ['stedɪ] a. ①稳步的 ②稳固的 ③沉稳的，可靠的 v. ①使平稳，稳住 ②稳定下来 ad. 稳步地，持续地，稳固地
steadily ['stedɪlɪ] ad. ①有规则地 ②稳固地，不动摇地
steadiness ['stedɪnɪs] n. 稳定性，坚定性

46. The chairman was blamed for letting his secretary _____ too much work last week.

A) take to   B) take out
C) take away   D) take on

▶▶ **take to** ①开始做 ②对某人、某事产生好感，喜欢，沉溺于

▶▶ **take out** ①拿出，取出，去掉 ②扣除

▶▶ **take away** 取走

47. "You try to get some sleep. I'll _____ the patient's breakfast, "said

the nurse.

 A) see to   B) stick to

 C) get to   D) lead to

▶▶ see to ①负责，确保 ②注意

▶▶ get to ①到达 ②接触到 ③开始

▶▶ lead to ①导致 ②通向

48. The London Marathon is a difficult race. _____ , thousands of runners participate every year.

 A)Therefore   B) Furthermore

 C) Accordingly   D) Nevertheless

▶▶ accordingly [əˈkɔːdɪŋlɪ]

[释义] ad. ①因此，于是 ②相应地

[同义] consequently, hence, therefore

49. The bank refused to _____ him any money, so he had to postpone buying a house.

 A)credit   B) borrow

 C) loan   D) lease

▶▶ postpone [pəustˈpəun]

[释义] v. 推迟，延缓

[同义] delay, put off, suspend

[同根] postponement [pəustˈpəunmənt] n. 延期，延缓，推迟

▶▶ loan [ləun]

[释义] v. 借贷，借出，借给 n. ①贷款，借出的钱 ②借出的东西

[同义] lend, let out

[词组] on loan 借来的

 short-term loan 短期贷款

 long-term loan   长期贷款

50. The more a nation's companies _____ factories abroad, the smaller that country's recorded exports will be.

 A)lie   B) spot

 C) stand   D) locate

▶▶ spot [spɒt]

[释义] v. ①使…有污渍，沾污 ②（从许多人或物中）认出，找到 n. ①污渍，污点 ②地点，场所，现场 a. ①当场的 ②抽样的 ③从现场广播的

[同根] spotless [ˈspɒtlɪs] a. 没有污点的

 spottable [ˈspɒtəbl] a. （织物等）容易沾上污渍的

 spotted [ˈspɒtɪd] a. 有斑点的，弄污的

 spotty [ˈspɒtɪ] a. ①多斑点的，多污点的 ②质量不一的

[词组] a spot of 少许，少量

 on/upon the spot ①当场，在现场 ②立刻 ③处于困难境地

 without spot 毫无缺点

51. Being ignorant of the law is not accepted as an _____ for breaking the law.

 A)excuse   B) intention

 C) option   D) approval

▶▶ ignorant [ˈɪgnərənt]

[释义] a. ①不知道的 ②无知的，愚昧的，无学识的

[同义] unaware, uneducated, uninformed, unintelligent

[反义] aware, educated, informed, learned

[同根] ignore [ɪgˈnɔː] v. ①不顾，不理，忽视 ②驳回

 ignorance [ˈɪgnərəns] n. ①无知，愚昧 ②不知 (of, about)

[词组] be ignorant of 不懂…，不知道…

▶▶ excuse [ɪkˈskjuːz]

[释义] n. ①借口，理由 ②假条 v. ①原谅 ②为…辩解

[同根] excusable [ɪkˈskjuːzəbl] a. ①可原谅的，可容许的 ②言之有理的

[词组] in excuse of 为…辩解

 make excuses for 为…找借口，推诿

 make one's excuses to 向…表示歉意

▶▶ **intention** [ɪnˈtenʃən]

[释义] *n.* ①意图，目的，打算 ②意思，含义

[同义] aim, goal, plan, objective

[同根] intend [ɪnˈtend] *v.* 打算，想要，计划

intent [ɪnˈtent] *n.* ①意图，目的 ②意思，含义 *a.* ①专心的 ②急切的

intentional [ɪnˈtenʃənəl] *a.* ①有意图的，故意的 ②与目的有关的

intentionally [ɪnˈtenʃənəlɪ] *ad.* 有意地，故意地

[词组] by intention 故意

have no intention of doing... 无意做…

without intention 无意中，不是故意地

52. Within two days, the army fired more than two hundred rockets and missiles at military _____ in the coastal city.

A) goals   B) aims
C) targets   D) destinations

▶▶ **target** [ˈtɑːɡɪt]

[释义] *n.* ①（欲达到的）目标，指标 ②靶子 ③（批评、嘲笑等的）对象 *v.* ①瞄准 ②把…作为目标 ③为…定指标

[同义] aim, goal, object, point

[词组] on target 击中要害的，准确的

off target 不对头的，不准确的

53. It is said in some parts of the world, goats, rather than cows, serve as a vital _____ of milk.

A) storage   B) reserve
C) resource   D) source

▶▶ **storage** [ˈstɔːrɪdʒ]

[释义] *n.* ①储藏，保管 ②贮藏（量），库存量 ③贮藏库

[同根] store [stɔː] *v.* ①贮备 ②存储 *n.* ①店铺 ②贮藏，贮备

54. "This light is too _____ for me to read by. Don't we have a brighter bulb some where?" said the elderly man.

A) mild   B) dim
C) minute   D) slight

▶▶ **dim** [dɪm]

[释义] *a.* ①昏暗的，暗淡的 ②模糊的，朦胧的 *v.* 使暗淡，使失去光泽

[同义] darkish, faint, indistinct, vague

[同根] dimness [ˈdɪmnɪs] *n.* 微暗，不清楚

dimmish [ˈdɪmɪʃ] *a.* 暗淡的，朦胧的

dimly [ˈdɪmlɪ] *ad.* 微暗，朦胧

[词组] take a dim view of 对…持悲观看法，对…持怀疑态度

▶▶ **minute** [maɪˈnjuːt, məˈnjuːt]

[释义] *a.* ①微小的 ②详细的，仔细而准确的

[ˈmɪnɪt] *n.* ①分钟 ②片刻 ③笔记 *v.* ①记录 ②测定时间

[词组] at the last minute 在紧要关头，在决定/危急时刻

on the minute 准时，一分不差

up to the minute 最新（式）的

55. We have arranged to go to the cinema on Friday, but we can be _____ and go another day.

A) reliable   B) probable
C) feasible   D) flexible

▶▶ **feasible** [ˈfiːzəbl]

[释义] *a.* ①切实可行的 ②可能的，合理的 ③可用的，适宜的

[同义] practicable

[反义] infeasible

[同根] feasibility [ˌfiːzəˈbɪlətɪ] *n.* 可行性，可能性

56. We are quite sure that we can _____ our present difficulties and finish the

task according to schedule.

A)get across   B) get over

C) get away   D) get off

▶▶ **get across** ①（使）越过 ②被理解

▶▶ **get over** ①克服 ②恢复 ③熬过 ④爬过

▶▶ **get away** ①逃脱 ②离开 ③把…送走

▶▶ **get off** ①下来 ②脱下 ③出发

57._____ recent developments, we do not think your scheme is practical.

A) In view of   B) In favor of

C) In case of   D) In memory of

▶▶ **in view of** ①鉴于，考虑到，由于 ②在…能看见的范围内

▶▶ **in memory of** 纪念，追念

58.Jessica was _____ from the warehouse to the accounting office, which was considered a promotion.

A)delivered   B) exchanged

C) transferred   D) transformed

▶▶ **transfer** [træns'fɜː]

[释义] v. ①调动，使转学 ②改变，转换 ③转乘，转搭（车或船）④转让 ['trænsfɜː] n. ①迁移，调任 ②已调动的人，已转移的东西

[同义] move, shift, handover

[同根] transference ['trænsfərəns] n.①转移，传递 ②调任，调动 ③（财产）转让

transferable [træns'fɜːrəbəl] a.①可转移的，可转换的 ②可传递的

transferred [træns'fɜːd] a.①转移的 ②调动的，转让的

[词组] transfer from...to... 从…调往…，从…转化为…

59.Mr. Smith asked his secretary to _____ a new paragraph in the annual

report she was typing.

A)inject   B) install

C) invade   D) insert

▶▶ **annual report** 年度报告

▶▶ **inject** [ɪn'dʒekt]

[释义] v. ①注射（药液等），给…注射 ②插（话），引入 (into) ③使（卫星、飞船）入轨道

[同根] injection [ɪn'dʒekʃən] n. ①注射 ②注射剂 ③（卫星等）射入轨道

injector [ɪn'dʒektə] n. 注射者，注射器，喷射器

[词组] inject...into... ①把…注入… ②给…增添…

inject with 注入…

▶▶ **invade** [ɪn'veɪd]

[释义] v. 侵入，侵犯

[同义] attack, intrude, overrun, raid, violate

[反义] withdraw

[同根] invader [ɪn'veɪdə] n. 侵略者

invasion [ɪn'veɪʒən] n. 入侵

60.There's the living room still to be _____ , so that's my next project.

A)abandoned   B) decorated

C) dissolved   D) assessed

▶▶ **decorate** ['dekəreɪt]

[释义] v. ①装饰，装潢 ②粉刷，油漆，裱糊 ③授勋（章）给

[同义] beautify, ornament

[同根] decorator ['dekəreɪtə] n. 装璜工人，室内装饰工人

decoration [ˌdekə'reɪʃən] n. ①装饰，装潢 ②装饰品 ③勋章，奖章

decorative ['dekərətɪv] a. 装饰性的，作装饰用的

[词组] decorate with... 以…装饰

▶▶ assess [ə'ses]

[释义] v. ①估定，评估 ②确定 ③征收

[同义] value, judge, estimate, evaluate

[同根] assessment [ə'sesmənt] n. ①估价，评价 ②被估定的金额
assessable [ə'sesəbl] a. ①可估价的 ②可征收的

61.The old paper mill has been _____ to make way for a new shopping centre.

A)held down   B) kept down

C) pulled down   D) turned down

▶▶ paper mill 造纸厂

▶▶ hold down ①压制 ②缩减 ③牵制 ④垂下

▶▶ make way for 让路给…，为…开路

62.It may be necessary to stop _____ in the learning process and go back to the difficult points in the lessons.

A)at a distance   B) at intervals

C) at ease   D) at length

▶▶ at a distance 在远处

▶▶ at intervals ①每隔一段时间/距离 ②不时地

▶▶ at ease 安逸，自在

▶▶ at length ①详细地 ②最后

63.You can hire a bicycle in many places. Usually you'll have to pay a _____.

A) deposit   B) deal

C) fare   D) fond

▶▶ fare [feə]

[释义] n. ①车/船费，飞机票价 ②乘客 ③伙食，饮食

64.My grandfather had always taken a _____ interest in my work, and I had an equal admiration for the stories of his time.

A)splendid   B) weighty

C) vague   D) keen

▶▶ splendid ['splendɪd]

[释义] a. ①有光彩的，灿烂的 ②壮丽的，豪华的 ③辉煌的，庄严的

[同义] brilliant, excellent, glorious, magnificent

▶▶ weighty ['weɪtɪ]

[释义] a. ①有分量的 ②有权势的 ③重要的，有影响的 ④严重的

[同义] important, influential, powerful

[同根] weigh [weɪ] v. 称…重量，称
weight [weɪt] n. ①重量，分量 ②重要性 ③势力 ④负担

65._____ quantities of water are being used nowadays with the rapid development of industry and agriculture.

A) Excessive   B) Extensive

C) Extreme   D) Exclusive

▶▶ excessive [ɪk'sesɪv]

[释义] a. ①过度的 ②份外的，额外的 ③非常的，格外的

[同根] exceed [ɪk'siːd] v. ①超过，比…更好 ②超越…的界限
excess [ɪk'ses] n. 超过，超出，过量，过份
excessively [ɪk'sesɪvlɪ] ad. 过分地，过度地

▶▶ exclusive [ɪk'skluːsɪv]

[释义] a. ①排斥的，排外的 ②专一的，唯一的，单独的 ③独享的，独占的

[反义] inclusive

[同根] exclude [ɪks'kluːd] v. 拒绝接纳，把…排除在外，排斥
exclusively [ɪk'skluːsɪvlɪ] ad. ①仅仅，专门地 ②单独地，独有地

66.John cannot afford to go to university, _____ going abroad.

A) nothing but
B) anything but
C) not to speak of
D) nothing to speak of

▶▶ **nothing but** 只有，只是，仅仅
▶▶ **not to speak of** （更）不用说
▶▶ **nothing to speak of** 没有什么，不值一提

67. Most laboratory and field studies of human behavior _____ taking a situational photograph at a given time and in a given place.

A) involve   B) compose
C) enclose   D) attach

▶▶ **at a given time and in a given place** 在特定的时间和特定的地点

68. If you don't like to swim, you _____ as well stay at home.

A) should   B) may
C) can   D) would

▶▶ **may/might as well** 最好…，不妨…

69. Dr. Smith was always _____ the poor and the sick, often providing them with free medical care.

A) reminded of   B) absorbed in
C) tended by   D) concerned about

▶▶ **free medical care** 免费医疗
▶▶ **remind of** 提醒，使记起

▶▶ **be tended by** 被…照管 / 护理

70. Thomas Jefferson and John Adams died on July 4, 1826, the fiftieth _____ of American Independence.

A) ceremony   B) occasion
C) occurrence   D) anniversary

▶▶ **ceremony** ['serɪmənɪ]
[释义] *n.* ①典礼，仪式 ②礼节，礼貌 ③规定的礼仪，惯例
[同根] ceremonial [ˌserɪ'məʊnɪəl] *a.* ①礼节的，礼仪的，仪式的 ②拘于礼仪的 *n.* ①礼节 ②典礼，仪式
[词组] stand on/upon ceremony 讲究礼节，拘泥礼节，讲客套
with ceremony 正式，隆重
without ceremony 不拘礼节地，随便地

▶▶ **occurrence** [ə'kʌrəns]
[释义] *n.* ①发生，出现 ②事件，发生的事情
[同义] affair, event, incident, instance
[同根] occur [ə'kɜː] *v.* ①发生 ②被想起，被想到
occurrent [ə'kʌrənt] *a.* ①目前正在发生的 ②偶然发生的

▶▶ **anniversary** [ˌænɪ'vɜːsərɪ]
[释义] *n.* 周年纪念（日）*a.* 周年的，周年纪念的
[同根] annual ['ænjʊəl] *a.* 每年的，一年一次的 *n.* ①一年生植物 ②年刊，年鉴

Answer Key									
41.C	42.B	43.A	44.B	45.A	46.D	47.A	48.D	49.C	50.D
51.A	52.C	53.D	54.B	55.D	56.B	57.A	58.C	59.D	60.B
61.C	62.B	63.A	64.D	65.B	66.C	67.A	68.B	69.D	70.D

41. People's expectations about the future may have more influence on their sense of well-being than their _____ state does.

  A) current   B) initial

  C) modern   D) primitive

▶▶ **have influence on** 对…有影响

▶▶ **well-being** ['wel-,bɪɪŋ]

[释义] *n.* 幸福，康乐，安康

▶▶ **the sense of well-being** 幸福感

42. After working all day, he was so tired that he was in no _____ to go to the party with us.

  A) taste   B) mood

  C) sense   D) emotion

▶▶ **sense** [sens]

[释义] *n.* ①意思，意义 ②感觉，知觉，见识 ③理解力，鉴赏力

[同根] sensation [sen'seɪʃən] *n.* ①知觉，感觉 ②引起轰动的人或事
sensible ['sensəbl] *a.* ①明智的，有判断力的 ②可感觉的，能注意到的
sensitive ['sensɪtɪv] *a.* ①敏感的，有感觉的 ②易受影响的 ③过敏的
senseless ['senslɪs] *a.* 无意识的，无感觉的，不省人事的

[词组] in a sense 在某一方面，就某种意义来说
in no sense 决不（是）
make sense ①讲得通，有意义 ②〈口〉言之有理，是合情合理的
make sense of 理解，弄懂…的意思

43. There is already clear _____ to show that plants and animals are being affected by climate change.

  A) witness   B) certification

  C) identity   D) evidence

▶▶ **certification** [sɜːtɪfɪ'keɪʃən]

[释义] *n.* ①证明，证书 ②合格证

[同根] certify ['sɜːtɪfaɪ] *v.* ①证明，证实 ②证明…合格，保证…的质量 ③担保 ④批准
certified ['sɜːtɪfaɪd] *a.* ①证明合格的，有保证的 ②持有证件的
certificate [sə'tɪfɪkət] *n.* ①证书，执照 ②凭证，单据 ③证明 [sə'tɪfɪkeɪt] *v.* ①发证书给… ②用证书证明
certificated 持有合格证书的，持有证明的

▶▶ **identity** [aɪ'dentɪtɪ]

[释义] *n.* ①身份，本身，身份证明 (identity card 常略作 ID) ②同一人，同一物 ③相同，一致 ④相同处，一致处

[同根] identify [aɪ'dentɪfaɪ] *v.* ①认出，识别，鉴定 ②认为…等同于
identification [aɪ,dentɪfɪ'keɪʃən] *n.* ①认出，识别，鉴定，验明，确认 ②有关联，认同，支持
identifiable [aɪ'dentɪfaɪəbl] *a.* 可辨认的，可识别的，可证明是同一的
identical [aɪ'dentɪkəl] *a.* ①同一的 ②（完全）相同的，一模一样的

44. Many women still feel that they

are being _____ by a male culture, particularly in the professional services sector.

A) held back   B) held forth
C) held on   D) held out

▸▸ **hold back** 阻碍发展，抑制（情感、情绪），阻止
▸▸ **hold forth** 长篇大论地讲，滔滔不绝地讲
▸▸ **hold on** ①（打电话时用语）请等一下，不要挂上 ②坚持
▸▸ **hold out** ①给予，提供 ②支持，继续 ③坚持，忍耐

---

45. The findings paint a unique picture of the shopping habits of customers, plus their motivation and _____ .

A) privileges   B) possibilities
C) possessions   D) preferences

▸▸ **finding** ['faɪndɪŋ]
[释义] *n.* ①（常作复数）调查 / 研究的结果 ②发现，发现物

---

46. It's good to know that quite a few popular English expressions actually _____ from the Bible.

A) acquire   B) obtain
C) derive   D) result

▸▸ **derive** [dɪ'raɪv]
[释义] *v.* 来自，起源于，派生出来
[同义] come from, result from
[词组] derive from... 得自…，由…来

---

47. Tom, did it ever _____ to you that you would be punished for cheating on exams?

A) happen   B) occur
C) reflect   D) strike

▸▸ **be punished for...** 因…而受惩罚
▸▸ **happen to sb.** 发生在…身上

▸▸ **occur to sb.** 被某人想到，被某人想起

▸▸ **reflect** [rɪ'flekt]
[释义] *v.* ①反射，照出，映出 ②反映，显示 ③深思，考虑
[同根] reflective [rɪ'flektɪv] *a.* ①反射的，反照的，反映的 ②思考的，沉思的
reflection [rɪ'flekʃən] *n.* ①反射，反照 ②反映，映像，倒影 ③思考
[词组] reflect on... 思考…，反省…

---

48. In the US, 88 percent of smokers had started before they were 18, despite the fact that it is _____ to sell cigarettes to anyone under that age.

A) liable   B) liberal
C) irrational   D) illegal

▸▸ **despite the fact that...** 尽管

▸▸ **liable** ['laɪəbl]
[释义] *a.* ①会…的，有…倾向的 ②有…危险的，可能遭受…的 ③负有责任的，有义务的
[同义] apt, likely, probable
[词组] be liable to do 易于…的，有…倾向的
be liable for 对…应负责任

▸▸ **liberal** ['lɪbərəl]
[释义] *a.* ①慷慨的，大方的 ②大量的 ③心胸开阔的，开明的 ④不严格的，自由的 *n.* ①自由主义者 ②自由党成员
[同义] generous, tolerant, freethinking
[同根] liberty ['lɪbətɪ] *n.* ①（行动、言论、选择等）自由 ②释放，自由
liberalize ['lɪbərəlaɪz] *v.* 使自由化，放宽限制，使不受官方限制
liberalism ['lɪbərəlɪzm] *n.* ①宽容，开朗，开明的思想 ②自由主义

▸▸ **irrational** [ɪ'ræʃənəl]

[释义] *a.* ①无理性的，失去理性的
②不合理的，荒谬的

[反义] rational, reasonable

[同根] irrationalize [ɪˈræʃənəlaɪz] *v.* 使
失去理性，使不合理
irrationally [ɪˈræʃənlɪ] *ad.* 不合理
地，无理性地

**49. According to the key witnesses, a
peculiarly big nose is the criminal's
most memorable facial _____.**
A) feature   B) hint
C) spot   D) signature

▶▶▶ **peculiarly** [pɪˈkjuːlɪəlɪ]

[释义] *ad.* ①特别，尤其 ②奇怪地，古
怪地 ③独特地，有特色地

[同根] peculiar [pɪˈkjuːljə] *a.* ①古怪
的，奇特的 ②特有的，独具的 ③特
别的，特殊的
peculiarity [pɪˌkjuːlɪˈærɪtɪ] *n.* ①奇
特，古怪 ②怪癖，怪异的东西 ③独
特性，特性

▶▶▶ **memorable** [ˈmemərəbl]

[释义] *a.* ①难忘的 ②值得纪念的 ③值
得注意的，重大的，著名的

[同义] notable, rememberable

[同根] memorial [mɪˈmɔːrɪəl] *n.* ①纪念
物，纪念碑，纪念仪式 ②历史记载
memorably [ˈmemərəblɪ] *ad.* 值得纪
念地，重大地，有影响地

▶▶▶ **signature** [ˈsɪgnɪtʃə]

[释义] *n.* 签名，盖章，画押

[同根] sign [saɪn] *v.* ①在…签字，签
名 ②签署，做手势 ③预示 *n.* ①标记，
标志 ②符号，记号 ③示意动作，手
势 ④招牌，广告牌

[词组] add/put one's signature to 在…上
签名/盖章

50. Brazil's constitution _____ the military

use of nuclear energy.
A) withdraws   B) forbids
C) interrupts   D) objects

▶▶▶ **nuclear energy** 核能

▶▶▶ **withdraw** [wɪðˈdrɔː]

[释义] *v.* ①收回，抽回 ②收回，提取
③撤退，撤回

[同根] withdrawal [wɪðˈdrɔːəl] *n.* ①收
回，取回，提款 ②撤回，撤退 ③退缩

▶▶▶ **forbid** [fəˈbɪd]

[释义] *v.* ①禁止，不许 ②阻止，制止
③不准进入/使用

[同义] ban, prohibit

[同根] forbidden [fəˈbɪdn] *a.* 被禁止
的，一般人禁止使用或进入的

**51. Some people argue that the death
_____ does not necessarily reduce
the number of murders.**
A) plot   B) practice
C) penalty   D) pattern

▶▶▶ **plot** [plɒt]

[释义] *n.* ①阴谋，秘密计划 ②情节
③小块土地 *v.* ①密谋，策划 ②设计
情节

[同义] scheme, intrigue

▶▶▶ **penalty** [ˈpenəltɪ]

[释义] *n.* ①惩罚，处罚 ②罚款，罚金
③[体] 罚球

[同义] punishment

[反义] reward

[同根] penalize [ˈpiːnəlaɪz] *v.* ①宣布
应处罚 ②对…处罚/处刑 ③使处于
不利地位，妨碍

[词组] death penalty 死刑
pay the penalty 遭受惩罚，自食其果

**52. Many personnel managers say it is
getting harder and harder to _____**

honest applicants from the growing number of dishonest ones.

A) distinguish   B) disguise
C) dissolve   D) discount

▶▶ **personnel manager** 人事主管，人事经理

▶▶ **disguise** [dɪs'gaɪz]

[释义] v. ①隐瞒，掩饰 ②伪装 n. ①伪装，化装 ②掩饰物 ③托辞，借口

[同义] conceal, cover, hide

[词组] disguise as... 伪装成…
in disguise 伪装，化装
in/under the disguise of 在…伪装下
throw off one's disguise 摘下假面具，露出真面目

▶▶ **discount** [dɪ'skaʊnt]

[释义] v. ①不全信，怀疑地看待 ②不重视，不理会 ③低估，贬低，减损
['dɪskaʊnt] n. ①折扣   ②不全信

[同根] discountable [dɪ'skaʊntəbl]
a. ①不可全信的   ②可享受折扣的

[词组] at a discount ①打折扣，不值钱的 ②不受重视的
with some discount ①打折扣 ②以保留态度

53. A study shows that students living in non-smoking dorms are less likely to _____ the habit of smoking.

A) make up   B) turn up
C) draw up   D) pick up

▶▶ **make up** ①构成，组成 ②和解，和好 ③化妆，化装 ④捏造，虚构

▶▶ **draw up** ①草拟   ② (汽车) 停在… ③逼近，追上

54. Almost all job applicants are determined to leave a good _____ on a potential employer.

A) illusion   B) reputation
C) impression   D) reflection

▶▶ **be determined to do sth.** 决心做…，决定做…

▶▶ **illusion** [ɪ'lu:ʒən]

[释义] n. ①幻觉，错觉 ②幻想，错误的观念

[同义] deception, misconception, delusion

[同根] illusionary [ɪ'lu:ʒənərɪ]
a. (=illusional) ①错觉的，造成错觉的 ②幻觉般的
illusioned [ɪ'lu:ʒənd] a. 充满幻想的，受幻觉影响的

[词组] be under the illusion (与 that 连用) 错误地相信

▶▶ **reputation** [ˌrepjʊ'teɪʃən]

[释义] n. ①名声，名气   ②好名声，声望，声誉

[同根] disreputable [dɪs'repjʊtəbl]
a. 声名狼藉的，破烂不堪的

[词组] of reputation 有名望的
of no reputation 声名狼藉的
live up to one's reputation 不负盛名，名副其实
lose/ruin one's reputation 名誉扫地

▶▶ **impression** [ɪm'preʃən]

[释义] n. ①印象，感想 ②影响，效果

[同根] impress [ɪm'pres] v. ①给…深刻的印象，使铭记 ②压印，盖戳
impressive [ɪm'presɪv] a. 给人深刻印象的，感人的
impressionism [ɪm'preʃənɪzəm] n. (绘画等的) 印象主义，印象派
impressionist [ɪm'preʃənɪst] n. 印象主义者，印象派作家

▶▶ **reflection** [rɪ'flekʃən]

[释义] n. ①反射 ②映像，反映 ③沉思

[同义] indication, image, thinking,

thought

[同根] reflect [rɪ'flekt] v. ①反射，照出 ②反映，表达 ③深思，考虑
reflective [rɪ'flektɪv] a. ①反射的 ②沉思的，熟虑的

55. A special feature of education at MIT is the opportunity for students and faculty to _____ together in research activities.

A) specialize   B) participate
C) consist   D) involve

▶▶ faculty ['fækəltɪ]

[释义] n. ①大／中学全体教师 ②才能，本领，能力 ③学院，系

▶▶ specialize ['speʃəlaɪz]

[释义] v. ①专门研究 ②深入 ③使专用于

[同根] special ['speʃəl] a. ①特殊的，特别的 ②异常的，独特的 ③专门的，特设的 n. ①专车，专机 ②特殊的人或物 ③特刊 ④特色菜
specialist ['speʃəlɪst] n. 专家
speciality [ˌspeʃɪ'ælɪtɪ] n. ①特性，特质 ②专业

[词组] specialize in 擅长于，专攻

▶▶ participate [pɑː'tɪsɪpeɪt]

[释义] v. ①参与，参加 ②分享，分担
[同义] join in, partake, take part in
[同根] participator [pɑː'tɪsɪpeɪtə(r)] n. 参与者，分享者
participation [pɑːˌtɪsɪ'peɪʃən] n. 分享，参与，参加

[词组] participate in 参加，参与，分享

56. Although they lost their jobs, savings and unemployment benefits allow the couple to _____ their comfortable home.

A) come in for   B) catch up with
C) look forward to   D) hold on to

▶▶▶ unemployment benefits 失业补助

▶▶▶ come in for ①得到（权益），接受（遗产等）②受到（责怪）

▶▶▶ catch up with ①赶上，与…并驾齐驱 ②抓住，找到证据，惩处 ③带来不良的后果

▶▶▶ look forward to 期望，期待，盼望

57. Although many experts agree that more children are overweight, there is debate over the best ways to _____ the problem.

A) relate   B) tackle
C) file   D) attach

▶▶ file [faɪl]

[释义] v. ①编档保存 ②提出，提交
n. ①文件夹，纸夹 ②档案，卷宗 ③纵队

[词组] on file 存档，有案可查
in file 成纵队，依次，鱼贯地
file away/off 排成一列纵队出发，归档
file in 鱼贯而入，陆续编入，编入档内
file out 鱼贯而出

58. An important factor in determining how well you perform in an examination is the _____ of your mind.

A) state   B) case
C) situation   D) circumstance

▶▶ the state of one's mind 心态

▶▶ circumstance ['sɜːkəmstəns]

[释义] n. （常用复数）①环境，条件，情况 ②事态，情势
[同义] condition, situation, state
[词组] under/in no circumstances 无论如何都不，决不
under/in the circumstances 在这种情况下

59. Research shows that there is no _____

relationship between how much a person earns and whether he feels good about life.
A) successive   B) subsequent
C) significant   D) sincere

▶▶▶ successive [sək'sesɪv]

[释义] a. ①连续的，连接的，依次的 ②接替的，继承的

[同根] succession [sək'seʃən] n. ①连续，交替 ②一系列，一连串 ③继任，继承

successor [sək'sesə] n. ①继承人，接班人 ②后续的事物

successively [sək'sesɪvlɪ] ad. 接连着，继续地

▶▶▶ subsequent ['sʌbsɪkwənt]

[释义] a. 后来的，随后的

[同义] following, later, succeeding

[反义] earlier, previous

[同根] subsequence ['sʌbsɪkwəns] n. ①随后，后来，接续 ②随后发生的事物

subsequently ['sʌbsɪkwəntlɪ] ad. 随后，后来，接着

[词组] subsequent upon 作为…的结果而发生的，接着…发生的

▶▶▶ significant [sɪg'nɪfɪkənt]

[释义] a. ①重大的，重要的 ②表示…的 (of) ③有意义的，意味深长的 ④相当数量的，值得注意的

[同义] marked, meaningful, vital, important

[反义] insignificant, trivial, unimportant

[同根] significance [sɪg'nɪfɪkəns] n. ①重要性，显著性 ②意义，含义 ③意思，意味

▶▶▶ sincere [sɪn'sɪə]

[释义] a. ①真诚的，真挚的 ②真实的，真心实意的

[同义] earnest, genuine, heartful, honest

[反义] insincere

[同根] sincerely [sɪn'sɪəlɪ] ad. 真挚地，真诚地，诚实地

sincerity [sɪn'serɪtɪ] n. ①诚实，真挚 ②真心实意

60.Sadly, as spending on private gardens has _____ , spending on public parks has generally declined.
A) heightened   B) lifted
C) flown   D) soared

▶▶▶ heighten ['haɪtn]

[释义] v. 提高，升高

[同根] height [haɪt] n. 高度，海拔

61.Lung cancer, like some other cancers, often doesn't produce _____ until it is too late and has spread beyond the chest to the brain, liver or bones.
A) trails   B) therapies
C) symptoms   D) symbols

▶▶▶ trail [treɪl]

[释义] n. ①痕迹，踪迹 ②小路 v. 跟踪，追踪

[同义] track, mark, path

[词组] trail off 逐渐减弱，缩小
trail after 追随

▶▶▶ therapy ['θerəpɪ]

[释义] n. ①治疗，疗法 ②治疗效果 ③理疗

62.With the increasing unemployment rate, workers who are 50 to 60 years old are usually the first to be _____ .
A) laid off   B) laid aside
C) laid out   D) laid up

▶▶▶ unemployment rate 失业率

▶▶▶ lay aside ①搁置 ②积蓄

▶▶▶ lay out ①摆开，展示 ②布置，安排

▶▶▶ lay up ①贮存，搁置 ②使某人卧床，

不能工作等

63. The physical differences between men and women can be directly _____ to our basic nature as hunters and child-bearers.

A) pursued   B) traced
C) switched   D) followed

▶▶ bearer ['beərə]

[释义] n. ①生育者 ②送信人 ③搬运者

[同根] bear [beə] v. (bore, borne, bearing) ①忍受，容忍 ②具有，显示 ③承担，负担 ④经得起（考验等）⑤写有，刻有 ⑥生（孩子），结（果实）n. 熊

bearing ['beərɪŋ] n. ①举止，风度 ②关系，关联 ③意义，意思 ④方面

bearable ['beərəbl] a. 可忍受的，支持得住的

▶▶ trace [treɪs]

[释义] v. ①追溯，追踪 ②查出，找到 ③描摹，勾画出 n. ①痕迹，踪迹 ②微量，少许

[同义] follow, track, trail

[词组] trace (back) to 追溯到，上溯到

without trace 无痕迹，无踪迹

trace out 描绘出

64. It is clear that the dog has a much greater _____ of its brain devoted to smell than the case with humans.

A) composition   B) compound
C) percent   D) proportion

▶▶ compound ['kɒmpaund]

[释义] n. 复合词，混合物，化合物 a. ①化合的，复合的，混合的 ②群体的

[同义] combination, composite, mixture

▶▶ percent [pə'sent]

[释义] n. 百分比，百分数

[同根] percentage [pə'sentɪdʒ] n. ①百分率，百分比 ②所占比例

proportion [prə'pɔ:ʃən] n. ①比例，比率 ②相称，均衡

[同义] percentage, portion, ratio, amount, balance

[词组] in proportion to ①与…成比例，与…相称 ②和…相比

in proportion 比例相称，协调

out of proportion 不成比例的

in the proportion of 按…的比例

65. American college students are increasingly _____ with credit card debt and the consequences can be rather serious.

A) boosted   B) burdened
C) discharged   D) dominated

▶▶ credit card debt 信用卡透支

▶▶ burden ['bɜ:dn]

[释义] v. ①使负担，加负荷于 ②加重压于 n. 负荷，负担

[同义] load

[同根] burdensome ['bɜ:dnsəm] a. 繁重的，烦人的，难以承担的

[词组] be burdened with... 被…所累

pass one's burden on sb. 把责任丢给某人

66. Numerous studies already link the first meal of the day to better classroom _____.

A) performance   B) function
C) behavior   D) display

▶▶ numerous ['nju:mərəs]

[释义] a. 为数众多的，许多的

[同义] many, abundant, plentiful

[同根] numerously ['nju:mərəslɪ] ad. 多数地，无数地

numerable ['nju:mərəbl] a. 可数的，

可计数的

67. The most successful post-career athletes are those who can take the identity and skills they learned in sports and _____ them to another area of life.

A) utilize   B) employ

C) apply   D) exert

▶▶ utilize [ˈjuːtɪlaɪz]

[释义] v. 利用

[同义] make use of, use

[同根] utility [juːˈtɪlɪtɪ] n. ①功用，效用 ②有用之物 ③公用事业 / 设备

utilization [ˌjuːtɪlaɪˈzeɪʃən] n. 利用，应用

▶▶ apply [əˈplaɪ]

[释义] v. ①运用，应用，实施 ②申请，请求 ③指定，把…用于 ④适用

[同根] application [ˌæplɪˈkeɪʃən] n. ①应用，实施 ②用法，用途 ③请求，申请

applicant [ˈæplɪkənt] n. 申请人

[词组] apply to sth. 应用于…，适用于…

apply for 申请…

▶▶ exert [ɪɡˈzɜːt]

[释义] v. ①用（力），尽力 ②运用，行使，施加

[同义] force, strain, try, apply, use, exercise

[同根] exertion [ɪɡˈzɜːʃən] n. ①尽力，努力 ②行使，运用，施加

[词组] exert oneself to do sth. 努力做…，尽力做…

exert an influence on 对…施加影响

68. The technological advances made it possible for the middle classes to enjoy what had once been _____ only to the very rich.

A) manageable   B) measurable

C) acceptable   D) affordable

▶▶ technological advances 科技进步

▶▶ measurable [ˈmeʒərəbl]

[释义] a. ①可测量的，可计量的 ②可预见的 ③值得注意的，重大的

[同根] measure [ˈmeʒə] v. ①测量，计量 ②打量 ③估量 ④斟酌，权衡

measured [ˈmeʒəd] a. ①标准的 ②慎重的，经过仔细考虑的 ③有节奏的，有韵律的 ④从容不迫的

measureless [ˈmeʒəlɪs] a. 无限的，无法度量的

measurement [ˈmeʒəmənt] n. ①测量法 ②测量 ③尺寸

▶▶ affordable [əˈfɔːdəbl]

[释义] a. ①花费得起的，担负得起的 ②经受得住的

[同根] afford [əˈfɔːd] v. ①担负得起费用，花费得起 ②经受得住 ③抽得出（时间）④给与，提供

69. Being out of work, Jane can no longer _____ friends to dinners and movies as she used to.

A) urge   B) treat

C) appeal   D) compel

▶▶ be out of work 失业

▶▶ urge [ɜːdʒ]

[释义] v. ①催促，力劝 ②驱策，推动 n. 强烈欲望，迫切要求

[同义] push, stimulate, encourage

[反义] discourage, hinder

[同根] urgency [ˈɜːdʒənsɪ] n. ①紧急，急迫 ②紧急的事 ③强求，催促

urgent [ˈɜːdʒənt] a. 急迫的，紧急的

urgently [ˈɜːdʒəntlɪ] ad. 迫切地，急切地

▶▶ compel [kəmˈpel]

[释义] v. ①强迫，强求，强使发生 ②驱策，驱使

[同义] drive, oblige, force, constrain

[同根] compelling [kəm'pelɪŋ] a. ①强制的，强迫的 ②激发兴趣的，引人注目的

70. _____ by the superstars on television, the young athletes trained hard and played intensely.

A) Imitated   B) Imposed

C) Insured   D) Inspired

▶▶ intensely [ɪn'tenslɪ]

[释义] ad. ①紧张地，认真地 ②强烈

地，激烈地 ③热情地

[同义] fiercely, severely, forcefully

[反义] mildly, moderately

[同根] intense [ɪn'tens] a. ①激烈的，强烈的，剧烈的 ②紧张的，认真的 ③热切的，热情的

intensify [ɪn'tensɪfaɪ] v. 加强，增强，（使）变尖锐

intensive [ɪn'tensɪv] a. ①集中的，加强的，密集的 ②集约（经营）的

intension [ɪn'tenʃən] n. ①增强，加剧 ②强度，烈度 ③专心致志

intensity [ɪn'tensɪtɪ] n. ①强烈，剧烈，紧张，极度 ②强度，烈度

Answer Key									
41.A	42.B	43.D	44.A	45.D	46.C	47.B	48.D	49.A	50.B
51.C	52.A	53.D	54.C	55.B	56.D	57.B	58.A	59.C	60.D
61.C	62.A	63.B	64.D	65.B	66.A	67.C	68.D	69.B	70.D

As a physician who travels quite a lot, I spend a lot of time on planes listening for that **dreaded** "Is there a doctor **on board**?" **announcement**. I've been called only once—for a woman who had merely fainted. But the accident made me quite **curious** about how often this kind of thing happens. I wondered what I would do if confronted with a real midair medical emergency—**without access to** a **hospital staff** and the usual emergency **equipment**. So when the New England Journal of Medicine last week published a study about in—flight medical events, I read it with interest.

The study estimated that there are an average of 30 in-flight medical emergencies on U.S. flights every day. Most of them are not serious; fainting and dizziness are the most frequent complaints. But 13% of them—roughly four a day—are serious enough to require a pilot to change course. The most common of the serious emergencies include heart trouble, strokes, and difficulty breathing.

Let's face it: plane rides are stressful. For starters, cabin pressures at high **altitudes** are set at roughly what they would be if you lived at 5,000 to 8,000 feet above sea level. Most people can **tolerate** these pressures pretty easily, but passengers with heart disease may experience chest pains as a result of the reduced amount of oxygen flowing through their blood. Another common in-flight problem is deep **venous thrombosis**—the so-called **economy class** *syndrome* (综 合 症) . Whatever happens, don't panic. Things are getting better on the in-flight-emergency front. Thanks to more recent legislation, flights with at least one **attendant** are starting to install **emergency medical kits** to treat heart attacks.

文章词汇注释

▶▶ **dread** [dred]

[释义] v. 惧怕，担心 n. ①恐惧，恐怖，畏惧 ②可怕的人（或物）

[同义] fear, be afraid of

[同根] dreadful ['dredful] a. ①可怕的，恐惧的 ②不愉快的，令人不快的

▶▶ **on board** 在飞机上，在轮船上

▶▶ **announcement** [ə'naunsmənt]

[释义] n. ①广播，通告，声明 ②言论，谈话

[同义] broadcast, declaration

[同根] announce [ə'nauns] v. ①广播 ②正式宣布，宣告，发表
announcer [ə'naunsə] n. ①广播员 ②告知者 ③报幕员

▶▶ **curious** ['kjuəriəs]

[释义] a. ①好奇的，求知的 ②稀奇的 ③难以理解的

[同义] inquisitive, odd, peculiar, unusual

[同根] curiosity [ˌkjuərɪ'ɒsɪtɪ] n. ①好奇心，求知欲 ②珍品，古董，奇人/事
curiousness ['kjuəriəsnɪs] n. ①好学 ②好奇
incurious [ɪn'kjuəriəs] a. ①无好奇心的，不感兴趣的 ②不爱追根究底的

[词组] be curious about sth. 对（某事物）感到好奇
be curious to (do) 很想（做），渴望（做）

▶▶ **without access to...** 无法得到…，不能使用…

▶▶ **hospital staff** 医务人员

▶▶ **equipment** [ɪ'kwɪpmənt]

[释义] n. ①设备，固定资产 ②供给

[同义] apparatus, supplies

[同根] equip [ɪ'kwɪp] v. ①装备，配备

②使做好准备，训练 ③使具备 ④装束

▶▶ **altitude** ['æltɪtjuːd]

[释义] n. ①海拔高度，地平纬度 ②高处 ③高级，高等

[同义] height, elevation

[词组] in one's altitude 自高自大，飘飘然

▶▶ **tolerate** ['tɒləreɪt]

[释义] v. ①容忍，宽容 ②忍受，容许

[同义] accept, bear, endure, permit

[同根] tolerant ['tɒlərənt] a. ①忍受的 ②宽容的
tolerable ['tɒlərəbl] a. ①可容忍的，可原谅的 ②尚好的，过得去的
toleration [tɒlə'reɪʃən] n. ①容许 ②忍受
tolerance ['tɒlərəns] n. ①(=toleration) 容忍，宽容 ②忍受能力 ③耐受力

▶▶ **venous** ['viːnəs]

[释义] a. ①静脉的，静脉中的 ②有脉的，多脉的

▶▶ **thrombosis** [θrɒm'bəusɪs]

[释义] n. 血栓症

▶▶ **economy class** 经济舱

▶▶ **attendant** [ə'tendənt]

[释义] n. ①服务员，侍者 ②伴随物，附属品 ③随从 ④出席者 a. ①出席的，在场的 ②随行的 ③伴随的

[同义] waiter, appendix, incidental

[同根] attend [ə'tend] v. ①出席，参加 ②照料，看护 ③陪伴，服侍
attendance [ə'tendəns] n. ①出席，到场 ②陪从，看护 ③保养，维护

▶▶ **emergency medical kits** 急救箱，急救设备

选项词汇注释

▶▶▶ **address** [ə'dres]

[释义] v. ①对…发表演说 ②称呼 ③写下收信人的姓名，地址 n. ①演说，讲演 ②称呼，通讯地址

[同根] addresser [ə'dresə] n. ①发信人，发件人 ②发言人
addressor [ə'dresə] n. 说话者，发言人

[词组] address oneself to 着手，致力于

▶▶▶ **condition** [kən'dɪʃən]

[释义] n. ①条件，状况，情况 ②环境，形势 ③地位，身份 v. ①使能适应 ②使处于良好状态 ③以…为条件

[同义] circumstance, situation, state, specification

[同根] conditional [kən'dɪʃnəl] a. ①有条件的，以…为条件的 ②条件的，假定的
conditioned [kən'dɪʃənd] a. ①受条件限制的 ②受调节的 ③适合…的，习惯于…的
conditioner [kən'dɪʃənə] n. 调节器，空气调节装置

[词组] be in condition 身体很好
be out of condition 身体不适
on condition that 条件是…

▶▶▶ **significant** [sɪg'nɪfɪkənt]

[释义] a. ①意义重大的，重要的 ②相当大的，相当多的

[同根] signify ['sɪgnɪfaɪ] v. 表示…的意思，意味，预示
significance [sɪg'nɪfɪkəns] n. 意义，重要性
significantly [sɪg'nɪfɪkəntlɪ] ad. ①相当地，显著地 ②有重大意义地，重要地

▶▶▶ **confine** [kən'faɪn]

[释义] v. ①限制，限定 ②监禁，禁闭 ③使离不开，受困于

[同义] contain, enclose, restrain

[同根] confinement [kən'faɪnmənt] n. ①限制，拘留 ②密封 ③界限
confining [kən'faɪnɪŋ] a. ①限制的，拘束的 ②狭窄的，偏狭的
confines ['kɒnfaɪnz] n. 疆界，范围，界线

[词组] be confined to（局）限于…，(被)限制在…
beyond the confine of 超出…的范围
within the confines of 在…（范围）之内
confine oneself to 只涉及，只限于

▶▶▶ **harshly** [hɑ:ʃlɪ]

[释义] ad. 严厉地，苛刻地

[同根] harsh [hɑ:ʃ] a. ①粗糙的 ②刺耳的 ③严厉的，苛刻的 ④残酷的，无情的
harshness ['hɑ:ʃnɪs] n. ①粗糙的事物 ②严肃 ③刺耳
harshen ['hɑ:ʃən] v. ①使粗糙 ②刺耳 ③使苛刻，使无情

▶▶▶ **reluctantly** [rɪ'lʌktəntlɪ]

[释义] ad. 不情愿地，勉强地

[同根] reluctant [rɪ'lʌktənt] a. ①不情愿的 ②难处理的，难驾驭的，反对的
reluctance [rɪ'lʌktəns] n. 不情愿，勉强

▶▶▶ **casually** ['kæʒuəlɪ]

[释义] ad. ①偶然地 ②随便地 ③临时地

[同义] by accident, incidentally, accidentally

[同根] casual ['kæʒuəl] a. ①随便的，非正式的 ②疏忽的，漫不经心的 ③偶然的，碰巧的

The part of the environmental movement that **draws** my firm's **attention** is the design of cities, buildings and products. When we designed America's first so-called "green" office building in New York two decades ago, we felt very alone. But today, thousands of people come to **green building** conferences, and the idea that buildings can be good for people and the environment will be **increasingly influential** in years **to come**.

Back in 1984 we discovered that most **manufactured** products for **decoration** weren't designed for indoor use. The **"energy-efficient"** sealed commercial buildings constructed after the 1970s energy crisis revealed indoor air quality problems caused by materials such as paint, wall covering and carpet. So far 20 years, we've been **focusing on** these materials **down to the molecules**, looking for ways to make them safe for people and the planet.

Home builders can now use materials—such as paints that release **significantly reduced** amounts of **organic compounds**—that don't destroy the quality of the air, water, or soil. **Ultimately**, however, our basic design strategy is focused not simply on being "less bad" but on creating completely healthful materials that can be either safely returned to the soil or reused by industry again and again. As a matter of fact, the world's largest carpet manufacturer has already **developed** a carpet that is fully and safely *recyclable* (可循环用的).

Look at it this way: No one **starts out** to create a building that destroys the planet. But our current industrial systems are **inevitably** causing these conditions, whether we like it or not. So instead of simply trying to reduce the damage, we are adopting a positive approach. We're giving people high-quality, healthful products and an opportunity to make choices that **have a** beneficial **effect on** the world. It's not just the building industry, either. Total cities are taking these environmentally positive approaches to design, planning and building. Portland, Seattle and Boston have said they want to be green cities. Chicago wants to be the greenest city in the world.

文章词汇注释

▶▶ draw one's attention 引起某人的注意

▶▶ green building 环保型建筑

▶▶ increasingly influential 越来越有影响的

▶▶ to come 未来的

▶▶ **manufactured** [ˌmænjuˈfæktʃəd]

[释义] a. 制造的，人造的

[同根] manufacture [ˌmænjuˈfæktʃə] v. ①（大量）制造，生产 ②把…制成用品，给…加工 ③捏造，虚构

manufacturer [ˌmænjuˈfæktʃərə] n. 制造厂，制造商，工厂主

manufacturing [ˌmænjuˈfæktʃərɪŋ] n. 制造业，工业 a. 制造业的，制造的，生产的

manufactory [ˌmænjuˈfæktərɪ] n. 制造厂，工厂

▶▶ **decoration** [ˌdekəˈreɪʃən]

[释义] n. ①装饰，装潢 ②装饰品

[同义] beautification, ornament

[同根] decorate [ˈdekəreɪt] v. ①装饰，装潢 ②粉刷，油漆，裱糊

decorator [ˈdekəreɪtə] n. 装饰者，装潢者

decorative [ˈdekərətɪv] a. 装饰性的，作装饰用的

decorated [ˈdekəreɪtɪd] a. 经装饰的，盛装的

▶▶ **energy-efficient** a. 节能的

▶▶ **focuse on** 把注意力集中在…

▶▶ **down to the molecules** 小到分子的

▶▶ significantly reduced 大大减少的

▶▶ organic compound 有机化合物

▶▶ **ultimately** [ˈʌltɪmətlɪ]

[释义] ad. 最后，最终

[同义] eventually, finally, last

[同根] ultimate [ˈʌltɪmɪt] a. ①最终的，极点的，绝顶的 ②基本的，首要的 ③最大的，决定性的 n. ①最终的事物 ②终点，终极

▶▶ **develop** [dɪˈveləp]

[释义] v. ①研制，开发 ②发展，使发达 ③冲洗（胶卷）

[同义] cultivate, process

[同根] developing [dɪˈveləpɪŋ] a. 发展中的

development [dɪˈveləpmənt] n. ①研制，培育 ②发展，进化 ③事态发展情况

▶▶ **start out** ①开始时打算，本来想要 ②出发，动身 ③开始从事工作，启用

▶▶ **inevitably** [ɪnˈevɪtəblɪ]

[释义] ad. 不可避免地

[同义] certainly, unavoidably

[同根] inevitable [ɪnˈevɪtəbl] a. ①无法避免的，必然（发生）的 ②照例必有的

inevitability [ɪnˌevɪtəˈbɪlətɪ] n. 必然性

evitable [ˈevɪtəbl] a. 可避免的

▶▶ **have an effect on** 对…有影响，对…起作用，产生效果

选项词汇注释

▶▶ **outlook** ['aʊtlʊk]

[释义] *n.* ①观点，看法 ②展望，前景 ③景色，景致 ④注视，瞭望

[同义] expectation, view, prospect

▶▶ **scheme** [ski:m]

[释义] *n.* ①计划，规划，方案 ②系统，体制 ③阴谋，诡计 *v.* 策划，图谋，搞阴谋

[同义] plan, plot

▶▶ **inward** ['ɪnwəd]

[释义] *a.* ①里面的，内部的 ②内心的，精神的 *ad.* 向内地

[同义] inner, inside, interior, internal

[反义] external, outward

[同根] inwardly ['ɪnwədlɪ] *ad.* ①在内部 ②向内地 ③思想上，精神上

▶▶ **stable** ['steɪbl]

[释义] *a.* ①稳定的，稳固的 ②持久的 ③坚定的，不动摇的 ④平稳的 *n.* 马厩

[同义] constant, firm, fixed, steady

[反义] unstable, unsteady, shaky

[同根] stabilize ['steɪbɪlaɪz] *v.* 使稳定，保持…的稳定，使稳固

stably ['steɪblɪ] *ad.* ①稳定地，稳固地 ②固定地，持久地 ③坚定地，不动摇地

stability [stə'bɪlɪtɪ] *n.* ①稳定性 ②永久（性），耐久（度）③坚定，坚决

▶▶ **descend** [dɪ'send]

[释义] *v.* ①下来，下降，下倾 ②递减 ③祖传，世代相传

[反义] ascend, rise

[同根] descending [dɪ'sendɪŋ] *n.* 下降的，下行的，递降的

descendant [dɪ'sendənt] *n.* ①子孙，后裔，后代 ②（某一原形的）派生物 *a.* ①下降的，向下的 ②祖传的，派

生的

[词组] descend from 从…下来

▶▶ **depress** [dɪ'pres]

[释义] *v.* ①使沮丧，使抑郁 ②消弱，抑制 ③使不景气，使萧条

[同义] discourage, dishearten, sadden, lower

[反义] cheer, encourage, increase, raise

[同根] depression [dɪ'preʃən] *n.* ①减少，降低 ②沮丧，抑郁 ③萧条

depressive [dɪ'presɪv] *a.* 令人沮丧的，压抑的，萧条的

depressing [dɪ'presɪŋ] *a.* ①令人抑郁的 ②抑郁的，阴沉的

▶▶ **anyhow** ['enɪhaʊ]

[释义] *ad.* ①不管怎么说，无论如何 ②不论以何种方式

[同义] anyway, in spite of, in any case, at all events

▶▶ **anyway** ['enɪweɪ]

[释义] *ad.* ①不管怎么说，无论如何 ②不论以何种方式

[同义] anyhow, in spite of, in any case, at all events

▶▶ **partial** ['pɑːʃəl]

[释义] *a.* ①部分的，局部的 ②偏袒的，偏向一方的

[同义] fractional, fragmentary, partly

[反义] impartial, total

[同根] partialize ['pɑːʃəlaɪz] *v.* ①使偏向一方，使偏心 ②偏袒

partially ['pɑːʃəlɪ] *ad.* ①部分地，局部地 ②不公平地，偏袒地

[词组] be partial to 对…偏心的，对…偏爱的

▶▶ **superficially** [suːpə'fɪʃəlɪ]

[释义] *ad.* ①表面地 ②肤浅地，浅薄地

[反义] deeply, profoundly, thoroughly

[同根] superficial [ˌsuːpəˈfɪʃəl] a. ①表面的 ②肤浅的，浅薄的

superficialize [ˌsuːpəˈfɪʃəlaɪz] v. 使表面化

▶▶ basic [ˈbeɪsɪk]

[释义] a. ①基本的，基础的 ②主要的，首要的 n. [pl.] ①基本原理，概要 ②基本规律 ③基本因素

[同义] essential, fundamental, underlying

[同根] base [beɪs] n. ①基底，底座 ②基础 ③基地 ④起点 v. 根据，基于

basis [ˈbeɪsɪs] n. ①基础，根据，基本原理 ②主要部分，主要成分

basically [ˈbeɪsɪkəlɪ] ad. 基本地，主要地

▶▶ originally [əˈrɪdʒənəlɪ]

[释义] ad. 最初，原先

[同义] firstly, initially

[同根] origin [ˈɒrɪdʒɪn] n. ①起源，由来，起因 ②出身，血统

original [əˈrɪdʒənəl] a. ①最初的，原始的 ②独创的，新颖的 n. 原物，原作

originate [əˈrɪdʒɪneɪt] v. ①起源，发生 ②发起，创办，发明 ③引起

▶▶ adjust [əˈdʒʌst]

[释义] v. ①调节，改变…以适应 (to) ②校正，校准 ③解决，调节

[同义] adapt, regulate

[同根] adjustive [əˈdʒʌstɪv] a. 调节的，校正的，调整的，适应性的

adjustment [əˈdʒʌstmənt] n. ①调整，调节，校正 ②调节装置，调节器

[词组] adjust oneself to... 使自己适应于…

adjust to 改变 / 调整以适应…

▶▶ functional [ˈfʌŋkʃənl]

[释义] a. ①功能的 ②职务上的 ③可使用的，可操作的

[同根] function [ˈfʌŋkʃən] n. ①功能，作用 ②职务，职责 v. ①（器官等）活动，（机器等）运行 ②起作用 ③行使职责

▶▶ precious [ˈpreʃəs]

[释义] a. ①珍贵的，贵重的 ②心爱的，受到珍爱的

[同义] costly, expensive, priceless, valuable

▶▶ entire [ɪnˈtaɪə]

[释义] a. ①全部的，整个的 ②完全的，完整无缺的 ③一贯的，连续的 ad. ①全部地，完整地 ②安全地，彻底地 n. 全部，整体

[同义] complete, thorough, total, whole

[同根] entirely [ɪnˈtaɪəlɪ] ad. ①完全地，彻底地 ②全部地，完整地

▶▶ full [fʊl]

[释义] a. ①充满的，完全的 ②丰富的，完美的 ③详尽的 ad. 完全地，十分

[同义] crowded, filled, loaded, packed

[同根] fully [ˈfʊlɪ] ad. ①充分地，完全地，足足 ②至少

▶▶ complete [kəmˈpliːt]

[释义] a. ①完整的 ②完成的 ③圆满的，彻底的 v. ①完成 ②使之完满

[同根] completion [kəmˈpliːʃən] n. ①成就，完成，实现 ②完备化

completely [kəmˈpliːtlɪ] ad. ①十分地 ②完全地

Do you wake up every day feeling too tired, or even upset? If so, then a new alarm clock could be just for you.

The clock, called Sleep Smart, measures your sleep cycle, and waits for you to be in your **lightest phase of sleep** before **rousing** you. Its makers say that should ensure you wake up feeling **refreshed** every morning.

As you sleep you **pass through a sequence of** sleep states—light sleep, deep sleep and REM (rapid eye movement) sleep—that repeats **approximately** every 90 minutes. The point in that cycle at which you wake can affect how you feel later, and may even have a greater impact than how much or little you have slept. Being roused during a light phase means you **are more likely to** wake up **energetic**.

Sleep Smart records the **distinct** pattern of brain waves produced during each phase of sleep, **via** a **headband equipped** with *electrodes*（电极）and a **microprocessor**. This measures the electrical activity of the wearer's brain, in much the same way as some machines used for medical and research purposes, and **communicates wirelessly with** a clock unit near the bed. You **program** the clock with the latest time at which you want to be wakened, and it then *duly*（适时地）wakes you during the last light sleep phase before that.

The concept was invented by a group of students at Brown University in Rhode Island after a friend **complained of** waking up tired and performing poorly on a test. "As **sleep-deprived** people ourselves, we started thinking of what to do about it," says Eric Shashoua, a recent college graduate and now **chief executive officer** of Axon Sleep Research Laboratories, a company created by the students to develop their idea.

文章词汇注释

▶▶ **light phase of sleep** 浅睡期

▶▶ **rouse** ['raʊz]

[释义] v. ①叫起，唤醒 ②惊起（猎物）③激起，使激动，唤起，使觉醒

[同义] awaken, provoke, stir, wake up

[同根] rousing ['raʊzɪŋ] a. ①使人觉醒的，激动人心的 ②活跃的，兴旺的 arouse [ə'raʊz] v. ①唤醒，唤起 ②鼓励，引起

[词组] rouse sb. from/out of... 把…从…中弄醒

▶▶ **refreshed** [rɪ'freʃt]

[释义] a. 感觉清新的，恢复体力的

[同义] enlivened, freshened, renewed, revived

[同根] refresh [rɪ'freʃ] v. ①使振奋精神，使恢复活力 ②使变得新鲜，使得到补充 ③使感到清凉 refreshen [rɪ'freʃ ən] v. = refresh refreshing [rɪ'freʃɪŋ] a. ①提神的，凉爽的 ②给人新鲜感的 refresher [rɪ'freʃə] n. ①提神清凉饮料 ②帮助记忆的东西或人

▶▶ **pass through** ①经历 ②通过 ③遭受
▶▶ **a sequence of** 连续的，一连串的

▶▶ **approximately** [ə'prɒksɪmətlɪ]

[释义] ad. 大约，近似地

[同义] roughly, inexactly, about

[同根] approximate [ə'prɒksɪmət] a. ①近似的，大概的 ②接近的，紧靠的 v. ①近似 ②粗略估计

▶▶ **be more likely to...** 更有可能…

▶▶ **energetic** [ˌenə'dʒetɪk]

[释义] a. ①精力充沛的，精神饱满的 ②能量的，高能的

[同义] vigorous

[同根] energy ['enədʒɪ] n. ①活力，干劲 ②能力，精力，力量 ③能量，能源 energetically [ˌenə'dʒetɪkəlɪ] ad. 精力充沛地，积极地

▶▶ **distinct** [dɪ'stɪŋkt]

[释义] a. ①明显的，清楚的 ②有区别的，不同的 ③明确的，确切的

[同根] distinction [dɪ'stɪŋkʃən] n. ①区分，辨别 ②差别，不同 ③特征，特点 ④荣誉，声望 distinctive [dɪ'stɪŋktɪv] a. 特殊的，特别的，有特色的

▶▶ **via** ['vaɪə, 'viːə]

[释义] prep. ①通过，凭借 ②经由，经过

▶▶ **headband** ['hedbænd]

[释义] n. ①（耳机）头环 ②头巾，头饰带

▶▶ **equipped** [ɪ'kwɪpt]

[释义] a. 装有…的，装备了…的 (with)

[同义] armed

[同根] equip [ɪ'kwɪp] v. ①装备，配备 ②使做好准备，训练，使有资格 equipment [ɪ'kwɪpmənt] n. ①装备，配备 ②设备，器具 ③才能，禀赋

[词组] be equipped for 准备好，对…有准备 be equipped with 装备有…，安装有…

▶▶ **microprocessor** ['maɪkrəʊˌprəʊsesə]

[释义] n. [计] 微处理器

▶▶ **communicate wirelessly with** 通过无线电与…交流，联系

▶▶ **program** ['prəʊgræm]

[释义] v. ①编程序 ②计划，安排 ③编排节目 n. ①计划，方案 ②节目 ③程

序 ④课程

▶▶ complain of/about 抱怨，埋怨，诉苦

▶▶ sleep-deprived *a.* 失眠的
▶▶ chief executive officer 首席执行官

选项词汇注释

▶▶ **dictate** [dɪk'teɪt]
[释义] *v.* ①听写，口述 ②命令，要求
[同根] dictation [dɪk'teɪʃən] *n.* ①命令 ②口授令人笔录，听写
dictator [dɪk'teɪtə] *n.* ①独裁者 ②口授者

▶▶ **remove** [rɪ'mu:v]
[释义] *v.* ①消除，去掉 ②移开，挪走 ③调动，迁移 ④脱下，摘下
[同义] eliminate, delete, transfer
[同根] removal [rɪ'mu:vəl] *n.* ①移动，调动，搬迁 ②消除，排除 ③免职，开除
removable [rɪ'mu:vəbl] *a.* ①可消除的 ②可移动的，可拆装的 ③可免职的
removed [rɪ'mu:vd] *a.* ①分离的，远离的 ②隔代的，隔辈的
remover [rɪ'mu:və] *n.* ①搬运工，搬运公司 ②去除剂，洗净剂
[词组] be removed from 从…开除/移开/去除

▶▶ **recall** [rɪ'kɔ:l]
[释义] *v.* ①记得，回想起，使人想起 ②叫回，召回 ③使（思想、注意力）重新集中
[同义] recollect, cast one's mind back

Language is the most astonishing behavior in the animal kingdom. It is the **species**-typical behavior that **sets** humans completely **apart from** all other animals. Language is a means of communication, but it is much more than that. Many animals can communicate. The dance of the honeybee communicates the location of flowers to other members of the *hive*（蜂群）. But human language permits communication about anything, even things like *unicorns*（独角兽）that have never existed. The key **lies in** the fact that the units of meaning, words, can **be strung together** in different ways, according to rules, to communicate different meanings.

Language is the most important learning we do. Nothing defines humans so much as our ability to communicate **abstract** thoughts, whether about the universe, the mind, love, dreams or ordering a drink. It is an **immensely complex** process that we take for granted. Indeed, we **are** not **aware of** most aspects of our speech and understanding. Consider what happens when one person is speaking to another. The speaker has to translate thoughts into spoken language. Brain imaging studies suggest that the time from thoughts to the building of speech is extremely fast, only 0.04 seconds! The listener must hear the sounds to **figure out** what the speaker means. He must use the sounds of speech to identify the words spoken, understand the pattern of **layout** of the words (sentences), and finally **interpret** the meaning. This takes somewhat longer, a **minimum** of about 0.5 seconds. But once started, it is of course a continuous process.

文章词汇注释

▶▶▶ species ['spi:ʃɪz]
[释义] *n.* ① [生] 种 ② 种，类，种类
　a. [生] 物种上的

▶▶▶ set...apart from... 使…与…分开／分离
▶▶▶ lie in 在于
▶▶▶ be strung together ①被串起，被连

在一起，被联系在一起 ②被用绳 /
线扎在一起

▶▶ **abstract** ['æbstrækt]

[释义] *a.* ①抽象的 ②深奥的 ③理论的
n. ①摘要，概要 ②抽象派艺术作品
③抽象概念 *v.* ①把…抽象出来
②做…的摘要 ③提取，抽取

[同根] abstracted [æb'stræktɪd]
a. ①心不在焉的，出神的 ②分离出
来的

▶▶ **immensely complex** 非常复杂的
▶▶ **be aware of** 意识到
▶▶ **figure out** ①理解，明白 ②合计为，
计算出

▶▶ **layout** ['leɪ,aut]

[释义] *n.* ①安排，设计，布局 ②（书刊、

广告等）版面编排 ③陈列（物）

▶▶ **interpret** [ɪn'tɜ:prɪt]

[释义] *v.* ①理解，了解 ②解释，阐明
③翻译，口译

[同根] interpreter [ɪn'tɜ:prɪtə] *n.* ①解
释程序，解释者 ②口译人员
interpretation [ɪn,tɜ:prɪ'teɪʃən]
n. ①解释，阐明 ②口译，通译
interpretable [ɪn'tɜ:prətəbl] *a.* 可阐
明的，可翻译的，可解释的

[词组] interpret as 理解为

▶▶ **minimum** ['mɪnɪməm]

[释义] *n.* 最小值，最低限度 *a.* 最小的，
最低的

[反义] maximum ['mæksɪməm]
n. 最大量，最大限度 *a.* 最高的，最
多的，最大极限的

选项词汇注释

▶▶ **transfer** [træns'fɜ:]

[释义] *v.* ①调动，使转学 ②改变，转
换 ③转乘（车或船）④转让
['trænsfɜ:] *n.* 迁移，调任

[同义] move, shift, handover

[同根] transference ['trænsfərəns]
n. ①转移，传递 ②调任，调动 ③（财
产）转让
transferable [træns'fɜ:rəbəl] *a.* ①可
转移的，可转换的 ②可传递的
transferred [træns'fɜ:d] *a.* ①转移的
②调动的，转让的

[词组] transfer from...to... 从…调往…，
从…转化成…

▶▶ **transmit** [trænz'mɪt]

[释义] *v.* ①播送，传送，发射 ②传播
③传染 ④传（热、声等）

[同根] transmission [trænz'mɪʃən]
n. ①传播 ②（信号、节目等）发射，

播送 ③传染
transmitter [trænz'mɪtə] *n.* 传达人，
发报机，发射机

▶▶ **consist** [kən'sɪst]

[释义] *v.* ①组成，构成 ②存在于，在于

[同义] comprise, include, make up

[词组] consist in 存在于
consist of 由…组成
consist with 与…一致

▶▶ **scale** [skeɪl]

[释义] *n.* ①规模，范围 ②刻度，标度
③衡量标准，尺度 ④等级，级别

[词组] in scale 成比例，相称
out of scale 不成比例，不相称
scale up 按比例增加
scale down 按比例减少

▶▶ **combine** [kəm'baɪn]

[释义] *v.* （使）联合，结合，组合

['kɒmbaɪn] *n.* ①联合企业 ②联合收割机

[同根] combination [ˌkɒmbɪˈneɪʃən] *n.* 结合，联合，化合，化合物

combined [kəmˈbaɪnd] *a.* ①结合的，联合的 ②由多方面协同完成的

▶▶ declare [dɪˈkleə]

[释义] *v.* ①宣布，声称 ②公布，发表 ③申报（纳税品等）

[同义] announce, assert, pronounce, state

[同根] declaration [ˌdekləˈreɪʃən] *n.* ①宣言，宣布 ②公布，披露 ③申报（纳税品等）

declared [dɪˈkleəd] *a.* ①公开宣称的 ②呈报的

declaredly [dɪˈkleərɪdlɪ] *ad.* 公然地

[词组] declare against sth. 声明反对某事

declare off ①宣布作废，毁约 ②宣布退出

▶▶ prescribe [prɪˈskraɪb]

[释义] *v.* ①指定，规定 ②开处方，给医嘱 ③限定，限制

[同根] prescription [prɪˈskrɪpʃən] *n.* ①指定，规定 ②处方，药方 ③解救方法，诀窍

prescriptive [prɪˈskrɪptɪv] *a.* ①指定的，规范的 ②约定俗成的

An earthquake hit Kashmir on Oct. 8, 2005. It took some 75,000 lives, injured 130,000 and left nearly 3.5 million without food, jobs or homes. Almost overnight, scores of tent villages bloomed across the region, tended by international aid organizations, military personnel and aid groups working day and night to shelter the survivors before winter set in.

Mercifully, the season was mild. But with the arrival of spring the refugees will be moved again. Camps that provided health care, food and shelter for 150,000 survivors have begun to close as they were never intended to be permanent.

For most of the refugees, the thought of going back brings mixed emotions. The past six months have been difficult. Families of as many as 10 people have had to shelter under a single tent and share cookstoves and bathing facilities with neighbors. "They are looking forward to the clean water of their rivers," officials say. "They are dreaming of free fresh fruit. They want to get back to their herds and start farming again. " But most will be returning to nothing but heaps of ruins. In many villages, electrical lines have not been repaired, nor have roads. Aid workers estimate that it will take years to rebuild what the earthquake took away. And for the thousands of survivors, the recovery will never be complete.

Yet the survivors have to start somewhere. New homes can be built from the stones, bricks and beams of old ones. Spring is coming and it is a good time to start again.

文章词汇注释

▶▶▶ **hit** [hɪt]
[释义] v. ①袭击，打击，击中 ②碰撞 ③偶然发现，伤…的感情 n. ①打击，打，碰撞 ②讽刺 ③（演出等）成功

▶▶▶ **overnight** ['əʊvə'naɪt]
[释义] ad. ①一下子，突然 ②在整个夜间 ③在头一天晚上 a. ①似乎一夜间发生的，突然的 ②持续或住一夜的，只供一夜使用的 ③头一天晚上的 ④一整夜的

▶▶▶ **scores of** 许多，大量

▶▶▶ **bloom** [bluːm]
[释义] n. ①大量出现，突然激增 ②开花，草木丛生 / 茂盛 ③处于繁盛时期
[同义] flourish, develop, blossom
[反义] wither
[同根] blooming ['bluːmɪŋ] a. ①有花的，开着花的 ②青春健美，精力旺盛的 ③兴旺的
[词组] be out of bloom 花已落
come into bloom 开花
in full bloom 花盛开着
take the bloom off sth. 使…失去光彩，使成就

▶▶▶ **tend** [tend]
[释义] v. ①照管，护理 ②趋向
[同根] tendency ['tendənsɪ] n. ①趋向，倾向 ②（性格）倾向
[词组] tend toward / to 倾向
tend on 招待，照料
tend to 注意，趋向

▶▶▶ **international aid organization** 国际救援组织

▶▶▶ **military** ['mɪlɪtərɪ]
[释义] a. 军事的，军用的

[同根] militant ['mɪlɪtənt] n. 好战者，好战分子 a. 好战的，积极从事或支持使用武力的

▶▶▶ **personnel** [ˌpɜːsə'nel]
[释义] n. ①人员，职员 ②人事部门 a. ①员工的 ②有关人事的
[同义] staff
[同根] personal ['pɜːsənl] a. ①私人的 ②亲自的 ③私营的
personality [ˌpɜːsə'nælɪtɪ] n. ①个性，人格 ②名人

▶▶▶ **shelter** ['ʃeltə]
[释义] v. ①庇护，保护，掩蔽 ②为…提供避难所 ③躲避，避难 n. 掩蔽处，庇护所，避难所
[同义] defend, guard, protect, shield
[同根] sheltered ['ʃeltəd] a. 受保护的，受庇护的
[词组] shelter oneself 掩护自己，为自己辩护

▶▶▶ **survivor** [sə'vaɪvə]
[释义] n. 幸存者
[同根] survive [sə'vaɪv] v. ①幸存，幸免于 ②比…活得长
survival [sə'vaɪvəl] n. 幸存（者），残存（物）

▶▶▶ **set in** ①（季节、时期等）开始，来临 ②患上（某种疾病）③（潮汐）上涨 ④[喻] 流行，盛行

▶▶▶ **mercifully** ['mɜːsɪfulɪ]
[释义] ad. ①不幸之中算幸运地，（因结束痛苦而）受欢迎地 ②仁慈地
[同根] mercy ['mɜːsɪ] n. ①仁慈，怜悯，宽恕 ②幸运，侥幸
merciful ['mɜːsɪful] a. ①仁慈的，慈悲的 ②（因结束痛苦而）受欢迎的，

不幸之中算幸运的

▶▶ **mild** [maɪld]

[释义] *a.* ①温和的，温柔的 ②轻微的 ③淡味的 ④适度的

[同义] gentle, moderate, tender, soft

[反义] fierce, severe

[同根] mildness [maɪldnɪs] *n.* 温和，温暖

mildly ['maɪldlɪ] *ad.* ①温和地 ②适度地 ③略微

▶▶ **refugee** [,refju(:)'dʒi:]

[释义] *n.* 流亡者，难民 *v.* ①流亡，逃难 ②亡命国外 ③迫使流亡 ④接纳…避难

[同根] refuge ['refju:dʒ] *n.* 庇护，避难，避难所

▶▶ **health care** 卫生保健

▶▶ **be intended to be** 规定为，确定为

▶▶ **permanent** ['pɜ:mənənt]

[释义] *a.* ①长期不变的，固定（性）的，常在的 ②永久（性）的，永恒的 ③耐久的，永不退色的

[同义] lasting, endless, eternal, unceasing

[反义] impermanent, temporary

[同根] permanence ['pɜ:mənəns] *n.* 永久，持久

permanently ['pɜ:məntlɪ] *ad.* 永存地，不变地

▶▶ **emotion** [ɪ'məʊʃən]

[释义] *n.* ①感情，情绪 ②激动，激情

[同根] emotional [ɪ'məʊʃənl] *a.* ①易动感情的，情绪激动的 ②情绪/情感上的 ③表现强烈情感的，催人泪下的

emotionless [ɪ'məʊʃənlɪs] *a.* 没有感情的，冷漠的

▶▶ **facility** [fə'sɪlɪtɪ]

[释义] *n.* ①[pl.] 设施，设备 ②设备，工具 ③灵巧，熟练 ④容易，便利

[同根] facilitate [fə'sɪlɪteɪt] *v.* ①使容易，使便利 ②促进，助长 ③援助，帮助

facilitation [fə,sɪlɪ'teɪʃən] *n.* ①简便化，促进 ②使人方便的东西

[词组] give facilities for 给予…方便

with facility 容易，流利

▶▶ **look forward to** 期待，盼望

▶▶ **herd** [hɜ:d]

[释义] *n.* ①牧群（尤指牛群），兽群 ②人群，〈贬〉百姓 ③一大批，大量 *v.* ①（使…）集在一起，把…赶在一起 ②使入群

▶▶ **heaps of** ①一堆一堆的 ②许多，大量

▶▶ **ruin** [rʊɪn;'ru:ɪn]

[释义] *n.* ①废墟，遗迹 ②毁灭，崩溃 *v.* ①毁坏，毁损 ②毁灭，使成为废墟

[同义] destroy, spoil, damage

[同根] ruined ['rʊ(:)ɪnd] *a.* 毁灭的，荒废的

ruinous ['rʊɪnəs,'ru:ɪ-] *a.* 灾难性的，破坏性的

ruinously ['rʊɪnəslɪ] *ad.* 毁灭地，破坏地

[词组] go/come/fall to ruin 毁灭，灭亡，崩溃

ruin oneself 毁掉自己

in ruins ①成为废墟 ②遭到严重破坏

▶▶ **take away** ①拿走，夺走，拆去 ②使离开，带走 ③使消失，消除（病痛等）

▶▶ **beam** [bi:m]

[释义] *n.* ①梁，桁条，横梁 ②（光线的）束，柱，电波 ③高兴的表情或微笑 *v.* ①发出光与热，放射 ②高兴地微笑 ③发送，传送

选项词汇注释

▶▶ **scarcely** [ˈskeəslɪ]

[释义] *ad.* ①几乎不，简直没有 ②刚刚，才

[同义] rarely, hardly

[反义] plentifully

[同根] scarce [skeəs] *a.* ①缺乏的，不足的 ②稀有的，难得的

scarcity [ˈskeəsɪtɪ] *n.* ①缺乏，不足 ②罕见，难得

▶▶ **rank** [ræŋk]

[释义] *n.* ①职衔，军衔 ②地位，社会阶层 ③排，行列 *v.* 把…分等，给…评定等级

[同义] class, grade

▶▶ **equipment** [ɪˈkwɪpmənt]

[释义] *n.* ①设备，固定资产 ②供给

[同义] apparatus, supplies

[同根] equip [ɪˈkwɪp] *v.* ①装备，配备 ②使做好准备，训练 ③使具备 ④装束，穿着

▶▶ **installation** [ˌɪnstəˈleɪʃən]

[释义] *n.* ①安装，装置 ②就职

[同根] install [ɪnˈstɔːl] *v.* ①安装，安置 ②使就职

installment [ɪnˈstɔːlmənt] *n.* ①分期付款，债款的分期偿还数 ②分期连载的部分 ③就职，任职 ④安装，安置

▶▶ **emergence** [ɪˈmɜːdʒəns]

[释义] *n.* ①出现，显露 ②浮现，露头

[同根] emerge [ɪˈmɜːdʒ] *v.* ①（问题、困难等）发生，显现，（事实、意见等）显出，暴露 ②浮现，出来

emergent [ɪˈmɜːdʒənt] *a.* ①出现的 ②突然出现的 ③必然发生的

emergency [ɪˈmɜːdʒnsɪ] *n.* ①紧急情况，突发事件 ②急需 ③急症 *a.* ①紧急的，应急的

▶▶ **transfer** [trænsˈfɜː]

[释义] *v.* ①调动，使转学 ②改变，转换 ③转乘，转搭（车或船）④转让 [ˈtrænsfɜː] *n.* ①迁移，调任 ②已调动的人，已转移的东西

[同义] move, shift, handover

[同根] transference [ˈtrænsfərəns] *n.* ①转移，传递 ②调任，调动 ③（财产）转让

transferable [trænsˈfɜːrəbəl] *a.* ①可转移的，可转换的 ②可传递的

transferred [trænsˈfɜːd] *a.* ①转移的 ②调动的，转让的

[词组] transfer from...to... 从…调往…，从…转化为…

▶▶ **puzzled** [ˈpʌzld]

[释义] *a.* 迷惑的，不解的

[同根] puzzle [ˈpʌzl] *v.* ①迷惑，使困惑 ②使苦思 ③思索而得 *n.* ①不解之迷，疑问 ②智力游戏，谜

puzzling [ˈpʌzlɪŋ] *a.* ①令人费解的 ②令人迷惑的，莫名其妙的，使为难的

puzzlement [ˈpʌzlmənt] *n.* ①迷茫 ②困惑

▶▶ **contrast** [ˈkɒntræst]

[释义] *v.* 使与…对比，使与…对照 *n.* 对比，对照

[词组] by contrast 相比之下

in contrast 与…相反

in contrast to 和…形成对比

▶▶ **implement** [ˈɪmplɪmənt]

[释义] *n.* ①工具，器械 ②装备，家具，服装 *v.* ①贯彻，执行 ②使生效

③向…提供工具 ④弥补

[同义] apparatus, appliance; carry out, complete

[同根] implementation [ˌɪmplɪmenˈteɪʃən] n. 执行，履行

▶▶ **appliance** [əˈplaɪəns]

[释义] n. ①（用于特定目的的）器具，器械，装置 ②适用，应用

[同根] apply [əˈplaɪ] v. ①运用，使用 ②涂，敷 ③使（自己）致力于，专注于 ④申请，请求

applied [əˈplaɪd] a. 应用的，实用的

applicant [ˈæplɪkənt] n. 申请人，请求人

application [ˌæplɪˈkeɪʃən] n. ①申请，请求，申请表 ②应用，实施 ③用法，用途 ④敷用，施用

applicable [ˈæplɪkəbl] a. 可适用的，可应用的

▶▶ **seek** [siːk]

[释义] v. ①寻找，寻求 ②请求，征求 ③探索，追求 ④尝试，设法

[同义] search, hunt, look for

[同根] seeker [ˈsiːkə] n. 寻找者，探索者，追求者

[词组] seek after ①寻求 ②追求，追逐

seek out 找出，搜出，挑出

seek for 寻找，探索，寻求，追求

seek through 找遍，搜查遍

▶▶ **cultivate** [ˈkʌltɪveɪt]

[释义] v. ①耕作，栽培 ②培养，养成 ③发展，建立

[同义] nurture, develop, improve

[同根] cultivation [ˌkʌltɪˈveɪʃən] n. ①培养，修养 ②耕作，栽培 ③发展，建立

cultivated [ˈkʌltɪveɪtɪd] a. ①耕种的 ②有教养的

▶▶ **nourish** [ˈnʌrɪʃ]

[释义] v. ①养育，滋养 ②培育，助长，支持，鼓励

[同义] feed, nurture, maintain, nurse

[同根] nourishing [ˈnʌrɪʃɪŋ] a. 滋养的，富有营养的

nourishment [ˈnʌrɪʃmənt] n. 食物，营养品

nutrition [njuːˈtrɪʃən] n. ①营养，滋养 ②营养物，滋养物

nutritional [njuːˈtrɪʃənəl] a. 营养的，滋养的

nutritious [njuːˈtrɪʃəs] a. 有营养的，滋养的

▶▶ **current** [ˈkʌrənt]

[释义] n. ①（空气、水等的）流，电流 ②潮流，趋势，倾向 a. ①现时的，当前的 ②流行的，流传的

[同根] currency [ˈkʌrənsɪ] n. ①流传，流通 ②传播通货，货币

currently [ˈkʌrəntlɪ] ad. ①普遍地，通常地 ②现在，当前

[词组] against the current 逆流而行，不同流俗

go current 流行，通用，流传，见信于世

go with the current 随波逐流

▶▶ **account** [əˈkaunt]

[释义] v. ①解释，说明 ②报账 ③认为，把…归结于 n. ①户头，账户 ②解释 ③记述，报导，报告 ④理由，根据

[同根] accounting [əˈkauntɪŋ] n. ①会计，会计学 ②帐，记帐，清算帐目

accountant [əˈkauntənt] n. 会计（员），会计师

accountancy [əˈkauntənsɪ] n. 会计师之职，会计学

▶▶ **evaluate** [ɪˈvæljueɪt]

[释义] v. ①估计 ②对…评价，为…鉴定 ③估…的值，定…的价

[同义] estimate

[同根] evaluation [ɪˌvæljuˈeɪʃən] n. 估

算，评价

evaluative [ɪ'væljʊeɪtɪv] a. 可估价的，可评价的

evaluable [ɪ'væljʊəbl] a. 可估值的，可评价的

evaluator [ɪ'væljʊeɪtə(r)] n. 估价者，评价者

▶▶ **reservation** [ˌrezə'veɪʃən]

[释义] n. ①保留，保留意见，异议 ②预定，预约 ③（公共）专用地，自然保护区

[同根] reserve [rɪ'zɜːv] v. ①保留，储备 ②预定，定 ③保存，保留 n. ①储备（物），储备量 ②（常作复数）藏量，储量

reserved [rɪ'zɜːvd] a. ①储备的 ②保留的，预定的 ③有所保留的，克制的 ④拘谨缄默的，矜持寡言的

reservior ['rezəvwɑː] n. ①贮水池，水库 ②贮藏处 ③贮备

▶▶ **retreat** [rɪ'triːt]

[释义] n. & v. ①撤退，（使）后退 ②退避，躲避 ③改变主意，退缩

[同根] retreatism [rɪ'triːtɪzəm] n. 逃避现实，退却主义，逃跑主义

retreatant [rɪ'triːtənt] n. 深居者，静修者

[词组] retreat from 放弃，退出
beyond retreat 没有后退的可能
cut off the retreat 截断退路

▶▶ **replacement** [rɪ'pleɪsmənt]

[释义] n. ①归还，复位 ②交换 ③代替，更换 ④代替物

[同义] substitute

[同根] replace [rɪ(:)'pleɪs] v. ①代替，接替 ②更换，调换 ③归还，赔还 ④把…放回原处

replaceable [rɪ'pleɪsəbl] a. ①可代替的，可更换的 ②可归还的，可复位的

One factor that can **influence consumers** is their mood state. Mood may be **defined** as a **temporary** and mild **positive** or **negative** feeling that is **generalized** and not **tied** to any particular circumstance. Moods should **be distinguished from emotions** which are usually more **intense, related to specific** circumstances, and often conscious. **In one sense,** the effect of a consumer's mood can be thought of in much the same way as can our **reactions** to the **signal** of our friends-when our friends are happy and "up", that tends to influence us positively, but when they are "down", that can have a negative **impact** on us. Similarly, consumers operating under a **given** mood state tend to react to *stimuli* (刺激因素) in a direction **consistent** with that mood state. Thus, for example, we should expect to see consumer in a positive mood state evaluate products **in more of a favorable manner** than they would when not in such a state. Moreover, mood states appear **capable of enhancing** a consumer's memory.

Moods appear to be readily influenced by **marketing techniques.** For example, the **rhythm**, **pitch**, and **volume** of music has been shown to influence behavior such as the **amount** of time spent in supermarkets or **intentions** to purchase products. **In addition**, advertising can influence consumers' moods which, **in turn**, are capable of influencing consumers' reactions to products.

文章词汇注释

▶▶▶ **influence** ['ɪnfluəns]

[释义] *v.* 影响，支配 *n.* ①影响 ②支配力，势力 ③有影响的人、事

[同义] affect, impact

[同根] influential [ˌɪnfluˈenʃəl] *a.* ①有影响的 ②有权势的

[词组] exert an influence on 对…施加影响 through the influence of 靠…的力量

▶▶▶ **consumer** [kənˈsjuːmə]

[释义] *n.* ①消费者，顾客 ②消耗者，毁灭者

[反义] producer

[同根] consume [kən'sju:m] v. ①消耗，花费 ②吃，喝 ③毁灭 ④挥霍，浪费

consumption [kən'sʌmpʃən] n. ①消耗，挥霍，浪费 ②消费，消费量，

consumptive [kən'sʌmptɪv] a. ①消耗的，浪费的，毁灭的 ②消费的

▶▶ define [dɪ'faɪn]

[释义] v. ①（给…）下定义 ②限定，立界限 ③详细说明

[同根] definition [,defɪ'nɪʃən] n. ①定义，解说，阐明 ②限定 ③明确

definite ['defɪnɪt] a. ①明确的，明白的 ②肯定的，无疑的 ③限定的

indefinite [ɪn'defɪnɪt] a. ①无定限的，无限期的 ②不明确的，含糊的 ③不确定的，未定的

definitive [dɪ'fɪnɪtɪv] a. ①确定的，最后的 ②权威性的

[词组] be defined as 被定义为…

▶▶ temporary ['tempərərɪ]

[释义] a. 暂时的，临时的，短暂的

[同义] momentary, transient

[反义] permanent

[同根] temporarily ['tempərərɪlɪ] ad. 暂时地，临时地

contemporary [kən'tempərərɪ] a. 当代的，同时代的

▶▶ positive ['pɒzətɪv]

[释义] a. ①积极的 ②有把握的，确信的 ③确定的，肯定的 ④ [数] 正的，[电] 阳的

[同义] affirmative, assured, convinced, definite

[同根] positiveness ['pɒzətɪvnɪs] n. 肯定

positively ['pɒzətɪvlɪ] ad. 肯定地，积极地

▶▶ negative ['negətɪv]

[释义] a. ①消极的，反面的，反对的

② 否定的，表示否认的 ④负的，阴性的

[反义] positive

[同根] negation [nɪ'geɪʃən] n. ①否定，否认，表示否认 ②反面，对立面

▶▶ generalized ['dʒenərəlaɪzd]

[释义] a. 笼统的，无显著特点的，不能适应特殊环境的

[同根] general ['dʒenərəl] a. ①一般的，普通的 ②笼统的，大体的 ③全体的，总的，普遍的 n. 将军

generalize ['dʒenərəlaɪz] v. ①归纳，概括 ②推广，普及

generality [,dʒenə'rælɪtɪ] n. 一般性，普遍性，通（用）性

generalization [,dʒenərəlaɪ'zeɪʃən] n. 概括，归纳，普遍化

generally ['dʒenərəlɪ] ad. 大体，通常，一般地

▶▶ be tied to 依靠，被…约束，被…限制
▶▶ be distinguished from 与…不同

▶▶ emotion [ɪ'məʊʃən]

[释义] n. ①感情，情绪 ②激动，激情

[同根] emotional [ɪ'məʊʃənl] a. ①易动感情的，情绪激动的 ②情绪/情感上的 ③表现强烈情感的，催人泪下的

emotionless [ɪ'məʊʃənlɪs] a. 没有感情的，冷漠的

▶▶ intense [ɪn'tens]

[释义] a. ①强烈的，剧烈的，激烈的 ②热切的，热情的

[同义] strong, powerful, passionate

[反义] moderate

[同根] intensify [ɪn'tensɪfaɪ] v. 加剧，加强，增强，强化

intensive [ɪn'tensɪv] a. ①加强的，集中的，密集的 ②集约的，精耕细作的

intension [ɪn'tenʃən] n. ①决心，专

心致志 ②强度，烈度 ③增强，加剧

intensity [ɪn'tensɪtɪ] n. ①强烈，剧烈 ②强度，亮度

intensification [ɪn,tensɪfɪ'keɪʃən] n. 增强，强化，加剧，加紧

▶▶ related to 与…有关

▶▶ specific [spɪ'sɪfɪk]

[释义] a. ①明确的，具体的 ②特定的，特有的

[同义] definite, explicit, particular, special

[反义] general

[同根] specify ['spesɪfaɪ] v. 具体指定，详细说明

specification [,spesɪfɪ'keɪʃən] n. ①详述 ② [常作～s] 规格，工程设计（书），详细计划（书），说明书

▶▶ in a/one sense 从某种意义上说

▶▶ reaction [rɪ(:)'ækʃən]

[释义] n. ①反应 ②看法，意见，态度 ③（化学）反应，作用 ④反动

[同根] act [ækt] n. ①行为，举动 ②法案，法令 ③（戏剧的）幕 v. ①行动，采取行动，起作用 ②演戏，表演 ③执行职务

action ['ækʃən] n. ①行动，动作，作用，行为 ②诉讼 ③战斗

active ['æktɪv] a. ①积极的，活跃的，活动的 ② [语法] 主动的

react [rɪ'ækt] v. ①做出反应，反应 ②影响，起作用 ③（化学）起反应 ④反动

reactor [rɪ(:)'æktə] n. 反应堆

interact [,ɪntər'ækt] v. 互相作用，互相影响

interactive [,ɪntər'æktɪv] a. 相互影响的，相互作用的

▶▶ signal ['sɪgnl]

[释义] n. 信号 v. 发信号，用信号通知

[同根] sign [saɪn] n. ①标记，符号，手势 ②指示牌 ③足迹，痕迹 ④征兆，迹象 v. ①签名（于），署名（于），签署 ②做手势，示意

signify ['sɪgnɪfaɪ] v. 表示…的意思，意味，预示

significance [sɪg'nɪfɪkəns] n. 意义，重要性

significant [sɪg'nɪfɪkənt] a. 有意义的，重大的，重要的

significantly [sɪg'nɪfɪkəntlɪ] ad. 重要地，重大地

▶▶ impact ['ɪmpækt]

[释义] n. ①影响，冲击 ②冲击（或撞击）力 v. ①压紧 ②充满，挤满

[同义] influence, effect

[同根] impaction [ɪm'pækʃən] n. ①压紧，楔牢 ②冲击，撞击

impacted [ɪm'pæktɪd] a. 压紧的，结实的

[词组] have/make a great/strong /full impact on 对…有巨大影响

▶▶ given ['gɪvn]

[释义] a. (give 的过去分词) ①一定的，特定的，指定的 ②已知的，假设的 ③给予的，赠送的

[词组] given that... 考虑到…，倘若…，假定…

▶▶ consistent [kən'sɪstənt]

[释义] a. ①和…一致的（with）②一贯的 ③坚实的 ④相符合的

[同根] consist [kən'sɪst] v. ①由…组成 ②存在于 ③与…一致 ④并存

consistence [kən'sɪstəns] n. 一致性，连贯性

▶▶ in a manner 在某种意义上
▶▶ more of 更大程度上的…，更多的…

▶▶ favorable ['feɪərəbl]

[释义] a. ①有利的 ②赞许的，赞成的

读真题记单词大学英语

四级词汇

③讨人喜欢的，起促进作用的

[反义] adverse, unfavorable

[同根] favor ['feɪvə] n. ①恩惠，善行 ②喜爱，好感 ②赞同，支持 ③优惠 v. ①支持，赞成 ②偏爱，喜爱 ③有利于，有助于

favorite ['feɪvərɪt] n. ①最受喜爱的人（或物）②心腹，幸运儿 a. 最受喜爱的

favorably ['feɪərəblɪ] ad. 赞成地，有利地

▶▶ **capable of** 能够…的

▶▶ **enhance** [ɪn'hɑːns]

[释义] v. ①增强，增进，提高（质量、价格、吸引力等），增加 ②（价格）上涨，（价值）上升

[同义] better, improve, uplift, strengthen

[同根] enhancement [ɪn'hɑːnsmənt] n. 增进，增加

enhanced [ɪn'hɑːnst] a. 增强的，提高的，放大的

▶▶ **marketing techniques** 销售术，销售法，销售学

▶▶ **rhythm** ['rɪðəm,'rɪθəm]

[释义] n. 韵律，节奏，拍子

[同根] rhythmic ['rɪðmɪk] a. 节奏的，合拍的

rhythmicity [rɪð'mɪsɪtɪ] n. 节奏性，韵律性

rhythmist ['rɪðmɪst] n. 有节奏感的人，诗人，研究韵律的人

▶▶ **pitch** [pɪtʃ]

[释义] n. ①音高 ②沥青 ③投掷 v. ①投，

掷 ②丢弃，抛弃 ③为…定音高

[词组] make a pitch for... 为…作宣传／说好话

pitch in ①动手干，使劲干 ②协力，作出贡献

pitch into ①迫使处于，迫使接受 ②猛烈攻击，痛打，大骂 ③动手干

pitch on（随便）选出，选定，决定

▶▶ **volume** ['vɒljuːm; (US)-jəm]

[释义] n. ①音量 ②体积，容量 ③份量，额 ④书卷，卷

[同根] speak volumes (for sth.) 有力地说明，充分证明

▶▶ **amount** [ə'maʊnt]

[释义] n. ①量，数量，数额 ②总的含义，全部价值 ③总数，总额 v. ①合计，共计 (to) ②（在效果、意义、价值等方面）等同，接近

[词组] any amount (of) 极大量（的…）

no amount of 即使再大的…也不

be of little amount 不重要，无价值

in amount 总之，结局，总计

never amount to anything 一事无成

▶▶ **intention** [ɪn'tenʃən]

[释义] n. 意图，目的

[同义] aim, goal, plan, objective

[同根] intend [ɪn'tend] v. ①想要，打算 ②意指，意谓

intent [ɪn'tent] n. 意图，目的，意向

intentional [ɪn'tenʃənəl] a. 有意图的，故意的

▶▶ **in addition** 另外，此外

▶▶ **in turn** ①依次 ②反过来

234

选项词汇注释

▶▶ derive [dɪˈraɪv]

[释义] v. ①取得，形成 ②追溯…的起源（来由），说明…的起源（或来由）

[同义] acquire, gain, get, obtain, receive

[同根] derivation [derɪˈveɪʃən] n. ①得到，溯源，推论 ②起源，由来

derivative [dɪˈrɪvətɪv] a. 被引申出的，被推论出的 n. 派生物，转成物

derivatively [dɪˈrɪvətɪvlɪ] ad. 衍生地

[词组] derive from 得自…，由…衍生而来

▶▶ descend [dɪˈsend]

[释义] v. ①下来，下降 ②下倾 ③递减 ④祖传，世代相传

[反义] ascend, rise

[同根] descendable [dɪˈsendəbl] a. ①可下降的 ②可世袭的，可遗传的

descendant [dɪˈsend(ə)nt] n. ①子孙，后裔，后代 ②（某一原形的）派生物 a. ①下降的，向下的 ②祖传的，派生的

descending [dɪˈsendɪŋ] n. 下降的，下行的，递降的

[词组] descend from ①从…下来 ②是…的后裔，源于

descend on ①突然袭击 ②突然拜访某人

descend to 转而提到

▶▶ refer [rɪˈfɜː]

[释义] v. ①嘱咐（病人）转诊于，叫…求助于 ②提到，谈到，指称 ④参考，查阅 ④询问，查询

[同根] reference [ˈrefərəns] n. ①参考，参阅 ②提到，论及 ③引文（出处），参考书目 ④证明书（人），介绍（人）

[词组] refer oneself to 依赖，求助于

refer to ①提到，谈到，涉及 ②参考，查阅 ③认为与…有关

refer to sb./sth. as 称某人/物为…

▶▶ attach [əˈtætʃ]

[释义] v. ①系上 ②使附属，使依恋 ③加于…之上

[同义] connect, fasten, put together

[反义] detach

[同根] attached [əˈtætʃt] a. ①连接的 ②附属的 ③（一般作表语）喜爱的，依恋的

attachment [əˈtætʃmənt] n. ①连接，参加 ②附件，附加装置 ③爱慕，依恋 (for, to)

[词组] attach oneself to ①依附 ②参加（党派等）②热爱，依恋

attach... to... ①认为…有（重要性、意义等）②把…归因于…

▶▶ associate [əˈsəʊʃɪeɪt]

[释义] v. ①（在思想上）把…联系在一起 ②使联合，结合，使有联系 ③ (with) 结交、交往 n. 伙伴，同事，合伙人 a. 副的

[同根] association [ə,səʊsɪˈeɪʃən] n. ①协会，联盟，社团 ②联合，结合，交往 ③联系，联想

associated [əˈsəʊʃɪeɪtɪd] a. 联合的，关联的

associative [əˈsəʊʃɪətɪv] a. ①联合的 ②联想的

[词组] associate oneself with 参加到…中去，公开对表示赞成（或支持）

be associated with 与…有关

▶▶ gesture [ˈdʒestʃə]

[释义] n. ①手势，示意动作 ②姿态，表示 v. ①作手势，用动作示意 ②用手势表示

▶▶ provided [prɜːˈvaɪdɪd]

[释义] conj. (=on the condition that) 假如，如果，倘若…，在…条件下

▶▶ **sensitive** ['sensɪtɪv]

[释义] a. ①敏感的，神经过敏的，神经质的 ②容易生气的，易受伤害的 ③高度机密的，涉及国家机密事务的

[同根] sense [sens] n. ①官能，感觉，意识 ②赏识，领悟 ③判断力，见识 ④意义，意味 v. 感到，理解，认识

sensitivity ['sensɪ'tɪvɪtɪ] n. ①敏感性 ②灵敏度

sensible ['sensəbl] a. ①明智的，有判断力的 ②感觉得到的，意识到的

sensibility [,sensɪ'bɪlɪtɪ] n. ①感觉（力）② (情绪上的) 敏感，善感 ③鉴赏力

sentiment ['sentɪmənt] n. ①情操，情感，情绪，②伤感 ③意见，观点

sentimental [,sentɪ'mentl] a. 感伤的，感情脆弱的

sensation [sen'seɪʃən] n. ① (感官的) 感觉能力 ②感觉，知觉 ④引起轰动的事件（或人物）

sensational [sen'seɪʃənəl] a. 使人激动的，轰动的，耸人听闻的

[词组] be sensitive to 对…敏感

▶▶ **grant** [grɑ:nt]

[释义] v. ①同意，准予，授予 ②承认 n. ①授予物 ②给予，授予 ③财产转让

[词组] take...for granted 认为…理所当然

granted that ... (=granting that ...) 假定…，即使…

▶▶ **resistant** [rɪ'zɪstənt]

[释义] a. ①抵抗的，防抗的 ② (复合) 抗…的，耐…的

[同义] opposed to, defiant, opposing

[同根] resist [rɪ'zɪst] v. ①抵抗 ②抗，耐 ③按捺，忍住

resistance [rɪ'zɪstəns] n. ①抵抗 ②抵抗性，抵抗力 ③耐性

resistable [rɪ'zɪstəbl] a. 可抵抗的，抵抗得住的，可抗拒的

▶▶ **persistent** [pə'sɪstənt]

[释义] a. ①持续的，顽强地存在的 ②坚持不懈的，执意的

[同义] continuing

[同根] persist [pə(:)'sɪst] v. ①坚持，固执 ②持续，存留

persistence [pə'sɪstəns] n. ①坚持，固执 ②持续，存留

persistently [pə'sɪstəntlɪ] ad. ①持续地，顽强地存在的 ②坚持不懈地，执意地

▶▶ **insistent** [ɪn'sɪstənt]

[释义] a. 坚持的，不容反对的

[同义] firm, persistent

[同根] insist [ɪn'sɪst] v. ①坚决要求 ①主张，坚持

▶▶ **retailer** ['ri:teɪlə]

[释义] n. ①零售商，零售店 ②详述者，复述者，传播者

[同根] retail ['ri:teɪl] n. 零售，零卖 a. ①零售的 ②批零的，小量的 v. ①零售，零卖 ②详述，复述，传播

retailing ['ri:teɪlɪŋ] n. 零售业

▶▶ **manufacturer** [,mænju'fæktʃərə]

[释义] n. 制造商，厂商

[同根] manufacture [,mænju'fæktʃə] v. 制造，加工 n. 制造，制造业，产品

manufactory [,mænju'fæktərɪ] n. 制造厂，工厂

▶▶ **critical** ['krɪtɪkəl]

[释义] a. ①决定性的，关键性的 ②吹毛求疵的 ③批评的，评判的

[同根] critic ['krɪtɪk] n. ①批评家，评论家 ②吹毛求疵者

critique [krɪ'ti:k] n. ① (关于文艺作品、哲学思想的) 评论文章 ②评论

criticize ['krɪtɪsaɪz] v. ①批评，评判，

责备，非难 ② 评论，评价

criticism ['krɪtɪsɪzəm] n. ① 批评，评判，责备，非难 ②评论文章

critically ['krɪtɪkəlɪ] ad. ①吹毛求疵地 ②批评地，评判地 ③决定性地，关键性地

▶▶ cultivate ['kʌltɪveɪt]

[释义] v. ①培养，养成 ②耕作，栽培 ③发展，建立

[同义] nurture, develop, improve

[同根] cultivation [ˌkʌltɪ'veɪʃən] n. ①培养，修养 ②耕作，栽培 ③发展，建立

cultivated ['kʌltɪveɪtɪd] a. ①有教养的 ②耕耘的

▶▶ cautiously ['kɔːʃəslɪ]

[释义] ad. 慎重地，小心翼翼地

[同义] carefully

[同根] caution ['kɔːʃən] n. ①小心，谨慎 ②注意（事项），警告 v. 警告，劝…小心

cautious ['kɔːʃəs] a. 十分小心的，谨慎的

▶▶ rarely ['reəlɪ]

[释义] ad. 很少地，罕有地

[同根] rare [reə] a. ①稀罕的，珍贵的 ②稀疏地 ad. 非常

▶▶ currently ['kʌrəntlɪ]

[释义] ad. ①现在，当前 ②普遍地，通常地

[同义] at present, presently

[同根] current ['kʌrənt] a. ①现在的 ②通用的，流通的 n. ①潮流 ②水流，气流，电流 ③趋势，倾向

currency ['kʌrənsɪ] n. ①通货，货币 ②（货币的）流通，通行 ③流通时期

▶▶ extent [ɪks'tent]

[释义] n. ①范围，程度 ②广度，长度，大小

[同义] degree

[词组] to a certian extent 在一定程度上，有几分，部分地

to some extent 某种程度上，（多少）有一点

to the extent of 到…的程度

▶▶ scope [skəup]

[释义] n. ①（活动）范围，机会，余地 ②眼界，见识

[同义] extent, range, space

[同根] microscope ['maɪkrəskəup] n. 显微镜

telescope ['telɪskəup] n. 望远镜

▶▶ capacity [kə'pæsɪtɪ]

[释义] n. ①容量，可溶性，吸收力 ②生产量，生产力 ③最大限度

[词组] at full capacity 以全（部）力（量），满功率，满负载

be filled to capacity 客满，挤得满满的

to capacity 达最大限度，满负载

capacity of /to / to do … 的能力

▶▶ reflection [rɪ'flekʃən]

[释义] n. ①映像 ②反射，反照 ③深思，考虑，反省

[同义] consideration, meditation, contemplation

[同根] reflect [rɪ'flekt] v. ①反射（光，热，声等）②映出，照出 ③反映，表明，显示 ④深思，考虑，反省

reflective [rɪ'flektɪv] a. ①反射的，反照的，反映的 ②思考的，沉思的

reflector [rɪ'flektə(r)] n. 反射器，反射镜，反射物

▶▶ in depth ①深入地 ②彻底地，广泛地

Universities are **institutions** that teach **a wide variety of** subjects **at advanced levels**. They also **carry out** research work **aimed at extending** man's knowledge of these subjects. The **emphasis** given to each of these **functions** varies from university to university, according to the views of the people **in control** and according to the **resources available**. The smaller and newer universities do not **possess** the staff or equipment to carry out the **maximum** research projects possible in larger institutions. But most experts agree that some research activity is **essential** to **keep** the staff and their students **in touch with** the latest developments in their subjects.

Most students **attend** a university mainly to **acquire** the knowledge needed for their chosen profession. Educationists believe that this aim should not be the only one. Universities have always aimed to produce men and women with judgment and wisdom as well as knowledge. For this reason, they encourage students to meet others with differing interests and to read widely to broaden their understanding in many fields of study. After a secondary school course, a student should be interested enough in a subject to enjoy gaining knowledge **for its own sake**. He should be prepared to **make sacrifices** to study his chosen field **in depth**. He should have an **ambition** to **make** some meaningful **contribution** to man's knowledge.

文章词汇注释

▶▶▶ **institution** [ˌɪnstɪˈtjuːʃən]
[释义] *n.* ①（教育、慈善、宗教等）公共机构 ②制度，习惯
[同根] institute [ˈɪnstɪtjuːt] *v.* ①建立，设立，制定 ②实行，开始，着手 *n.* ①学会，协会，学院，（大专）学校 ②<美>（教师等的）短训班，

<英>成人业余学校
institutional [ˌɪnstɪˈtjuːʃənəl] *a.* ①社会公共机构的 ②制度上的

▶▶▶ **a wide variety of** 种类繁多的，许多种的

▶▶▶ **at advanced levels** 先进水平，较高

水平

▶▶ **carry out** ① 进行，实行，执行 ②完成，实现

▶▶ **aim at...** ①旨在，针对… ②瞄准… ③志在…

▶▶ **extend** [ɪk'stend]

[释义] v. ①扩展，扩大…范围 ②给予 ③继续 ④延长

[同义] widen, expand, enlarge

[同根] extension [ɪks'tenʃən] n. ①延长，伸展 ②扩展，扩大 ③推进，发展 ④（电话）分机

extensive [ɪks'tensɪv] a. ①广大的，广阔的 ②广泛的，全面的

▶▶ **emphasis** ['emfəsɪs]

[释义] n. （对事物、意义、重要性等的）强调，（事实、观点等的）重点

[同根] emphasize ['emfəsaɪz] v. ①强调，着重 ②唤起对…的注意

[词组] give emphasis to 着重，强调

lay / place / put emphasis on / upon 注重，着重于，强调，加强（语气）

▶▶ **function** ['fʌŋkʃən]

[释义] n. ①功能，官能 ②作用，用途 ③职责，职务 v. ① 工作，活动，运行 ② 行使职责

[同根] functional ['fʌŋkʃənl] a. ①实用的，为实用而设计的 ②官能的，机能的

[词组] function as... 起…的作用

▶▶ **in control** 有控制（掌握，管理）能力的

▶▶ **resource** [rɪ'sɔ:s]

[释义] n. ①资源 ②储备力量，资财，财力 ③谋略，对策，应付方法 ④（消息等的）来源

[同根] resourceful [rɪ'sɔ:sful] a. ①资源丰富的 ②足智多谋的

[词组] as a last resource 作为最后一着

be full of resource(s) 富有机智的

▶▶ **available** [ə'veɪləbl]

[释义] a. ①可利用的，可获得的，在手边的 ②可取得联系的，有空的

[同义] convenient, obtainable, ready, handy

[反义] unavailable

[同根] avail [ə'veɪl] v. 有用于，有助于 n. [一般用于否定句或疑问句中] 效用，利益，帮助

availability [ə,veɪlə'bɪlɪtɪ] n. 利用（或获得）的可能性，有效性

▶▶ **possess** [pə'zes]

[释义] v. ①拥有,占有 ②具有（品质等）③（想法、感情等）影响,控制,缠住,迷住 ④懂得，掌握

[同根] possessor [pə'zesə] n. 持有人，所有人

possessive [pə'zesɪv] a. 所有的，物主的，占有的 n. 所有格

possession [pə'zeʃən] n. ①持有，私藏 ②拥有，所有权，所有物 ③财产（常用复数）

▶▶ **maximum** ['mæksɪməm]

[释义] a. 最高的，最大的，最多的 n. 最大限度，最大值，顶点

[反义] minimum

[同根] maximal ['mæksɪməl] a. 最大的，最高的

maximize ['mæksɪmaɪz] v. 使增加（或扩大）到最大限度，充分重视，充分利用

▶▶ **essential** [ɪ'senʃəl]

[释义] a. ①不可少的，必要的 ②重要的，根本的，实质的 ③精华的 n. [pl.] ①本质，实质，精华 ②要素，要点 ③必需品

[同义] indispensable, requisite, necessary, crucial, vital

[同根] essence ['esəns] n. ①本质，本

体②精髓，要素，精华
essentially [ɪˈsenʃəlɪ] ad. 本质上，本来，根本
[词组] be essential to 对…必要的

▶▶ keep...in touch with 使…与…保持联系

▶▶ attend [əˈtend]
[释义] v. ①上（学、教堂），出席，到场 ②注意，留意 ③照看，照料
[同根] attention [əˈtenʃən] n. ①注意，专心，留心 ②注意力 ③考虑，关心，照料 ④礼貌，客气
attentive [əˈtentɪv] a. ①注意的，留心的 ②关心的，体贴的，有礼貌的 ③殷勤的
[词组] attend school 上学
attend a lecture 听讲课
attend church 去教堂
attend a wedding 出席婚礼

▶▶ acquire [əˈkwaɪə]
[释义] v.（尤指通过努力）获得，学到
[同根] acquired [əˈkwaɪəd] a.（尤指通过努力）获得的，后天的
acquisition [ˌækwɪˈzɪʃən] n. ①获得

②（尤指有用或受欢迎的）获得物，增添的人/物
acquisitive [əˈkwɪzɪtɪv] a. ①（对金钱、财物等）渴望得到的，贪婪的 ②能够获得并保存的
acquisitiveness [əˈkwɪzɪtɪvnɪs] n. 渴望得到，贪婪，占有欲

▶▶ for its own sake 为了…自身，由于…自身的原因

▶▶ make sacrifices 作出牺牲，付出，奉献

▶▶ in depth 深入地（的），全面地（的），彻底地（的）

▶▶ ambition [æmˈbɪʃən]
[释义] n. 志向，抱负，野心，雄心
[同根] ambitious [æmˈbɪʃəs] a. ①有雄心的，有抱负的 ②由野心或雄心引起的 ③费劲的，要求过高的
[词组] achieve/fulfil/realize an ambition 实现报负
cherish/nurse/harbour an ambition 有志向，心怀雄心，怀有抱负

▶▶ make contribution to 对…做出贡献

选项词汇注释

▶▶ prospect [ˈprɒspekt]
[释义] n. ①［常作 ~s］（成功、得益等的）可能性，机会，（经济、地位等的）前景，前途 ②将要发生的事，期望中的事 v. 勘探；勘查
[同根] prospective [prəsˈpektɪv] a. 预期的，盼望中的，即将发生的
prospector [prɒˈspektə] n. 勘探者，探矿者
[词组] in prospect ①可期待，有 ... 希望 ②在考虑中
open up prospects (for) 为…开辟前景

▶▶ involve [ɪnˈvɒlv]
[释义] v. ①涉及，包含，包括 ②使卷入，使陷入，拖累 ③使专注
[同义] contain, include, engage, absorb
[同根] involved [ɪnˈvɒlvd] a. 有关的，牵扯在内的，参与的，受影响的
involvement [ɪnˈvɒlvmənt] n. ①卷入，缠绕 ②复杂，混乱 ③牵连的事务，复杂的情况
[词组] be / become involved in 包含在…，与…有关，被卷入，专心地（做）
be / get involved with 涉及，给…缠住

▶▶ spare [speə]

[释义] v. ①宽容，饶恕，赦免 ②节约，吝惜 ③免去，解除

[词组] spare no expense 不惜代价

▶▶ virtual ['vɜ:tjuəl,-tʃuəl]

[释义] a. ①实际上起作用的，事实上生效的 ②（用于名词前）几乎 ③[计] 虚拟的

[同根] virtually ['vɜ:tjuəlɪ] ad. 事实上，实际上，差不多

▶▶ optional ['ɒpʃənəl]

[释义] a. ①可选择的，选修的 ②随意的 ③非强制的 n. 选修科

[同义] elective, voluntary, open

[反义] compulsory, forced

[同根] option ['ɒpʃən] n. ①选择，选择权，可选择的事物 ②选修课 ③买卖选择权

optionally ['ɒpʃənəlɪ] ad. 随意地

▶▶ coordination [kəu,ɔ:dɪ'neɪʃən]

[释义] n. ①协调 ②同等，同位，对等

[同义] harmonization

[同根] coordinate [kəu'ɔ:dɪneɪt]

v. ①调节，协调 ②（使）同等，（使）同位 a. 同等的，同格的，同位的，并列的

coordinative [kəu'ɔ:dɪneɪtɪv] a. 并列的，协调的

coordinator [kəu'ɔ:dɪneɪtə] n. 协调人，统筹者

▶▶ accordance [ə'kɔ:dəns]

[释义] n. ①一致，符合 ②授予，给予

[同义] conformity，agreement

[同根] accord [ə'kɔ:d] v. ① 相符合，相一致 (with) ②授予，给予 n. ①一致，符合 ②（尤指国与国之间的）谅解，协议

accordant [ə'kɔ:dənt] a. 一致的，和谐的，相符合的

according [ə'kɔ:dɪŋ] (~ to) prep. 根据，依照

disaccord [,dɪsə'kɔ:d] v. & n. 不一致，不和

discord ['dɪskɔ:d] n.（意见、想法等）不一致，不协调，争论，冲突

[dɪs'kɔ:d] v. 不一致，不协调

[词组] in accordance with 根据，依照；与…一致，合乎

▶▶ endure [ɪn'djuə]

[释义] v. ①忍耐，容忍 ②持久，持续

[同义] bear，tolerate，carry on，keep on，last

[同根] duration [djuə'reɪʃən] n. 持续时间，为期

durable ['djuərəbl] a. 持久的，耐用的

durably ['djuərəblɪ] ad. 持久地，耐用地

▶▶ ensure [ɪn'ʃuə]

[释义] v. ①保证，担保，保证得到 ②使安全

[同义] guarantee，insure

[同根] assure [ə'ʃuə] v. 有信心地说，向…保证 ②使确信，使放心

insure [ɪn'ʃuə] v. ①给…保险 ②保证，确保

assurance [ə'ʃuərəns] n. ①保证，表示保证（或鼓励、安慰）的话 ②把握，信心 ③（人寿）保险

insurance [ɪn'ʃuərəns] n. ① 保险，保险单，保险费 ②预防措施，安全保证

▶▶ procession [prəu'seʃən]

[释义] n. ①（人、车、船等的）行列，队伍 ②接续，连续

[同根] process ['prəuses] n. ①过程，进程 ②程序，步骤，作用，方法 v. 加工，处理

processible ['prəusesəbl] a. (= processable) 适合加工（或处理）的，

可加工（或处理）的

[词组] in process 在进行中

in process of time 随着时间的推移，渐渐

▶▶▶ **possession** [pə'zeʃən]

[释义] n. ①有，持有 ②所有物，财产 ③拥有，所有权

[同根] possess [pə'zes] v. ①具有 ②拥有 ③懂得，掌握 ④影响，控制

possessed [pə'zest] a. ①着魔的，疯狂的 ②拥有的，具有…的

possessive [pə'zesiv] a. ①拥有的，占有的 ②占有欲强的

[词组] be in possession of sth 拥有（或占有、持有）某物

come into sb.'s possession 落入某人手中

have possession of 拥有

▶▶▶ **typical** ['tɪpɪkəl]

[释义] a. ①典型的，有代表性的，象征性的 ②（品质、性格等方面）特有的，独特的

[同根] type [taɪp] n. ①类型，种类 ②典型，模范 v. 打字，翻印

typically ['tɪpɪkəlɪ] ad. ①通常 ②典型地，有代表性地 ③果然，不出所料地

typicality [ˌtɪpɪ'kælɪtɪ] n. 典型性，代表性，特征

▶▶▶ **prompt** [prɒmpt]

[释义] v. ①促使，怂恿 ②刺激，激起 ③提示 a. 敏捷的，及时的

[同根] promptly ['prɒmptlɪ] ad. 迅速地，敏捷地

▶▶▶ **provoke** [prə'vəuk]

[释义] v. ①激起，引起 ②对…挑衅，激怒

[同根] provoking [prə'vəukɪŋ] a. 恼人的，挑动的

provocative [prə'vɒkətɪv] a. ①挑衅的，煽动的 ②引起讨论的

provocation [ˌprɒvə'keɪʃən] n. ①惹人恼火的事，激怒的原因 ②激怒，刺激

▶▶▶ **anticipate** [æn'tɪsɪpeɪt]

[释义] v. ①预期，期望，预料 ②早于别人做…，先于…行动

[同义] expect, foresee

[同根] anticipation [ˌæntɪsɪ'peɪʃən] n. ①预期，预料，预感 ②预先采取的行动

▶▶▶ **lengthen** ['leŋθən]

[释义] v. 延长，伸长，拉长，（使）变长

[反义] shorten

[同根] length [leŋθ] n. ①长度，（时间的）长短 ②期间 ③一段，一节

lengthy ['leŋθɪ] a. 长的，（演说、文章等）冗长的，过分的

[词组] lengthen out 过分延长

▶▶▶ **enforce** [ɪn'fɔːs]

[释义] v. ①实施，使生效 ②强迫，迫使，强加

[同义] compel, execute, force, oblige

[同根] force [fɔːs] n. ①力量，武力，暴力 ②说服力，感染力 ③有影响的人或事物，军事力量 v. ①强迫，迫使 ②（用武力）夺取 ③勉强作出

enforcement [ɪn'fɔːsmənt] n. 执行，强制，实施，加强

reinforce [ˌriːɪn'fɔːs] v. 加强，增援，补充，增加…的数量

reinforcement [ˌriːɪn'fɔːsmənt] n. 增援，加强

▶▶▶ **specify** ['spesɪfaɪ]

[释义] v. 指定，详细说明，列入清单

[同根] special ['speʃəl] a. ①特殊的，特别的 ②异常的，独特的 ③专门的，特设的 n. ①专列，专车，专机 ②特殊的人或物 ③特刊 ④特色菜

specific [spɪ'sɪfɪk] a. ①明确的，具

体的 ②特定的，特有的

specified ['spesɪfaɪ] *a.* 规定的，指定的

specification [ˌspesɪfɪ'keɪʃən] *n.* ①详述 ② [常作～s] 规格，工程设计（书），详细计划（书），说明书

▶▶ **object** ['ɒbdʒɪkt]

[释义] *n.* ①物体 ②目标，对象 ③宾语 [əb'dʒekt] *v.* 反对，拒绝，抗议

[同根] objective [əb'dʒektɪv] *a.* ①客观的，公正的 ②客观上存在的，真实的 ③目标的 *n.* ①目标，目的，任务 ②客观事实，实在事物

objectivity [ˌɒbdʒek'tɪvətɪ] *n.* 客观性，客观现实

▶▶ **scope** [skəup]

[释义] *n.* ①（活动）范围，机会，余地 ②眼界，见识

[同义] extent，range，reach，sphere

[同根] microscope ['maɪkrəskəup]

n. 显微镜

telescope ['telɪskəup] *n.* 望远镜

▶▶ **radical** ['rædɪkəl]

[释义] *a.* ①根本的，基本的 ②激进的，极端的 *n.* 激进分子

[同义] extreme

[反义] conservative，superficial

[同根] radicalism ['rædɪkəlɪzəm] *n.* 激进主义，激进政策，激进

radically ['rædɪkəlɪ] *ad.* 根本上，以激进的方式

▶▶ **initial** [ɪ'nɪʃəl]

[释义] *a.* ①最初的，开始的 ②声母的，首音的 *n.* 首字母

[同根] initialize [ɪ'nɪʃəlaɪz] *v.* 初始化

initialization [ɪˌnɪʃəlaɪ'zeɪʃən] *n.* [计] 初始化

initially [ɪ'nɪʃəlɪ] *ad.* 最初，开头，首先

Playing organized sports is such a common experience in the United States that many children and teenagers **take** them **for granted**. This is especially true among children from families and **communities** that have the resources needed to organize and **sponsor** sports programs and make sure that there is easy **access** to participation opportunities. Children in low-income families and poor communities are less likely to take organized youth sports for granted because they often lack the resources needed to pay for participation fees, equipment, and **transportation** to practices and games and their communities do not have resources to build and **maintain** sports fields and **facilities**.

Organized youth sports first appeared during the early 20th century in the United States and other wealthy nations. They were originally developed when some educator and developmental experts realized that the behavior and character of children were strongly influenced by their social surroundings and everyday experiences. This led many people to believe that if you could organize the experiences of children in particular ways, you could influence the kinds of adults that those children would become.

This belief that the social environment influenced a person's **overall** development was very encouraging to people interested in progress and reform in the United States at the beginning of the 20th century. It caused them to think about how they might control the experiences of children to produce responsible and **productive** adults. They believed strongly that democracy depended on responsibility and that a growing **capitalist** economy depended on the productivity of works.

文章词汇注释

▶▶ take...for granted 认为…是理所当然的

▶▶ community [kə'mjuːnɪtɪ]
[释义] n. ①由同宗教，同种族，同职业或其他共同利益的人所构成的团体②社区，社会③共享，共有，共用
[同义] colony, district, people, society, town
[词组] community of goods 财产的公有
community of interest(s) 利害的一致，利害相通

▶▶ sponsor ['spɒnsə]
[释义] v. ①资助，赞助，负责 ②发起，主办 ③（尤指议会中）支持（法案等），倡议 n. ①发起人，主办者，②（法案等的）倡议者，提案人 ③保证人 ④赞助者
[同义] supporter
[同根] sponsorship ['spɒnsəʃɪp] n. 赞助者的地位，任务等

▶▶ access ['ækses]
[释义] n. ①接近（或进入）的机会，享用的机会②接近，进入 ③入口，通道 v. ①[计] 存取，访问②接近，使用
[同根] accessible [ək'sesəbl] a. ①可（或易）得到的，易相处的 ②可（或易）接近（进入）的
[词组] be easy/hard/difficult of access 容易 / 难接近
give access to 接见，准许出入
have/gain/get/obtain access to 得接近，得会见，得进入，得使用
open access （图书馆）开架阅览

▶▶ transportation [ˌtrænspɔː'teɪʃən]
[释义] n. 运输，运送，[美] 运输机关 / 工具

[同根] transport [træns'pɔːt] v. ①搬运，传送，运输 n. ①搬运，传送，运输②运输工具，交通工具
transportable [træns'pɔːtəbl; trænz-; trɑːn-] a. 可运输的，可搬运的
transporter [træn'spɔːtə] n. 运输者

▶▶ maintain [meɪn'teɪn]
[释义] v. ①维修，保养 ②坚持，保持 ③供养，赡养
[同义] ① preserve ② keep, uphold, sustain, retain
[反义] abandon
[同根] maintenance ['meɪntɪnəns] n. ①维持，保持 ②维修，保养 ③赡养费，扶养费 ④扶养
maintainer [meɪn'teɪnə] 养护工，维护人员
[词组] maintain a family 供养家庭
maintain good relations 维持良好的关系
maintain one's composure 保持冷静
car maintenance 汽车维修

▶▶ facility [fə'sɪlətɪ]
[释义] n. ① (pl.) 设施，设备，工具 ②简易，便利 ③熟练，机敏
[同根] facile [fæ'saɪl] a. 过于简易的，肤浅的
facilitate [fə'sɪlɪteɪt] v. 使容易，使便利，促进
[词组] give/afford facilities for 给予…方便
with facility 容易地，流利地

▶▶ overall ['əʊvərɔːl]
[释义] a. 总的，全面的，全部的 ad. ①总共 ②大体上，一般地 n. (pl.) 工装裤，

读真题记单词大学英语
四级词汇

长罩衣
[同义] total, whole
[词组] overall impression 总体印象
   overall situation 总的形势，全局

▶▶▶ **productive** [prəˈdʌktɪv]
[释义] a. ①多产的，有生产能力的，能生产的 ②出产…的，产生…的
[同义] creative, prolific, fruitful
[反义] ① unproductive, destructive
[同根] produce [prəˈdjuːs] v. ①生产，产出 ②拿出，出示 ③制作，出版 [ˈprɒdjuːs] n. 产品（尤指农产品）
   producer [prəˈdjuːsə] n. ①生产者，制造商 ②制片人
   product [ˈprɒdəkt] n. ①产品，产物 ②结果，成果 ③创作，产品
   production [prəˈdʌkʃən] n. ①生产，

制造 ②生产过程 ③产量 ④戏剧，影片，广播节目
   productivity [ˌprɒdʌkˈtɪvɪtɪ] n. 生产力，生产率
[词组] productive of 造成…，产生…

▶▶▶ **capitalist** [ˈkæpɪtəlɪst]
[释义] a. 资本主义的 n. 资本家，资本主义者
[同根] capital [ˈkæpɪtəl] n. ①资本，资金，资产 ②首都，首府 ③大写字母 a. ①首都的 ②重要的 ③死罪的 ④大写的
   capitalism [ˈkæpɪtəlɪzəm] n. 资本主义
   capitol [ˈkæpɪtəl] n. 国会大厦，州议会大厦

Kimiyuki Suda should be a perfect customer for Japan's car-makers. He's a young, successful **executive** at an Internet-services company in Tokyo and has plenty of **disposable** income. He used to own Toyota's Hilux Surf, a sport **utility** vehicle. But now he uses mostly subways and trains. "It's not inconvenient at all," he says. Besides, "having a car is so 20th century."

Suda **reflects** a **worrisome trend** in Japan; the automobile is losing its emotional **appeal**, particularly among the young, who prefer to spend their money on the latest electronic devices. While mini-cars and **luxury** foreign brands are still popular, everything in between is **slipping**. Last years sales fell 6.7 percent, 7.6 percent if you don't count the mini-car market. There have been larger one-year drops in other nations: sales in Germany fell 9 percent in 2007 **thanks to** a tax increase. But experts say Japan is **unique in that** sales have been decreasing **steadily** over time. Since 1990, yearly new-car sales have fallen from 7.8 million to 5.4 million units in 2007.

Alarmed by this state of **decay**, the Japan Automobile Manufacturers Association (JAMA) **launched** a **comprehensive** study of the market in 2006. It found that a widening wealth gap, *demographic* （人口结构的）changes and general lack of interest in cars led Japanese to hold their vehicles longer, replace their cars with smaller ones or give up car ownership altogether. JAMA **predicts** a further sales decline of 1.2 percent this year. Some experts believe that if the trend continues for much longer, further **consolidation** in the automotive **sector** is likely.

文章词汇注释

▶▶ **executive** [ɪɡ'zekjutɪv]

[释义] n. ①经理主管人员，执行者 ②行政部门，（工会、党派等的）执行委员会 a. ①执行的，实行的 ②行政的，经营管理的

[同义] n. ① administrator, manager, director ② management a. ① & ② administrative, managing

[同根] execute ['eksɪkju:t] v. ①实行，实施，执行 ②处死
execution [ˌeksɪ'kju:ʃən] n. ①实行，实施，执行 ②死刑，处死刑
executor [ɪɡ'zekjutə] n. 执行者，实行者
executioner [ˌeksɪ'kju:ʃənə] n. 死刑执行人，刽子手

[词组] the executive（政府的）行政部门
executive body/committee 主管机构 / 委员会

▶▶ **disposable** [dɪs'pəuzəbl]

[释义] a. ①可自由支配的，可（任意）处理的 ②一次性使用的，无法回收的

[同根] dispose [dɪs'pəuz] v. ①处理，处置 ②部署 ③布置，安排 ④除去
disposal [dɪs'pəuzəl] n. ①处理，处置 ②布置，安排 ③除去
disposed [dɪ'spəuzd] a. ①愿意的，乐意的 ②有…倾向的
disposition [dɪspə'zɪʃən] n. ①性情，性格 ②安排，部署 ③处理，处置

[词组] disposable income 可支配收入

▶▶ **utility** [ju:'tɪlɪtɪ]

[释义] n. ①实用，效用，有用 ②（常用复）有用的东西 ③公共事业 v. 实用的，有多种用途的

[同根] utilize [ju:'tɪlaɪz] v. 利用，应用

utilitarian [ju:tɪlɪ'teərɪən] a. 实用的，功利的

[词组] of no utility 没用的，无益的

▶▶ **reflect** [rɪ'flekt]

[释义] v. ①反映，表达，表现 ②反射 ③思考，考虑（on/upon）

[同义] ① express, show ② mirror ③ think, deliberate, muse, speculate, consider

[同根] reflex ['ri:fleks] n. ①反射作用，条件反射 ②影像，倒影
reflection [rɪ'flekʃən] n. ①影像，倒影 ②（热、声音等的）反射 ③沉思，熟虑
reflector [rɪ'flektə] n. 反射体，反射镜
reflective [rɪ'flektɪv] a. 沉思的，反射的

▶▶ **worrisome** ['wʌrɪsəm]

[释义] a. 令人烦恼的，使人焦虑的

[同义] troublesome

▶▶ **trend** [trend]

[释义] n. ①趋势，趋向 ②（海岸、河流、山脉等）走向，方向 ③时髦，时尚

[同义] tendency

[同根] trendy ['trendɪ] a. 流行的 n. 新潮人物，穿着时髦的人
trendily ['trendɪlɪ] ad. 时髦地

▶▶ **appeal** [ə'pi:l]

[释义] n. ①吸引力，感染力 ②呼吁，恳求 ③上诉 v. ①吸引，有感染力，吸引人 ②呼吁，恳求

[同义] v. ① attract, please ② plead, beg, petition, pray

[同根] appealing [ə'pi:lɪŋ] a. ①有感染力的，吸引人的，②恳求的

[词组] appeal to ①投合…的心意，引起…的兴趣 ②向…呼吁 / 请求
appeal for ①对 … 的吸引力 ②呼

呼⋯，请求⋯

appeal for aid 恳求援助

▶▶ **luxury** ['lʌkʃərɪ]

[释义] *a.* 奢华的，豪华的 *n.* ①奢侈品 ②奢侈 ③豪华

[同义] ② extravagance, indulgence ③ magnificence, splendor

[同根] luxurious [lʌg'zjuərɪəs] *a.* 奢侈的，豪华的

[词组] a life of luxury 奢华的生活

luxury apartment/flat/car 豪华的房间 / 套房 / 汽车

be lapped in luxury 穷奢极欲

wallow in luxury 沉迷于灯红酒绿的生活

▶▶ **slip** [slɪp]

[释义] *v.* ①滑落，跌跤，降低，减少 ②溜走，悄悄过去 ③跌落，变坏，④犯小错误 *n.* ①疏漏，差错 ②失脚，滑倒 ③不测事故，不幸事件 ④下降，下跌

[同根] slipping ['slɪpɪŋ] [美俚] 渐渐不行了的，渐渐松驰的

[词组] give sb the slip 摆脱或避开（尾随者或追逐者）

a slip of a child 瘦削的孩子

a slip of the pen/tongue 笔误 / 口误

▶▶ **thanks to** 由于，因为，多亏

▶▶ **unique** [juːˈniːk]

[释义] *a.* ①独特的，无可匹敌的 ②唯一的，（书籍）孤本的 ③稀罕的，不同寻常的

[同义] ① matchless, rare ② sole, single, exclusive

[反义] ① common

[词组] be unique to 只有⋯才有的

▶▶ **in that** 因为，在于

▶▶ **steadily** ['stedɪlɪ]

[释义] *ad.* ①稳定地，固定地，有规律

地 ②稳地，平稳地

[同根] steady ['stedɪ] *a.* ①稳的，平稳的 ②稳定的，固定的 *v.* (使) 稳定，(使) 稳固

steadiness ['stedɪnɪs] *n.* 稳固

▶▶ **decay** [dɪˈkeɪ]

[释义] *n.* ①衰败，衰退 ②腐朽，腐烂 *v.* ①使衰弱，使衰退 ②使腐败，使腐烂

[同义] *v.* ① spoil ② rot,decompose

[同根] decayed [dɪˈkeɪd] *a.* ①腐朽的，腐烂的，腐败的 ②衰减的，衰退的

decadent ['dekədənt] *n.* 颓废的，衰落的，堕落的

[词组] be far gone in decay 衰弱过甚，凋落不堪

go to decay (=fall into decay) 腐朽，凋谢，衰微，年久失修

▶▶ **launch** [lɔːntʃ; lɑːntʃ]

[释义] *v.* ①发动，开展，着手进行 ②发射，投射，使 (船) 下水

[同根] launcher ['lɔːntʃə; 'lɑːntʃə] *n.* ①发射者 ②创办者

launching ['lɔːntʃɪŋ; 'lɑːntʃɪŋ] *n.* ①下水 ②发射

[词组] launch out ①出航，乘船去 ②开始，着手

launch (out) into ①开始从事，投身于 ②大发 (议论)，出 (恶言)

▶▶ **comprehensive** [ˌkɒmprɪˈhensɪv]

[释义] *a.* ①综合的，广泛的，全面的 ②有理解力的，容易了解的

[反义] incomprehensive

[同根] comprehend [ˌkɒmprɪˈhend] *v.* ①领会,理解 ②包括 (包含),由⋯组成

comprehension [ˌkɒmprɪˈhenʃən] *n.* 理解，包含

▶▶ **predict** [prɪˈdɪkt]

[释义] *v.* 预言，预料，预报

[同义] forecast, foresee, foretell, anticipate

[同根] prediction [prɪ'dɪkʃən] n. ①预言，预料 ②预言的事物，预报的事物

predictable [prɪ'dɪktəbəl] a. 可预言的

predictive [prɪ'dɪktɪv] a. 预言性的，有预报价值的

predictor [prɪ'dɪktə] n. 预言者，起预报作用的事物

▶▶ consolidation [kən,sɒlɪ'deɪʃn]

[释义] n. ①合并，统一 ②巩固，加强

[同义] ① combine ② strengthen

[同根] consolidate [kən'sɒlɪdeɪt] v. ①把…联为一体，合并 ②巩固，加强

consolidated [kən'sɒlɪdeɪtɪd] ① 合并的，统一的 ②加固的，加强的

▶▶ sector ['sektə]

[释义] n. ①（活动、领域的）部门，部分 ②扇形，地区 v. 使分成部分，把…分成扇形

[同义] n. ① section, zone, portion

[同根] sect [sekt] a. 派别，宗派

section ['sekʃən] n. ①部分，片断 ②部件，零件 ③（书，文件等的）节，项，段 ④（组织机构中的）处，科,组等 ⑤（城镇,国家或社会内的）地区，区域

Older people must be given more chances to learn if they are to **contribute to society** rather than be a **financial burden**, according to a new study on population published recently.

The current approach which focuses on younger people and on skills for employment is not adequate to meet the challenges of *demographic* (人口结构的) change, it says. Only 1% of the education **budget** is **currently** spent on the oldest of the population.

The **challenges** include the fact that most people can expect to spend a third of their lives in retirement, that there are now more people over 59 than under 16 and that 11.3 million people are over state **pension** age.

"Learning needs to continue throughout life. Our historic concentration of policy attention and resources on young people cannot **meet** the new **needs** ," says the report's author, Professor Stephen McNair.

The major **portion** of our education budget is spent on people below the age of 25. When people are changing their jobs, homes, partners and lifestyles **more often than ever**, they need opportunities to learn at every age. For example, some people are starting new careers in their 50s and later.

People need opportunities to make a "midlife review" to **adjust to** the later stages of employed life, and to plan for the *transition* (过 渡) to retirement, which may now happen **unpredictably** at any point from 50 to over 90, says McNair.

And there should be more money **available** to support people in establishing a sense of **identity** and finding **constructive** roles for the "third age", the 20 or more years they will spend in healthy retired life.

文章词汇注释

▶▶ **contribute to society** 贡献社会
▶▶ **financial burden** 财政负担

▶▶ **budget** ['bʌdʒɪt]
[释义] *n.* 预算 *v.* ①做预算，编入预算 ②设计使用
[词组] on a budget 节省费用
budget one's time 安排自己的时间

▶▶ **currently** ['kʌrəntlɪ]
[释义] *ad.* ①现在，当前 ②普遍地，通常地
[同义] ① presently, at present
[同根] current ['kʌrənt] *a.* ①现时的，当前的 ②流行的，流传的 *n.* ① （空气等的）流，电流 ②趋势，倾向，潮流
currency ['kʌrənsɪ] *n.* ①流传，流通 ②通货，货币

▶▶ **challenge** ['tʃælɪndʒ]
[释义] *n.* 挑战，艰苦的任务，努力追求的目标 *v.* ①向…挑战，对…质疑 ②刺激，激发 ③需要，要求
[同义] *v.* ① question, defy, doubt, dispute, confront
[同根] challenging ['tʃælɪndʒɪŋ] *a.* 挑战性的，引起兴趣的，令人深思的，挑逗的
challenger ['tʃælɪndʒə(r)] *n.* 挑战者
[词组] accept /take a challenge 应战
face the challenge 遇到问题，面向挑战
issue the challenge 提出任务
beyond challenge 无与伦比，无可非议
rise to the challenge 接受挑战，迎战，迎着困难

▶▶ **pension** ['penʃən]
[释义] *n.* ①养老金，退休金，抚恤金 ②津贴，补助金，年金

▶▶ [同根] pensioner ['penʃənə(r)] *n.* 领养老金（或退休金、抚恤金、补助金等）的人，年金者，靠养老金（或退休金、抚恤金等）生活的人

▶▶ **meet … needs** 满足…的需求

▶▶ **portion** ['pɔːʃən]
[释义] *n.* 部分，一份 *v.* 分配，把…的一份分给某人

▶▶ **more often than ever** 比以往更经常
▶▶ **adjust to** 调整使适应…

▶▶ **unpredictably** [ˌʌnprɪ'dɪktəblɪ]
[释义] *ad.* 不可预测地，不可预知地
[同根] predict [prɪ'dɪkt] *v.* 预言，预测
predictable [prɪ'dɪktəbəl] *a.* 可预言的，可预测的
predictive [prɪ'dɪktɪv] *a.* 预言性的，前兆的
prediction [prɪ'dɪkʃən] *n.* 预言，被预言的事物

▶▶ **available** [ə'veɪləbl]
[释义] *a.* ①可得到的，可使用的 ②在手边的 ③可取得联系的，有空的
[同义] ① obtainable, accessible ② on hand, existing ③ vacant, free
[同根] avail [ə'veɪl] *v.* 有益于，有帮助，有用，有利
availability [ə,veɪlə'bɪlɪtɪ] *n.* 可用性，有效性，实用性
[词组] readily/freely available 容易得到的

▶▶ **identity** [aɪ'dentɪtɪ]
[释义] *n.* ①身份，本体 ②个性，特性 ③相同处，同一（性）
[同义] ① personality, character ② individuality, uniqueness, distinctiveness
[同根] identify [aɪ'dentɪfaɪ] *v.* ①认明，

识别 ②认同 ③鉴定

identification [aɪˌdentɪfɪ'keɪʃən]
n. ①认出，确认，识别 ②身份证明

identical [aɪ'dentɪkəl] a. 完全相同的，同一的

identically [aɪ'dentɪkəlɪ] ad. 同一地，相等地

[词组] mistaken identity 错误身份

sense of identity 自我意识

cultural/ethnic/social identity 文化 / 民族 / 社会认同

identity card 身份证

▶▶▶ constructive [kən'strʌktɪv]

[释义] a. ①建设性的，积极的，肯定的 ②构造的，构成的

[同义] helpful, useful, worthwhile

[反义] ① destructive

[同根] construct [kən'strʌkt] v. ① 制造，编造 ②建造，构筑，组成 ['kɒnstrʌkt] n. ①建造物，构成物 ②观念，概念

construction [kən'strʌkʃən] n. 建筑，建筑物

constructor [kən'strʌktə] n. 建造者，施工者

We **commonly** think of **sportsmanship in connection with** athletic contests, but it also **applies to** individual outdoor sports. Not everyone who picks up a fishing rod or goes out with a gun is a sportsman. The sportsman first of all obeys the fish and game laws, not because he **is liable to** be punished as a **violator**, but because he knows that **in the main** these laws are made for his best interests.

The following are some of the things that those who would **qualify** for membership in the sportsmanship *fraternity* (圈内人) will do.

Take no more game than the **bag limit** provided for by the fish and game laws. The person who comes back from a trip boasting about the large number of fish or game taken is not a sportsman but a *game hog* (贪得无厌的捕猎者).

Observe the unwritten rules of **fair play**. This means shooting game birds only when the birds are "**on the wing**". For the same reason, do not use a shotgun to shoot a rabbit or similar animal while it is sitting or standing still.

Be careful in removing illegal or **undersized** fish from the hook. This should be done only after wetting the hands. This is necessary because the body of the fish is covered with a thin, **protective film** which will stick to your dry hands. If the hands are dry when the fish is handled, the film is torn from the body of the fish. Without the protective film, the fish is more easily attacked by diseases. If you wish to release a fish that is hooked in such a way that it will be impossible to closed to the hook as convenient. In a **remarkably** short time, the hook will break down and the fish will remain almost unharmed. Fish have been known to feed successfully while hooks were still in their lips.

Be sure of the identity of your target before you shoot. Many useful and harmless species of wildlife are **thoughtlessly** killed by the **uninformed** person who is out with a gun to kill whatever flies **within range**.

文章词汇注释

▶▶ **commonly** [ˈkɒmənlɪ]

[释义] *ad.* 普通地，一般地，平常地

[同义] usually, normally, generally

[同根] common [ˈkɒmən] *a.* ①共同的，公共的 ②普通的 ③通俗的 ④无特权的

▶▶ **sportsmanship** [ˈspɔːtsmənʃɪp]

[释义] *n.* ①诚实公平的精神 ②运动家精神／品质

▶▶ **in connection with** 关于…，与…有关

▶▶ **apply to** 适用于，运用于

▶▶ **be liable to do sth.** 易于…的，有…倾向的

▶▶ **violator** [ˈvaɪəleɪtə]

[释义] *n.* 违犯者

[同根] violate [ˈvaɪəleɪt] *v.* ①违反，违犯 ②侵犯，妨碍，打扰 ③亵渎

violation [ˌvaɪəˈleɪʃən] *n.* ①违犯（行为）②妨碍,侵害（行为）③亵渎（行为）

▶▶ **in the main** 大体上，基本上，就一般而论

▶▶ **qualify** [ˈkwɒlɪfaɪ]

[释义] *v.* ①（使）合适，（使）胜任 ②准予 ③限制，限定，修正

[同根] quality [ˈkwɒlɪtɪ] *n.* ①特性 ②品德，品质 ③质量，优质 ④身份，地位，作用

qualification [ˌkwɒlɪfɪˈkeɪʃən] *n.* ①资格，合格证书 ②取得资格 ③限制，限定

qualified [ˈkwɒlɪfaɪd] *a.* ①有资格的，胜任的 ②有限制的，有保留的

[词组] qualify as 取得…资格

qualify for... 有…资格，使能担任…

qualify to do sth. 使有资格做某事

▶▶ **bag limit**（法律允许的）最大捕猎量的限制

▶▶ **observe** [əbˈzɜːv]

[释义] *v.* ①遵守，奉行（法律、习俗、规章等）②观察，注意到 ③纪念，庆祝

[反义] disobey, disregard, neglect

[同根] observance [əbˈzɜːvns] *n.* ①（法律、习俗等的）遵守，奉行 ②纪念，庆祝

observation [ˌɒbzɜːˈveɪʃən] *n.* ①观察 ②陈述，评论

observatory [əbˈzɜːvətərɪ] *n.* 天文台，气象台

▶▶ **fair play** 公平比赛，公平对待

▶▶ **on the wing** 在飞行中

▶▶ **undersized** [ˈʌndəsaɪzd]

[释义] *a.* 比普通的小的，个儿小的

▶▶ **protective film** 保护膜

▶▶ **remarkably** [rɪˈmɑːkəblɪ]

[释义] *ad.* 非常地，显著地，引人注目地

[同义] extraordinarily, amazingly, extremely

[同根] remark [rɪˈmɑːk] *v.* ①说，评论说 ②注意，觉察 *n.* ①言辞，评论 ②注意，察觉

remarkable [rɪˈmɑːkəbl] *a.* ①值得注意的 ②非凡的，出色的 *n.* 引人注目的事件，知名人物

▶▶ **thoughtlessly** [ˈθɔːtlɪslɪ]

[释义] *ad.* ①欠考虑地 ②粗心地，轻率地 ③自私地，不关心他人地

▶▶ **uninformed** [ˌʌnɪnˈfɔːmd]

[释义] *a.* ①无知的 ②无生气的 ③未被

通知（或告知）的

[同义] ignorant

[同根] inform [ɪnˈfɔːm] v. ①通知，告诉，报告 ②告发，检举

information [ˌɪnfəˈmeɪʃən] n. ①通知，报告 ②消息，情报，资料 ③知识，见闻

informed [ɪnˈfɔːmd] a. ①有知识的，有情报（或资料）根据的 ②有教养的，明智的

▶▶▶ within range ①在…射程以内 ②在…范围以内